OWLKNIGHT

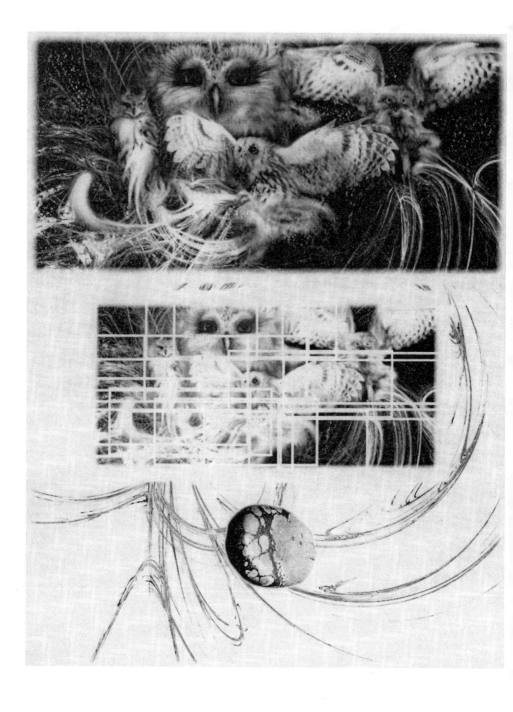

OWLKNIGHT

MERCEDES LACKEY

AND LARRY DIXON

VICTOR GOLLANCZ

LONDON

Copyright © 1999 Mercedes R. Lackey and Larry Dixon
All rights reserved

Interior illustrations by Larry Dixon

The right of Mercedes R. Lackey and Larry Dixon to be
identified as the authors of this work has been asserted
by them in accordance with the Copyright, Designs
and Patents Act 1988.

This edition first published in Great Britain in 2000 by
Victor Gollancz
An imprint of Orion Books Ltd
Orion House, 5 Upper St Martin's Lane,
London WC2H 9EA

To receive information on the Millennium list, e-mail us at:
smy@orionbooks.co.uk

A CIP catalogue record for this book
is available from the British Library

Printed in Great Britain by
Clays Ltd, St Ives plc

To our wonderful, loyal fans.

We've got soul.
We've got each other.
We've got the whole world to embrace.
This one's for you.

OFFICIAL TIMELINE FOR THE

by Mercedes Lackey

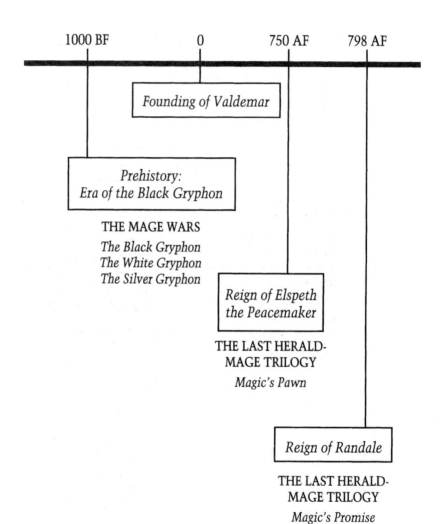

1000 BF   0   750 AF   798 AF

Founding of Valdemar

*Prehistory:
Era of the Black Gryphon*

THE MAGE WARS

*The Black Gryphon
The White Gryphon
The Silver Gryphon*

*Reign of Elspeth
the Peacemaker*

**THE LAST HERALD-
MAGE TRILOGY**

Magic's Pawn

Reign of Randale

**THE LAST HERALD-
MAGE TRILOGY**

*Magic's Promise
Magic's Price*

*BF Before the Founding
AF After the Founding*

HERALDS OF VALDEMAR SERIES

Sequence of events by Valdemar reckoning

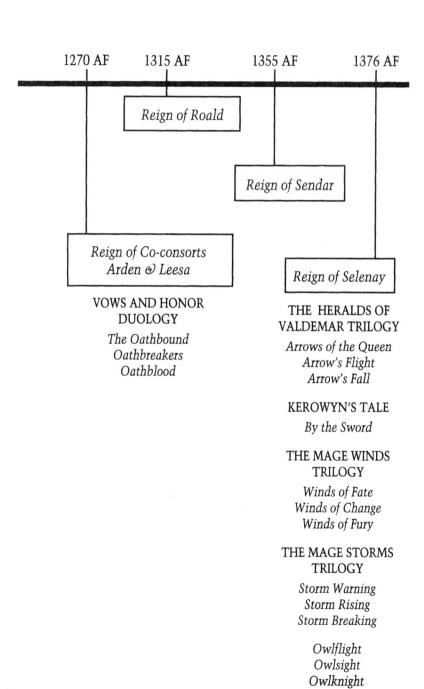

1270 AF   1315 AF   1355 AF   1376 AF

Reign of Roald

Reign of Sendar

*Reign of Co-consorts
Arden & Leesa*

Reign of Selenay

**VOWS AND HONOR
DUOLOGY**

*The Oathbound
Oathbreakers
Oathblood*

**THE HERALDS OF
VALDEMAR TRILOGY**

*Arrows of the Queen
Arrow's Flight
Arrow's Fall*

KEROWYN'S TALE

By the Sword

**THE MAGE WINDS
TRILOGY**

*Winds of Fate
Winds of Change
Winds of Fury*

**THE MAGE STORMS
TRILOGY**

*Storm Warning
Storm Rising
Storm Breaking*

*Owlflight
Owlsight
Owlknight*

One

A shrill whistle caught Darian's attention, and he looked up and over the lake of k'Valdemar Vale, shading his eyes with his hand. As he expected, he saw Snowfire waving at him from his "balcony," three-quarters of the way up the side of the cliff that edged the far side of the lake.

Actually, it would have been more accurate to say that he saw a tiny figure with white hair waving from the balcony—at this distance he couldn't have said for certain that it was Snowfire. It wasn't Nightwind, though; her hair was still raven-wing black.

The sky above the cliff shimmered with a light, pearly opalescence, although it was perfectly possible to see the clouds and blue sky beyond the new Veil, a magic shield that protected k'Valdemar.

I would never have believed we'd get a Veil so quickly, he marveled once again. *If anyone had told me that the Heartstone would support a Veil this soon, I would have told him he was wildly optimistic.* It wasn't a *full* Veil, which would have excluded all weather; this simply kept things at a constant, pleasant temperature, no matter the season. Rain came through, and snow fell to the ground as rain once it passed through the Veil, so they still got some weather. They couldn't do without roofs *yet*.

He whistled back at Snowfire, and waved his arm in the direction of the Council House, the newly built structure that housed all Joint Council sessions. It wasn't much of a structure; now that the Vale had protection, it didn't need to be much of a structure. It had "walls" of wicker work covered in vines, a roof that was half skylight and half slate, a floor of natural turf which flourished in the light. For furniture, in deference to the Valdemar contingent of the Joint Council, there were chairs and a table, but the chairs were of woven grapevine and wicker with soft cushions, and the table was a compass-rose shape of tree-trunk sections, topped with three rising layers of polished wood with one section for each member of the Council. The Tayledras of k'Valdemar, of course, felt no need for formal furniture, and neither did the tribesmen of the Ghost Cat clan.

Up on the cliff, Snowfire waved both arms back, signifying that he understood the Council was gathering. He disappeared into the dark opening in the cliff face behind him, presumably to fetch his mate, Nightwind. His errand of notifying Snowfire and Nightwind completed, Darian Firkin k'Vala k'Valdemar turned back and entered the shaded and secluded pathways of his Vale, heading for the Council House himself.

An odd and sometimes seemingly contradictory combination of qualities was Darian. A Journeyman-level Mage, from a land which did not have such things until very recently—a citizen of the country of Valdemar, yet also a Hawkbrother of the once-secretive Tayledras, adopted into the clan of k'Vala—even his clothing reflected those contradictions.

He wore soft fabrics of Hawkbrother manufacture; the loose trousers, gathered at the ankle, that both sexes wore, and the wide-sleeved, open-collared shirt that was also a staple among the Tayledras. Good, strong dyes were readily available in the Vale, so the rich gold of his shirt and brown of his trousers were commonplace *inside* the Vale, though not necessarily in the Valdemaran lands beyond.

But the embroidered, fitted vest he wore, though not of Valdemaran manufacture, was definitely of the local *style*. Of light brown leather lined in darker brown silk, it was embroidered in a motif of owls. Once again, contradiction—the cut of the vest was Valdemaran, the motif was clearly Tayledras.

So there it was, contradictions implied in his very dress,

contradictions that sometimes confused others, but never confused him. For all the contradictions, Darian was comfortable in his dual citizenship, and sometimes took an impish delight in how *un*comfortable it made others.

He looked up at the sound of a crow's catcall just above his head, laughing when he saw a falcon playing "tag" with a crow, flying in and out of the branches. In open air, the falcon would have had the advantage, but not in among the trees. The streamer trailing from the falcon's bracelets was less than half its original length, but the crow still had most of his streamer, and mocked the falcon enthusiastically. Both were bondbirds, of course, the specially bred, highly intelligent companions of the Hawkbrothers, and the falcon seemed to be taking his imminent defeat in good humor. Crows took just about everything in good humor; of all the birds bred by the Hawkbrothers as bondbirds, the crows had the liveliest sense of humor. Ravens were more sardonic, most of the falcons tended to be quick-witted but extremely focused, hawks a little slower but more deliberate, and owls somewhat ponderous in their thinking. Darian's own bondbird was an owl; in fact, it was one of largest birds in the Vale. Kuari was an eagle-owl, a bird which dwarfed all other birds except the bondbird eagles. Since there were no Tayledras with eagles in this Vale, Kuari and his parents Hweel and Huur were the largest birds here.

Now that the temperature was under control, the flora of the Vale was in the process of undergoing a shift from what had been native to this place to plants and even trees that could only be found in Tayledras Vales. There were more flowers; they were not necessarily bigger, but they bloomed all year long, their subtle perfume filling the air. The leaves of these new plants were enormous, and not just green—veins traced scarlet pathways, and pinks, oranges, and even blues made patterns that resembled flowers, enormous insects, or abstract collages on their surfaces.

It would take a very long time before this Vale looked anything like k'Vala, several generations, perhaps, but the beginnings were there, and Darian took a great deal of pleasure in seeing them. As he walked along the sand-softened pathway, he glanced up now and again, catching brief glimpses of new *ekeles* in the enormous trees. The treehouses of k'Valdemar were a bit more inventive than the ones in k'Vala; perhaps spurred on by *hertasi* creativity, there were experiments in Hawkbrother housing going on up there. Not *all* of them were successful, but the failure rate was low, and failures were never disasters. If one plan didn't work out, would-be home builder and *hertasi* just put their heads together and tried a new direction.

All this building had been spurred on by the existence of the Veil, making it possible to have *ekeles* that took full advantage of the constant balmy conditions. The hedonistic Tayledras loved it. So did those ubiquitous residents of established Vales, the hummingbirds and messenger-birds. Strictly off-limits as dinner or snacks for the predatory bondbirds, these feathered gems frolicked fearlessly from the ground to the treetops. The messenger-birds sported feathers of every hue possible, and in combinations that sometimes made Darian blink. Their natural voices were a bit shrill, but fortunately the heavy foliage tended to disperse and muffle their joyful shrieks. The voice they used to repeat messages was a bit more pleasant, a kind of hoarse chuckle, and when they chose to permit someone to scratch or tickle them, they would chortle and chirp their pleasure in a way that was quite funny.

A flock of the messenger-birds hurtled overhead, screaming with delight, apparently in pursuit of the falcon and the crow. A hummingbird hovered at a flower cluster just beside the path, paying no attention to Darian as he walked by.

He should have been contented; there should have been nothing more he could have wanted. But underneath, he was restless and uneasy.

Perhaps it had been the dream he'd had last night, that had sent him up out of sleep with a feeling of something threatening. He couldn't remember it though, that was the problem. All he *could* recall were the eyes of the Ghost Cat he had seen so long ago, and an odd sort of raven with the same kind of eyes. . . .

It's probably just that I've gotten used to crisis, he told himself wryly. *Once you get to the point that you watch for signs of crisis everywhere, totally innocuous events seem like grave portents. I should be glad that the worst crisis is where we're going to put the latest batch of "pilgrims" to the "Holy Dyheli!"*

That was an ongoing problem; every new group that made it down from the tribal lands of the North seemed to arrive with the potential to spread a new and different illness. Keeping them all quarantined from Ghost Cat and from each other until their ailments were identified and a cure devised required the tact of a diplomat, the organizational ability of the Kingdom Seneschal, and the tactical ability of a general. Although those qualities were not all combined in a single person, among them all, the Council members managed, though there had been a few emergency sessions in the past.

The meeting planned for today, however, was the routinely scheduled monthly meeting. Lord Breon and his son would be there for Kelmskeep, as would the Chief and Shaman of Ghost Cat for the Northerners, representatives from Errold's Grove, and from all the races resident at k'Valdemar Vale. Darian didn't figure he'd hear anything more exciting than progress reports—perhaps some complaints or requests from farmers.

The vague murmur of conversation mingled with the rustle of leaves reached him before he actually saw the Council House. He stepped past the vine-covered, wicker-work screen shielding the entrance, and joined the others in a "room" that seemed very much an extension of the lush forest outside.

Of the representatives for k'Valdemar, only he and the snow-haired, aged Starfall were present at this moment; Nightwind and Snowfire and the others were presumably on their way. Lord Breon and Val had arrived last night, staying overnight in the guest lodge, and now were in their chairs chatting comfortably with Chief Vordon and Shaman Celin of Ghost Cat. *Hertasi* moved about the table, putting beverages and light snacks within reach of the Council members on the topmost tier of the table. No one shuffled papers on the lowest table tier today, which was a good omen for a short meeting. The table itself was in the shape of an open rose seen from above, with the layers in trimmed wood forming the petals. The original concept had been for a square table, yet someone had observed that only allowed for comfort for four parties. The way things had been going who knows how many more powers might come to stay in this area!

The Lutters were no longer the ones making the decisions

for Errold's Grove—oh, they *thought* they were, but the real work was done by the Village Council, and two representatives from that body were the new glass-maker, Harrod Dobbs, and Barda of the Fellowship. Harrod was always glad of an excuse to come to the Vale for a chance to use the bigger glass furnaces here and trade tips and lessons from the Vale glass-makers. There was very little overlap in what he produced and what the Vale artisans did; Harrod only rarely made anything that wasn't utilitarian, as the demand for glass bottles and jars and common drinking vessels would always exceed his output. Still, he liked to turn out a nice set of goblets now and again, and most of what the Tayledras produced was lampwork and blown glass, so he was able to teach them molding techniques. The latest result of that was a series of small, flat medallions to hang in a window that they called "sun-catchers," formed of colored glass, with a decorative impression molded into each. They were an adaptation of an Eastern style, very popular within the Vale; whether they would become popular outside it had yet to be determined.

The nonhuman members of the group, Kelvren, Ayshen, Tyrsell and Hashi, had not yet appeared either—but just as Darian took his own seat and exchanged greetings with the rest, the *hertasi* entered, followed by the king stag and the *kyree.*

And right after them, Snowfire and Nightwind appeared. "Sorry we're running a bit late," Nightwind apologized, pulling her ebon hair away from her finely honed face. "Kel will be here in a minute, too—we had to pry the baby away from him and get her put down for her nap."

As if that had been a cue, the wicker walls shook with the thunder of enormous wings outside, and leaves blew, and Kelvren the gryphon joined the group, shouldering past the screen. He shook his dark brown feathers to settle them after his flight (and the baby Moonshadow's sticky hands) and looked around.

Ayshen, the leader of the lizard-folk called *hertasi,* sat beside Nightwind on her left. The Kaled'a'in smiled a welcome and swept her trailing sleeves out of the way for him, and he put the tray of her favorite berry tartlets he had brought on the top tier of her table section. To her right sat Snowfire, and the section of Tayledras concluded with the silver-haired mage Starfall, the eldest of the group. Then came Darian, then Lord Breon's sturdy son, Val, then the Lord himself. Between Lord Breon and the two Ghost Clan representatives sat Barda and Harrod. The *dyheli* stag Tyrsell stood beside Kelvren the gryphon along the back wall. Val's arm was in a sling again; he'd probably managed to sprain it at fighting practice.

"It ssseeemsss everrryone isss herrre," Kel said genially, and arranged himself along the wall, lying down on the turf out of the way. Hashi the *kyree* lay down next to him. "Good! I am sssorrry I was delayed. Who will ssstarrrt?"

"Actually, I will," Lord Breon said, looking uncommonly cheerful. Although his hair was threaded with gray, no one in his right mind would ever challenge Breon to a fight; he kept his well-muscled fighter's frame in top trim. "I have some excellent news to start the Council session with—we're getting our own, permanent, resident Herald-Mage!"

"No, really?" Snowfire exclaimed, blue eyes widening, as the others murmured their surprise. "When did you hear this?"

"Just before we left; news came by messenger." Lord Breon was extremely pleased, and well he should be. Giving this corner of the world a resident Herald meant that Queen Selenay and her Council judged the land that held Breon's keep to be of significant importance. That meant Breon's status had risen from that of a minor noble to that of a key landholder here in the Northwest.

"Actually," Breon continued, with a shamefaced glance at Starfall, "I probably ought to have told you last night, but—"

"But there was no point in repeating the story half a dozen times, when you could tell us all at once," Barda said bluntly, her plain, no-nonsense face showing no annoyance at all. "So, please, give us the details!"

"The Herald-Mage we're getting is a fellow called Anda; I gather he was trained by the mages that came in with the Princess and her lot, so he's got some experience in the war."

That got Kelvren's attention. "Trrruly?" he exclaimed. "Trrrained forrr warrr-magic?"

"That's what they told me, Kel; you'll have to ask him yourself if you want to know more." Breon nodded at the gryphon, whose ear-tufts were sharply erect with interest.

"Skandranon Rashkae wasss a warrr-mage." Kelvren turned

his head sideways to speak to the *kyree* who no doubt already knew, and the king stag who likely didn't care. "I could be one like him, with a good teacherrr." Hashi licked Kelvren's beak. Tyrsell just stared briefly at the gryphon, his expression typically unfathomable, then turned back to face Lord Breon.

"War-trained though he is, the Heraldic Circle feels that his experience in dealing with mages of so many different cultures will be useful here among us. I'm told that since the war he's been riding circuit on the Karse and Hardorn borders, so he's been running liaison with Sunpriests and Imperials. But that's not the whole of the news—he's bringing your Shandi back with him!"

Darian's eyes widened in surprise equal to Snowfire's. "Already?" he said cautiously, wondering if Shandi had somehow gotten herself in deeper trouble than she could get herself out of. It had been three years, perhaps less, since she had gone to the Collegium; surely she couldn't have gotten her Whites yet!

"Already," Lord Breon said with satisfaction. "The girl's got her Whites—not the record, maybe, but she's ready for other duties. Anda hand-picked her himself as his assistant, so she'll be groomed for permanent service here!"

"Breon! That's excellent news!" Barda said heartily, beaming at him. "I hope she's as happy with the posting as her parents will be! Well, heyla, with all this increase in attention, perhaps we can see some funding for better roads and a second bridge!"

"I don't know why she wouldn't be," Breon replied—and behind his back, Val rolled his eyes at Darian, who smothered a grin. Val and his lady were about to take Breon's place at Court, and Val could hardly wait to get away, out from under his father's well-intentioned restrictions. Not that Val was going to be irresponsible when the parental ties were severed—he wasn't the adolescent who'd yearned for "the clash of sword on sword" two years ago. It had been Darian who'd seen how he chafed under the burden of being "only" the son, but it was Starfall who'd suggested that Val would make an excellent representative for his father at Haven and the Court.

That Lord Breon had embraced the suggestion so readily told Darian that he himself hadn't worked out what to do with a young man full of energy and ideas with nothing to do.

"I want Herald Anda to meet you, Val," he said, turning to his son, who quickly assumed a more appropriate expression. "But as soon as he's settled in, it'll be a good time for you to leave; any later and I might not be able to spare you a proper escort."

Val grinned back at his father. "I'd have been disappointed if you'd asked me to go to Court before he arrived," he assured his father. "If there was ever an excuse for a Tayledras celebration, this will be it!"

Snowfire grinned, and Kel chuckled. "What an excellent suggestion, Val!" Snowfire said facetiously. "We would never have thought of that, we are so completely serious-minded. We'll take it under advisement!"

Val knew the Hawkbrothers too well now not to recognize the teasing for what it was, and just grinned back. "I'd be happy to advise you on the menu as well," he suggested.

Nightwind raised an eyebrow. "Not that you would ever volunteer to *cook* any of the proposed menu," she said dryly.

"You beat me to it," chimed in Ayshen.

"You wouldn't even suggest that if you had ever tasted his cooking, lady," Lord Breon replied with an exaggerated shudder. "I won't even let him make tea when we are out on a hunt."

Val opened his mouth to protest, then realized that he might get himself into something he didn't want, and shut it again. Darian smirked.

"Well, before we get into too many celebration plans, I've got a protest to lay before the Council," Barda announced. "Ard Kilmer and Fern Holl are not happy with Ghost Cat at the moment, and they want me to make a formal objection."

Chief Vordon looked surprised. "What could this problem be?" he asked. "Not Boys' Raids again, surely?"

He was referring to the last protest against Ghost Cat, when boys wanting to earn their Manhood status had begun raiding villagers. Everything that was taken was returned, and the items taken were all of little value—but the fact that those items had come from *inside* people's homes, and had been taken in the dead of night, had been more than a little unsettling to the good people of Errold's Grove. They did not like the idea of "half-wild barbarian boys" creeping around in their homes while they slept, and who could blame them? After all, their daughters might be next to be stolen, and the daughters might not *want* to be returned!

The Chief and Shaman, after long consultation with the Council, had agreed to a new way of earning Manhood tallies that would demonstrate even more raiding skill than snatching things from villagers. Now the boys who wanted to count coups had to slip up close enough to a sleeping *dyheli* to put a handprint in paint on its side. Tyrsell liked this game; it forced the herd to regain some of the alertness it had been losing since life at k'Valdemar was so unchallenging. The young bucks of the herd appreciated it as well, and had taken to "counting coup" back, sneaking up behind a stalking boy and giving him a sharp nudge with a horn to his backside.

"No, not Boys' Raids," Barda replied. "They've heard your folk have been buying their *chirras* with intent to breed, and they're afraid you're going to challenge their market."

"Fair is fair, Barda," Lord Breon protested. "They wouldn't have any room to protest if it was someone *else* from *their* village that was raising chirras in competition."

"I know that," Barda replied irritably, "but it's my job to present the protest. So I have."

"If they are so concerned, they could sell us only geldings," Chief Vordon rumbled, "And then we will take our trade goods elsewhere. Our people came here hungry. The memory of crying bellies has not left us. We seek to breed those animals, so we will have enough food to keep a reserve. If they do not consider our value as peaceful neighbors they help feed, then we will seek out others farther away who will sell to us."

"That could get ugly." Val whispered to Darian.

:*Competition keeps the breed strong,*: was Tyrsell's only comment.

The Chief looked to Lord Breon for further support, and possibly advice, and Breon was not loath to give it. "I move that the protest is noted but not valid—they're only protesting because they think the Chief won't know it's groundless and they think they can get a settlement from the Council for nothing. In fact, I move the protest be dismissed. All in favor?"

A show of hands (and talons, paws, and hooves) all around— including Barda's—made it unanimous without Chief Vordon having to get involved at all. Since Lord Breon was the one on record as putting it to the vote, and countering the protest, it was unlikely that anything more would be said by the two farmers.

Barda sighed. "That was the stickiest bit. Market prices are down, but they can't blame anything but the good crop of early vegetables. The Fellowship wants to send a parcel of wedding shawls with your boy as presents to people he thinks might do us some good."

"You mean bribes, don't you?" Vordon asked slyly.

"Anybody who understands bribery can't be that much of a barbarian," Val whispered.

"Presents, bribes, whatever." Barda shrugged the insinuation away. "We aren't asking for anything specific, and I certainly don't want him to go giving them to tariff-officials, or anything of the sort. These are a different design that we're hoping will catch on, and we're looking for someone who'll give us a decent price for the privilege of exclusivity. We made too many agreements back when the village wasn't as prosperous with traders who are making a great deal of money from our work. We aren't going to go back on those agreements now, but—well, you know."

Lord Breon turned to Val. "Think you can handle that?"

Val took his time in answering, his dark brows knitted as he thought. "If you don't expect results immediately," he said at last. "If you trust me with this, I need to take my time with it. And I'll want the use of a couple as outright gifts from Kelmskeep to important people."

"That's reasonable," Barda agreed. "In fact, that might well whet the right appetites, if you give those gifts out first. Nothing like having someone with influence take a liking to your work for getting traders interested. It's always better for the buyer to come to you."

"Done, then," Val said instantly, and another agreement was concluded.

"We want someone as—" Chief Vordon searched for the word he wanted and finally leaned over and whispered something in Starfall's ear. Starfall whispered back, and Vordon straightened. "As *agent,*" he said carefully. "For our goods. Someone who bargains well."

Barda nodded. "I didn't want to mention this before, because I didn't know how your people would feel about it, but

I've been thinking you could get better return if you had someone in the village working for you."

Harrod bobbed his round head earnestly, and his lank, blond
hair fell into his eyes. "My wife will do it, if you like," he
offered diffidently. "She's sharp enough that the Lutters com-
plain all the time about the prices they have to pay for jars. If
you'd rather pick someone else, though, just say so."

"No, no, your wife-mate will be good," the Chief said instantly, giving Darian the feeling that he'd been on the wrong
end of a bargain with Harrod's wife himself a time or two.
"Honest and—what was it?—sharp. Good."

The rest of the meeting was concerned with other such
things; requests from the village for Tayledras products and
that Lord Breon supply the new village militia with some replacement arms, since the blacksmith of Errold's Grove,
though good with ploughs and hinges, knew little of arms and
armoring. The *kyree* wanted permission to dig emergency
lairs in the bluffs along the river near the village, and the *hertasi* wanted help from Ghost Cat on a fishing expedition.
Most meetings were like this, where the details and difficulties of three cultures living in the same area got taken care
of and smoothed over. Sometimes there were arguments, and
twice there had been a point when Darian thought things
might come to blows, but somehow everything got sorted out
under the eyes of the Hawkbrothers. They'd even established
a Council common treasury as the means of paying for things
that all factions needed, and to pay off aggrieved parties if
there was no other way to settle a dispute. The cash was anything but petty, but they were all in agreement that when
time and diplomacy could not solve a problem, sufficient pay-
off would. As he had hoped, k'Valdemar was proving to be a
neutral ground where the territory's difficulties *could* be dealt
with. The fact that it was the most pleasant and most relaxing
place of all the possible spots where meetings could be held
helped tremendously to get things settled peacefully. It was
no accident that the Vale had turned out that way either.
Tayledras were past masters at the strategic use of pleasure
and comfort.

There weren't going to be any serious arguments today, that
was clear enough. Darian suspected that the imminent arrival
of this Herald might have something to do with that. Barda

had been awfully quick to drop the Errold's Grove protest, and even voted against it herself—perhaps because she knew that if she supported the protest, it would certainly come up again in front of the Herald.

No one wants to look bad in front of the important stranger, he thought, with a mental smile. *As if he won't have had to deal with arguments just as petty, or even more so, before this.* Of all of them, Darian had the most experience with Heralds; when k'Vala had helped the people of Valdemar clean out some nasty pockets of trouble left over from the mage-storms, he'd been the one, as the only Valdemar native, who spent the most time with their Heraldic liaisons. Stories came out over the campfire, often very funny stories, and Darian had about as good an idea of what it was like for a Herald on circuit as anyone who wasn't himself a Herald.

"Is that it, then?" Lord Breon asked, looking around the table. "Everything taken care of?"

"As much as we can in one meeting," Harrod replied, and Starfall nodded his agreement to that.

"Well, then, I have a proposition to make. We can take it as read that we're going to have a bloody great celebration to welcome Heralds Anda and Shandi, right?"

Starfall laughed. "And you can take it as read that k'Valdemar will host it. No one else has the facilities—unless it was held outside, and it's springtime, and you know what that means. Mud."

Breon made a face. "Rain. Mud. Guaranteed. If it doesn't rain on the welcome, it'll rain on Spring Faire. At least if it rains in the Vale, it'll be a warm rain."

"I think we can even spare the magical energy to keep rain out of the Vale for a single day," Starfall replied evenly. "A little borrowing from some other sources should make up the difference. Clearly, though, you have a request for the plans?"

Breon cleared his throat. "You all remember that I made Val a Knight when we decided he'd go to represent us at Court? Did I ever explain why?"

Snowfire wrinkled his brow in thought as the Errold's Grove representatives looked blank; they hadn't sat on the Council at the time. "Not that I recall. I thought it was simply something your people did from time to time."

"We-e-ell, yes, in a way. A Knighthood confers rank—like

Chief, or Warchief, Baron, or Elder. Not equal rank to those, but similar in concept," Breon explained, using examples familiar to everyone around the table. "Most rank in Valdemar comes with land attached, though—Knighthood is the only one that doesn't. It matches the ones that do, however—it's meant to serve as notice to other people that the Knight is someone to be honored and respected, someone with the power to make decisions. It goes to younger sons who won't inherit, for instance, or someone like Val who is going to serve as a representative for his parents. But it can also be used to reward people who've distinguished themselves; there're Knights in the Guard, for instance. It's a way of ennobling someone who's not highborn and make them equal to the nobles."

"All right," Nightwind said. "So?"

"So I'd like to make young Darian a Knight of Valdemar." Lord Breon sat back in his chair and enjoyed the various reactions of the rest of the Council.

Darian paled. He was too surprised—and concerned—to take any notice of the others. His first reaction was elation, but immediately following that was worry. "Lord Breon," he said, before anyone else could voice their opinion, "I appreciate the honor, but why? And—I've already got other commitments; I *am* adopted into the Tayledras, and I couldn't take any oaths that would conflict with that—"

Breon shook his head. "No troubles there, lad. There're a fair number of Valdemaran Knights that are envoys of other countries—well, there's the Karsite ambassador, Karal, for one. The oaths you swear aren't even in the name of a specific god; the phrasing is 'by all I hold holy and dearest' and you basically swear to defend the defenseless, uphold the right, that sort of thing. You're the real liaison between Valdemar and the Hawkbrothers—but without some sort of title, I'm afraid this Herald might overlook you." He gave a shrewd glance at Starfall, who nodded slowly. "Make you a Knight, though—and do it as part of his welcoming party—well, it'll say without saying anything out loud that *you* rank equal with *him*."

"Asss it ssshould be," Kel rumbled.

"I take it, then, that he's to be stationed *within* the Vale?" Starfall asked.

Breon nodded. "See what I'm working at, here? It's an honor, oh my yes, but I don't want a bunch of city-bred soft-heads thinking that they can make up for all their neglect by sending us a Herald, or even a Herald-Mage."

"And if he is expecting to be stationed in the Vale. . . ." Starfall ruminated on that for a bit. "If Darian is his equal, then it is clear that he is in the Vale as our *guest*, and not as anyone who has any real authority over us."

Breon looked satisfied, but said nothing. He didn't have to. *So far as he is concerned, the Joint Council is the only body with any right to make decisions around here,* Darian reflected. *He doesn't intend to give up the tiniest speck of his authority and autonomy to Haven bureaucrats, and he figures Starfall and Vordon feel the same way.*

He was probably right—definitely right, so far as Starfall was concerned. Vordon would side with what benefited his clan.

And as far as I'm concerned, that is right too. Darian understood completely what Lord Breon meant, when he'd spoken of the neglect that this part of the country had suffered. Granted, there had been an excuse for it—the war with Hardorn had drained Valdemar of every able-bodied fighter, putting them out on the front lines—but excuses didn't make things right, and one Herald-in-residence *wasn't* going to make up for it.

"Then I would very much like to accept the offer, Lord Breon," he replied firmly. Breon smiled broadly.

"Hah!" the Shaman said, getting their attention. "If you make this Knight-business, we will make Darian-of-the-Owl a Clan-brother! Yes, and at the same celebration!"

"An excellent idea!" Snowfire said with enthusiasm. "A *very* good idea! Let Herald Anda be on the right footing with all of us from the moment he arrives!"

Now Darian was more than surprised, he was stunned. "But—" he began. *Isn't this an awful lot of commitments to make? Can I honestly honor them all?*

Snowfire chuckled, and made a gesture that was supposed to be reassuring. "It's all right, Darian; Clan-brother is the equivalent of Wingbrother. The ceremony is a bit different, but you'll enjoy it."

Darian gulped down his protests. If Snowfire, who had

spent more time with the Ghost Cat Shaman than all of the rest of them combined, said it was all right, then he would have to take his word for it.

:While we are at it, perhaps my herd ought to hold the rite that makes him the king stag's prime doe,: Tyrsell said into their minds, his tone as dry as old papers. *:Then again— perhaps he wouldn't enjoy that particular ceremony.:*

Darian blushed a furious scarlet. Lord Breon, Val, Barda, and Harrod, who had no idea what Tyrsell meant, looked blank. But the Tayledras and the Ghost Cat representatives, who had an altogether *too* healthy taste for the bawdy, laughed themselves into exhaustion. Even Kel howled with laughter.

And Darian was not about to offer the confused ones any kind of explanation. Not then. Not *ever.*

Two

As soon as the meeting was over, Darian was co-opted by Starfall and Ayshen. He'd expected it; the burden of planning for this celebration would fall on Ayshen's shoulders, with Starfall handling the rest of the details. Ayshen had no more notion of what would serve to "honor" a Herald than a fish would know how to honor a bird. Starfall had worked with Heralds, but had only a sketchy grasp of what one would expect socially.

Darian was used to the appearance of the *hertasi* after all these years, but he took a moment to consider what the Herald's reaction might be. Ayshen was a typical specimen of his race; he came to just about chest-high on a human; his blunt, lizardlike head boasted a formidable set of teeth, a rounded cranium, and eyes set so that he had binocular vision, like an owl or a human. His tough hide, covered with pebble-scales, was a healthy blue-gray. His stubby hands and feet had talons that he had used to good effect in the past. What would Herald Anda make of all that—when the owner of these attributes was also the chief cook for k'Valdemar?

Shandi will have warned him, he reminded himself. *Besides, anybody who partners with a talking horse shouldn't look crosswise at a talking lizard—especially if he wants second helpings.*

So Darian allowed himself to be dragged off to Ayshen's little "den"—a quasi-office space behind the main kitchens, from which he ruled over all things domestic in k'Valdemar. He had maps and models of the entire Vale, with a complex of *hertasi* tunnels marked out in pale blue—for, like a good general, Ayshen kept careful track of the terrain. His offices had been built, along with the rest of the kitchens, from rock dug from the cliffs. Those who live intimately with forests are uniquely conscious of the devouring power of fire, and there was as little that was flammable in the kitchens as was possible. Water, flour, and sand were near at hand in the event they would be needed to smother any errant flame. The chief piece of furniture was Ayshen's desk; low, and suited to his size. Besides Ayshen's desk chair, there were three adjustable stools with hinged seat backs; Starfall and Darian each took one, revolving it until it was comfortable for them to use.

Not that it was any hardship to be ensconced in the *hertasi* den. Though the aromas of the evening's supper offerings mingled into a single mouthwatering perfume that would have driven a hungry man mad, Starfall and Darian were not left for a moment to suffer that particular torture. They hadn't even sat down before *hertasi* came out of the kitchen bearing platters of their particular favorites, all the tastier for being fresh from the cookstove and oven.

It's a good thing that Tayledras live in trees, Darian thought, as he juggled a hot filled pastry from hand to hand until it cooled. *Otherwise we'd all be as fat as geese ready for market!*

Starfall did not look as if he had ever lived on anything more substantial than air, but Darian knew that beneath his fancifully embroidered and cut robes, that body wasn't thin—it was *lean*, lean and hard, and superbly conditioned. It took great physical conditioning to handle node-magic; a mage that was flabby in body was likely to be flabby of mind as well. Starfall's silver hair wasn't the result of age, it was the result of handling and using node-magic, and the slightly tamer magic of Tayledras Heartstones, all of his life. Starfall would find it no great task to run up the stairs to the highest *ekele* in the Vale, and run back down again within moments.

"We'll have a feast, of course," Ayshen stated, shoving aside recipe books and menus. "You can't have a celebration without a feast. But should we have high tables and all that? I'm not certain there's anywhere central that we could set up that many tables."

"Have the usual sort of Tayledras feast, with food set out all over the Vale, Ayshen," Darian recommended soothingly. "One thing, though; have a set of our clothing done up in white—Herald's Whites for inside the Vale. Leave them out in the guest lodge for him."

"Good notion," Starfall seconded, nodding, with the customary soft clattering of his hair beads. "Welcoming ceremony first, then we take him to the lodge to get settled. He won't feel as out of place if he has time to change into clothing of our style."

"He'll like our sort of feast, I think; he'll expect something different, and I think he'd be disappointed if he didn't get it," Darian told the *hertasi*. "Besides, I'm sure Breon will have his own welcoming feast after ours, and he'll get all the etiquette and high tables he wants there."

Ayshen's body language showed relief in the relaxation of his tail and stubby-taloned fingers. "So be it, then. If different is what he's expecting, we can supply that. What do you say to setting up a particular place just for this Herald fellow—a short platform with food-tables nearby, of course—and move entertainment in and out. We could put him in the Council House, for instance. We'll have the new roof trim done by then, and it is a good central location."

"That would be a good idea," Darian replied, as Starfall nodded. "I remember how easily I got lost the first time I was in k'Vala. When he gets tired, the guest lodge is right on the same path, within shouting distance. Is the deck on the guest lodge finished yet?"

"It will be by the time the Herald arrives; they're putting the finishing touches on it now," Ayshen replied without even consulting his schedules. "This afternoon they're sanding the hand-rails and setting the steps. Tonight the greenery will be placed."

"We're the hosts; it would be courteous if we all came to him, rather than trotting him about from entertainment to entertainment," Starfall agreed. "We can arrange things so that the people he will need to know spend a good portion of time with him in the beginning, then anyone who is curious can come to meet him. Will that make preparations easier for you, Ayshen?"

"Oh, yes, and after I've had a look at him, I can decide which *hertasi* to assign to him." The *hertasi* sighed. "Only *one* fancy, decorated serving table to set up. The rest of you never notice my artistic efforts anyway."

"We *do*," Starfall insisted. "You just overwhelm our ability to praise with a superfluity of talent!"

Ayshen simply gave the Mage a withering look by way of reply. "So—how does this strike you—we have the actual welcoming *ceremony* at the entrance of the Vale. Everyone will fit there easily enough since the weeds were cleared out last season. Then, we take the Heralds and our other guests to the Council House and feed them. We let them talk for a while, and when it sounds as if the talk is running out, I run in some entertainment. Then a little more food—and so on, until he gives up for the night. We can pick foods that will make him drowsy quickly, which reduces the amount of entertainment needed on such short notice. He'll leave to doze after just a few hours."

"Which will be long before any Tayledras would give up," Darian laughed. "That sounds perfect, Ayshen." He grinned wickedly. "Then, the next day, when he's been properly softened up for us, we give him to Tyrsell and have him stuffed with our language, Ghost Cat's, and Kaled'a'in, all at once."

Starfall gave him a look of mock-horror. "I thought you *liked* Heralds!"

"I do—that's why I suggested the languages come in all at once. It won't take Tyrsell that much longer to give them all to him, and the headache won't be that much worse, after. Better to get it over with, *I* say." Darian mimicked Starfall's look of horror. "Well? Wouldn't *you* rather have it all at once than strung out over several days? I should think that after the first experience, the subsequent dread would make the next sessions worse."

Starfall nodded, then turned to face the *hertasi* upon hearing a low hiss.

"We were discussing the celebration," Ayshen reminded them pointedly, baring his teeth for emphasis. "Now just how, precisely, would you suggest we greet him?"

"Just that," Darian replied. "Greet him as our guest. Our

welcome guest, our equal, who will be joining the leaders already here in their efforts to foster harmony among otherwise different peoples. He'll already be on best behavior to impress when he rides up, so having a good turn out but little ceremony would make him feel appreciative that he must not endure trial after trial. Getting his disposition in our favor right away would be valuable."

"And you thought you didn't have the talent to become a leader!" Starfall exclaimed. "Listen to you!"

"I'm just quoting what my excellent teachers would say in the same circumstances," Darian retorted. "Weren't you just agreeing with Lord Breon that we're to make certain Herald Anda understands he is one among equals here?"

"Huh. The boy finally pays attention," Ayshen muttered, but when Darian turned to fix him with a sharp glance, he looked as innocent as could be.

"On the whole," Ayshen continued blandly, "I am relieved. This is going to be much easier to plan and execute than a wedding, for instance. Should I pull some of the *ekele*-building crew to go to work on the Herald's permanent quarters, do you think?"

Starfall exchanged a glance with Darian, who shook his head slightly. "Not yet," Starfall told him. "Although Breon said he's expecting to stay here—I presume as a kind of envoy—he may decide that he prefers to lodge in the village, in more familiar surroundings. For all we know, he may decide to establish himself outside *all* of our enclaves. I can let him know at some point that we have the hands, and the rest will contribute materials, when he wants to have a permanent residence built, and that he can have it constructed where he pleases."

Darian nodded. "Instead, I suggest you pull a couple of builder crews off to add proper accommodations for the Companion; they'll want to be close to each other, and this will show that *we* understand that the Companion is as important as the Herald, and that they work together. It certainly wouldn't hurt to have Companion quarters attached to the guest lodge for future visiting Heralds."

Ayshen nodded his blunt snout decisively. "Right, then. Won't be difficult; knock a two-level door into one of the end rooms, add the stabling, bring water in for a fountain—I can have that finished in a few days." He scratched his nose. "Sawdust floor, I think. Maybe some mats. Outside door with a rope latch, so the Companion can let himself in and out."

"That sounds perfect to me," Darian replied, very much impressed with Ayshen's forethought.

"So . . . just the welcome to plan for now, and the extra building." Ayshen wrote out a note in silverstick, folded it into a pyramid, and stuck it on the model of the guest lodge as a reminder. "That's manageable. Well, are you two going to sit there all day, eating everything in the kitchen? Shoo! I have work to do!"

Laughing, Darian and Starfall left the *hertasi* to his own devices, as he began rummaging about for more paper, muttering about menus.

Keisha stood at the open door of Darian's vine-covered house, hefting first one wicker pannier basket, then the other, to judge roughly which was heavier. Above her head, the trees met to form a ceiling over the house and path; songbirds and colorful messenger-birds chattered and sang, and hummingbirds chased each other around the branches. She had not gone to the meeting; as the chief Healer to both Vale and village, she spent roughly equal time in each—and that left her feeling a bit odd about representing either. Instead, Nightwind served as the mouthpiece for the Healers unless there was some pressing reason for Keisha herself to be there.

She had to check her packs anyway, for she was about to make another trip back to the village to make sure anyone who needed her services was properly tended to. The baskets were laden with various medications, most of them for animals rather than humans. The villagers were uncommonly healthy this summer, with half the normal number of accidents, even among the children. Perhaps that was due to increasing prosperity; well-fed and well-rested people resisted disease and didn't have nearly so many mishaps. Ever since the events of recent times, the Crown had sent more funding for rebuilding and renewing the area than it had ever received before in half a decade. Newer tools were invariably more reliable, safer tools out here. Even the old mill had been rebuilt into a safer operation—she had not had to deal with a single injury from it since its reopening.

She wore full Greens now, the forest-hued colors of a full Healer, with a silk scarf serving as a sash around her waist, laid over a matching one of cotton. Healers always had a use for a scarf—to sling an arm, tie off a cut artery, or dry a child's tears. They were not official parts of Healer's uniform, but their use was so common they might as well have been. Keisha paused, considering the Healer's uniform she wore. It had taken her a while to get used to that—and some persuasion as well. It was finally the argument that it would be better for her *patients* to see her in the colors of a Healer, because they would be under less stress, that tilted the balance. She refused to don anything elaborate, though; the loose trews and long-sleeved tunic were fancy enough for everyday wear—and when she wanted something festive, she opted for something that didn't display her status for all to see.

The good thing about being in the Vale was that she no longer had to make her own medicines unless she really felt like it; all she had to do was give the *hertasi* instructions, and they would see to the preparation for her, presenting her with neatly labeled pots and jars of anything she needed or wanted. A great deal of her time in the past had been spent in the actual concoction of medicine, time she now had leisure to spend in other ways.

So now I spend it riding to and from the village, instead! she thought wryly, as she made sure the two pannier baskets that her *dyheli* would carry were finally balanced as evenly as she could manage without actually weighing them.

She shared Darian's quarters—and yes, his bed—when she was in the Vale, and since he had never yet accompanied her to Errold's Grove when she went on her weekly visits, the touchy problem of whether he would share *her* home had never come up. Her parents, of course, had no idea that they were anything but friends, and everyone else had the sense not to betray their ongoing relationship to the village. It was true that she was old enough to do as she wished; it was also true, as Kerowyn had remarked before she left, that no child is "old enough" in her parents' eyes. She could own an estate, command a dozen servants, and have gray hair, yet she would not be "old enough."

She ducked back inside for a moment to make sure she hadn't forgotten anything, then returned to wait in the sunshine for her *dyheli* to arrive. *It's a given. If Shandi were to come back for more than a fortnight, she'd be treated the same way—as if she was no more than fourteen, and unable to make any decisions for herself. The only reason she doesn't get treated that way is because before Mother has a chance to get her lectures set fair in her head, Shandi's gone again.*

Besides, Keisha wasn't entirely sure how long this particular liaison was going to last. Darian was a very handsome lad, and every village female unspoken for (and some who were) had made it very clear that they found him fascinating. There were plenty of girls who would be only too happy to find out what life was like in a Vale. What if he got tired of her?

What if I got tired of him? Well, she couldn't see that happening, but she had a lot of responsibilities, more than she had ever had before.

And so did he.

That was part of the problem. His responsibilities kept him here, but that was not so with hers. Yes, she was—for now— the chief Healer for k'Valdemar. She was also still the Healer for Errold's Grove, and she wouldn't blame him if he got tired of finding her gone half the time. She couldn't devote herself to him the way her mother had devoted herself to her family. It just wasn't going to happen that way.

She rubbed her temple with one finger, and stifled a sigh. Sooner or later, the Vale would get a Tayledras Healer as well, and then all her energies would go to the village. She wouldn't have a reason to stay in k'Valdemar anymore. *He* certainly wouldn't move back to Errold's Grove. Then what? She couldn't keep going back and forth between here and the village when she didn't need to be here. People would start to wonder why. Saying she was studying under the Tayledras Healer would hold for a while, but what then?

She bent over to tie her baskets closed, certain now that she had everything she intended to take with her. Her vision was suddenly blocked by a pair of hands in front of her eyes; she seized Darian's wrists and spun herself around to meet his merry brown eyes and cheerful grin, reflecting dappled sunlight.

There was a crumb of pastry tangled up in a lock of his hair—and he was too fastidious to have left it there for very long. He must have just eaten minutes before. She sniffed, experimentally. "You've been eating garlic sausage rolls!" she accused.

"Well, you weren't going to be here tonight, so the garlic wouldn't matter, would it?" he retorted, and gave her a redolent kiss. "If you change your mind, there's still time to help yourself, and we'll both have garlic breath. Besides, you know how good garlic is for you!"

Not that she minded garlic breath, at least not when they both had it. Her main objection was that he would have been perfectly happy if everything he ate was spiced with garlic, and she didn't like it *that* much. . . .

Another thing we don't share. . . .

"Not a chance; if I don't make my trip, the Trilvy family will probably come get me. Rana Trilvy is *that* close—" she replied, holding her thumb and forefinger an infinitesimal distance apart. "And even though I've told her a hundred times that she's fine, she's still convinced that if I don't see her every week, something is bound to go wrong and her baby will be born with nine heads. Never, ever, try to argue with a nervous mother-to-be; you haven't the chance of a pigeon in a cattery of winning the argument."

Something about his expression made her wary; he had that devilish look he always got when he was keeping a secret, that made his sharp features look even more fox-like. "What happened at the Council meeting?" she continued, as if she hadn't noticed.

"Mostly the usual, but Breon had some news." He was *much* too casual; something was definitely up. Whatever Lord Breon had brought in the way of news was something he knew she'd want to hear.

She decided that two could play that game of feigned indifference. "Oh? Anything important, or can it wait until I get back?" She fooled with the baskets a bit more, taking care not to look directly at him.

"You'll probably hear it on the way back anyway, since you're going with Barda and Harrod. We're getting resident Heralds." He watched her closely, and she knew from the way he was acting that although this was momentous news, it wasn't the biggest part of his secret.

"Really?" she exclaimed anyway. "Heralds? As permanent residents? More than one?"

He nodded. "Two of them; an older, experienced Herald-Mage, believe it or not, and his personally selected trainee. Or maybe I should say, protegé, since she's got her Whites, and this is taking the place of her 'first circuit.' "

"A Herald-Mage! *That's* certainly something!" It was, too; there still weren't that many Herald-Mages about, and to have one of them assigned permanently to Errold's Grove said a great deal for how the status of this area had risen. "They must think we're high on their list of priorities now!"

"But it's not the *biggest* news, not for you, anyway. The other Herald is your sister Shandi." He grinned as her jaw dropped, and she looked at him in disbelief. "No, really, it is! I suppose they figure that they might as well assign her here, since she's likely to assign *herself* here, given half a chance. Even without half a chance, she's likely to turn up anyway."

"But—it hasn't been much more than two years—" She still couldn't believe it; Shandi had said nothing of this in her letters! She'd only complained now and again of how busy she was and how much she was expected to absorb.

Is that why she hasn't spent more than four weeks here in the last two and a half years? Because she's been rushing—or rushed—through her studies?

"Breon said she hadn't gotten the record for graduating quickly, but she was close. He was fairly impressed." Darian grinned at her reaction. "Mind you, he shouldn't have been surprised. Look at how well you've done, and you haven't had a Collegium full of teachers to help you! When I first met you, you would have barely qualified as a Healer trainee, at least as far as your Gift went. Now even the Sanctuary Healers call you their equal."

"Pfft." She dismissed her own prowess with a wave of her hand, not the least because she was not nearly as impressed with her "accomplishments" as he seemed to be. "How soon will they be here?"

"Cut your visit to Errold's Grove as short as you can; I got the impression it's just a matter of days before they arrive. For now, they'll be staying at the Vale. We're going to put on a celebration for them. Oh, the senior one's name is Anda; I don't suppose you recognize it, do you?" He tilted his head to the side, curiously.

She thought for a moment. "It sounds vaguely familiar;

Shandi must have mentioned him now and again." She kissed him quickly, then pushed him gently away, and turned back to her baskets, tying them shut deftly. "The sooner I'm gone, the sooner I'll be back. Don't work too hard while I'm off; but do try to see that Ayshen doesn't try to do *everything.*"

He sighed melodramatically, then bent to help her with her baskets. "You ought to know by now that keeping Ayshen from overwork is beyond *my* powers. I suppose it's of no use to ask if you'd like to stop all this, find a replacement, and settle down permanently here with me, is it?" he asked.

"When someone is getting ready for a journey, it's the wrong time to ask about settling down, Darian." She told her stomach to stop bouncing, and put on an air of calm. "The answer still hasn't changed."

"I didn't think it had, but a fellow can ask. It's just that we're awfully good together. . . ." To her intense relief, he didn't pursue the subject. She was saved from having to say anything more by the arrival of her *dyheli,* a young buck this time.

He didn't ask the question every time she left, but it was at least once a month. Was it only a sense of duty that kept him asking? He couldn't possibly understand what it meant to be bound to a calling; being a Healer meant being tied into her avocation even more tightly than being wedded.

Without being asked, Darian saddled the *dyheli* and fastened the baskets on either side of the arm-thick pad seated just over the stag's rump. She grabbed hold of the handle that was built in place of a saddle-horn, put her foot in a stirrup, and swung herself up into place. *Dyheli* had no reins to take up; they would never have permitted so undignified a contraption as a halter on their heads.

:*Good day, Healer,*: the buck said formally. :*I am Talen.*:

:*Thank you for your help, Talen,*: she replied just as formally. :*Are Barda and Harrod ready to return yet?*:

:*They await us at the Vale entrance. Shall we go?*: Talen responded, his thoughts glossed with a skimming of impatience. The bucks were almost always a little impatient; it seemed to go with the gender.

"I heard—go and come back soon, Keisha." That was all Darian said, but beneath the words was a great deal more that Keisha just didn't want to have to deal with. Talen felt her assent, and leaped away, keeping her from having to do any-thing more than wave back over her shoulder.

Within the Vale, the *dyheli* kept to a fast lope, but as soon as he burst through the tenuous curtain of the Veil and caught up with the other two, he stretched out into a full run. *Dyheli* often seemed as tireless as Companions; he'd have all of them in Errold's Grove well before suppertime.

Barda and Harrod hung on grimly; they were used to travel by *dyheli*-back, but not as accustomed to it as Keisha was. Although she could not (as Heralds were rumored to do) have fallen asleep in Talen's saddle, she moved easily with her mount.

If only she could have been as easy with her own thoughts.

Firesong k'Treva finished the last of his stretches, moving smoothly and slowly, while his partner Silverfox watched, alert for any sign of strain. Such alertness was as natural for him as breathing, after so many decades of body study. They shared this ritual every morning; Silverfox insisted on it, and Firesong had to admit he'd felt more like his younger self since he'd begun.

Being limber does have its advantages.

"Well?" he asked, as he finished the exercise and stood, arms hanging at his sides, completely relaxed, yet energized, tingling with the song of the body rather than of magic, on the uppermost deck of their *ekele.*

"You'll do," Silverfox replied, smiling slightly. "You *might* even be in better shape than you were before the Storms. I told you this would loosen you up, and you wouldn't believe me."

"I didn't have you to keep me active, before the Storms," Firesong pointed out, slipping on a robe of scarlet silk, embroi-dered with white-and-gold firebirds, over his form-fitting sleeveless tunic and trews.

"In other words, you were a lazy sluggard," the *kestra'chern* replied, and ducked as Firesong mimed a blow at him. The Healing Adept's firebird, Aya, who had been watching all of this activity with keen interest, let out a derisive squawk. The bird opened his snowy wings and dropped down onto Fire-song's shoulder, fixing his talons carefully into the padded fab-ric. The long white tail trailed gracefully down Firesong's back, curling around the thick, silver braid of Firesong's hair.

"Whose part are you taking, mine or his?" Firesong asked, looking into his bird's diamond-dust eyes. "Never mind. I don't want to know."

"And Aya is too smart to answer, anyway," the *kestra'-chern* laughed. "Not when he knows he can get treats from both of us this way."

It was Firesong's turn to make a noise of derision; Aya stretched his head and neck under Firesong's chin, and the Adept answered the silent request by scratching the firebird's chin. Aya crooned with pleasure. "Don't listen to him, little one," he said into Aya's ear. "He thinks everyone is as self-centered as he is—or more."

"Of course I do—since I'm not at *all* self-centered," Silverfox replied matter-of-factly. He took Firesong's elbow, and steered him in the direction of the staircase that curved around the trunk of their tree. "And don't look now, but your pet is trying to coax me into tickling him, too."

Aya opened one eye and gave Silverfox a withering look at the word "pet," but did not pull his head away from Silverfox's fingers.

Firesong felt a smile stretching the stiff, pitted and scarred skin of his face. Although life was nothing like he'd anticipated when he left his home Vale, it was very good. *What's more, I'm not sure if I'd be willing to do any of it over, since the end result is so—comfortable. It's amazing now that I can wear so many faces here without any of them being a mask—and wear a mask without hiding my feelings.*

Silverfox followed him down past the bedroom to the main public room of the *ekele*. The tree wasn't large enough to support an *ekele* very high off the ground, or for more than one room to be on a single level, but now that the Veil was in place, he'd had the *hertasi* construct an external stair linking all the rooms, so that the area that had been used for the internal staircase could be converted into usable space. Wide decks circled each level of the *ekele*, and the staircase threaded its way around and through them. All the windows were open to the balmy air, and flowering vines grown from k'Vala cuttings had been trained around each of the windows to scent the breezes.

There were plenty of masks hanging on the walls, but Firesong didn't trouble to reach for any of them as he and Silverfox entered the room. Here in his own home, no one would trouble him who had not been invited—and no one who had been invited would be shocked or disturbed by his burn-scarred appearance.

Some of Silverfox's handiwork hung on the walls as well—gryphon feathers, shed by some of the residents of k'Valdemar when they molted. These were all primaries, secondaries, or tail-feathers, and the smallest was as long as Firesong's forearm. Silverfox decorated the quills with beadwork, and painted the broad expanses with sinuous designs echoing the colors of the beads. Dyed leather and ribbons of strong textures complemented the interlace and lilt of the line-work. Feather artworks hung between each mask, and Firesong never tired of resting his eyes on them.

He lifted Aya off his shoulder and set the firebird down on a perch mounted in the wall, one indulgently made of silver in the form of a vine-wrapped branch with a hammered brass reflector behind it as tall as a *hertasi*. Aya roused all his feathers and shook himself vigorously; bits of fluff flew off of him and rode the air currents of the room like wayward insects, and sparks of false fire crackled around him.

"Wasn't the Joint Council meeting this morning?" he asked Silverfox, as he sank into his favorite chair and reached for a book. Before he could even make up his mind that he wanted something, one of his *hertasi* appeared at his elbow and left a tall glass of cooled juice on the table where his book had been.

"Yes, and Keisha was going back to Errold's Grove with the village representatives, so Darian will probably be a little late." Silverfox sighed, but didn't say anything more; Firesong assumed that the sigh was for Darian's situation with the girl. And it *was* too bad; but it was also Darian's and Keisha's choice to keep things hanging this way. Darian didn't allow it to affect his mage-studies; only if it had, would Firesong have had any right to stick his own nose into the affair.

It was later than Firesong would have expected, though, when Kuari came in to land on the railing of the porch, signaling that Darian could not be far behind. Lunch was long over, and Firesong was well into his book by then; Silverfox had already gone below to his workrooms at the foot of the tree to administer to some of his massage clients.

The Healing-Adept laid his book aside after reading a passage that made him smile, since it echoed his own teaching philosophy so well. *Teach what you know, regardless of when you have learned it—teach what you learned yesterday sagely, as if you have known it all your life, and teach what you have known for decades with enthusiasm, as if you learned it only yesterday.* He marked that page with a scarlet-jay feather and waited for Darian's step on the stair, and saw by the young man's face that there was unexpected news.

"Lord Breon said we're going to get a permanent, resident Herald," were the first words out of the young man's mouth.

"Really?" Firesong was a little surprised at the "we." "I take it he is expected to reside *here?* In k'Valdemar?"

Darian picked a seat and settled into it. "So Lord Breon says—unless the Herald decides it would be more politic to actually live outside the Vale. He's supposed to be a Herald-Mage, too. Keisha's sister Shandi just got her Whites, and *she's* coming too, as his protegé. I don't know if that's for the long term, but she'll certainly be here for a year."

"Hmm. We're having a welcome, obviously." Firesong knew there was something more, but Darian would get to it quickly enough; it was his nature not to hold anything back, for good or ill.

"Yes, and I—well, I suppose you could say that *I'm* going to be the chief entertainment," Darian replied ruefully, his expression a comical mixture of chagrin, embarrassment, and pride. "Lord Breon got this idea—"

He related exactly what had happened at the Council Meeting with remarkable facility—but then, the young man hadn't been *out* of the circles of power since he was about fourteen or fifteen. *Starfall is probably only waiting for him to reach the status of a full Mage before resigning from the Council, having Snowfire take his place, and graduating Darian into Snowfire's slot.*

Well, if that was indeed Starfall's plan, Firesong's own plans fit right into that. And now was a good time to set those plans in motion.

"Well, in that case," he said casually, "it is a pleasant enough day. I have had a good breakfast. Before you get too involved in all these other ceremonies, perhaps we'd better put you through your Mastery Trial."

Darian's face went completely blank; Firesong had the satisfaction—which was not happening often, these days!—of catching the young man completely by surprise. Firesong may as well have said, "I had a nice nap, so let's dig up this forest and make a pretty lake, eh?" The look on Darian's face was delicious.

"So, let's get that little exercise taken care of, shall we?" he continued, with mischievous casualness, as he got to his feet. "Come along."

He didn't stop to see if Darian was following as he headed for the stairs; Darian would follow, because Firesong hadn't given him any time to actually *think* about what he was going to do. Darian was ready—but the more time he had to stew about the Trial, the more likely it was that he'd work himself up into a nervous state over it, and risk failure. Firesong had never intended to give him that chance. Too many young mages froze up and couldn't even remember the simplest of spells when allowed to dwell on the upcoming Trial; it was a mistake some teachers made that would not happen with Darian.

The steps behind him creaked under Darian's weight, and Firesong smiled to himself. By this evening, the Vale would have yet another piece of news to talk about. Or at least they would, if Firesong had anything to say about it. Firesong usually got his way—although these days, when he didn't get what he wanted, he just changed his mind until he was happy with what he had.

Darian, however, would do very well in the coming trial, he knew. Firesong could feel intuitively that he would get exactly what he wanted. He had confidence in his pupil, and the Vale would have something more to celebrate by nightfall—the first new Master Mage of a new Vale. His student. Magnificent!

Three

Darian shivered as he followed Firesong down the stairs to the dome complex nestled at the foot of the tree. Most of that structure belonged to Silverfox, but Firesong kept one private room for himself, protected with the tightest permanent shields inside k'Valdemar. Layer upon layer, unseen buttress against invisible firewall, every sort of stabilized, strengthened magical protection known to the Adept had been firmed up. Over the past years they had been cast and enchanted into virtual patterns of stone, as if mortared by an expert, with the equivalent of pockets and drains for excess power to collect. This was Firesong's workroom, where he had taught Darian for two years; many of the shields were not meant to keep anything out but rather, to keep Darian's "mistakes" from escaping.

There hadn't been a great number of those mistakes—no more than three, all in his first few months with Firesong, and all minor ones—but the existence of those shields allowed him to work without worrying about the consequences of an accident to the rest of the Vale. The first had resulted in no worse than a burned hand and singed eyebrows, the second a splitting headache for both of them, and the third, a scorch mark on the floor surrounded by frost, which resulted in an intensive series of lessons on why resilient shields were more important than rigid ones. Darian had known all along that every lesson would lead up to a Mastery Trial, but he'd assumed he would have time to prepare for it, and undergo days of special readiness rituals.

Why now? Why not give me some time to work up to this? he asked himself, anticipation setting his nerves afire. He had *no* idea just what was going to be expected of him—

And it was too late for second thoughts. Firesong had reached the bottom of the staircase, palming something from one of the dozen narrow shelves of ornaments and oddities, and held open the door to the workroom for Darian. His scarred face showing nothing except pleasant anticipation, quite as if this were just another, perfectly ordinary lesson. Darian entered the door into the windowless room, lit from above by a blue-tinted skylight, and Firesong closed the door behind them both. He dropped a latch that all but seamlessly blended into the interlaced trim that ran around the room.

With the closing of the door, the shields sprang up and into place all around them, creating a kind of hum in the back of his head and a tingle along his skin. Firesong leaned casually against the doorframe, folded his arms across his chest, and nodded. "The usual," was all he said laconically.

So Darian began with "the usual," the building of his own shields, spreading them outward to encompass the room, then integrating them with Firesong's shields that were already in place, leaving some layers fragile so they could collapse back in case of a surge. He could have done this much in his sleep; it took scarcely a thought to shape his own energy to his will now. It hadn't always been that way.

But next came an addition to his shields, a shunt to drain off excessive heat. He had never actually *needed* this shunt before, but unused mage-energy, if not properly grounded and sent back to its source, or energy that came in to the mage at a rate greater than he could handle, manifested in waste heat. At the level a Journeyman worked, this was a trivial concern; the worst that happened was that the area got a bit too warm for comfort—or the occasional flash, like the earlier accidents. In fact, if working in the dead of winter and there was energy to spare, some Journeymen deliberately eliminated the shunt so as to warm the area they worked in. This ability to deliberately create heat made mages very popular in cold climes and seasons, and some weather-work was based directly on that effect.

But at the level a Master worked, improperly handled energy could be deadly; the shunt was a necessity—as Firesong's own scars testified. At the end of the Mage Storms, when trying to avert magical catastrophe, Firesong and his allies had done everything *right*, but the energies they had dealt with had been greater than any mage before or since had ever faced— even Adepts working in concert with Avatars of the Star-Eyed Goddess of the Shin'a'in had not been able to prevent all the damage such an overwhelming force could conjure.

"Now locate all the Heartstones of all the Clans," his mentor told him. Darian nodded, and unfocused his eyes to better invoke OverSight and see into the plane of mage-energy, searching out each active Stone and tracing the intricate web of ley-lines that surrounded them. First, his own—k'Valdemar was a lesser Stone by any estimation, but it was growing, its power increasing daily. He was rather proud of that, for some of the energies invested in the Stone were of his harvesting. Each bit of power he had added over the past two years had made the Stone stronger and more stable, so that now it was possible to turn this into a real Vale by all Tayledras standards.

Then—the Heartstone under the Palace at Haven. This one was a bit peculiar; *very* old, *very* powerful, but quiescent. The shields had held through the last of the mage-storms, making it just about the only magical artifact outside of a Vale that *had* survived complete and untouched. There wasn't much pull on it at the moment, for there were not that many Herald-Mages about who could use it. Someday, perhaps, Haven would be the Valdemar version of a Vale—but for now, the Stone slumbered. Like a war horse asleep in its stall, it wouldn't take much to rouse it to fury, but the proper hands could control it with a mere touch of the reins or a whisper in its ear.

However, *his* were not those hands; that power was there for the service of the Heralds. It was theirs, and theirs alone. They were sealed to it by their very nature, and by the bonds they had with their Companions. It helped to maintain a different sort of web of power, one that linked all Heralds and Companions together.

Next, k'Vala Vale, the nearest to k'Valdemar. Its Stone was old, too, though not nearly as ancient as the Palace Stone, and unlike that Stone, this one was fully awake and active, with much power flowing out as well as into it. There were plenty of demands on the k'Vala Stone, and it responded to those demands as smoothly as a masterful juggler kept an impossible number of toys in the air. It wasn't *quite* alive, not *quite* sentient, yet there was a quality of "life" and "personality" to it that was the hallmark of every Heartstone. That wasn't surprising, considering how closely linked to the life of a Vale the Heartstone was.

Darian found and identified all of the stones, holding them all balanced within his mind, shining points of brilliant light in the web of life-energy. Firesong followed his work closely, and nodded when Darian found and touched the last of the lot, and the farthest, the Stone of k'Treva Vale.

"Good." Firesong seemed satisfied that Darian had done the job with a minimal expenditure of his own energies. As a Journeyman, that was all he could really draw on for sustained and heavy use; the energies he himself produced or stored. He *could* recharge himself with the little trickles of power produced by all the living things around him, but that was akin to filling a cup with the dew collected on leaves. He could also make use of the tiny rivulets of energy as the living power collected in trickles and flowed toward the ley-lines. But not until he reached Master could he use the lines themselves—or the Heartstone.

Most schools of mage-craft built and maintained pools of power available to their Masters, but none except the Tayledras invested the energies not only of their own members but actually ran ley-lines into their power-pools and terminated them there. That was perhaps because only the Tayledras knew how to construct the Heartstones, to keep energy flowing out so that it never overloaded; of all of those outsiders who had tried, only one had succeeded—and that one was the legendary Herald-Mage Vanyel, Adept, and Tayledras-trained. Hundreds of years ago, Vanyel had invested the energies in the web that linked his Heralds, and a spell that had kept (or, more truthfully, irritated) "foreign" mages out of Valdemar, providing that steady drain; the Vales invested the excess in weather-control, shielding, and luxuries like the hot pools. When anyone else tried, the focus of power quickly destabilized in a manner quite destructive and usually fatal to all concerned.

"Now," Firesong continued, unperturbed, "without disturbing the ley-lines in any way, link yourself to the ones feeding our Stone."

He knew how to do that. He'd "watched" Firesong do it a thousand times—he'd practiced everything short of touching the lines themselves—and now was the moment of truth. He would either be able to call this hawk he'd trained back to his gloved fist, or fail—and feel its talons sink into his flesh, or watch it soar away out of reach forever.

He noticed that Firesong had no personal shields up whatsoever in case of failure. Knowing Firesong, that might be just another way to increase Darian's confidence, but it was a trust that touched him deeply.

Except for a brief stab of something sharp, a mingling of fear and excitement, he didn't let himself think or feel. He just acted.

He "reached" out, moving surely, but not too quickly. He caught hold of the nearest ley-line, and without permitting himself to hesitate, seized it, opening himself to it.

He knew enough to brace himself for the shock, but it still rocked him; it was like opening up his veins to a flow of white-hot glass! For a fraction of a second, he was immersed, blinded by the fiery incandescence, as pathways within him felt the caress of energies they had never known until this moment. Every breath seemed thicker, and every color more intense. All at once, he was drunk, delirious with power, dizzy with its intoxicating song, and disoriented.

Then everything he'd learned, from Starfall, from Firesong, from the mages of k'Vala Vale, came surging to the fore, and it was *he* who was in control, not the power.

It was still dizzying, still intoxicating, but the heady draught no longer overwhelmed him. He'd ridden horses in Valdemar, some very spirited and powerful horses. This was very like riding such a horse. He commanded; the power obeyed, but only because he had the skill to command and the strength of will not to succumb to the seductive song and be lost in it.

Darian still remembered that lesson outside k'Vala Vale when he'd nearly gotten lost in the shift and flow of the simple life-powers of everything around him. Having experienced that, he knew would not make that mistake again. He made sure that he was still anchored in himself and let his channels become accustomed to the new sensations. Then, metaphorically, he sat back and allowed himself to experience the moment. The wonder of Tayledras teaching was that it permitted the student to accept those things, to comprehend them, but never to become numbed to them; it was a way of understanding, not just using. Now he understood as a Master would. It would never happen like this again, this first taste of power, this seductive latent drunkenness; Darian wanted to be able to remember it, however dimly.

:*A remarkably mature sentiment,:* came a dry mental voice, after an interval. :*But you, my young student, are a Healing-Mage. So what* else *do you see, feel, or sense?:*

What else? Was there anything else?

But even as he asked himself that, his own Mage-Senses answered him, and he knew that, of course, there was. Within the stream of power that was the ley-line, there were a myriad of little subcurrents, and each of those threads told him of the health of the place it originated from. Eddies and obstructions in the flow as he traced it back out of the Vale showed him where the line itself needed alteration or mending. Two other mages—both Hawkbrothers—had tapped into this particular line; he sensed their presence at the same moment they sensed his. They acknowledged each other briefly, and went on with what they were doing. As did he; his touch moved by instinct and, sure from long practice, he mended the line, smoothing out the eddies, altering the flow until it ran swift and unimpeded.

:*Good. So, then, catch!:* Just as he completed this work, Firesong flipped something at him. Before it had gone half the distance between them, he lanced out a coruscating line of force and caught it in a gentle net of power, holding it in mid-air. It was only a river stone, but as he met Firesong's eyes and saw the approval in them, he was very glad that he had chosen to cradle it, and not blast it aside.

:*Well done. Now tap into the Heartstone,:* the voice commanded. :*You're keyed to it. Now use it. Without dropping the rock, that is.:*

Without releasing his hold on the line *or* the rock, Darian did exactly as he had been ordered, reaching for the Heartstone, touching it, then melding with its outer edges. He sensed it test him (or was it "taste" him?) and recognize him. That was all there was to it; he joined with the Stone, and all its power was his for the taking.

He'd expected an even wilder rush than the ley-line had fed into him; instead, this was like sinking into a peace-filled globe of light, or a blissfully hot pool of water. There was no sensation of heat, no exquisitely flickering inflow of energy; just the *presence* of enormous power, and the knowledge that he could do whatever he wanted with it.

This was no spirited horse, obedient to his will, but a kind of partner; a reservoir with a mind of its own, that acknowledged his right to drink of it.

Some mages signaled their achievement of Mastery with the production of "fireworks" that other mages of the same school could see and identify. But the Tayledras considered themselves no more than temporary custodians of their power. The Star-Eyed had granted them the use of that power for the purpose of healing the land after the Mage-Wars, and it wouldn't even have occurred to them to make such a frivolous use of it as a peacocklike display of achievement with that power.

Theirs was a different tradition; to leave their mark upon the Vale itself, creating some change that would improve the lives of all those dwelling within. And Darian knew just what his mark would be, as the first new Master of a new Vale. He had been thinking about it for some time, ever since he had been told of the tradition, and the last time he'd been in Ayshen's office, he'd checked the maps and models carefully for a place that would be open and suitable for his gift.

The lake at the far end of k'Valdemar was fed by several springs; he examined each of them in turn, to determine which would be the best candidate for his purpose. When he found one whose source was deeper than any of the others, he persuaded it to change its channel, to sink a little deeper, move nearer to the white-heat at the root of the Heartstone, before bubbling again to the surface.

Now with its waters warmed, it would serve as the water source for the first of the outdoor bathing pools. It wouldn't take the *hertasi* long to notice the change, and within days they would cap the new flow and be building great pools to receive the hot waters. By the end of the month, there would be Tayledras soaking in the soothing waters under the stars, and there would be room for anyone who needed a hot soak to come and take one. The current hot pools were all inside one of the first buildings to be constructed here, and there wasn't enough room to accommodate everyone at the same time.

:*A fine choice of gifts to your Vale, Master Dar'ian.*: Firesong's mind-voice held a smile of approval, and Darian blushed a little.

Just as carefully as he had taken control of Heartstone and ley-lines, he released them, but not before he replenished the power he had used to create his hot spring. He opened his eyes on Firesong's little workroom to see his mentor's eyes full of warmth and congratulations.

Then he took a deep breath, and sat down carefully, right there on the floor, as exhaustion hammered him with a blow that made his legs go weak. He put out his hand and caught the river stone squarely in his right palm, as it dropped.

"Put it all back, did you?" Firesong asked rhetorically. "Well, that's proper, but you didn't have to put all the energy back at one time. You could have 'borrowed' some of it."

"I didn't?" he asked. "But with all the preparations for the celebrations, we're going to be strengthening the Veil for a few days, and I thought we'd need every bit of energy now."

"Hmm. A kind thought. Never mind, you'll recover by this evening," Firesong interrupted, helping him up and keeping him on his feet with a hand beneath his elbow. He dismissed his shields, and Darian recaptured his own, feeling a little better as he took the power he'd expended on them back into himself again. Firesong didn't take him far, only past the door and into one of Silverfox's consultation rooms.

This was a very small room, used only for counseling. It had both a large window and a skylight, but the furniture was minimal. There was a soft, dark-green sling couch there, though, and Darian was very happy to lie down on it, dropping onto the silk-covered, down-stuffed cushions with his head spinning a little.

"Just lie there, and don't move," Firesong cautioned. He needn't have bothered, as Darian had no intention whatsoever of moving. He felt as if he'd run all the way to Errold's Grove and back.

Maybe a few magical fireworks would have been a better idea, he thought as he closed his eyes.

He woke again, suddenly, sweating, out of a dream that, like the one last night, he could not recall. His heart pounded in alarm, his hands were clenched on the fabric of the couch. An irrational feeling of dread hung over him, and he opened all of his senses in an effort to discover if there was anything wrong in the Vale at all.

But there was nothing. The Vale was as it had been; crafters working at their tasks, *hertasi* scuttling about, gryphons dozing in the sun. His heart slowed, the sweat dried, and he was too weary to maintain his state of alarm. Gradually he relaxed, and slept again.

The next time he opened them, he was feeling much better, and both the skylight above him and the open window beside him were dark. Someone had come in and covered him with a light blanket, then left a sweetly scented candle burning in a blue glass holder mounted on the wall. He felt better—but he didn't much feel like moving.

There didn't seem any real reason to move, either; Firesong knew where he was, and had presumably told anyone else who needed or wanted to know. Silverfox wouldn't mind him taking over the consultation room. And since Keisha wasn't going to be home, there was no great urgency to get back to his own ground-bound *ekele*. He was perfectly content at the moment to lie surrounded by warmth and softness, let his thoughts drift, and listen to the night noises outside.

Keisha's going to be surprised. Pleasantly, he hoped. This would put him on an equal footing with her, rankwise, though he very much doubted that would change anything in their relationship. *She'll be happy for me, that much I know for sure.* All the other honors that had been planned for him were really nothing more than titles to impress other people; reaching the rank of Master meant a real achievement of his own, felt in his heart.

"And how is our new Master Mage doing?" Firesong asked from the doorway, and Darian let out a little *yip* of startlement.

Firesong chuckled, and moved out of the shadows of the hallway and into the dim light from the candle.

"Serves you right for all the times you've sent me out of my skin," Firesong said. "Especially that time you shaved a year off my life when you managed to sneak up on me in my own *ekele*. How are you feeling?"

"Tired and hungry," Darian replied, suddenly feeling that hunger rise up and growl in his gut. "Very hungry, actually."

"No headache? Nausea? Dizziness?" As Darian shook his head at each question, Firesong smiled in satisfaction. "Good. Then you not only pass, you pass with all honors. And *tired* is easily fixed—find a ley-line."

"Now? Without shields?" Darian asked dubiously.

"You'd already integrated your shields into a coherent whole once you became a Journeyman; now you don't need to protect anyone from your mistakes anymore, because you aren't going to *make* any." Firesong sounded more confident in Darian's ability than Darian was, and he looked impatient for the first time as Darian wavered. "Look now, do you bother with special shields anymore when you use OverSight? Or gather low-level energy?"

"Well, no . . ." Darian took himself in hand without any further prodding. Firesong was right; by now, everything he'd learned was as familiar to him as the act of speaking or reading. Drawing on that confidence he'd had this afternoon, he closed his eyes, invoked Mage-Sight, and reached for the nearest ley-line, then opened himself. As thirsty earth drank in rain, his power-depleted self soaked in the raw strength of the line, and when he opened his eyes and released it again, he felt as good as he had when he'd awakened this morning.

Firesong gave him a lopsided grin. "Next time, don't wait to be reminded. I won't always be around, you know." He stood up, and Darian finally noticed that he'd changed his clothing from this afternoon. Now he wore blue and green, a loose-sleeved, body-hugging tunic with a high, embroidered collar, and skin-tight trews with matching soft boots. And in one hand he carried one of his many masks, a delicate thing of green scales and wispy blue plumes, that dangled loosely in his long fingers.

"Are you going somewhere?" he asked, for Firesong seldom donned a mask unless he planned to leave the shelter of his *ekele*. He didn't wear his masks to spare himself—he did it to spare others the sight of the burn scars that pockmarked his face from scalp to chin, but for a strip across his eyes where his equally burned forearm had saved his vision. But there was also the very real possibility that he had another reason as well; if there was one thing that Firesong loved to cultivate, it was an aura of mystery, and the wearing of his masks was an integral part of that mystery.

"As a matter of fact, I am," Firesong replied. "I'm taking you to your party." He grinned again. "You don't for a moment think we'd pass up such a fine excuse to have at least a *little* celebration, do you? It wouldn't be Tayledras!"

Firesong was inordinately proud of his pupil, though he wasn't about to let Darian know that. At least, he didn't want Darian to know *how* proud he was. One of the reasons he'd been contemplating giving up taking on pupils was because the last couple had, for one reason or another, never quite come up to his expectations of them. They were not bad people at all, nor stupid, just . . . less than optimal. Perhaps part of that had been a failure to mesh their personalities, or that some of his pupils had been as interested in *him* as they had been in learning what he taught. Part of that, of course, might just have been that they were discouraged; it would be a very long time before anyone was able to casually work the kind of large-scale magics that had been possible before the Mage-Storms disrupted everything. His pupils would be very old before they had power available to them to duplicate Firesong's own feats as a young and headstrong Master. It was likely that it would take another generation before there was the abundant power on hand to duplicate the lesser feats of an Adept. Gating was out of the question for at least a hundred years—safe and reliable Gating, anyway. It was no wonder they saw no reason to acquire proficiency in skills it was unlikely they would ever be able to use.

But Darian had a touch as sure and skilled as a fine craftsman, and he *never* left loose ends, or a job unfinished. Firesong was not yet certain he would reach Adept status, but as careful a worker as he was, given the current state of things and barring disaster, he would become one of the best mages of this generation. Darian was willing to follow brusque or peremptory instruction without thinking of Firesong as a tyrant; he had confidence that when he had done what he was told, it would be explained to him.

Always provided, of course, that nothing happened that interfered with his continued learning.

So Firesong decided that it was time to do a little delicate prodding. Not *meddling*—more on the order of information gathering. He never called his meddling by that unflattering name. Unsolicited guidance, discreet help, a "nudge," but never *meddling*.

"So, how do you think Keisha will feel about this?" he asked, as he walked beside his protegé, past the outer door of Silverfox's workrooms and out into the cool half-light of the Vale at night. It wasn't dark beneath the trees; lanterns tended by the *hertasi* and set along the path at intervals saw to that. They tried to replicate the blue of twilight, just after the sun has set and the sky to the west is luminous with afterglow, and Firesong thought that they succeeded very well.

"She'll be pretty pleased, I think," Darian replied. "She'll probably pretend to be annoyed that *I* don't have to wear uniforms, though. She's still awfully self-conscious about being in Greens."

"Mmm." Firesong made a noncommittal sound. "She did make rank before you did, though. There was an imbalance."

"That's probably why she'll be pleased; she's not very comfortable with being at a higher rank than people around her." Darian sounded as if he found that difficult to understand, but then, Darian was, beyond any doubt, a natural leader himself. *Which means he doesn't yet really understand Keisha's motivations. That could be a point of potential conflict, especially if she is put into a position where she has to make a leader's decisions.*

Firesong continued to probe, interspersing his personal questions with those of a much more casual nature, and got the distinct impression that Darian was having some difficulty with the young Healer. It wasn't enough to break their pairing—yet—but any time that conflict didn't get resolved in one way or another, there was always the potential for it to happen. An unhappy Master Mage was a potentially reckless or careless one, and there was a long Hawkbrother tradition of taking good care of compatriot mages. More than that was the fact that Firesong genuinely liked young Darian on a friendly basis, and he did not want to see him troubled.

While he continued to exchange banter with his student,

half of Firesong's mind was elsewhere, pondering what, if anything, could be done. *Goddess help me, I've turned into an inveterate matchmaker,* he thought with a mingling of amusement and dismay. *If I don't watch my step, I'm going to have anxious fathers coming to me yet. Well, I have before, actually, but daughters weren't involved. . . .* Nevertheless—

I'll ask Silverfox to look into the matter and have a word with one or both of them, he decided at last. Silverfox was infinitely more skilled at such things than he—as well he should be, since it was one of the duties of a *kestra'chern,* to keep all the interpersonal relationships running smoothly within the group to which he or she belonged, be it city or Vale, army or Clan.

Let Silverfox make what he can of it, he decided. And at that point, it was past time to do any more thinking of his own—he stepped aside at a particular point in the path marked by a lamp-standard shaped like an elongated gryphon, holding the glass globe of the lamp in one extended claw. Darian paused when Firesong did, looking faintly puzzled, and Firesong drew aside the curtain of flowering vines that had hidden a clearing at the foot of a tree too small as yet to support an *ekele.* He gave Darian's shoulder a push, sending him into the center of the clearing, where he was surrounded by friends and well-wishers, all eager to congratulate him on his new status. *Hertasi* had been waiting for just this moment, and as soon as Darian was escorted to a seat of cushions piled up against the trunk of the tree, they swarmed him with offerings of food and drink.

Firesong stayed for a time, but kept his silence, as those who were mages monopolized the conversation. Those of Master rank and above—Starfall, Snowfire, and others—related their own Mastery Trials, as those who had not yet attained the rank of Master listened eagerly and a little enviously, then pelted the others with questions.

It was altogether too much like a gathering of scouts comparing the latest skills of their bondbirds. Each and every nuance and tactic was described and debated in staggering detail. When anyone asked Firesong a question directly, he answered it, but otherwise kept silent.

Although he hid it well, he was just as tired as Darian, and with as much reason; he had cultivated an appearance of calm, even indifference, but beneath it he had laid careful safety precautions, planning for the very worst. All of those safeguards had been integrated into his shields, of course, ensuring that Darian wouldn't notice them—it was good for the young man's confidence. Doing so had cost him a great deal in terms of work. The energy could be replaced, but the physical labor meant he needed his own rest. He'd also had an emotional stake in the trial that had worn him out; he was ready for relaxation, not a seminar.

So he waited until the celebration was well underway, and he knew he would not be missed, before he slipped out.

Once on his own, he took off his mask and used it as a fan—not that he was very hot, but it was pleasant to feel the cool air on his face. He walked slowly back to the *ekele* he shared with Silverfox, taking note as he walked of all of the improvements that the *hertasi* had made along the trail. He liked to be able to compliment them on specifics; it made them very happy when their handiwork was noted in detail.

For instance, the lamps had been replaced recently, so that they all matched. Much effort had gone into color matching the opaque, blue glass globes that protected the flames of the lamps from being blown out. All of the oil reservoirs matched, too—now they were made of green porcelain that harmonized with the blue glass. It was a very effective touch.

A Vale to match my outfit. How nice.

The standards themselves remained the same. Along this path they were all in the shapes of living things, inhabitants of the Vale. The gryphon at the entrance to the clearing was just one example; the standard Firesong was just passing was in the shape of an elongated *hertasi,* and the one just ahead in the form of an attenuated *dyheli.* Sometimes Firesong wondered if they were portraits of particular individuals, but he had never asked, and since none of the standards were of humans, he couldn't tell by examining them in passing. Individuals of each species had distinctive markings and proportions, of course. Representations of those weren't apparent, not in the ones he had seen, at any rate. It certainly didn't detract from their beauty.

The path he was on crossed with another—the *hertasi* had not yet gotten around to replacing the lamps here to make them match. The bell-shaped glass covers were also blue, but they were of differing sizes and shapes, and were not all of the same color of glass. The standards, however, were all similar; simple wooden poles with vines trained to climb up them. The effect was more rustic and less baroque, and reminded him of all of the makeshifts that they had used when the Vale was first settled.

Two lamps marked the entrance to Silverfox's home, a structure very much like Darian's, a dome made of stone with rounded corners on the added chambers. It was covered with vines, so that it looked from outside as if there was nothing there except a heap of greenery. Somewhat to Firesong's surprise, Silverfox was waiting for him, leaning against the doorframe with his arms crossed over his chest.

"Well, stranger, what are you doing out here?" he asked, pausing to admire the view. Silverfox had always been a handsome fellow, but in Firesong's opinion, he had improved with age. He had lost some of the softness along his jawline that had made him look younger than he actually was, and the silver streak running from his temple all through his waist-length hair had grown wider by no more than a finger's-width. Somehow he always managed to wear garments that harmonized with Firesong's—blue and black, for instance, to Firesong's current blue and green.

"Waiting for you; I knew you wouldn't be too late at the party," came the easy reply. "You never did care much for discussions of technique, and that's *all* they're going to get into tonight—hmmm. Well, you won't be involved in— magical power technique, anyway." He cast his eyes upward a little, as if he was calculating something. "By now I expect they've reached the stage of drawing diagrams on whatever surface is available."

Firesong laughed. "I expect you're right," he replied. "I'd rather keep discussions of technique for lessons; it's not my notion of conversational material."

"Come on, then," Silverfox said, standing up straight and beckoning. "I have refreshments cooling on the top deck, and there's a good breeze."

By the time Firesong got to the upper deck of the *ekele*, his weariness had completely caught up with him, and he was perfectly happy to sink down into a chair next to Silverfox and accept a cool drink. "I've got a bit of a favor to ask you,

ashke," he said, as Silverfox took the chair next to him, pulling his hair over his right shoulder to avoid sitting on it.
"Would you keep an eye on Keisha and Darian? I've got the
feeling that all is not comfortable between them, and I think
they could use a little advice."

"That's what I'm here for," Silverfox replied easily. "I'll be
glad to look into it. You mustn't be angry at me, though, if the
outcome is that they decouple themselves."

That took Firesong aback. "Why should they?" he asked, a
little more sharply than he intended. "Do you already know
something I don't?"

Silverfox shrugged. "No, actually, I don't. But remember,
my job is to get the best possible outcome. I'm not a matchmaker. If our chief Healer and eventual Vale Elder are better
off apart than together, that's what I'll counsel them. Short-
term unhappiness is much better than long-term misery, and
very few liaisons are lifebonds."

Firesong was a touch disappointed in that answer, but he
had to admit that Silverfox was right. "Well, if that's what
happens, I can't promise you that I won't be upset, but I won't
be angry, and certainly not with you."

"Very sensible of you—and I'm only reminding you of the
worst possible situation." Silverfox reached over and took his
hand, squeezing it reassuringly. "We could have the very opposite here, with both of them wanting a committed relationship, and both holding back because of some idealistic
nonsense or other—"

"Like, for instance?" Firesong put a teasing note into his
voice, knowing what Silverfox was likely to say. "Idealism *is*
always nonsense when it isn't *your* idealism, eh?"

"Pest. Like, for instance, that they both are under the illusion that all successful relationships *have* to be lifebonds,"
Silverfox replied.

"You mean they don't?" Firesong asked innocently.

"Oh, no, no, no. Spells aren't needed to make magic, and
lifebonds aren't needed to make love. Here—" Silverfox put
his drink down, and stood up in a single fluid, gliding motion,
to lean over Firesong's chair. His long hair made a curtain that
shut out the rest of the world. "Allow me to demonstrate. . . ."

Four

Darian watched the shadows dance among the lamp-lit leaves overhead, supremely relaxed and content with his lot. The talk had settled to a murmur over to one side, with the rest of the small gathering of friends simply enjoying an all-too-infrequent moment of doing absolutely nothing.

"This isn't really a proper party," Wintersky complained, for after the drowsy laziness that inevitably followed a round of excellent food and drink set in, bodies sprawled over cushions as if in the aftermath of a massacre, and no one was inclined to do much more than listen to crickets sing. It had been a massacre, of sorts. The refreshments and supper brought by eager *hertasi* had been slaughtered down to the last drop and crust. Darian was wondering if he would make it to his bed after all, or just give up and fall asleep where he was, when Wintersky's complaint broke the silence.

The bodies stirred and sat up, but no one replied to Wintersky, who continued in a firmer tone of voice. "No, it's just nothing like a real party, and if anyone among us deserves a big celebration, it's you, Dar'ian," Wintersky stated authoritatively. "We ought to have one, that's what we should do!"

"What, on top of everything else we're planning?" Darian replied, appalled at the very idea. "Aren't you all going to make me enough of an entertainment as it is? And think of the poor *hertasi*! They're already working their tails to stubs just to get ready for the Heralds, and now you want to add *another* party to their burden?"

"He's right, Wintersky," Sunleaf responded from the far corner of the clearing. Sunleaf, a contemporary of Snowfire, had been eager and willing to assist Darian in his studies when none of the greater mages were available, and the two had become good friends. "But Dar'ian, Wintersky is right, too," he continued, nodding his shaggy head. "Keisha isn't here, for one thing, and it doesn't seem fair to me that we leave her out. Why don't we just do this all over again as soon as she gets back? We'll just call this a practice for the real party—or better yet, just a little gathering of friends. Say we just made a spur-of-the-moment picnic to congratulate you, and it's not a party at all. Because really, that's all it was."

Darian didn't have to think about it. He knew that Keisha would be hurt if she thought she'd been left out of the celebration. He did *not* want to hurt her feelings, nor did he want to make her think that he had forgotten all about her in the rush of euphoria after passing the Trial. "I'm glad you thought of that," he replied gratefully. "So long as we don't overburden our *hertasi* friends, that's what we ought to do."

Sunleaf laughed. "Oh, trust me, it's in my own best interest," he answered, and from across the clearing, Darian saw him wink. "I know what she'd do to me if she found out we had a party without her!"

"Do to *you*? Have pity, I have to sleep with her—what do you think she'd do to *me*? I'd be afraid to close my eyes!" Since the attendees at this little celebration were all males, and mostly bachelors, the entire gathering laughed at both of them, and Darian was momentarily ashamed to speak so of Keisha. *On the other hand, Snowfire has said the same thing about Nightwind, to her face, and she just pretends to threaten him.* "We should keep it very casual, but give Keisha and the other girls a chance to dress up." There; that should make up for his lapse.

One of the *hertasi* that had adopted Darian and Keisha—a young striped male called Meeren—was picking up discarded and empty cups. At this sally, he hissed a laugh of his own. "Very well, then, do not worry about the preparations," the leather-capped *hertasi* put in. "It is of manageable difficulty.

In fact, with this much notice, we can have a few delicacies set aside for you. I will arrange for the *official* party to take place when Keisha returns."

Darian relaxed; Meeren was one of Ayshen's most valued assistants, a specialist in logistics. Whatever Meeren organized was certain to be a success.

Now the young *hertasi* turned to sweep the clearing with his gaze, his tail counterbalancing his movement as he turned. "And what Dar'ian has said makes me think. Do *you* young Tayledras think to be inviting some females, so that Keisha will not be the only one of her gender here? It will not only be Keisha who is disappointed to learn that there was a gathering to which no one thought to bring a friend."

"That's an even better idea—how *did* this end up as an all-male party, anyway?" asked Wintersky, looking around himself in astonishment. One of the *shaych* scouts replied with a laugh, "We were just lucky?"

"Don't ask me—I was the last one to be invited," Darian countered, tossing a cushion at the scout. "It wasn't any idea of mine!"

Keisha was unusually glad to see the entrance of the Vale ahead of her. The twin pillars with the shimmer of the Veil between them beckoned her with all the warmth and welcome of an old friend. She was equally glad to ride through the cool shadows under moss-covered trunks and dismount at her very own door again. She removed the panniers resting across the back of her *dyheli*, but before she could touch the tack, a *hertasi* had come and taken it, and the *dyheli* trotted off to rejoin his herd.

How do they do that? Appear out of nowhere and just take over things? She stared at the retreating *hertasi* tail. *I am never going to get used to it. It's like they are always around, and always watching, no matter what we do—and then they know what we need next.* She picked up the empty panniers, one in each hand, and with her foot nudged open the green-painted door.

It wasn't that she was tired—that was far from the case; she had enjoyed the ride back enormously. Spring was her favorite season, and this spring was turning out to be particularly lovely. So far it had rained just enough, and only at night, so

that blue skies graced the daylight hours. Everything was
growing or in bloom. There were already spring vegetables
coming in to the market, weeks before the usual time. It
hadn't been too cold *or* too hot. In fact, if the entire region had
been seated beneath a Veil, the weather couldn't have been
more perfect.

No, the problem was not that Keisha was tired—unless it
was that she was tired of Errold's Grove. When she returned
to her childhood home, she increasingly felt as if she was trying to squeeze into clothing that she had long since outgrown.
Every time she made her weekly visit it was the same thing,
whereas the Vale was constantly changing. The only change
in the village was the occasional new pile of rocks, a fresh
border around a flower bed, or a new shirt worn out-of-season
so that everybody noticed. Other than that, it was the same
little complaints, the same village gossip—

The same lectures from Mother about still being single.

She dropped her panniers into their corner, and frowned,
feeling a sullen anger well up in her again. Back in Errold's
Grove she had fought it down, but now she allowed herself to
admit it. *I wanted so badly to tell her exactly what I thought.*
What was so *bad* about *not* being married? It wasn't as if she
was the *only* one in the family expected to produce grandchildren—there were already two squalling infants bearing the
Alder name and features, one each from her two oldest brothers. What on earth could she do as a married woman—besides
produce legitimate grandchildren—that she couldn't do as a
single one? Could she be any more valued? Would she have
any higher rank?

*If she doesn't stop giving me the "you'll grow old, lonely,
and abandoned" lecture every time I'm ready to leave, I
swear, I'm going to stop visiting her,* Keisha thought sullenly.
What's more, I'll let everyone in the village know why *I
stopped visiting her!*

She wouldn't and she knew it, but the idea was very, very
tempting. As she walked into the outer room with its comfortable furnishings of woven branches and overstuffed beige
cushions, its walls of soft cream, and tiled floor, she took her
first completely free breath since she'd left. This was home,
from the mask and decorated gryphon-feather hanging on the

wall, gifts from Firesong and Silverfox, to the flowering vines around the skylight of the bathing room.

I'm stale, that's what it is. All I ever see these days are farm animals, idiot men as dumb as farm animals, women as stubborn as farm animals, pregnant mothers-to-be, cuts and scrapes, and the occasional sniffle. It wasn't that she wanted Errold's Grove to suffer a disaster. Nothing of the sort could be farther from her mind! But she didn't even get to see the interesting diseases the Northern tribes brought down with them anymore. The Sanctuary Healers got all of those. All she was left with were the all-too-ordinary problems.

Havens, people are taking such care these days that I never even see an infected puncture anymore!

She dropped all of her soiled clothing from the trip into the basket-hamper they kept for the purpose just outside the bathing-room door. She stripped off the tunic and trews she wore, and added them to the pile, then entered the bathing room. In the echoing room, tiled floor-to-ceiling, she knelt beside the square tub sunken into the floor and drew herself a bath. They had hot water now, although it came from a tank perched up in a tree, shared by several other *ekele* and heated by the sun rather than by magic.

Maybe we'll get that, too, in a few years, though it seems a pity to waste the sun's heat when it costs us nothing. She was no mage, but she was acutely sensitive to the cost in magical energies of every act of magic. Living here in a new Vale as much as living with Darian had made her very aware of such things. Darian was in superb physical shape, even to a Healer's eyes, and when she saw the physical exhaustion he bore after some of his lessons, she had no doubts remaining about magic's costs.

When the tub was full, she added herbs and scented salts, and soothing fragrance rose in the steam that condensed on the leaves of the vines planted in boxes around the skylight above her. She eased into the tub, to just over her breasts, and soaked for a good long time, allowing herself to run through all of the emotions she had repressed. Nightwind had told her that holding them in did no good and much harm, so she let them run their course. Disappointment led to anger, which gave way in turn to a seething despair.

What am I doing with myself? Nothing, that's what! Is

Mother right? Am I going to die a cross old maid, lonely and abandoned? How long is it going to be before this makes me sour, and Darian gets tired of me and starts looking for a prettier girl? It was going to happen; she was just sure of it. Then what?

Then, I suppose, I'll go back to my little house in the village. Eventually they'll start to treat me the way they treated Justyn. . . .

A hard lump of self-pity rose in her throat, a sob that she choked down lest one of the *hertasi* was about. If they caught her in this mood, they'd be upset and concerned, and entirely sure it was their fault that she was unhappy.

The hertasi *like me anyway. . . .*

She couldn't get herself out of this mood; it felt as if she had fallen into a pit and was too tired to climb out. She squeezed out a few bitter tears, a distillation of it all, and then, suddenly, felt much better. It was as if those few tears had taken all of her self-pity with them.

Not that crying had changed anything.

But with the tears out, she started to think past them, realizing how silly she would have sounded to anyone else, and in a moment, she laughed weakly at her own absurd thoughts. *In the very worst case, it's not as if I would lose everything! Even if Darian gets tired of me, we'll still be friends, I'd still be a full Healer, and I'm entitled to ask to be sent wherever I want. And Shandi is coming back, so how bad can things be, really?* Darian gave no hint that he had lost interest in her, anyway—so why was she borrowing trouble?

Worry about that when the time comes, if it ever happens at all. And if it does—well, there's no reason why I can't exchange positions with one of the Sanctuary Healers, is there? I'll bet one of them would be willing to take over the village for a few months' rest! Or even longer—there's no telling how any of those Trainees are going to turn out, and if any of them turns out like old Gil Jarred, with a weak Gift, then Errold's Grove is the right place for him and I can take his place in the Sanctuary permanently. That will give me plenty of excitement! The very fact that she had come up with an alternative to moldering in the village cheered her up immensely.

So what if Darian has more and more duties—and Firesong keeps heaping him with more complicated lessons. I might end up being sent off by the Healer's Circle, too—things happen. Crying about them before they've happened isn't going to stop them.

She stopped herself before she could step off the edge again, and fall into that pit of depression. *I think I'd better talk to Nightwind.*

She scrubbed off the sweat and dirt of the journey, feeling as if she was scrubbing away all her frustrations as well. She washed her hair, then ran more clean water for a thorough rinse. Sometimes it seemed like water was her best friend of all; it was nearly impossible to feel *too* badly when in a refreshing soak or a warm rain. When she emerged from the bathing room, cleansed and wrapped in thick towels, she found that one of the *hertasi* had been in the bedroom before her, and had laid out—a garment she didn't recognize.

What— Havens, what is this?

She lifted one sleeve of the dress that had been put out for her to don. A springlike leaf green, it was absolutely charming—of light Tayledras-made silk with billowing sleeves caught into long cuffs, and a high collar. Both collar and cuffs were ornamented with silver embroidery, and there was a second, sleeveless gown of a slightly heavier weight in a darker green to wear over it. This sleeveless gown had a beautiful embroidery of silver-thread vines, leaves, and flowers running from the left shoulder to the hem, and all around the bottom.

This was *not* the simple green tunic-and-trews she had expected. She did not recall that there had been anything special planned for her return.

But next to the dress was a note attached to a new hair ornament—one of Aya's sparkling white tail-feathers with green crystal beadwork ornamenting the shaft. She picked it up and read it.

You are invited to share a small celebration in honor of Darian Firkin k'Vala k'Valdemar on the occasion of his attaining the rank of Master Mage. Follow the firebird feathers. And there was a postscript, in a rougher hand. *We decided to postpone this until you came home; it wouldn't be a proper celebration without you.* She didn't need a signature to recognize Darian's handwriting on the postscript, and only the elegant Silverfox could have penned the invitation.

She forgot her anger completely. Surprise was followed immediately by such a rush of cheer that she might as well have downed an entire beaker of wine by herself.

She dropped her towels on the floor and hurried into the lovely gown, fastening the hair clasp into her damp hair. The feather trailed down along the side of her face, brushing her cheek in a graceful curve. Although the feather ceased to drip false sparks once it was no longer attached to Aya, it did retain the ability to sparkle as if it had been dusted with minute particles of gemstones.

With her skirts caught up in one hand, she ran out the front door and caught sight of the first of the firebird feathers. This was a smaller, body-feather; it hung from a strand of beads fastened to the lamp-standard marking the beginning of the lefthand path, fluttering and twisting in the light breeze.

The feathers were easy enough to spot—each one was within sight of another—and she soon met someone else following the same trail.

Wintersky's current partner, a Tayledras scout called Ravenwing, waved to Keisha just as Keisha caught sight of her. She, too, was dressed for a celebration, in tunic of gold deerskin and trews of black silk. The tunic had beading in black and metallic gold across the shoulders and around the collar, with fringes along the sleeves and bottom hem that cascaded past her knees. Her bondbird, a handsome little cooperihawk, perched on a light gauntlet she wore on her left hand.

"Heyla!" Ravenwing called cheerfully. "Have you any idea what's been planned? I got out of my bath to find an invitation next to my clothing!"

Keisha shook her head, admiring Ravenwing's new hair patterns. Many of the Tayledras had snow-white hair by their early twenties at least, simply because they lived within a place where extremely powerful mage-energies were a part of everyday life, but the scouts often had their hair dyed in camouflage colors so that they blended in with their surroundings. Ravenwing's patterns were brand new, the colors and edges crisp and unfaded—and it was obvious to Keisha's experienced eyes that the reason she'd been in the bath was because she had been washing out the excess dyes.

"I love your new patterns!" she exclaimed—for Ravenwing's hair had been dyed to resemble the wings of the enormous brown-eye butterflies that thronged the Vale. It was still camouflage, but it was anything but drab.

"You do? Thank you!" Ravenwing looked pleased, and ran her fingers through her loose hair with obvious pleasure. "I just got so tired of looking like I had a nest of old leaves on my head!"

"Once the others see it, they'll want to copy it," Keisha assured her. "It looks wonderful!"

Ravenwing caught her up on the news as they followed the trail of beaded feathers at a brisk walk. Keisha learned that she hadn't missed much, other than Darian attaining Master status. "Everybody's too caught up in getting ready for the Heralds to arrive," Ravenwing concluded, and looked curiously at Keisha. "Is it true that one of them is your sister?"

"So they tell me! I'll be glad to see her. Until she was Chosen, she was my best friend besides being my sister." Keisha fingered the feather in her hair thoughtfully. "I hope she hasn't forgotten that."

"How could she? Don't be silly." Ravenwing seemed very sure of that. "She'll be just as happy to see you as you are to see her. And if she's anything like you, I can't wait to meet her. There aren't enough girls our age around this Vale, not nearly enough to get into the kind of trouble we used to cause back in k'Vala!"

Ravenwing's eyes sparkled with amusement as she said that, and Keisha had to laugh. The Tayledras girl had been very free with her tales of the scrapes she and her gang of friends had perpetrated, and Keisha had, more than once, wished she had gotten a chance to join in the mischief. "Believe me, Shandi can cause enough trouble for three! If she hasn't gone all sober on us now that she's a Herald, we'll have a fine time—oh, look—" She interrupted herself. "That must be where the party is!"

Meeren, her own *hertasi*, stood beside the path, holding aside a curtain of vines for someone who had come from the opposite direction. He saw them, and beckoned them on; they hurried their steps and he grinned, showing all his teeth, as they reached him.

"Ah, the final pair!" Meeren exclaimed. "With you, we are ready to begin the celebration at last!"

Keisha ducked under the slant of vines, and was seized from

behind by a pair of strong arms. "Keisha!" Darian crowed, spinning her around and around until she was dizzy. "You found my presents!"

"What? The dress? The feather?" she asked, trying to catch her breath, her head swimming as he finally stopped whirling her around. "Never mind, thank you for both—oh, Darian, congratulations! This is—wonderful!"

She cupped both her hands around his chin and pulled his head down for a long, heartfelt kiss. She heard the others whooping behind her, and for once, was not embarrassed by their rowdy attentions. She was wholeheartedly proud of him, and happy for his achievement, and she wanted him to know it beyond a shadow of a doubt. His arms closed around her as he drew her close, and for a time the cheers and hoots faded into a faint murmur as her ears filled with the pounding of both their hearts.

Then he let her go, and she took a step backward, smiling breathlessly up into his wide grin. She hadn't even gotten her scattered wits together when he seized her hand and led her ceremoniously to a seat on the far side of a little clearing, where two enormous cushions had been braced against back-rests placed on the ground. "My lady," he said, gesturing broadly as he bowed to her, his grin as wide as ever, "if you will choose your seat, we can begin."

She took the seat to the right; he dropped onto the cushion at the left, and a steady stream of *hertasi* moved into the clear-ing, each carrying a platter. As was usual at these casual cele-brations, the *hertasi* carried each platter around the circle of diners, and they helped themselves. If the platters still had anything left on them, they made the rounds a second time. *Hertasi* then returned bearing drink, pouring each cup full of a light spiced wine. There was very little alcohol in this wine; Tayledras drank it for the taste, not with the purpose of intoxi-cation. That was one of the things that Keisha liked so much about living among the Tayledras. Celebrations in the village inevitably ended in drunks staggering about and making themselves nuisances, and the morning after inevitably brought a parade of hung-over sufferers to her door. But the rare intoxicated Hawkbrother took himself away to sleep it off as soon as he or his friends realized the extent of his intoxi-cation, and he either found his own hangover remedy or quietly suffered the punishment for his overindulgence.

Every morsel was delicious—even though most of it wasn't special "feast" food. She quickly gathered that this was not a formal celebration, probably to spare the *hertasi* from any more extra work. The few special dishes could very well have been culled from the ones already in progress for the Heralds' welcome. That made her feel easier; like Darian, she knew how hard the *hertasi* worked, and like him, she had not grown up accustomed to having them around. Putting any extra burden on them made her feel guilty.

As the dinner proceeded, each of Darian's friends in turn voiced a wish for the new Master, and when it came time for Keisha to give hers, she knew precisely what she wanted to say.

"I salute our own Darian," she said. "May he always be properly recognized for his accomplishments, and may he never regret a moment spent in achieving them."

She raised her glass, and the others joined her. Now, if this had been the kind of celebration one would find in Errold's Grove, now would be the time that Darian made a speech. But the Hawkbrothers didn't have that particular tradition, and Keisha was just as glad; Darian didn't much care for making speeches, and he already had plenty he was going to have to produce when the Heralds arrived.

Instead, those of the participants who cared to took turns entertaining the rest. About half of the population of this Vale were amateur musicians, and three of Darian's guests had brought their chosen instruments with them—Silverfox being one, blindingly quick-fingered with a hand drum. One scout got up to teach a sculptor a step, and in no time at all, impromptu dancing had started. Keisha began to tap her fingers in time to the infectious beat, and Darian's left foot did the same, until Darian could bear inactivity no longer.

"Come on!" Darian urged her, jumping to his feet and holding out his hand to her. She loved dancing, and did not hesitate a moment in allowing him to help her to her feet, and joining him in the circle.

They danced until the musicians were tired of playing, pausing only for cold drinks and a moment to catch their breath. She had danced with every male at the celebration, including Firesong (in a striking mask made of Aya's feathers and polished quartz beads), and was just about out of energy. By that time, it was late enough that everyone agreed it was time to bring the party to an end. A final round of iced teas and juices—the ice cut during the winter and stored deep in *hertasi*-dug caves during the warmer months—allowed the heated dancers to cool down.

Keisha leaned against Darian's shoulder, tired, permitting herself the luxury of forgetting all about the duties of a Healer, and giving herself up completely to the pleasure of the moment. And the moment was glorious; glimpses of a sky full of stars appeared as the great tree above them moved its branches in a light wind. The air, perfumed faintly with night-blooming flowers, had cooled just a trifle since sundown but was still perfectly comfortable. Now that the musicians were done in, the murmur of conversation and the song of insect and bird provided another sort of melody.

"So, Keisha, how was your visit?" Darian asked, shifting just a little so that she could settle more comfortably against his shoulder, and putting one arm around her to hold her steady.

She groaned. "Mother managed to get me into a corner again. Other than that, it was the usual, nothing of any great urgency. I think they don't need me so much as the potions I bring with me."

"We could always send your medicines over with the Council members," he suggested. "You could cut your visits to every other week or so, instead of going once a week."

The idea was tempting. "Perhaps after Rana Trilvy's baby comes. I wouldn't care to upset a first-time mother." Darian's shoulder was warm, and his arm around her comforting. She shoved all of her doubts and misgivings into a corner of her mind and shut a door on them. "This was lovely; thank you for waiting for me."

His arm tightened slightly around her; she squeezed his hand in reply. "I knew you'd be disappointed if I didn't. Besides, you don't get nearly enough of a chance to simply enjoy yourself. When the village has a celebration, you spend most of the time dealing with accidents and drunks, and the next day with hangovers and belly-aches."

"Well, thanks to you, I'm going to get *quite* a few chances to do so in the near future," she said, and laughed when he sighed. "Come on, it won't be that bad, will it?"

"I'm not so sure. The easiest is likely to be the Ghost Cat ceremony—and for that, all of the men will be stripping down and cramming into the sweat house until we're equally parboiled. Then I exchange blood with the Shaman—I gather we each cut our palms and clasp hands—he declares that I'm his true son, with his blood in my veins and mine in his."

"That doesn't sound too difficult," Keisha observed. "Other than the parboiling part. By *all* the men, are you just talking about the Ghost Cat folk?"

She heard the grin in his voice. "Oh, no, this includes Lord Breon and Val—Snowfire and Wintersky have to get in on this too, and maybe Starfall—and certainly Herald Anda. Should be very interesting to see how *he* reacts."

She giggled. "It should be very interesting to see how Lord Breon takes it!"

The rest of the guests had started to slip away, by twos and fours, while they talked. She took a quick glance around, and realized that they were completely alone; not even a single *hertasi* had remained behind.

He was still caught up in thinking about the ordeals he was about to undergo. "Before that, there's the knighting thing. I've got to do a night-long vigil, then Breon gets to put on his show, which is supposed to take the rest of the day. Oathtaking, knighting, ceremony following the knighting, speeches, tournament, feast, more speeches. The Ghost Cat people are probably going to be bored silly—and I know I will be, at least during the speeches."

"You will not—you'll be making mental notes like you always do," she retorted. "You'll be figuring what people are thinking by what they say and don't say, and who they look at while they're talking. You'll tuck all that away in your mind, and when we most need it and least expect it, you'll pull something out in a Council session that will solve everything."

"Oh, come now!" he protested, laughing, "I'm not anywhere near that good!"

"You only *think* you aren't. The rest of us know better." He didn't say anything, but she could tell he was embarrassed. "You'd better get used to it; people rely on you, Darian, and you're good enough to be depended upon," she added. "I know, and Starfall, Firesong, and Snowfire know, that you've got the instinct. You read people beautifully."

"I don't like to think that I'm manipulating them, though," he replied, his voice uncertain. "That seems so unethical."

She chose her words carefully. "It isn't that you're manipulating them, it's that you're getting them to see things they wouldn't think of for themselves. Eventually, when the problem is over, they *do* see, and the next time you won't have to prompt them or coax them into it. I don't think that's manipulation, that's education. Besides, in a sense, we all manipulate each other; that's what happens when you are friends, when you trust and love someone. *I* manipulate people as a Healer, but it's with skill and good intent. Sometimes I have to trick them in order to make their medicine work."

"I don't know. . . ." He still sounded reluctant. "It just seems that I'm getting people to do things they'd rather not do at the time, and I wonder if that's right."

"But aren't they more inclined to do the same thing on their own, later, once you've persuaded them into it the first time?" she countered. "Think of Val! If you hadn't shown him how awful fighting and warfare really is, he'd have been inclined to throw himself into the thick of battle the first chance he had! *Now* he takes the time to think things through, and see if there isn't a way to solve a situation without killing anyone. I don't doubt for a moment that if fighting turns out to be the only answer, he'll still be right up in the front of it—you didn't turn him into a coward, because that's not in his nature. All you did was bring out a part of his nature he hadn't bothered to develop before you talked to him."

"But what if he *had* been fearful, and I *had* turned him into a coward?" Darian replied.

"What's better? That he discover that he was really timid about fighting when he was in the middle of a fight, or when he was sitting safe at home?" she said instantly. "Which does the most harm—or the least? It seems to me that if he'd discovered he couldn't bear the battlefield, he'd have had plenty of opportunity to cultivate courage or find an alternative place to be useful where he didn't have to actually fight. But *you* know what kind of havoc a single fighter can wreak just by turning and running."

Darian sighed. "I guess you're right."

She clasped both her hands over his and squeezed them. "You know I am, you mean. You never use your abilities with people to make them do something that's alien to their nature—you just make them see alternatives and then *try* those alternatives. Some day it might happen that you run up against someone who doesn't like the alternative you offer, and goes into it reluctantly, but you don't nock an arrow to your bow and force him into it. He can always say no."

"But people don't want to say no when I ask them to do something," he protested. "It makes them feel guilty to turn me down, so they go ahead and do what I ask even though they don't want to—"

"Then it's *their* job to grow a stronger spine." As far as she was concerned, that was the end of that argument. "And here we are, wasting a perfectly lovely evening by agonizing over things that haven't ever happened! I can think of much better things to do with our time."

She hadn't expected an immediate response, but she was very pleased when she got one. "So can I," he replied, and turned so that she was no longer resting on his shoulder so that he could kiss her.

Her body began to tingle pleasantly as he prolonged the kiss, nibbling delicately on her lip as she responded. She shifted a little so that she could put both her arms around him, losing herself in sensation. *Meeren will see that the "privacy" sign is set up by the time we need it,* she thought—and gave herself up to loving.

Five

Darian stepped back from the golden-oak wall panel he'd been holding up, and admired all of the new *hertasi*-work ornamenting the Companion stables. The structure was finished just in time. *Thank goodness for gryphons. If we hadn't had warning, we could have been caught in mid-addition.*

For the past several days, especially swift gryphons had been patrolling the main road to Errold's Grove, on the watch for the approaching Heralds; even at the speed a Companion moved, a gryphon in the air traveled faster. A rough calculation gave them about a day's warning before the visitors arrived. Last night the two had finally been spotted just before sunset, and the gryphon in question, a gyrfalcon-type with amazing speed, had come rushing back to the Vale as fast as she could with the news. She was exhausted when she arrived, but two more gryphons had been eager to take the news to Errold's Grove and Lord Breon's Keep, giving everyone advance notice that their very special guests were soon to appear.

The basic structure of the attachment to the guest lodge meant to house the Companions had been finished quite quickly, but Ayshen (no mean architect) had planned for the ornamentation and elaboration to be completed in stages. No matter *when* the new residents arrived, the stables would appear finished. The first change had been to the fountain that supplied fresh running water; the initial installation had been a simple trough with water constantly flowing through it running along the rear of all three stalls. Utilitarian, but not very impressive; certainly not Tayledras. "There is power in style," was all Ayshen would say concerning the redesign. Now each of the three stalls held a separate handsome terra-cotta basin, with a constant flow of fresh, clean water bubbling up from the bottom and drained by a pipe just beneath the rim at the rear. Outside, the pipes joined into one, which drained into an ornamental pond. Ayshen figured the fish wouldn't mind secondhand water.

The second change had been to add separate mangers for different sorts of foodstuffs; a hay rack just for hay, and smaller mangers and basins for oats, sweet-feed, and hot mashes. The hay rack had been fastened at the front of the stable for all three to share, but each stall had its own "special treat" containers; the latter were actually more terra-cotta basins which fitted into twisted-wire racks. The basins were removable, so that they could be taken away to be cleaned after use. The old wooden mangers that served for all food and were not removable for cleaning had been left in place, but trimmed with braided rope.

Then the dirt floor was replaced with brick, laid over a layer of gravel, over which in turn first sawdust, then clean straw was spread. Since Companions *weren't* horses, a "latrine stall" with a slanted brick floor was added, with a sluice to wash the waste away, and a drain to carry the waste to the waste tanks to be purified and turned into fertilizer. The Companions themselves could operate the sluice with a pull-rope, as they would be able to open all doors with a pull-latch and could come and go as they liked.

The last set of improvements was to give the place ornamentation; paneled woodwork, carvings along the beams, shelves and a proper tack room. Whenever Darian found himself with a moment to spare, he'd gone to help the building crew, and he'd been holding a wall panel in place when the news had come that the Heralds were within a few hours of arrival.

I'd be perfectly happy to live here, he thought, looking around at the fine carvings, the solid appointments, the beautifully made door into the guest lodge itself, which was actually a double door. It was a regular door divided in half, so that the upper half could be left open for the Companions to stick their heads into the room.

"You've done a terrific job, friends," he said aloud to the crew of *hertasi* picking up their tools. "I can't see anything that could be improved upon."

One of the nearest looked up at him. "I can," the *hertasi* responded. "And if I can, you know that Ayshen will, too."

"This is better and far more gracious than anything outside of Haven," he told the *hertasi* firmly. "I'll tell Ayshen that myself. Besides, I think any further changes ought to be made after you consult with the Companions themselves, not before."

The *hertasi*, who appeared to be the work-crew chief, looked around, and nodded after a moment. "You're probably right," it admitted. It (it was usually impossible for humans to tell which *hertasi* was male and which female) stowed the last of its tools in its toolbox, then bent and picked up the heavy box as easily as if it had weighed no more than a basket of eggs. The other *hertasi* cleared out as the crew chief took a last look around and nodded again. "It's solid," the *hertasi* said, the ultimate compliment that any *hertasi* would ever pay to its own work. "Even Ayshen will agree to that."

It trotted out with a wave of farewell to Darian, who shook his head and had to laugh.

He left through the door into the guest lodge just as more *hertasi* arrived, bearing bales of hay and bags of grain. More were following, carrying cleaning supplies, although he could not imagine how the place could possibly be any cleaner. But then, he wasn't a *hertasi*.

The guest lodge had been cleaned and polished until every surface gleamed; the mattresses taken out and restuffed, new linens made for the beds, new blue gauze curtains hung on the windows. There were flowers in all the rooms, scented candles in holders on every table, with bundles of additional candles tied with a ribbon stocked in an open cabinet in the main room. Last year a bathing room had been added to the guest lodge since not every guest cared to bathe in company; like Darian's, this bathing room was supplied with sun-heated water from a tank above the roof. He took a quick peek, and saw that everything possible had been supplied here, as well. In two of the rooms, a set of white clothing designed by the *hertasi* was laid out on the bed. Presumably one set had been made to Shandi's measurements. As for Herald Anda, perhaps the *hertasi* had simply guessed at the size for the other set. It was easy enough to tell which room had been designated for each Herald, though. The room that was to be Shandi's held some of her old possessions brought from Errold's Grove, and a specially chosen basket of sewing and embroidery supplies.

Obviously there was nothing more he needed to do here. As Darian walked out onto the covered porch that surrounded the Lodge, he nearly ran into another *hertasi*, an adolescent by its build. "Dar'ian—you are to prepare!" the youngster blurted out before he could apologize for his clumsiness. "The guests are less than two hours distant!"

He glanced up at the sky, trying to tell where the sun was through the trees, and judged that it was early afternoon. The Heralds had made good time, but the Vale was ready for them.

All except me! he reminded himself, and bolted up the trail to his *ekele*.

It was empty when he arrived; Keisha had probably gotten ready hours ago. He had seen her outfit earlier; the *hertasi* that had adopted the two of them had outdone themselves in the way of clothing for her. She now had a set of Greens that would be the envy of every Healer who saw them. There would be plenty of Healers to impress, too; every Sanctuary Healer that could get away had been arriving all morning. Even if they hadn't been anxious to meet the new Heralds, no one wanted to miss a Vale-wide Hawkbrother celebration. K'Valdemar had a far-flung reputation for its hedonistic hospitality on such occasions.

The *hertasi* hadn't exactly shirked when it came to Darian's outfit either, but at the moment he wasn't concerned with his clothing. After helping with the stables since early morning, what he needed most was a bath.

Once clean, he hurried into the first of his four sets of "welcoming" garb. This first set, the most exotic and·ornamental of the lot, was for today, when the Heralds were formally greeted and welcomed into k'Valdemar Vale. This was to mark his primary allegiance to his Vale and Clan. Tomorrow, he would wear Valdemaran formal military garb, although it would not be in Guard blue, but in brown, with badges of owls rather than the winged horse of Valdemar. This outfit included light ornamental armor and came complete with embroidered surcoat displaying his new arms. But the arms were not in Valdemaran style, but in the mode of the Hawkbrothers—the fluid, sinuous curves and stylization they had developed over the course of centuries. And the device itself was not Valdemaran either, for there was not a single noble family in all of the land that used an owl for their device. It seemed odd to him, but it was so. Lord Breon told him that owls were considered ill-omened in some parts; it was said that if an owl landed on one's house three nights in a row and called, someone in the house would die. Others swore that owls were the eyes of evil spirits, because they flew so silently and attacked in the darkness when no other creature could see. There were plenty of nocturnal creatures besides owls, including animals no one thought of as evil—but there was no arguing with superstition. The good part was that there was no one to argue with when he planned his device around a stylized portrait of Kuari coming in to land, wings spread wide.

He would spend the night in that outfit, in vigil. The next morning he would change into his third outfit, Valdemaran Court garb, with a more elaborate version of his embroidered surcoat, this one sparkling with gold-and-silver thread and tiny gemstones. He had no idea how the *hertasi* had managed to get not one, but *two* embroidered surcoats done in time, yet they had. There was always the belief that there were more *hertasi* than anyone ever actually saw, down in their burrows—and since so many looked alike to human eyes, who could count for sure just how many there were to make the goods they brought? That outfit was for the feast celebrating his knighting. Hopefully they'd let him get a nap before he had to endure hours of a formal Valdemaran feast. . . .

But that wasn't the end. On the fifth day—they were going to allow him a day to rest before he took up the trial again—he would don a set of clothing that was a blend of Ghost Cat and Hawkbrother styles. Crafted mostly of supple leather, it was decorated with Kuari's feathers, ornaments of carved bone harvested from Kuari's kills, beadwork with an owl-and-feather theme, and finished with a belt and dagger-sheath carved with a frieze of standing owls. Under it all was a draped loincloth, woven with a decorative pattern of feathers. He would put it all on only to take it off again (except for the loincloth), for this was his costume for his presentation at the Ghost Cat sweathouse.

At least both Heralds would have to keep him company through most of this. They would stand guard to make certain he didn't fall asleep during the vigil, and Anda would join all the men in the sweat-house ceremony while Shandi waited with the women in the drum-circle outside. The women had their own rituals, which were held secret from the men; all he knew was that they involved drumming for the men in the lodge.

Right now, however, he had best concentrate on today's ordeal.

This was not the sort of outfit he would have chosen to wear to a celebration, but fortunately, like the clothing that Snowfire and Nightwind wore for their wedding, he was going to be able to abandon part of it once the most formal portions of the evening were over. The base was a comfortable, soft sleeveless tunic of silk the color of red amber, and a pair of dark brown silk trews. Over this went a hip-length vest woven with a pattern of owl feathers, buttoned with amber toggles. Over *that* went an ankle-length coat, this cut of and lined with silk the color of honey amber, with a high collar, sleeves scalloped to resemble great wings, and so completely embroidered with owl feathers that very little of the original silk showed through. It was belted over the hips with a belt made of plaques of tiger-eye stone carved with more owls, no two of which were alike. The belt clasp was the mask of an owl, made in two halves that met so perfectly that it looked like a solid piece when buckled. The eyes were amber, the beak of creamy shell all the way from Lake Evendim, and the owl mask of carved horn, each feather individually carved and fitted to a metal backing plate. His boots of warm brown leather were inlaid on each calf with a design of an owl feather in four different shades of brown deerskin.

The coat was infernally heavy; not hot, but heavy. The weight of all that beading and embroidery hung on his shoulders like the heaviest pack he'd ever had to hike with.

Once the entire outfit was on, he waited for Meeren to return to inspect him and put the finishing touches on his appearance.

He certainly couldn't put the finishing touches on himself; he could hardly move without knocking something over with his sleeves.

It wasn't long until Meeren trotted in the door, clad himself in a coat made of thousands of tiny black octagonal scales of metal, forming a "fabric" as flexible as silk. Meeren examined him closely, looking at him from all angles, before pronouncing his satisfaction. "You'll do," the *hertasi* said. "Now sit, and let me make you presentable."

Darian sat gingerly on a low stool, and Meeren moved in, brush and comb in hand. Despite his apprehension, Meeren did not pull every hair out of Darian's head; in fact, he was remarkably gentle. Darian had allowed his hair to grow long, Tayledras-fashion, so that he could braid feathers and beads into it as his Clan-brothers did. It took a defter hand than his to achieve the kind of effects that Firesong or Starfall managed, and that was where Meeren came in.

He sat patiently as Meeren worked, wondering what was going on, but unable to tell anything from the gentle tugs and pulls on his hair. Meeren didn't take long, not as long as the *hertasi* must have taken with Keisha, but Darian was very impatient to see his handiwork, and shifted restlessly on his stool.

"All right, all right, I'm finished!" Meeren exclaimed. "Go ahead and look—but don't admire yourself too long; they're waiting for you at the Vale entrance."

He got up carefully, mindful of his costume, and moved into the bedroom to peer into the only mirror in the house.

It was a pleasant surprise, for he had been a little afraid that Meeren would overdo the decorations; Meeren had worked Kuari's feathers, a few strands of amber beads, and leather thongs finished with tiny silver feathers and figurines into his hair without making him look like a walking display of hair-jewelry. In fact, with his hair pulled back from his face and given a little more discipline, he looked a few years older than he actually was. That was exactly the effect he'd hoped for, but when he turned to thank the *hertasi*, Meeren was already gone.

It's time for me to be gone, too. He took a last look at him- •

self, satisfied himself that everything was fastened in firmly and wasn't going to come apart, then headed for his destination at a trot that would have been a run if not for the weight.

The Veil distorted the view past the entrance, but there was no doubt that everyone who could possibly appear to greet the Heralds had made it his business to come. As he passed the Veil itself, the tingle along his skin and down his spine seemed a bit stronger than usual; that probably meant Starfall and Firesong had gotten the Veil strengthened enough to keep out rain and inclement weather. *Of course, now that they've got the "umbrella" up, it won't rain.*

When he emerged on the other side and surveyed the crowd beneath trees that were only large by the standards of those who lived outside a Vale, he saw Keisha wave at him, then run to meet him. She looked a great deal more comfortable in her Greens than he was in his costume; her outfit was a butterfly-sleeved, calf-length tunic over long trews, belted with silver. Silver embroidery of leaves and vines on all hems was the extent of ornamentation, for the real emphasis in her costume was the fabric, which somehow managed to ripple through every possible shade of green as she moved. She seized his arm and tugged him to the right, looking relieved. Out in the crowd, there were at least two brightly painted inflated kick balls being tossed about randomly from person to person.

"Are they here yet?" he asked, wondering if he had missed the ceremony somehow.

"No, no, not yet, but Kel has them in sight." She gestured upward, and he followed her pointing finger to a patch of blue sky in the canopy of leaves. A small black speck rode a thermal in a slow, lazy circle overhead. *Kel is obviously planning on making an impressive entrance,* he thought with amusement. *His favorite hobby, besides being preened.*

But Keisha was tugging on his arm again, and he followed her obediently out past the restless mob of his fellow Hawkbrothers. Anticipation hung thickly in the air, and mingling with the Tayledras were members of Ghost Cat, villagers from Errold's Grove, and Lord Breon's people. Errold's Grove would get its own chance to greet the Heralds, but that wouldn't take place until the sixth day, and Darian intended to avoid that particular festival if he possibly could. He fully expected to be passed out in his bed then by the time all parties involved had gotten done with him.

There was no elevated platform setting the greeting committee apart from the rest, but one wasn't needed. If nothing else, the costumes marked all of the principal players out; the last time Starfall, Snowfire, and Nightwind had worn their elaborate outfits had been at Snowfire and Nightwind's wedding. Since then, the heavily embroidered and embellished items had been serving as wall art, as Darian's own costume eventually would. Firesong had outdone all of them; if sheer magnificence of clothing was the standard of importance, Herald Anda would surely think that *he* was the leader in this Vale. Silverfox lacked Firesong's impressive mask, but that was all he lacked; in every other respect, he was Firesong's reverse-image twin. The two of them were clad in blue and gold; where Firesong had gold in the patterns of beading and embroidery, Silverfox had blue, and vice versa. What first appeared to be subtle streaks of gold or blue in their hair became, on closer inspection, strings of tiny beads, ending in minute feathers. Aya sat on Firesong's shoulder, and as Darian neared, Kuari hooted a greeting from a branch above Starfall. His parents, Hweel and Huur, sat beside him. Starfall's falcon was on his gloved fist, and even the glove was beautifully made, with appliqued designs made of layers of dyed deerskin set into the cuff. Birds called, crowed, or screamed to each other, and a yellow kick ball bounced off Kuari's branch, making him hoot in indignation.

"Sorry!" someone called.

"Well, the boy cleans up rather nicely," Firesong said to Starfall, with a wink. "Perhaps we won't have to pretend he's a servant after all."

"Hey!" Darian protested, pointing an accusing finger at Firesong. "*I'd* been working on the stables all morning. What were *you* doing?"

"Making certain that rain would not interrupt our greetings," Firesong replied blandly, with a toss of his head that made the beads chime together like tiny bells. "Delicate work, that, requiring the skill of an expert."

Starfall rolled his eyes and snorted in derision. "Yes it did, which is why you *helped*," he corrected. "Or at least, you called it helping."

Firesong pretended to be greatly offended, and Silverfox just shook his head at both of them. "Indeed! I was there to make certain that instant corrections could be made if you upset something with your blundering. After all, Father, you *are* getting a bit forgetful lately."

"Forgetful? My blundering!" Starfall exclaimed. "What about—"

"Enough, you two," Nightwind interrupted them, then giggled. "Some of the outsiders might begin to believe that you two hate each other."

Starfall grinned, and behind the mask, Firesong mockpouted. "Oh, *Mother*—" he began, in imitation of a whining child.

"Don't!" Nightwind warned, hands on hips. "Just don't. Act like the baby, and I'll send you to your room like a baby!"

Firesong chuckled. "She's getting rather good at that, isn't she?" he said in an aside to Snowfire. "That whole mother thing, I mean."

Snowfire nodded ruefully. "It's a good thing, too, since the baby has me completely under her control. One teary-eyed look, and any resistance I had just evaporates."

He might have elaborated on that subject, but a shout of "Here they come!" interrupted him. There were several whistles, and the kick balls mysteriously vanished amid the crowd.

The entire group peered up the trail; Firesong and Darian both shaded their eyes with their hands. At first Darian couldn't see anything, but then a ray of light falling slantwise through the branches glanced off something white, which resolved into two distant riders.

Was it only two years ago that I stood here waiting for my new teacher, only to find out that he was the famous Adept Firesong? So much had happened since then; he had been so busy he hadn't even had much time to visit the village except for the seasonal Faires. *When I'm not off settling minor disputes, arbitrating trades, or helping the Vale understand the village, I've been caught up in Firesong's training. No wonder time has gotten away from me!*

He wished for a breeze, feeling the weight of his coat even more; for once, a breeze sprang up in answer to his wish. The riders neared at a steady pace, and he broke off his musing to examine them at his leisure. They both wore the Herald "working garb" of leather trews, a leather jerkin, and a plain white shirt tied loosely at the neck; it was pretty clear that they hadn't been expecting a formal reception or a major celebration. It had been a year since he'd last seen Shandi, and it seemed to him at least that she had gotten taller. Her face had thinned out a bit, but aside from that, her new status didn't seem to have put much of an outward stamp on her.

However, her Whites were *obviously* new, compared to the well-worn costume of the man riding beside her. So was her Companion's tack, and Darian made a mental note to have one of the *hertasi* look it over for stiffness and give it a good oiling with the special lanolin they used on hawk-furniture.

Herald Anda had probably not been very young when he demonstrated Mage-Gift and was selected for training by Darkwind and Elspeth. Now he was in late middle age, brown hair generously streaked with gray, and his weathered face as wrinkled as any shepherd's of the same age. He was in perfect health and excellent condition, however; despite a ride of many days' duration, he sat his Companion easily with little hint of fatigue.

The crowd behind Darian stilled, with hardly more than a murmur or two from those waiting. The two Heralds rode up in silence, with only the music of the forest behind them and the sound of their Companions' hoofbeats to punctuate it. They didn't use their reins, but the Companions came to a graceful halt about two wagon-lengths from Starfall. Herald Anda was in the lead, but by no more than a pace; neither he nor Shandi looked surprised at the size of the crowd waiting for them. *While they probably weren't thinking about a big, formal reception, I suppose they would be expecting a big crowd—this is one of the most important things to happen around here since we established the Vale. Besides, Heralds are rare enough around here that even an "ordinary" Herald draws a crowd.*

Karles, Shandi's Companion, tossed his head and looked around at the huge crowd with deep interest. The Heralds dismounted together, in a movement as perfectly timed as if they had rehearsed it. There were some murmurs of admiration from the crowd; Ayshen was right, there *was* power in style.

But of course, they don't have to practice moving together— not when they're Mind-linked to their Companions, and perhaps to each other as well. It certainly gave a good impression, however, making it look as if they had been a team for a very long time.

Again, Shandi remained a pace or two behind Herald Anda, who approached the little group that stepped forward to welcome him. Firesong and Silverfox in their turn lagged a little behind the rest, as Starfall took the lead with Darian beside him.

All right, here I go. Darian felt Anda's eyes rest on him for a moment, before the Herald turned his attention to Starfall.

"Herald Anda, we bid you and your Companion welcome to k'Valdemar Vale," Starfall said gravely. "Shandi and Karles, of course, we already know. We are glad to welcome them as well. We hope this new partnership will be a fruitful one for all of us, and we are pleased to be part of this new venture with Valdemar."

Darian stepped forward with his own well-rehearsed words. "We of k'Valdemar Vale invite you to partake of our hospitality and fellowship for as long as you desire," he told them. "We hope, in fact, that you find it so welcome that you take up residence permanently within the Vale. Now, if you will permit—I am Darian Firkin k'Vala k'Valdemar." He gave his full name with permissible pride, and bowed his head in the brief nod of equal to equal. "This is Adept Starfall k'Vala, this is his son Healing-Adept Firesong k'Treva." Starfall nodded, and Firesong moved forward a little and did the same. They had agreed on the order in which they would be introduced when they decided that Darian would make the introductions. "With Firesong is the *kestra'chern* Silverfox k'Leshya of the Kaled'a'in. I also introduce to you Mage-Scout Snowfire k'Vala and *trondi'irn* Nightwind k'Leshya of the Kaled'a'in."

Anda nodded to each of the people introduced, and if he didn't know what a *kestra'chern* or a *trondi'irn* was, he didn't show it.

Now the nonhumans came forward; Hashi wearing a collar and breastplate of appliqued leather, Ayshen in a coat of metal-scale like Meeren's, and Tyrsell sporting jeweled caps to his horns and a jeweled collar. "Here also are Hashi, chief of the *kyree*, Ayshen, leader of the *hertasi*, and Tyrsell, King-Stag of the *dyheli* of k'Valdemar Vale."

Evidently Anda had been warned, or had seen enough of intelligent nonhumans that he showed no sign whatsoever of surprise. He was, however, about to get a bit of a start.

Because just as Darian had figured, Kel had planned all along to make an impressive entrance. So he did—plunging through the branches of the trees with folded wings, to open them with a sudden snap at the last moment, and thunder in to a perfect landing. He kicked up such a wind that the Heralds both had to protect their eyes with their hands from the flying debris, and the Hawkbrothers, male and female alike, seized their hair to avoid ending up with a tangled mess.

Kel settled back onto his haunches, and regarded the Heralds with a mild gaze. He was in the full panoply of a Silver Gryphon; harness, collar, gems on his ear-tufts, and feathers painted and gilded. "And this is Silver Gryphon Kelvren, chief of the k'Valdemar gryphons," Darian finished, determined to look as if Kel's entrance had been planned from the beginning. Kel bowed his head regally—then lost every bit of his dignity at Anda's reply.

"I am very pleased to meet all of you at last," the Herald replied. "As is my Companion Eran. I am sure you already know that Shandi and Karles are overjoyed to be here as well. I am personally pleased to meet again with gryphons, since I was taught the use of magic by Treyvan and Hydona; I came to know them well, and consider them to be two of my best friends."

Kel's beak opened, and his eyes pinned in surprise. "You were taught by Treyvan and Hydona? You arre frrriends with the great onesss?" he gasped, and could not manage to say more, so overcome he was with the shock. Darian smoothly took up his speech again, covering Kel's dumbfounded astonishment.

"We comprise the Elders and Council of k'Valdemar," he told Herald Anda. "And as such, we open the Vale to you."

That was all that he was supposed to say, and as he stepped back, Starfall took over. "If you will allow us, we will conduct you and your Companions to your temporary home." He followed his speech with a gesture. "When you are settled and refreshed, we have planned a welcome feast and festival in honor of your arrival. We hope our customs will soon seem comfortable to you."

"Thank you, for all four of us," Anda replied, and took his place at Starfall's right, with his Companion Eran following. They all turned to face the gathering waiting behind Starfall, who had been holding their collective breath the better to hear the speeches.

That was the signal for everyone assembled to greet the new Heralds with a rousing cheer that shook the leaves and probably frightened every bird for furlongs about into silence.

The gathering split in two, making a path for Starfall and Anda. Behind them followed everyone else, with Shandi, Karles, and Keisha bringing up the rear. Shandi had her head together with Keisha, and Darian figured that they wouldn't miss his presence, so he stayed right behind Starfall. He was easily within hearing distance, and so caught most of the men's conversation.

"I am quite glad to take up this position, Adept Starfall," Anda was saying earnestly. "I have had enough traveling for two lifetimes. It will be good to finally settle into one place."

"I was under the impression that Heralds generally did *not* settle, is that true?" Starfall asked.

"In the past, yes, that has been true," Anda admitted. "Our saddles were usually our homes. We certainly spent more time on roads than in bedsteads. However, it occurred to Her Majesty that those with Mage-Gift would be of less use to the Crown in an emergency if it was impossible to lay plans knowing where they were, or if they were too far into the hinterlands to do any good. She decided that, insofar as it was possible, it would be better for Herald-Mages to assume permanent residencies, especially since there are so few of us. She has stationed about half of us as instructors at the Collegium, made Elspeth, Darkwind, and myself ambassadors, and the rest will be taking new stations such as mine, in important places along the Border."

"So you are intended to become the permanent ambassador here?" Starfall's satisfaction at that admission was evident in his voice.

"When you have gone to the trouble of creating a perfect place for all of the peoples of this area to come together, we would have been rather foolish to ignore the tacit invitation,"

Anda said dryly, and Starfall chuckled. "And to be blunt, in doing so, you saved Haven the trouble of making such a place and even better, saving them, if not a king's ransom, certainly a duke's!"

I think he's going to fit in just fine. He certainly has the right sense of humor, Darian mused.

"Now, did I understand your young spokesperson to say that our quarters are temporary?" Anda continued. Starfall nodded, and gestured to Darian to join them.

"We didn't want to assume your requirements, so we're putting you in the guest lodge until you have decided what you want," Darian said diffidently. "You'll want to see the Vale, of course, and we took into consideration that there is always the possibility that you might decide you would rather have your permanent headquarters outside it."

"Possible, but unlikely; why put the embassy in the countryside rather than the diplomatic capital?" Anda smiled slightly. "By the way, I'm given to understand that you have some method of imparting language in a candlemark or so. I would be very grateful if you could arrange for me to undergo the 'lesson' as soon as possible."

Starfall coughed slightly. "It leaves one with a dreadful headache," he warned.

Herald Anda shrugged. "Extended use of any mind-magic leaves one with a dreadful headache," he replied, as Darian stifled a grin of triumph. "The cost, however, is well worth the benefit. If you can arrange for this, I should like very much to have all of the languages in use here. I understand that Shandi has already acquired the necessary tongues."

"I will arrange for it with pleasure," Starfall told the Herald. "And you will curse me for it afterward. Meanwhile, we do have a great deal scheduled for you over the next few days."

Darian watched Herald Anda very closely, and thought he detected a faint hint of dismay as Starfall outlined all of the ceremonies ahead. *Surely he must have expected something of the kind.* Or maybe not. Although Heralds were important people, he hadn't seen a lot of ceremony involving them or honoring them—maybe because they tended to swoop in, take care of their business, and ride out again.

Poor Anda! He has no idea of what he's in for now! For the first time since all this had been planned, Darian felt a little better about his role as "entertainment." If his guess was right, Anda was just as dismayed at the prospect of a week of "performing" as Darian was. There was some small comfort in shared misery after all.

Six

According to Val, those about to be knighted generally spent their vigil in a chapel, on their knees. Darian had no intention of following that particular tradition; if Lord Breon wasn't satisfied with *his* way of keeping vigil, the man shouldn't have offered to knight him.

He wasn't going to spend the night indoors, and he absolutely wasn't going to spend it on his knees. The point of the vigil was to contemplate, to meditate on the things that had brought him here and what would follow. The point was definitely not to dislocate kneecaps, and besides that, he did his thinking better outside.

So after the requisite instructions from a Senior Knight (Val, coached by his father), Darian retired to the rear of the Keep and the gardens. He carried Kuari, and was accompanied by Val and Herald Anda. Women about to be knighted, it seemed, were always accompanied by females, and men by males, which let Shandi off easily. Or maybe not; now she would have to endure the feast, as the representative Herald.

Together, they watched the sun set behind the trees and the stars appear in the darkening sky. Darian had picked a spot with a garden bench to sit on, surrounded by bushes; as Val and Anda withdrew a little to hunch over a strategy game, he settled himself for the night. He gingerly helped Kuari down onto the trimmed grass; Kuari looked up at him hopefully.

:*Hunt now?*: the owl begged. Kuari loved hunting Lord Breon's lands; there were pastures and grain fields that attracted rabbits, with no cover for them to hide in. Kuari raised his wings a little, looking up into Darian's face with his enormous golden eyes.

:*Of course you can hunt now,*: he told the owl affectionately. Kuari didn't hesitate; with a soft croon, he spread his wings wide and shoved off from the ground with his powerful legs. Darian's dark-adapted eyes had no trouble following him; for the first several wagon-lengths, Kuari flew at knee height, pumping his wings to gain speed. Then, just at the edge of the garden, he surged upward and flew off into the trees. From there, he would scout for a good place to wait at the edge of the fields.

He would be back as soon as he had made his kills and fed; for now, Darian was content to sit on the stone bench and take in the night alone.

This was the dark of the moon, so nothing was going to obscure the stars. It wasn't as quiet as he would prefer; Lord Breon had several important guests, nobles from "nearby" holdings, who had come especially for the week-long festivities. The preknighting feast was still going on inside, and there was a fair amount of loud conversation coming from the Great Hall. More noise came from the kitchens; the rattling of pots and pans, the clatter of dishes, the shouts of the servants. There was a group of minstrels in there somewhere, trying manfully to produce music for the occasion, but they were losing the battle against the noise.

It was quite a contrast with last night's celebration at the Vale; it was always possible to talk to someone without raising the voice, for instance. Right now Darian heard a dozen different conversations going on, all shouted—someone was holding forth on sheep, someone else lamented the fact that he had three daughters, all within a year of each other in age and all betrothed, who were determined to have separate weddings rather than the money-saving triple wedding their father wanted. A round of laughter erupted when someone bawdily suggested a connection between the two subjects. Another old grouch bellowed out that things were *different* when he was knighted, no foreigners in fancy outfits and no disobedient daughters, either—

Darian stifled a laugh at that last; even in the Vales there were old grouches who growled that way. The same old tune would be sung in the future, and probably back in the time of Urtho there had been someone complaining how things had been *different*. . . .

At a Vale feast, though, the grouches kept their grumbles at a lower volume, so no one had to listen to them except other grouches who agreed with them. Obvious pockets of malcontent were easily avoided.

There wasn't anyone like that at k'Valdemar yet; no one moved here who wasn't prepared, indeed eager, for change. There was a surprising number of truly elderly Tayledras who had indicated that they would like to come, now that there was a Veil in place. He couldn't blame them for not wanting to share in the relative hardship of the first two years, and he had told the others that he thought encouraging the older folk to try k'Valdemar for size was a good idea. A Vale composed of folks mostly between the ages of sixteen and forty seemed very unbalanced to him; he wanted to see more children, and more people over the age of fifty.

No grouches, though.

He heard Keisha's sudden laugh ring out above the background noise, and Shandi's a moment later. He smiled at that; he was glad they were enjoying themselves. Shandi had walked Herald Anda through all the intricacies of last night's festivities, with Keisha helping. Shandi had looked very handsome in her Vale-made Whites, and so had Anda, though there had been some last-minute adjustments of hems and waistbands, or so Meeren had said. Virtually identical to the celebration of Nightwind and Snowfire's wedding, with the exceptions being that there were no displays of magic, and that there were a great many folk from outside the Vale taking part, the official celebration took place in and around the Council House. Anda stayed there; Shandi didn't, once she knew that Anda had things well in hand and was comfortable. She knew very well that the little clearings and the hot pools were the best places for fun, and as soon as she could reasonably assume that Anda would be all right on his own, she and

Keisha slipped out. Darian joined them very shortly thereafter, leaving Anda to a discussion of mutual acquaintances with Firesong and Silverfox.

And right now, I expect they wish they could slip out again! he thought. It was much better out here, in the clear, cool air, watching the stars. He had the feeling that even Val felt the same way, although it was too bad that Val would have to keep himself awake, and could not retire to the bed he shared with his pretty young wife.

It certainly wasn't going to be the first time Darian had stayed awake until dawn. Some of Firesong's lessons had involved fasts, vigils, enduring extremes of heat and cold, and other discomforts. He'd had to learn how to shut out what he had to, in order to keep his concentration on the task at hand, and how to force himself to the limits of his endurance and even a bit beyond.

Sitting and thinking until dawn is a walk down a Vale path by comparison.

He supposed that most of those who came to their knighthood vigils had plenty to think about. They would ponder the circumstances that had brought them here, and wonder if they could live up to the expectations of those who had chosen to honor them. For Darian, this wasn't so much an honor as a tool; a tool to help him handle his responsibilities more effectively. Still, there were those oaths—once a knight, courage was not applauded, it was assumed. Honesty was required. All the virtues he displayed would simply be expected of him— the only things that would be noticed would be his lapses.

So that's probably why most people aren't knighted until they've proved themselves, he reflected. *At that point, I suppose that virtue becomes a habit.*

The level of noise from the Keep behind him was tapering off as the candlemarks passed. The feast was probably over; the ladies had retired, leaving the men to serious drinking and progressively more incoherent conversation. *What a stupid custom!* he thought, amused. Then again, there came one of his old, departed Master Justyn's lessons: "Young Darian, your great speech is always mindless prattle to someone else, just as they are certain their prattle is a great speech." The old man had been right about so many things that only with experience made sense now.

At around midnight last night, the festivities had also slowed down. That was because most of the outsiders had left the Vale for their camps outside; only a few had been invited to stay within the Veil, and not only the guest lodge, but several *ekele* were hosting overnight visitors. Lord Breon's party cut their celebrating short as well, knowing they would have to ride back to the Keep in the morning. They wanted to have clear heads and steady stomachs for the journey. The villagers were still wary of staying too long in the strange Vale, especially after dark, and most of them had cleared out long before midnight. Only Ghost Cat tribesmen had stayed to "help" the Hawkbrothers see in the dawn.

Darian had stayed up past midnight, but not far past. Unlike Lord Breon's people, he knew he would be able to sleep late; the *dyheli* that took him to the Keep was much swifter than a horse, and even if he left just before noon, he would catch up with Lord Breon before his group arrived at the Keep. Nevertheless, he was not interested in seeing two dawns in two days, not with so much yet to do.

Herald Anda had retired at midnight; Shandi had not. There was some very interesting interplay going on between Shandi and Steelmind, a Tayledras herb- and plantmaster; what it meant, he didn't know, but it was certain that Shandi had made a deep impression on the other.

Shandi had a confidence about her that he dearly wished Keisha could acquire. What was it that had made Keisha so uncertain of herself? She was completely self-assured when it came to Healing, so why was she so unsure about everything else, especially her standing with him?

I've got to have a word with Silverfox, he decided. If there was such a thing as an expert in emotions, it would be a *kestra'chern.* Maybe Silverfox could give him the clue he needed to help Keisha.

But that brought something else to mind. *I'd better explain what a* kestra'chern *is to Anda as soon as the opportunity presents itself. Silverfox can do a great deal that Anda wouldn't even guess on his own.* It had taken Darian the better part of a year to *really* understand just what it was that Silverfox did.

A *kestra'chern,* a good one like Silverfox, anyway, was the oil that kept friction within a group to a minimum. But the tools he used to deal with incipient trouble were just about unlimited, up to and including taking someone into his bed, if that was what was needed. He was very like a Herald with a limited "community" to serve, but without careful explanation, Darian was afraid that Herald Anda would not necessarily see things that way.

Another difference between a Herald and Silverfox was that a *kestra'chern* tended to wait until people with problems came to him, rather than reaching out to deal with the problems. There were exceptions, but as Silverfox had once said, succinctly, "I am no one's nursery maid. Sometimes the children have to fight their quarrels without intervention." A Herald, of course, would plunge right in, but because Heralds rode a circuit rather than living in a particular community, real problems were usually at the point where they required intervention by the time a Herald got *to* them.

And the things that people can and should handle by themselves are usually kept quiet when the Herald is around. Reluctance to show the dirty linen in public saves Heralds from having to deal with it.

Darian decided that he'd had enough of sitting thanks to the numbness that usually came from sitting on stone, and got up to take a slow walk around the garden. He looked back at his two watchers, dark shapes against the backdrop of the light stone of the Keep, and the golden gleam of the lighted windows. Anda waved at him to show that he'd seen Darian stand.

In the dark, senses besides sight were heightened, and perceptions shifted in wondrous ways if one made himself open to them. Night birds called, at distances farther than he could have seen through the forests in daylight. Insects and what must have been thousands of tiny peeping frogs filled the air with their songs. It wasn't too difficult to keep to the garden paths, even in the darkness. The paths were graveled, and the moment he stepped off them, the sound alone told him. It was still a bit early for the garden to be fully in flower, but there were hints of scent as he passed certain beds—the sweetness of honey-climber, the intoxicant edge of the tiny flowers of the lily-bell, the subtle scent of violet. He knew which beds had recently been turned by the tang of fresh earth, and where the lawn had just been clipped by the sharpness of the newly cut grass. The sound behind him was definitely dying, and a quick glance back at the Keep showed more than half the windows had gone dark. Perhaps it was just as well that the guests had all faced that long ride this morning; the wine had gotten to them all the easier. With luck, less than half of them would be nursing hangovers in the morning when he was knighted.

When the dawn first painted the eastern sky with thin, gray light, Darian was still wide awake, but poor Val had fallen asleep where he sat! Darian pretended not to notice, turning his back so that Herald Anda could wake the young man discreetly. Kuari had returned with a sated appetite after Darian had finished his walk; now he, too, dozed, perched on the bench beside Darian with one foot tucked up. From time to time Darian worked his fingers in through the soft feathers to scratch Kuari's round head; when he did that, the owl crooned in his sleep and clicked his beak.

Footfalls behind him woke Kuari, who swiveled his head halfway around to glare at the interlopers. Darian stood up and turned to grin at Anda and a sleepy-eyed Val.

"Ready?" Anda asked casually. Darian nodded, then coaxed Kuari up onto his arm.

:Time to go find a tree to sleep in,: he told the owl, who looked a little ruffled at having his nap disturbed. *:I have to go inside now, and if you don't find a secure place, you know that the crows will harass you.:*

Kuari sighed, but agreed. Darian gave him a boost, and he labored off to a thick evergreen close to the Keep, where he could find a roost near the trunk, and the songbirds wouldn't see him. At the moment, the songbirds were too busy heralding the day and warming up their muscles to pay any attention to Kuari.

Darian followed Anda and Val back inside, to the Great Hall, where a group awaited them. Again, knighting was usually done in the chapel, but Darian had voiced a mild objection to that. Breon had readily agreed, since the chapel at the Keep wouldn't have held the full group that wanted to witness the knighting anyway.

Breon's Keep was not very old; it dated back no more than a century or so. As a consequence, it didn't have the same air of gloom that many of the older buildings of Valdemar did. In the Great Hall, the stone walls had been plastered over and whitewashed, then hung with tapestries. Above the tapestries, clerestory windows let in the early-morning daylight. Wooden beams supported the roof, and the battle banners of Breon's family hung from them. Because of the windows and plastering, although the Hall was cool, there was none of that feeling of dankness and damp that made older versions of this room that Darian had seen in Valdemar so uncomfortable.

Breon waited on the stone dais that held the High Table; behind him the table had been set for breakfast, which would follow the ceremony.

That certainly shows where my importance is, Darian thought with great amusement. *First, we get the ceremony over with, and then we can eat!*

The rest of his witnesses were gathered below Breon. The sturdy Breon was wearing a surcoat that reached down past his knees, embroidered with the arms of his family and his own personal device. This was a relatively new item of his wardrobe, replacing the one he had worn for *his* investiture as a knight. The *hertasi* had made it for him as a birthday gift in time for Val's knighting, and it was just as splendid as the one Darian would wear to tonight's feast. Anda and Val led the way to the foot of the dais, with Darian following about four paces behind. From here on, the knighting would follow strictly traditional lines.

"Who comes before me in the light of the new sun, and why are you here?" Breon rumbled, in a voice that sounded a little hoarse—no doubt from all the shouted conversation last night. The wording had a weighty air of the ancient about it, a nearly palpable reinforcement that a knighting was anything but a casual lark.

Val answered, as the Senior Knight for this ceremony. "The Knighted Heir of Lord Breon, Sir Valyn, and the Herald-Mage Anda; we present a candidate for the honor of Knighthood, and stand as his sponsors."

"And has he passed all tests of valor and virtue, of word and deed?" Breon replied, looking sternly down at his son and the Herald.

This time it was Anda who answered. "He has passed all tests and more, by the words of his mouth, and the deeds of his body. It is his actions of virtue and nobility that bring him before you this dawn."

That last was an acknowledgment that Darian hadn't been required to undertake any physical trials to prove his fitness for combat. Val had, because he had never actually fought, but Darian had faced—and struck down—the barbarian shaman of the northern Blood Bear tribe that had ravaged Errold's Grove, and he had done so entirely by himself at the ripe age of fourteen. That alone probably would have qualified him.

Although I'm not sure how noble the weapons of a bucket and a pitchfork are. . . .

"Has he stood his vigil as ordained by tradition?" asked Breon.

The back of Val's neck flushed with embarrassment at his own lapse, but he answered stoutly, "He has, waking the night through, alone with his thoughts, fasting, and in contemplation of his past and future."

At that reminder of "fasting," Darian's stomach protested his lack of breakfast. At least it didn't growl.

Breon nodded ponderously. "Therefore present him to me now, that I may see him with my own eyes,"

Val and Anda each stepped to the side, and Darian stepped forward. In his capacity as Herald—in the most ancient sense of the word—Anda presented Darian.

"Here we bring to all eyes and powers Darian Firkin, adopted of k'Vala clan of the Hawkbrothers, founder of k'Valdemar Vale, and worthy candidate for the honor of knighthood." Anda's voice rang out with strength, filling the Great Hall without sounding as if he was shouting.

Well, that's one trick I'd certainly like to learn.

Breon looked down at Darian, and gave him a quick wink. Darian raised his eyebrows slightly in acknowledgment, but otherwise kept his expression properly sober.

"Darian Firkin, adopted of clan k'Vala, founder of k'Valdemar, is it your will that you be presented for the honor and responsibilities of Valdemaran Knighthood?" Breon asked, managing to get through the k'Vala and k'Valdemar without any trouble, though Val said he'd been fumbling the titles in practice. That was one reason why they'd broken up Darian's name the way they had.

Darian nodded. "It is my will and my wish, Lord Breon," he said, pitching his voice a little deeper than usual.

"Kneel, then." Lord Breon held out his hand, and Val put Darian's sheathed sword hilt-first into his palm. Breon held out the sword hilt-first toward Darian, who knelt and put his right hand on the hilt. "Do you swear, Darian, by this blade which is your honor, that you will use your strength for good and not ill, to aid and not oppress; that you will defend the weak and helpless against those who would oppress them, that you will seek good with all your heart, seek the light with all your soul? That you will serve as an example to those who would follow you, as a rock of fortitude for those who have gone before you; that you will uphold the law when the law is in the right, and oppose the law when it serves oppressors; that you will work for the greatest good, with all you may bring to bear, even in the face of death and fear?"

"I do swear," Darian replied firmly.

"Do you swear to strive for honor, for courage, for valor, for virtue, all for their own sake and not for the acclaim of the multitude, nor for gain, nor for the power they might bring you?"

"I do swear," Darian repeated in the same tones of resolve.

"Do you accept the honor of knighthood as a responsibility as well as a title? Will you hold to the standards of all those before who have ever borne the title of Knight?"

"I do so accept it," Darian said, wondering if Breon knew just how long he had pondered that very question, wondering if he dared take on another responsibility. But he had come to the conclusion that it represented giving his current responsibilities a more recognizable name, and as such, he felt comfortable in accepting it. "And I will hold to those standards, keeping them ever in my heart and mind."

Breon reversed the sword, unsheathed it, and laid the naked blade once on each shoulder, tilting the sword after each so that the cold steel laid against Darian's bare neck. "Then accept these blows in token of the ones you shall take that others be spared—and rise, never to kneel to another again, unless you deem that other to be worthy of your profoundest esteem. Kneel only to honor what is holy or in recognition of one whose nobility exceeds the common."

Darian stood, and Breon sheathed the sword. "Accept from me this blade, Sir Darian, and wield it forever in honor."

Darian took the sword and belted it on over his surcoat, buckling and latching it securely, then turned to face the group behind him. Once again, Anda raised his voice. "Ladies and Lords, Knights, gentlemen, and guests, I present to you Sir Darian Firkin k'Vala k'Valdemar, Owl Knight of the Tayledras!"

There were enough friends in the crowd—and those who had just recently gained genuine admiration for him, too—that the cheer took on a distinctly enthusiastic note as Darian was escorted by Val and Anda out of the Great Hall, down the special strip of Valdemaran-blue carpet that had been laid for him to walk on.

Once past the doors, Darian sagged a little, and Val slapped him on the back. "To bed with you," the young man declared. "I'm your champion and representative at the tournament, so you don't even have to put in a token appearance if you don't feel up to it."

"No, I should open it, at least," Darian responded. "That's only right." He grinned and straightened up. "Besides, think of all those young fighters out there who've been dying for a look at the weird Tayledras knight—they at least deserve to see that I don't have two heads. I'll call Kuari in to land, on my shoulder, you know, give them a show. Then I'll retire."

He didn't have any feelings of guilt over the fact that Val wasn't going to get a nap, not when he knew from Val's relative freshness that his friend had probably had a good long doze in the darkness. Anda had big, dark rings under his eyes, but Anda was going to be able to get some sleep as well; he wasn't needed at the tournament at all.

"In that case, let's get this tourney open, so the hotbloods can start beating on each other," Val replied heartily. Anda took his leave of them, and they headed for the front of the Keep, where a well-worn stand and a tourney-field had been set up outside the walls. Tournaments were a good place for fighters to demonstrate their skills to a potential employer, and to have a chance to earn some prize money into the bargain. Since this tournament was sponsored by k'Valdemar, the prizes weren't money, but were Tayledras-produced items that could readily be converted into money—or into dowries—bolts of silk, glassware, and jewelry. The prizes had been on display at last night's feast, and Darian didn't doubt that most examples, if not all of them, already had several potential buyers from among Breon's guests.

Darian climbed up into the grandstand, and looked down at the sea of helmets below him. With the early-morning sun to his right, he couldn't see faces inside those helmets, only dark eye-slits. It was a little unnerving, but only a little.

It was a good thing he'd memorized a speech for this, too, since fatigue was starting to catch up with him. He smiled, waved, made his speech, and exhorted the fighters to display not only strength and courage, but honor and brotherhood. In fact, there was an award for the fighter who behaved the best on the field and off it. Despite some mental disgruntlement from his owl, who had been awakened for the flight, Kuari's appearance and wide-winged, silent landing as Darian declared himself by the title Owl Knight raised a cheer from everyone. Kuari then left Darian in a ground-skimming flight down the length of the tourney grounds past every competitor, and disappeared into the shadows of the forests. Exclamations of amazement and murmurs of approval resounded. It seemed Ayshen was proven right yet again. Darian turned the proceedings over to Val, who took over with relish. As Darian's Champion, Val was going to get to do some fighting against the few knights among the fighters, and he had his eye on the prize to give to his wife. He could have gotten the same sort of prize by just asking Darian for it, but it wouldn't have been as satisfying to Val to just ask for it, as it would be fun to win it by pounding everyone else into the ground. Darian happily left him to it.

Darian dismounted the grandstand and managed not to stagger as he made his way to the little room he'd been given. It was deep within the Keep, not even a clothes closet by Tayledras standards, with a bare arrow-slit for a window. It was only large enough for a narrow cot, at the foot of which waited a tray with his breakfast on it—but right now, it suited his purposes perfectly. It had a bed, and nothing at the moment was needed more. Now he had no more duties until this evening, when he would be presented to all the guests, preside over the distribution of the prizes, and take the seat of honor at Breon's right hand at the High Table.

*   *   *

Darian struggled against a heavy weight on his chest; for some reason, he couldn't open his eyes or even move—

Finally he wrenched his head around, and his eyes flew open.

A huge, translucent cat lay laconically on him, covering him from his neck to his toes, hindquarters spilling over the cot and onto the floor. It looked into his eyes and breathed softly on his face; its breath held the same scent as the winter wind just before a storm.

It looked up suddenly, its shimmery golden eyes wary and alert. Darian found his gaze pulled to the tiny slit of a window.

A raven the size of the huge cat—and just as eerily translucent—peered in through the slit, first one eye, then the other, then tried to force its way into the room.

Impossibly, first the beak, then the head, then the body and wings flattened themselves and oozed into the room with him.

Both cat and raven stared at him, as if expecting him to answer a question of life-or-death importance—

But he had not the faintest notion what the question was.

He fought to cry out, but his throat was frozen—

And he sat bolt upright on the floor, with a shout.

He was alone. No bird, no cat; the heavy weight on his chest had been the cot; he had overset it on top of himself.

Hot with embarrassment, he was just grateful that no one had come in answer to his shouting , or the ruckus he must have made as he fought with his bedding. Still clumsy with fatigue, he managed to fumble the cot upright again, and lay back down, this time to sleep dreamlessly.

The next day he was safely back in k'Valdemar, and although he'd had some doubts about his performance at the feast, Anda assured him that he had done splendidly. "*I* caught the sarcasm," Anda said, when he'd expressed his guilt over some of his remarks to one of Breon's grouchy guests, "But trust me, Lord Talesar wouldn't recognize irony if you loaded it into a catapult and flung it at him. You did well; people I talked with said they couldn't believe how patient you were with the old goat."

Today was a rest day for him; Anda and Shandi were getting

their formal reception at Errold's Grove. Keisha had gone along as moral support for Shandi, figuring that with both of them there, her mother wouldn't be able to single either of them out for attention.

The first place he went when he arrived was the hot pools; the one thing he truly needed at this point was a long soak. As always, Meeren knew the moment he'd passed the Veil, and he had no sooner gotten settled into the water than the *hertasi* appeared with cold drinks and finger food.

"Well?" Meeren asked, perching on the rocks beside Darian. "How did it go?"

Darian gave the *hertasi* a complete description of the events of the past two days, knowing that Meeren would be providing all the details to the other, insatiably curious *hertasi* of the Vale, and to the *kyree* who served as their historian. Meeren sat rock-still, interrupting Darian only for questions about details, and at the end let out an enormous sigh of satisfaction.

"Excellent job," he said, bestowing the *hertasi* vote of approval on him. "You gave them a good show, and you've made a fine impression on Lord Breon's neighbors. I anticipate more trade agreements from this, especially now that they've seen the quality of our goods. We could use more trades for meat; those gryphons are eating the larder bare, and red meat fills them up better than herd birds." Meeren rubbed his hands at the prospect; when trade agreements were conducted in the Vale, he usually served as Ayshen's assistant—of late he had even conducted them himself under Ayshen's supervision. Darian often wondered when he found the time to take care of the *ekele* and his other responsibilities.

Then again—if he couldn't take care of twenty major things at once, Ayshen would never have picked him as an assistant.

"So tomorrow is the Ghost Cat ceremony," Meeren went on. "I don't foresee any problems there."

"I wouldn't think so," Darian agreed. "No speeches, for one thing. I've been to their sweat-house gatherings before. Anything you say is supposed to be right out of your head, and spontaneous. Nobody minds if you aren't very articulate."

Meeren chuckled. "That should certainly suit *you*," he teased. "You're at your best when you're inarticulate."

"Oh, *thank* you," Darian replied sarcastically. "Have you been taking lessons in sarcasm from Firesong? By the way, you might want to consider adding needlework to your list of potential trade items; most of Breon's lady-guests were positively drooling over our surcoats."

"I doubt any of them could afford what we would charge for work like that," Meeren said dryly. "But I'll keep it in mind. Who knows? There might be potential in selling small motifs for ladies to add their own work around."

Having satisfied himself that he had pried everything worth hearing out of Darian for now, Meeren left him to his soak and dinner, pausing only to add, over his shoulder, "Oh, and by the way—good work on the hot spring."

Once he was ready to come out, the building had started to fill up with folk coming in from hunting and labor. He left the pools to them, and sought his bed, hoping Keisha was having a good time at the village. He was still so tired from the vigil, his nightmare, and the feast that followed that he'd almost fallen asleep on his *dyheli's* back, and that was no mean feat.

Breon's guests, no longer hindered by the need to be alert and fresh the following day now that the tournament was over, had kept him awake far longer than he'd wanted to be. It was just a good thing he'd been able to opt out of the Errold's Grove welcome; he really pitied poor Anda.

When he got back to his *ekele* and into the bedroom, he found that Meeren had left a mug of something on the bedside table with a note attached. In the spiky *hertasi* script, it read, "Drink this, and nothing will wake you up until I do."

He contemplated the mug for a moment. He wanted to be awake when Keisha came back from the village—but he really didn't want any of those uneasy dreams he'd been having off and on. *So I suppose the question is, how much do I want to greet Keisha, versus how much I want to avoid having a nightmare.*

He yawned, closed his eyes for a moment, and caught himself starting to drop off. That decided him.

The question isn't "want" but "need." I need sleep. They're going to have the sweat house packed and hot, and I can't leave it without losing face. If I don't get enough sleep, I won't be able to take the heat, and I might even pass out.

There was danger in that possibility as well; if he passed out, it was possible that no one would notice in the darkness until he was in serious trouble.

And wouldn't that be a bad omen where everyone was concerned! No, Keisha's Healer enough to expect me to be sleeping, and she'd probably get mad at me if I wasn't getting the rest I need.

He picked up the mug and drank the contents off as quickly as he could, resolutely ignoring the bitter taste that no amount of honey could conceal.

Before the potion could go to work on him, however, he wrote a note for Keisha on the other side of Meeren's. *The hertasi want me to sleep, so I'm going to be obedient. Otherwise I might wake up to find all my clothing tied in knots. Sorry I couldn't wait up for you,* ashke.

Only after he had propped the note up on the empty mug did he lie down, and it was a good thing he did, because when the potion hit, it hit without warning, and not even an earthquake would have awakened him.

Seven

The Ghost Cat enclave was near enough to k'Valdemar that the inhabitants could send runners to the Vale for protection in case of disaster or attack. In the first few weeks, that had given Darian an odd feeling—that Northerners would be running *to* the Tayledras, and for protection! By now, though, he was so used to it that it only occurred to him on the occasions when Ghost Cat tribesmen dressed up in their ceremonial regalia, and once again, his sense of *difference* woke up. What the tribesmen wore for everyday use was similar to Tayledras scout gear but for the looser seams, and grew more so all the time as Ghost Cat adopted Hawkbrother materials and styles. The people he had first thought of as barbarians turned out to be very appreciative people, even going so far as to honor their benefactors by becoming like them whenever they could.

When Darian woke up with Meeren shaking him, Keisha was already up and dressed, looking down at him with laughter in her eyes. She, too, had donned a special costume for the occasion, the female version of Shaman Celin's garb. On her head, because she was a Healer and allied with the Tayledras, she wore a hood made to resemble an enormous hawk head. Darian thought he detected the delicate touch of Firesong in the placing of the feathers, and Ayshen's talons in the carving of the beak, which had clearly been modeled after Kel's. The headdress was attached to a feathered cloak, complete with pseudo-wings, and while the feathers of the head had been made from the molted feathers of k'Valdemar raptors, the cloak had been built out of the body-feathers of the gryphons. Keisha's deerskin dress, fringed and beaded, had the badge of the Healers worked in beadwork on the breast just under her throat. Little bone carvings dangled amid the fringes, but unlike Darian's, which were of predators and prey, Keisha's were of flowers and leaves, with the occasional hawk. Her dress ended at the floor, but the deerskin had been slit into fringe from the floor to the knee, giving her great freedom of movement. She wore boots with leaves appliqued along the outer calves and lacings up the inner side. Once again, the *hertasi* had outdone themselves . . . but then again, Meeren and Loshi found Keisha and Darian very undemanding when it came to clothing.

I don't think we've asked for anything new for . . . more than a year anyway. The outfits that Loshi had designed might well have been in production, or even finished, waiting for a special occasion to finally be presented.

Well, not the two surcoats—but the uniforms, the festival garb, and the Ghost Cat regalia could have been made. There was bound to be something *of importance at Ghost Cat eventually.*

"You know—" Darian paused to yawn, and accepted a warm mug of something from Meeren. "You look amazing in that outfit."

"I think I like it," Keisha replied, turning to the right and left to look down at herself. "I didn't think it would be comfortable, but it is."

Darian downed the drink, which was mouth-puckeringly tart, and handed the mug back to Meeren before he got out of bed; his mind felt very fuzzy, and he hoped whatever it was that Meeren had given him was a dose to help clear the effects of the sleeping potion. "How did the village welcome go?"

"I think I am going to be in Shandi's debt for at least a year," Keisha replied, still looking as merry as she had before Darian broached the subject. "She's gotten Mother to think of something besides me."

She looked so tickled that Darian could only say, "Dare I ask how?"

"Shandi can answer that for herself, thank you," Shandi replied, poking her head in at the bedroom door. "Mother made the mistake of asking about—no, actually making *prying* questions about the overnight arrangements Heralds have, meaning me and Anda of course. So I told her."

Shandi's lips twitched as she tried not to laugh. "Oh, but that wasn't the best part," Keisha put in. "She turned bright pink, and practically shouted, 'You mean you *sleep* with him?'"

"And I answered, quite matter-of-factly, 'Why, no, do you think I should?' It's the first time I've ever seen her speechless." Shandi couldn't hold back the laughter any longer, and Keisha and Darian joined her.

Darian wiped his eyes, which were damp with tears of laughter. "Both of you had better go get something to eat before all the good stuff is gone. I'll catch up with you. It won't take me long to get dressed."

Shandi vanished, and Keisha took the hint. Only then did Darian get out of bed. He'd gone to sleep last night not wearing much, and he wasn't sure he wanted to get out of bed in front of Shandi. She didn't have Tayledras sensibilities, after all.

Meeren had his entire outfit ready and waiting, and in next to no time he was trotting up the trail toward the building where most people in the Vale ate together; food was always kept ready and waiting there, but at the usual mealtimes hot, fresh dishes were brought from the kitchen in a steady stream. He actually did catch up with Keisha and her sister just before they reached the door; they helped themselves, then took a small table near one of the open windows. Gauzy curtains and vines framed them as they began their meal.

He ate lightly, but drank plenty of water; he hoped someone had warned Anda to do the same. "Where's your senior?" he asked Shandi, as she did justice to a stack of flat-cakes.

"He's already over at Ghost Cat," she replied. "You should have seen his face when I told him what he was going to be doing today!" She rolled her eyes and grinned. "It's a good thing he has patience and a sense of humor. I pointed out that he wasn't the only one making this round of ceremonies, and that it's all in his honor anyway. He just sighed, and said, 'I wish they were a little less glad to see me, then.'"

"How long have you known him?" Keisha asked, curiosity writ large all over her expression. "You mentioned him now and again, but I didn't think he was anything more than one of your teachers."

"All the way from the time I arrived—what I didn't know is that there's a kind of fast way through the Collegium, if you arrive older than about fifteen and are already educated by Collegium standards." She paused to take a bite or two. "I didn't have to go through most of the academic courses, because I had the basics already—and imagine my surprise to discover that all of those useless lessons in 'manners' we had to go through turned out to be identical to all the courtly protocol Heralds need for dealing with the nobility!"

It was Darian's turn to drop his jaw. "No! Are you serious?"

"Absolutely." Shandi nodded and grinned. "Even the book they use is the same one old Widow Clay uses. There were three examinations, which I passed—those old lessons saved me from a *year* of schooling in 'Courtly Graces.' To cut it all short, by doubling up a fair amount and not taking as many holidays as everyone else, I finished in two intensive years instead of four. In order to do that, I had to have a mentor assigned to me to help. It was no accident that I got Anda. As soon as the Queen and her Council realized what you lot were up to, they planned to send an ambassador and picked Anda for the job, and he mentioned that I was from the region. The Queen herself gave the nod about me, can you believe it? And so then I was being tutored by Anda. He was learning as much from me as he could while I was stuffing *my* head full of Collegium classes, and he tutored me when I wasn't quite getting things. He's a lot like your Starfall, Darian. Very dry sense of humor, but it goes deep. He took to dragging me around with him socially, once he knew I wasn't going to embarrass him, so I got to know the gryphons and some of the other ambassadors. We got on so well that they waited until I had my Whites and sent us both, so I could coach him on local politics and customs while *I* learn about how to be a diplomat."

"Are you going to stay after your field-year?" Keisha asked.

I'll bet she wants Shandi to stay, Darian thought. *I think it would be a good thing if she could.*

Shandi shook her head. "I don't know; it may depend more on what happens here than anything else. If Anda thinks I need more experience elsewhere, then I'll be sent off. If he decides he needs me to help out here, then I'll stay. Heralds don't have much say in where they're sent; we go where we're needed."

"But why send a Herald-*Mage* and not assign another Herald-Mage as his junior?" Keisha wanted to know.

Good question. Darian was as interested to know the answer to that as Keisha—maybe even more.

Shandi took her time in finishing her breakfast before answering. She pushed the plate away as a sign that she was done with it, and took a long drink of juice while Keisha waited with admirable patience.

"I can only tell you what I *think* is the reason," she replied, putting down her glass. "I haven't asked that question myself, partly because right now I'm supposed to be learning to figure out answers on my own. I think that the reason a Herald-Mage was sent in the first place is twofold. First, the Circle wants to know more about how to use that Heartstone they've got simmering under the Palace, and they hope Anda can pick up some answers from you lot. Second, magic comes as naturally to the Hawkbrothers as breathing, and someone who didn't have Mage-Gift might make some wrong assumptions or give the wrong impression to them."

"I don't know if you're right, but it certainly sounds logical," Darian agreed. "But why not pick a junior who has the Gift?"

"Two reasons again. One, there aren't a lot of Heralds with Mage-Gift, and there might not have been anyone to send. It's entirely possible that I'll be replaced by someone who has it. Second—our generation is used to magic; we've grown up with it. We know what we can reasonably expect a mage to do and how he'll think. Or—maybe I should say, the *Heralds* of our generation will; ordinary folk might be just as perceptive or completely oblivious." She chuckled and winked at Keisha. "The point is, for someone to assist Anda, or even take over the post when he steps down, a Herald of *our* generation is perceptive enough to handle the job. Plus, they told me that my particular Gifts will be very useful to a diplomat."

She didn't elaborate on what her Gifts were, leaving Darian to wonder just what it was she had. He knew about the limited ForeSight—which could presumably keep a diplomat from making a disastrous decision—but what else would apply?

Keisha was staring at her sister with a mingling of surprise and chagrin. "Shandi, you have *changed* out of all recognition!" she managed. "When you left, you were—well, kind of dreamy and careless. Now—"

Shandi waved her hand at her sister. "It's all in having a sense of purpose and a job to do. *You* were the one who always had that; there didn't seem to be any place for me that made any sense. I didn't really see myself as getting married no later than seventeen and raising ten or a dozen littles. The only thing I really liked was sewing, but you can't make a life around fancy-work. I just drifted, right up until the moment Karles Chose me. *Then,* for the first time, I had a place that was my own, and an important job no one else could do." She shrugged. "I haven't so much changed as woken up, you could say, and as soon as I did, I started making up for lost time."

"With a vengeance!" Keisha looked at her sister as if seeing Shandi for the very first time. "No wonder you were able to render Mother speechless!"

Now I'm happier than ever that Shandi's here, Darian thought, surveying the two sisters, who were more alike than they would have guessed two years ago. *She's like fuel for Keisha's fire.*

"Time to go, people," Darian reminded them. They all shoved away from the table, which was promptly swarmed by *hertasi,* and by the time they had reached the doorway another group had taken it over.

The sweat house was very dark inside, with only a little light leaking in around the blanket over the door. Sweat literally ran from every pore of Darian's body as he sat knee-to-knee in the circle around the hot rocks in a pit in the center of the house. Thick with steam, redolent with the scent of cedar, the air was so hot it would have been torture to anyone who hadn't been in the circle from the time the first rock was brought in.

A hand touched Darian's right elbow, and he accepted the bucket of water passed to him, taking up the dipper made of gourd floating on the top and drinking eagerly of water that tasted strongly of the bundles of herbs that had been soaking

in it. Once in a *very* great while, and only under extreme conditions, there were herbs in there that were supposed to make
"seeing the other side" easier, according to Shaman Celin
Broadback Caller. That wasn't the case today; this ceremony
was meant to make Darian one of the tribe, not meant to be a
vision-seeking. The herbs in the bucket were those that aided
endurance and heat tolerance, nothing more esoteric.

Still, even with that help, the heat in here had climbed considerably past the point that Darian had experienced the last
time he was undergoing a ceremony. He was glad that they
were on the last round, and from here on, although it wouldn't
get cooler, it wouldn't get hotter either.

This round was for silence; the rounds alternated, silence
and speech. With each round, more hot rocks came in, fresh
from the fire. They had been warming in the heart of the fire
stack for half the day and hissed as they were brought in,
glowing red from every pit and crevice. Poignant to Darian
only perhaps was the fact that they were brought in scooped
by a pitchfork. The ceremony began with a round of speech,
and ended in a round of silence, or rather, listening. Outside
the sweat house, the women surrounded the building, drumming. Six of the Eldest sat in a half-circle around a huge drum
made from a section of tree trunk; the rest were placed around
the sweat house with hand-drums. All of them beat the same,
simple rhythm during the silence rounds, the rhythm of a
heartbeat. Darian felt as if he were sitting in the middle of
the earth's own heart as the drumbeat throbbed around him,
vibrating deep in his chest. It was a magnificent effect, felt
deep in the bones and lungs.

He passed the bucket on to Anda, who was on his left, and
stared at where the rock pit was, just in front of him, no more
than a hand's length away from his feet. He couldn't see the
rocks glowing anymore, but he certainly felt the steam coming off them when the Shaman tossed another ladle of cedar
water on them. The rocks hissed as the water splashed on
them, and it rose in clouds of heat that felt like a blow to the
skin of his face.

And yet he had to admit that all this felt curiously comforting, if not comfortable. There was no one partaking of this
ceremony who did not want Darian to be there, the Shaman
and Chief Vordon had seen to that. Unlike the ceremony of

knighting, literally everyone here was a friend, and fully pleased to welcome Darian and *his* friends into their tribal circle. Even Anda must have sensed that, for now there was no hint of the earlier tension that Darian had sensed to his left.

Outside, had the drumbeats quickened a little? It was the women who determined the length of the rounds of silence, signaling an end by increasing the speed of their rhythm until the drum song ended in three decisive beats.

He thought there was tension in the air that had not been there a moment before. Perhaps the drums had sped up, and the women were about to set them all free into the cool air of early evening. He knew every nuance of the symbolism here; he and Shaman Celin had discussed the ritual for many long nights once Ghost Cat had decided to bring him into the tribe. This was in every sense a birth—did Anda know or sense that? He wasn't sure how much the Shaman had told the Herald before the ceremony began.

Tension increased; the air throbbed around him, pressing in on him. There was the recurring sensation that his skin no longer held him, but rather that his flesh and blood extended out into the sultry air, a vapor. Celin threw another dipperful of water on the stones. A second rhythm joined the first, both sets of drums driving onward, pace increasing slowly, but steadily.

In the general area of the stone pit, a hazy hint of a glow appeared. At first Darian thought that his eyes were playing tricks on him; then he figured that Celin had opened the blanket over the door a trifle, and there was a ray of light reflecting and diffusing into the steam. But when he glanced to the side, the blanket was still firmly down, yet the glow had strengthened.

Is anyone else seeing this?

To his right, there was no sign that Kala saw anything but darkness—but to his left, he felt Anda stir and lean forward, peering at the glow.

Little whispers of sound between the drumbeats told him that there were others who were seeing something, too. The glow brightened, and began to pulse in time to the drums.

Celin hadn't said anything about *this!*

Now even phlegmatic Kala tensed; the glow was bright

enough at this point to see the faint outlines of rocks piled beneath it.

As the drums sped up, with each beat the glow pulsed and condensed, assuming a definite shape.

A large four-legged shape.

Suddenly, in the rounded area that could have been a head, a pair of fiery eyes appeared, exactly as if the mist-creature had just opened them. And the eyes were fixed on Darian.

Darian caught his breath and sat very still, although his heart outraced the drums outside.

A moment more, and the final pulse of light brought form and detail to the shape—but Darian had known from the moment those eyes focused on him what that shape would be. It was the Ghost Cat, the totemic spirit of Ghost Cat tribe. It was the size of a pony, with blue eyes exactly the color of a blue-white flame. This wasn't the first time he'd seen it— though there had only been one other moment he had looked into its eyes while wide awake.

The drums outside rose to a crescendo of frenzy.

It paced toward him, putting one enormous, snowshoe-sized-paw in front of the other, until it literally stood nose-to-nose with him. Then it slowly bent its head—he thought he felt a puff of cold breath on his feet—he couldn't think through the frantic drumbeats that filled his body—

Thud! Thud! Thud!

With the last of the three beats signaling the end of the ceremony, the Ghost Cat vanished. From outside, the Eldest of the women flung the blanket up, and light and cool air poured into the sweat house as the steam rushed out. The steam glowed, but with natural, reflected light; swirls of fresh air entered and began to dissipate it.

Those to the left and immediately at the door began crawling out, Shaman Celin first; although Darian was still trying to wrap his mind around what he'd just seen, he managed to respond when Kala nudged him and joined the rest to crawl in single-file out the sweat-house entrance.

The light of the setting sun half-blinded him; as his head emerged, the women set up a mighty chorus of ululation; two of the Elder Women came forward and seized him under each elbow, pulling him to his feet. A third came forward with a bucket of cold water—which, after the heat of the lodge, felt like knives of ice!—and drenched him with it.

He yelped, then performed as expected, gasping and sputtering; the women howled with laughter, then the two Elders wrapped him in a blanket and rubbed him down briskly, as impersonally as if he'd been a horse. They spun him three times around, then thrust him forward, staggering, to where a fourth woman waited to help him on with his clothing. Shandi and Keisha stood by on the sidelines, bent over with laughter, but he didn't mind. He'd known exactly what was coming, and *he* was the one who had asked for Ghost Cat to invite both the girls to participate.

The Shaman, clothed and dry, but with damp hair slicked back, came forward as soon as Darian was dressed; he grabbed Darian's right hand and swiftly slashed a flint blade across his palm, in the fleshy padded part between the base of the thumb and the wrist. He did the same with his own, and before Darian's cut had even begun to sting, Shaman Celin clasped their two bloody hands together, and raised them to the sky.

"This is our new son, Kurhanna, whose blood is in my veins as mine is in his!" the Shaman shouted. "Welcome him to our circle!"

A great cheer arose, and although the Shaman gave Darian a considering look that portended a long discussion at a later time, he said nothing. Instead, he stepped back and allowed the members of his tribe to carry their newest member off to their version of a formal feast.

It had taken Anda a little time to get used to sitting on the ground and eating meat with only a knife, but now he seemed right at home among the tribesmen. With a leaf-wrapped strip of meat in his left hand and his knife in his right, Anda fed himself just as the tribesmen were doing, setting his teeth into the meat and cutting off a bite-sized portion, the blade coming perilously close to his lips. Despite the fact that he needed translations to understand what the men around him were saying, he managed to carry on tolerable conversations.

In a situation unusual for Ghost Cat, and prompted by the wish to honor *both* Heralds, women mingled with men around the fire. Normally women had their own meals and fire, but that would have separated Anda from Shandi. The women were enjoying the novel situation, although the oldest of them had formed a little circle of their own off to the side. The unmarried women were taking full advantage of this unique opportunity to flirt, though the Elders among the women tried to quell them with disapproving glances.

Evidently most of the men had gotten over their initial surprise and had simply accepted the appearance of their tribal totem as a unique demonstration of the spirits' approval. The Clan would not be where it was now—namely alive and safe—if not for visions of the Ghost Cat in the past, the Tayledras agreed. It was not something simply made up or hallucinated; it had been there those times, as it was in the sweat house today. No one had said anything to Darian about it yet.

Anda cast Darian a questioning glance now and again, but he had not pursued the subject of what they had seen any more than the other tribesmen had.

Now it seemed that he had forgotten it entirely—or at least, he intended it to appear that way. Anda, as Darian had observed, was a very deep fellow, and if he didn't want you to know how he felt about something, he could be as opaque as a sheet of stone.

Darian was quite sure that every single person in that sweat house had seen the Cat, but had what seemed extraordinary behavior to *him* been something easily accepted by the rest of the men? Only the Shaman seemed to think it needed more examination.

They're used to seeing the Cat; after all, it led them here. Maybe the Cat always comes to greet new members of the tribe, and they were only startled because they hadn't expected it to greet an obvious outsider like me.

But that then posed the question, why didn't Celin simply accept the explanation as well? What did the Shaman know that the rest of his kinsmen didn't?

Stupid question; a great deal, obviously, or he wouldn't be the Shaman.

This celebration reminded him of the time he'd spent with the k'Vala delegation that had gone into Valdemar to help clean out the problems created by the mage-storms. When they hadn't been guested in someone's keep—which was mostly, especially in good weather—they'd camped like this. The Vale was never completely dark, and it never had the feeling of *wilderness* that the land outside it possessed. Here, beyond the circle of firelight, was the *dark*. Within the lighted circle was fellowship—but beyond it, there was no telling what could lie in wait.

But I fly an owl, and the night holds no mystery for me. That's what my Northern name means, after all—Nightwalker.

Night-walker, Owl Knight, Tayledras—he was taking on a great many identities lately.

He absently answered a question from the tribesman to his right, and movement to his left caught his gaze. Shaman Celin watched him closely, the old man's eyes gleaming with reflected flames, and when he saw that he had gotten Darian's attention, he gave a nod, then jerked his head toward his own lodge. Darian gave an amusing answer to his friend which sent the fellow into gales of laughter. With that for an ending to his conversation, he got up. As soon as he did so, the Shaman did likewise, and as Darian walked away from the fire, the Shaman joined him.

One benefit of having been formally adopted was that Shaman Celin came right to the point as soon as they were out of easy earshot of the rest. Darian was now a member of the tribe, and no secrets need be kept from him.

"You saw the Cat," the Shaman said bluntly.

"Everyone saw the Cat, Eldest," Darian replied, just as brusquely. "Even Anda. I hope you have an explanation for him, because he's bound to ask me, and I don't know what to tell him."

The Shaman grimaced. "I was hoping you would have one for me—why the Cat came to your feet—and why he left *this* on the ground where you sat."

The Shaman held something out to Darian, something small and dark, difficult to identify in the flickering firelight. Darian took it from him gingerly.

It was a black feather, roughly as long as his hand, probably from a corvid, like a crow, or perhaps a raven.

Darian shook his head and fingered the feather thoughtfully. "I wish I had an answer for you, Celin," he said candidly, and rubbed his head. "Perhaps the Cat didn't leave it. Are you certain the feather wasn't in there before we started?"

"Yes," Celin replied. Darian did not doubt him for a moment; Celin was very thorough in his duties; if he said the feather wasn't in the sweat house before the ceremony began, then it hadn't been there.

"I suppose one of us could have brought it in accidentally," he said, but he was hesitant, because he hadn't seen any corvids hanging about the enclave. And he didn't see how anyone from k'Valdemar could have brought a feather this far—and tracked it into the sweat house after completely disrobing.

Someone might have brought it in on purpose, but why? And why leave it where Darian had been sitting? Even if one of the men in the ceremony had secretly been resentful, there was no particular "message" that such a feather could have carried. The raven was not a bird of ill omen for the Northerners; in fact, the raven was one of their prominent totems. Yet since the raven was not a Ghost Cat totem, leaving a raven feather would mean exactly nothing, neither approval nor disapproval.

And Celin would have made careful note of everything the Cat did anyway; if he said that the Cat had left this feather, whether or not Darian noticed it at the time, it was a fairly good bet that the Cat had done just that.

"If it had been an owl feather, that would have made some sense. An obvious message of approval," Celin said, thinking out loud. His eyes crinkled around the edges. "Spirits give clear messages when a clear message will accomplish more . . . they give riddles when the act of solving the riddle accomplishes more. Or, when the riddle itself is part of the answer. Are you certain this means nothing to you?"

A very vague recollection of his uneasy nights prodded at him. *I owe it to him to tell him as much as I can remember, even if it isn't enough to be useful.* "I've had some—dreams—of late," he said slowly. "But I don't remember a great deal. I *think* I remember the Cat, and maybe a raven, but that's all. I was exhausted."

Shaman Celin nodded. "Spirits often wait until we are exhausted. Sometimes it is easier to reach us then. Sometimes it is to make the messages firmer to us." He hissed out a long sigh. "Dreams are important," he said somberly. "It was a dream that sent us south, and visions along the way that kept us going. Some were riddles no more obvious than this one. I wish you could remember more." He shook his head and sighed again. "If it comes again, this dream—"

"If it comes again, I shall wake myself and write down all I can," Darian told him. "I can promise you that, even if it doesn't help us now."

The weariness of six days of celebration—or "suffering" the celebrations—had taken their toll, and when Darian elected to cut his participation short, Anda and the rest followed his lead with no regrets. As they walked back to the Vale together, beneath a waxing moon, Darian had the feeling that Anda was seething with questions, and was not quite certain how to broach them. Finally, Anda asked the most obvious, and least likely to offend.

"Did I really see a—a ghostly cat in there? One like the name of the Clan?" the Herald asked, as if he was not really certain of his own senses.

In the darkness Anda might not be able to see him nod, but Darian nodded anyway by pure reflex. "You did," he said shortly. "That was the Ghost Cat totem; the creature itself. They say it led them here."

"You saw the Ghost Cat again?" Shandi asked excitedly. *That* certainly got Anda's attention.

"What do you mean by *again?*" he asked sharply, turning his head to look back at her.

"Darian, Keisha, and I all saw it—well, actually everyone saw it—when we stopped Ghost Cat and Captain Kero's force from fighting," Shandi said, freeing Darian from having to say anything more, for which he was very grateful. Anda turned his attention to the person he knew best in the group, and left him alone for the moment, beckoning Shandi to walk beside him so that he could talk to her.

Shandi gave him all the details of that final moment when she and Karles had brought the child that Keisha had cured back to the tribe—and a Companion and the Ghost Cat spirit had interposed themselves between the two forces, themselves in obvious truce. Anda either had not heard this before, or had not taken much note of the appearance of the spirit, for he questioned Shandi, and then Keisha, very closely.

"It wasn't an illusion," he muttered, as if to himself. Darian judged it safe to put in his own word.

"No, Herald, it wasn't—not when Keisha and I first saw the Cat, leading the boy's brother to us, and not back there in the sweat house." Darian put as much firmness into his tone as he could. "By that time I was enough of a mage that I would have been able to sense an illusion—assuming anyone in Ghost Cat was *capable* of producing such an illusion, which they aren't. Firesong is very certain that no one in the tribe has Mage-Gift."

Anda sighed. "I've never seen a spirit," he admitted reluctantly. "And I'm ashamed to admit that I've been a bit doubtful that anyone else has, in spite of everything that I've heard from folk I trust. Now I'm not sure what to think. I suppose . . . I suppose the fact that it appeared and came over to you means that you've been accepted without reservation into the tribe, not only by the people, but by the spirits who guide them."

"It sounds that way to me, Herald Anda," Shandi put in eagerly. "And that's good, really. In fact, it's excellent that *you* saw the Cat; it means that the Cat approves of you being here. If I were you, I'd let the Shaman know."

Anda pondered that for a moment. "I would rather that you or Keisha mentioned it, rather than it coming directly from me," he said, finally. "Say that I saw it, and wondered what it meant."

Darian admired his restraint—if it had been *his* experience, he'd probably have gone straight to Celin and demanded to know what had happened. But coming from Shandi or Keisha as an aside, the Shaman would assume that Anda was perfectly used to seeing such portents, and had not been in the least alarmed. The Shaman would also assume, as Shandi had, that if the Cat had permitted Anda to see it, Anda's presence had been given spiritual approval.

That was all to the good, and would make Anda's job a great deal easier.

Now if only I could be certain of what it all meant.

Eight

Darian was cleaning and oiling *dyheli* tack outside the storage building when an adolescent *hertasi* appeared at his elbow. That was the only way to describe the phenomenon; one moment Darian was alone, sitting on a section of a tree stump outside the shed that held all the Vale's tack, the next moment there was a short, skinny lizard standing at his elbow. Darian had finally gotten used to the way *hertasi* just appeared without warning, and no longer jumped in startlement when it happened.

"Dar'ian," the youngster said diffidently. "You will please go to the meadow? Tyrsell has need of you."

"On my way," Darian replied, taking time only to finish cleaning the saddle strap he was working on and put away the cleaned tack. Tyrsell didn't just arbitrarily send for anyone, but he hadn't worded the message as if it was an emergency, so Darian didn't want to leave his mess for someone else to have to clean up.

It did sound urgent enough that Darian broke into a lope when he was on paths broad enough that there was a reasonable chance he wouldn't accidentally crash into anyone coming the other way. He thought he had an idea why Tyrsell needed him, though. Anda had been distinctly showing impatience at having to rely on Shandi as his translator, and Darian had the feeling he had taken matters into his own hands.

Not the brightest idea, when Tyrsell would assume he'd been told everything about the process of getting languages from the dyheli. As far as I know, he hasn't talked to anyone in detail about it.

The problem was, since Anda was a Herald, and the Heralds were taught the use of whatever Mind-Gifts they had, Anda might well assume that he knew everything there was to know about mind-to-mind communication. But a *dyheli* mind was only superficially like a human mind, and the close melding of the human and *dyheli* required for an instantaneous transfer of language had certain bewilderingly painful side-effects.

When he arrived at the meadow, he discovered that his guess was correct; Anda lay sprawled on his back in the grass, out cold, bleeding from both nostrils. Darian trotted over and knelt beside the unconscious Herald, then looked up at Tyrsell's long nose. "How long has he been like this?" Darian asked.

:*Longer than I anticipated, but I have never given anyone five languages at once before,*: Tyrsell replied.

"Five?" Darian raised an eyebrow. "I thought you were only going to give him three—*hertasi*, Ghost Cat, and Tayledras."

:*He wanted Kaled'a'in and* tervardi *as well. He also wanted Shin'a'in, but I have no command of that tongue.*: A deer-fly chose that moment to buzz around the *dyheli's* eyes. Tyrsell shook his head so that his ears flapped, and snapped at the fly in irritation. It took the hint and flew off, and Tyrsell resumed his contemplation of the Herald and Darian.

"He's a glutton for punishment, isn't he?" Darian asked rhetorically. "Typical Herald. They think they're invulnerable." He checked the prone Herald over with Mage-Senses and with the Healer tricks he'd picked up from Keisha. "Well, his pulse is good, he's breathing regularly, he didn't hit his head on a rock when he went down, and he seems all right otherwise. Where's his Companion? I'm sure Eran can give us some help here."

Tyrsell flattened his ears in chagrin. :*I beg your pardon. I didn't think to call him. A moment—*: He raised his head and looked off in the general direction of the Vale. :*He's coming.*:

Eran didn't look concerned when he trotted into the meadow; his behavior as he bent his head down and stared for a moment at Herald Anda's face confirmed Darian's "diagnosis." A moment later, Eran looked up again, into Tyrsell's eyes.

:Eran says that there is nothing wrong with Anda other than that he has overstrained his Mind-Gifts,: Tyrsell reported. :He says that he will pull Anda into waking, so that he can begin to recover properly.:

"Did you order the tea for his headache?" Darian asked. Tyrsell nodded.

:The same hertasi I sent for you should be arriving with it in a moment.: Tyrsell and Eran looked into one another's eyes again, exchanging another set of thoughts, and Tyrsell snorted in dyheli laughter. :Eran thinks we should withhold the tea so that Anda gets a lesson in humility.:

"Eran, that's not very nice of you!" Darian said in mock surprise. The Companion snickered—that was the only possible description of the sound that came from him. "No, really, I know you're annoyed with Anda, but his only real mistake was in thinking that his training in Mind-Gifts would prepare him to meld with Tyrsell. And I don't think he realized that taking in five languages instead of the three we recommended would hit him so hard."

The young hertasi came out of the trees carefully carrying a stoppered jug. "Nightwind gave specific instructions. She says that if this does not do the trick, you are to hit him in the head with it, for being too stupid to live," the hertasi told Darian solemnly.

"I heard that," Anda said from the grass.

:You were meant to,: Tyrsell observed dryly. :Or so I surmise.: He gave Eran a penetrating look, and the Companion tossed his head and snickered again.

Darian took the jug, unstoppered it, and discovered that it was not the tea that was commonly used for the treatment of mental strain, but the stronger and more concentrated decoction. Normally one only took two or three mouthfuls—Nightwind had sent an entire jug! A small jug, no bigger than a closed fist, but a jug nevertheless.

"Hit me in the head with it," Anda continued with a groan,

after briefly opening his eyes and closing them immediately. "I would prefer to die."

Darian laughed at the Herald's woebegone expression "What, and prove Eran and Nightwind right?"

"I will not be here to suffer their scorn," Anda pointed out logically, but squinted his eyes open and made an effort to sit up. When he finally got upright, he propped both elbows on his knees, and dropped his head into his hands with a moan. Two drips of blood from his nose spattered on his uniform.

It was quite clear that Anda had never suffered a reaction like this one to any of his attempts at mind-magic.

"Did Nightwind say how much of this he was to take?" he asked the *hertasi*, who stared at Anda in fascination.

"All of it," the adolescent said succinctly. He then looked upon Anda with sudden clear disdain and just muttered, "Blood on white," then disapprovingly shook his head.

She said he should drink all of it! Darian shook the jug to try to judge how full it was, then gingerly tilted it. It was *quite* full.

Well, Nightwind knows what she's doing.

"Here, you heard him," Darian said, pulling one of Anda's hands away from his face and pushing the jug into it. "Drink it. All of it."

"Only if you'll swear it's poison." But Anda clasped his hand around the jug and raised it to his mouth. He was obviously expecting it to taste foul (which, as Darian knew from experience, it did) so although he reacted to the flavor with a hideous expression, he drank it all down, as ordered, before dropping the jug into the grass and gasping, "Blessed *gods!* What does she make that out of, hoof scrapings? No, don't tell me, I don't want to know."

When Nightwind had given Darian this particular potion, she'd followed it with a drink that took the wretched taste out of his mouth. She'd sent no such drink with the *hertasi*— which meant she really was annoyed with Anda.

But the Herald was a resourceful fellow; he began pulling up pieces of grass and chewing them, then discreetly spitting them out. His attempt at cleansing his mouth evidently worked, as his mouth stopped puckering and his eyes gradually stopped watering.

"All right," he sighed. "I admit it. I was an idiot. I made

assumptions and acted on them without bothering to ask anyone first. Now is this vile medicine *really* going to work, or was this all a cruel hoax?"

"It works," Darian promised. "In fact, given how much of it you just drank, we'd better get you back to the guest lodge before it hits you."

Anda looked up at Eran, who relented, and knelt down beside the Herald. Anda used the Companion's back and Darian's arm to steady himself, and staggered to his feet. Eran rose as well, and Anda draped one arm over Eran's back, resting most of his weight on his Companion. With that support, and Darian on his other side, they walked slowly back to the Lodge. Tyrsell remained in the meadow, having a silent discussion with the young *hertasi.*

"By the way, had you noticed that you've been speaking and understanding Tayledras?" Darian asked casually.

"I have?" Anda replied, his astonishment momentarily superseding his pain. "Great good gods, I have!"

"Not only that, but you *really* understand the tongue," Darian pointed out. "You understand it the way you would if you'd grown up speaking it. *You aren't mentally translating it.* That's why you have the headache, because you just got the language dumped into your head whole and entire, the way Tyrsell first got it from a human. That's the way the *dyheli* remember things, but not the way a human does. You have to remember that when you do anything that requires closer contact than simple Mindspeech, Anda—*dyheli, tervardi, hertasi,* and *kyree* are not human, and if you aren't careful, you can get into trouble. Well, Havens, check your new memories about *dyheli* and how the king stag is chosen."

Darian kept silent and let Anda sort through the memories he'd gotten along with the language, and watched his eyes widen. Darian knew why—the king stag was chosen by having the strongest mind in the herd, which meant that, at any time he cared to, he could literally take over the minds of every *dyheli* in the herd and make the herd do what he wanted. This was useful in an emergency, when individuals might panic and throw the entire herd into chaos.

And Anda had probably realized that Tyrsell could do the same thing to a sizable number of humans as well, if he chose.

The fact was, no king stag treated that ability trivially, for if he did, he wouldn't remain the king stag. And that, too, would be in Anda's new memories.

"You have to get some rest, maybe sleep a little, and let things settle into your head," Darian continued. "Once you do, you'll be all right."

"Which is, I take it, the real purpose of the potion?" Anda replied, with a wry smile. "Not to kill the pain so that I can go back to work, but to make sure that I *don't?*"

"Precisely. And may I remind you that *you* are the one who got yourself into this in the first place? So do not get angry at us for seeing to your health."

Eran curved his head around, stretching out his long neck to do so, and looked Darian straight in the eye before snorting his agreement.

"At least I'll never have to repeat this experience," Anda sighed, as they reached the door of the guest lodge. By that time he wasn't resting his weight on Eran anymore, and Darian was only walking beside him in case he stumbled.

Darian turned to leave him—but could not resist replying over his shoulder, "Not unless you meet a *dyheli* who knows Shin'a'in."

Anda only groaned, and looked pitiable. "You're a cruel man, Darian. A very cruel man."

Darian laughed, and left him to return to his chore.

Since all of Keisha's handiwork was in the *ekele* that she shared with Darian, it only made sense to take Shandi there to demonstrate some of the needlework and dyes Keisha had been trying since she moved into the Vale. She'd learned some new techniques from the *hertasi,* who did most of the embroidery and beadwork for the Tayledras; the little lizards had been happy to share their passion with a fellow addict.

Shandi was just as enthusiastic as Keisha had been. They soon had threads, yarns, and strip samplers spread out all over the sofa and chairs, plus a few pieces of Keisha's finished work were down off the walls or out of the wardrobe. In the middle of an animated discussion of new dye colors, Shandi suddenly looked into nothingness, then laughed out loud. Keisha had learned enough by now, though, not to be alarmed at what might have signaled the onset of insanity in anyone but a Herald.

"What did Karles just tell you?" Keisha demanded.

"That Anda just pulled a typically stubborn and pig-headed male act, and went to Tyrsell to get the languages by himself. *Five* of them, all at once. And is suffering the consequences, with no pity from anyone." Shandi laughed again, shaking her head, as Keisha was torn between feeling sorry for Anda and wickedly pleased that he'd mounted his pride and let it carry him straight over the edge. "Nightwind sent a jug of something to him, with instructions to hit him in the head with it if the potion didn't do any good."

"Ouch! She's *annoyed!* This may be the best way to teach him that he doesn't know *everything,* though," Keisha said.

"Just because he's a Herald, you mean?" Shandi shrugged, but her eyes twinkled and her mouth twitched into a grin. "That tends to be our major fault, I suppose. It's difficult to remember that you might be wrong when you're almost always right."

Keisha rolled her eyes ceilingward. "Modest, aren't you?" Keisha replied dryly.

"Of course—that, and every other possible virtue," Shandi countered with a toss of her head, as she feigned a lofty attitude. "Are you trying to tell me you've lived all your life in Valdemar and haven't learned that yet?"

Keisha made a rude noise by way of an answer, and Shandi laughed heartily, throwing her head back. "Oh, it's good to be back here with you—I made a lot of friends at the Collegium, but there was never anyone that was a *sister.*"

Keisha knew exactly what she meant—more so, perhaps, because until she had begun living in the Vale, she hadn't had anyone she could really think of as a friend except Shandi. Now she could count Nightwind, Ravenwing, several friends among the *hertasi,* and was cautiously coming to think of Silverfox as a friend, though she was still rather intimidated by him. Firesong—well, she was completely intimidated by Firesong, though she'd never let *him* know that. But she knew that if she needed help, Firesong was someone she could count on, and wasn't that part of the definition of a friend? Friends weren't supposed to be identical in what they did, or what they meant to someone—otherwise, who would want or need more than one?

And then there was Darian. Darian was the best friend

she'd ever had, except for her sister, and always would be, no matter what happened between them. Now if only she could figure out exactly where she was going with him.

"So what's going on with you and Darian?" Shandi asked, as if she had been following Keisha's thoughts. Keisha looked at her, startled by the question.

"What do you mean by that?" she demanded, with a touch of sharpness.

Shandi leaned back into the cushions of the sofa, and fingered the soft silk of a skein of embroidery thread. "Well, since you asked, I couldn't help but notice that you seem restless, a little nervous, but *he* seems perfectly happy. So what's the matter? I should have thought you'd have been posting the banns by now—and I don't think it's his fault that you're not. I *also* don't think that you are looking for someone else, so what's the problem?"

"I'd . . . rather not talk about it just yet," Keisha demurred. *I'd rather not talk about it at all, actually. Maybe she'll take the hint and leave me alone.*

Shandi shrugged. "All right for now, but you're not going to avoid talking about this for too long. Maybe the folks here in k'Valdemar are too polite to get you to 'fess up, but I'm not. You're my sister, and I'm going to find out what's bothering you and fix it if I can."

Keisha eyed her sister cautiously; this was an entirely new side to Shandi that she hadn't suspected existed. What had brought this out in her? Was it being trained as a Herald, and being used to jumping straight in to solve problems whether the people involved wanted them solved or not? "How do you know what I'm thinking, anyway?" she demanded. "I thought you weren't supposed to go snooping around in people's heads." She couldn't help feeling resentful, even though this was *Shandi* who was trying to meddle. Hadn't she already had enough of her mother's meddling in her life?

"Not thinking," Shandi corrected. "Feeling. I know what you're feeling, which is hardly the same as knowing what you're thinking, especially when you make it so easy to read. And what do you expect, when my sister is such a strong Healer?"

That was such a complete non sequitur that Keisha could only look stupidly at her. "What?"

"Healer. Empath. Not thinking, *feeling*. That's what made them decide back at the Collegium that I'll be a good diplomat. It turned out when they got everything sorted out and started giving me *real* testing and training that my strongest Gift is Empathy." She chuckled. "Which is probably why I could never bear to hurt anyone's feelings."

"Why didn't you tell me this before?" Keisha asked.

"You didn't ask, and it was never relevant." Shandi was so matter-of-fact about it, that Keisha could hardly believe it. "You didn't need to know about it when we all handled the Ghost Cat crisis, and it didn't come up when I was visiting."

"Well, that's true enough," Keisha admitted. "I just thought—well, I suppose I wasn't thinking, actually."

Shandi raised an eyebrow at her. "I was trained by Queen's Own Talia, no less. Then again, Herald Talia is the only Empath currently among the Heralds, so she'd pretty much have to be the one who taught me, wouldn't she?"

Keisha was utterly speechless at this—and stared at her sister as if she had turned into a stranger. In a sense, she had—here was the girl that *Keisha* had taken care of and gotten out of scrapes, talking casually about being taught by the Queen's Own Herald of Valdemar!

"It developed fairly late, which they tell me was just as well," Shandi continued calmly, ignoring her sister's dropped jaw and goggled eyes. "But they said with a sister who turned out to have a strong Healing Gift the way you have, and as alike as the two of us are, it's not too surprising that I'd be an Empath. The only thing likelier would have been that I'd be an Animal Mindspeaker—or another Healer, but then I probably wouldn't have been Chosen. No Companion will Choose a Healer or a potential Healer, unless the Healing Gift is really, really minor, and some other Gift is a lot stronger."

"I suppose that Animal Mindspeech would have been useful," Keisha ventured, slowly gathering her scattered and wandering wits together.

"Not as useful as this." Interestingly, Shandi didn't seem particularly proud of her Gift, any more than a carpenter was proud of having an average, serviceable set of tools. "I can tell when people are lying, or trying to lie, without using the Truth Spell. I can tell when they're being pushed into saying or doing something against their will. All kinds of things that it's useful for a diplomat to know."

"Or a spy," Keisha said without thinking, and looked sharply at her sister.

But Shandi laughed at her. "Or a spy—which is sometimes an impolite name for a diplomat. You see? We even think alike. Now, since you won't talk about Darian, what was it you were saying about this golden yellow?" She held up the skein she'd been toying with.

Keisha went back to her yarns and dyes, but beneath the discussion, her mind was busy with all that Shandi had revealed in those few words. There were many things, it seemed, that she needed to learn about her sister, especially now that she would be living right under Shandi's nose.

And even the "old" Shandi had not been inclined to let sleeping problems lie undisturbed if she thought she could do something about them.

After a fruitful afternoon of cleaning and mending every bit of *dyheli* tack in the shed, Darian was ready to reward himself with a swim. He stowed the last bit of tack away, then tucked the cleaning supplies in their proper place, and closed the shed up. He was dirty and oily, but he knew the girls were in the *ekele* and he didn't want to disturb them. *I'll get clean enough in the lake,* he decided. *And the* hertasi *will take care of a change of clothing for me.* And as for the tack oil, it was lanolin, and his skin would absorb it.

Cleaning tack was most often a job for the *hertasi*, but they had enough to do just building, and catching up with the chores and projects that had been put back while the celebration and the preparations for it had been going on. When a job needed doing in the Vales, whoever had the skill took care of it. Except, perhaps, for the cooking chores—so far as the *hertasi* were concerned, there wasn't a human anywhere who could match *hertasi* cookery, and the making of a meal would be the very last job that the *hertasi* would give over to human hands.

I've come along a bit from the fellow who resented having to clean and mend. He chuckled at himself, and shook his head. *I guess that's what growing up is supposed to do to you.*

The tack shed, one of a group of storage sheds tucked into

an out-of-the-way corner screened with trees and ornamental bushes, was not all that far from the lake, and a direct pathway linked the two. The walk was barely long enough to get his muscles warmed up from sitting all afternoon.

Once the path opened up to the clear, quiet waters, he turned to the right to stroll along the edge of the lake on his way to the swimming beach. He wanted to see how the *hertasi* were coming with the hot spring he'd created. One of the reasons he had chosen that particular spring was its nearness to the lake; but another was that it emerged about a third of the way up to the top of one of the hills cupping that end of the valley. The water started from a point that was about the height above the lake of a five-year-old tree. That would make it perfect for a series of cascading pools, where the water moved downward from pool to pool, cooling as it went. Soakers could pick their preferred temperature by the height of the pool in the cascade.

The *hertasi* had already dug the series of soaking pools leading down to the lake, from the smallest (which would be the hottest) at the top, to the largest (big enough to hold thirty or forty soakers, and would be just comfortably warm) at the bottom, just like the ones at k'Vala. The first three pools had been sculpted and finished inside with formed rock; these three were in the process of curing. A crew of *hertasi* was laying the rock of the fourth pool, and the other pools each had one or two hertasi in them, sculpting the earth into seats, couches, and benches, which would be covered with the formed rock. At the moment, the hot water ran down a temporary channel into the lake, where it mixed directly with the lake waters, creating an area of warmth. Even now, that spot was in use, though it wasn't as hot as the finished pools would be, nor was the edge anything more than raw lake shore. As soon as the last pool was finished, the *hertasi* would plant the slope with heat-loving vegetation, and a specialist like Steelmind who worked at inducing plants to grow with amazing speed would soon have the place looking as if it had always been there. When the pools had cured, the *hertasi* would divert the water and they would begin filling. It would take at least a day for them to fill and come up to proper temperature. Then, no doubt, there would be an impromptu opening party.

Right now, though, Darian wasn't looking for a place to

soak; tack cleaning wasn't hard work, just tedious work. He didn't need to soothe sore muscles, he just needed to cool off and get cleaner. He was also hoping Kel would be out here, as this was the time of day that the gyrphon usually took his bath and he hadn't had a chance to talk to Kel in days. They'd both been so busy with the celebrations that there hadn't been time for anything else.

He was right on time for the gryphon's bath. Just as he neared the sloping rock-shelf that stretched for several wagon-lengths just under the surface where the gryphons usually bathed in shallow water heated by the sun, Kel flew in, hovered, and landed in the water. He skimmed in at a shallow angle, sending a huge rooster tail of water to the other side of his body before plunging. Gryphons bathed like birds, and Kel was no exception to that rule, slamming his head and shoulders into the water, then hunkering down and splashing vigorously with his wings. Even the smallest bird kicked up quite a bit of water when bathing; when a gryphon (twice the size of a warhorse, with a wingspread wide enough to shelter a small house) decided to take a bath, it tended to drench anyone within five or six furlongs. Darian knew this, of course, and stood well away as the gryphon ducked and splashed, ducked and splashed, until every feather was soaked so that it looked as if he were covered in quills instead of feathers.

Gryphons, like birds, also tended to be single-minded about their bathing, so Kel didn't look up and notice Darian until he was done and looking for the best spot to clamber out and sun himself.

"Ha! Darrrrian!" Kel exclaimed. "Have you rrrrecoverrred from all the cccelabrrrationsss?" He looked so ridiculous that Darian had to strangle his laughter, for otherwise he'd hurt Kel's feelings.

"Barely," Darian acknowledged. "I'm going for a swim. Mind if I join you afterward?"

"Be my guessst," Kel responded genially. "I will be verrry happy to ssshare a rrrock with you." The gryphon waded out, generously *not* shaking himself until Darian was out of range. And when he did go into a blur of motion, he carefully did so where a plot of flowers looked as if they could use the water, then saw to it they were fertilized, too.

Darian meanwhile stripped and waded in along the shallow

rock-shelf. The water here was tepid—fine for bathing gryphons, but not particularly refreshing. He wanted his swim in cooler waters, and as soon as he reached a place where the lake was deep enough, he dove in and struck for the opposite shore.

By the time he'd swum to the shore and back again, he felt relaxed and sufficiently cleansed of the oil and dirt of tack cleaning that he was ready to come out.

The ever-watchful *hertasi* had spirited his dirty, oil stained clothing away and left towels and one of the loose, enveloping robes where his clothing had been. He dried himself off and pulled the robe on over his head, cinched the various ties, then climbed out onto Kel's chosen rock to join him in the sun.

There were many flat-topped sheets of rock here, conveniently near the underwater rock-shelf, and Kel wasn't the only gryphon drying his feathers in the sunlight. All of the gryphons in k'Valdemar were young adults, looking to make reputations for themselves; Kel had the most experience and seniority of the lot. That could have been a cause for problems, because young and ambitious gryphons were like young and ambitious humans—they tended to forget they weren't immortal and took risks. Kel was not old enough to remain immune if the rest got excited, but they were all in the Silver Gryphons as well, and their senior officer was a Kaled'a'in of about fifty, imbued with plenty of caution and good common sense. Their *trondi'irn*, who cared for their injuries and ills, was Nightwind—and there wasn't a being in all of k'Valdemar who cared to annoy Nightwind by getting hurt by doing something stupid. With Nightwind and Redhawk supervising them, the young gryphons of k'Valdemar would probably not do anything intolerably risky.

Darian threw a towel down on the rock and stretched out beside Kel. Damp gryphon had an odd scent, not unpleasant, but different from the spicy-musky odor of dry gryphon. Kel smelled a little like spice, but more like a certain dark brown, salty sauce that Ayshen used for vegetables. Strange, really. He looked almost black, his feathers were still so laden with moisture; when he dried, he would be a beautiful golden-brown, with a sheen of bronze.

"So, have you gotten a chance to ask Herald Anda about studying with Treyvan and Hydona?" he asked lazily.

There was a long, and unexpected pause. "I darrre not," Kel confessed sheepishly. "Trrreyvan and Hydona! The Great Ones! Why, they arrre legendsss!"

"They're gryphons, like other gryphons, Kel. They're bone and blood and gristle. And Herald Anda is as fallible as anyone else; you don't have to be intimidated by him." He glanced over at the sunning gryphon, who had his head down on his outstretched forelegs, watching Darian with one golden eye. His ear-tufts were flat, a sign that he really was feeling as sheepish as he sounded.

"That iss not ssso easssy," Kel sighed. "It isss harrrd to rrregarrrd Herrrald Anda asss orrrdinarrry."

"Listen, you may not believe this, but the awesome Herald Anda just did one of the stupidest things I've ever heard of." Without sparing Anda, he related the Herald's blunder of the afternoon, and Nightwind's response to it. He watched for Kel's reaction, and saw the gryphon slowly lift his head, his ear-tufts picking up as he recounted the story.

"I sssuppossse—" he began, "that wasss not the brrrightesst of actionsss."

"Kel, it just proves that you don't have to be intimidated by him," Darian repeated. "You haven't done anything quite that stupid."

"It wasss not precisssely ssstupid," Kel protested, but his eyes sparkled. "Jussst—overrrconfidence."

"Call it what you will, *I* don't think that you need to feel as if he's some sort of minor god just because he was trained by your idols," Darian repeated. "Besides, didn't he say he was looking forward to getting acquainted with all the gryphons? You're the chief gryphon of this Vale. You've got as much rank as I do, Kel—which means you're Herald Anda's equal."

Kel perked up more. "I am, arrren't I?" His beak gaped in pleasure, and he looked around with contentment. "I believe I will find an imprrresssive enough placsse, and welcome Herrrald Anda on behalf of the otherrrsss—when he wakesss, in a few daysss, that isss."

Darian laughed. "That's a good choice, Kel," he agreed, and turned over onto his back, shading his eyes with a flap of towel. "I doubt very much that he wants to see anyone for quite a while."

He was half asleep when Kel's voice woke him. "Darrrian," the gryphon said. "What arrre you thinking?"

"Nothing, actually," Darian replied sleepily. "Why?"

"I wasss thinking, You arrre my frrriend, and I am yourrrsss. That we arrre of the sssame family of sssorrrtsss. We arrre wingmatesss and brrrotherrrsss, you and I." The gryphon paused to scratch an ear slowly, sending a freshly dried tuft of feather-down drifting in the breezes caused by his movement. "I wasss thinking, how prrroud my parrrentsss arrre of what I have done, and how yourrrsss would be the sssame if they knew."

Kel's words acted like that bucket of cold water after the sweat-house ceremony; they shocked him awake. "They would," he said, but his mind was elsewhere, sent careening on a new path—or rather, on an old path that he had not traveled in far too long.

I still don't know what happened to them. I meant to go out and hunt the old trap-lines to find out—or try—but I never did. How did I forget?

Guilt wracked him for a moment with a physical spasm. How could he have let himself get so involved in the life of the Vale that he forgot his parents?

Get hold of yourself. There's no reason to feel guilty. You did not forget, you were busy. You have thought of them constantly, you just didn't go do that one thing. You had too much else to do, including growing up, he told himself, though it was easier to tell himself that than it was to shed the guilt. *Two years aren't going to make any difference in the clues that are left—if there* are *any.* He was woods-wise enough to know that (in the worst possible case) bodies left out in the open were quickly torn apart by scavengers. The parts were carried off, scattered; summer insects found what was left to be irresistible. In a year, not even the major bones were likely to be left. Although it made him sick to even think of applying that to his parents—

After all this time, two years wouldn't make any difference, he repeated to himself. *Five, even ten wouldn't make any difference.*

Darian rubbed at his face with both hands, coping with the thoughts that Kelvren's innocent commentary had dredged up. He murmured a thanks to the gryphon, who responded by bumping him affectionately with a wing, then assuming another lounging position. Darian's thoughts stayed on his parents' fate. They could not have been lost in the Pelagiris this long—not even for a year. Blind, deaf, dumb and limbless they could find their way back to Errold's Grove by orienteering. They had been that good.

But if his parents *weren't* dead—then there was only one other thing that could have happened to prevent them from returning to him.

They had to have been caught in a Change-Circle. And if they had survived that experience, there was no telling what might have happened to them. What they might have become.

Or where they were.

His duties to his homeland, his adopted people, his friends and his mentor had been fulfilled, and then some. It was more than time for him to use his own tracking skills and resolve, and find out what he could about the past.

Nine

"I want to visit the Sanctuary," Anda abruptly declared, just as Keisha set her plate and cup down and joined the little group around the table he shared with Shandi and Darian. Shandi smiled at her sister and shrugged slightly; Darian kept eating. "How do I go about doing that?"

"Catch a disease?" Darian offered.

Anda was looking at Darian, but it was Keisha who answered seriously, ignoring her breakfast for the moment to shoot Darian a look of disdain. The meal was too hot to dig into immediately anyway; she might as well deal with Anda. She wasn't at all certain that he had learned the lesson of impatience. *If he's going to the Sanctuary, though, I'm going along.*

"I suppose I can take you there," she said. "When do you want to go?" She already knew the answer, of course. Anda had been running at full speed since the moment he arrived, and not even the exhausting welcome-week had kept him from what he saw as his duty to integrate himself into the life of Vale, village, and tribe.

"Today, if possible." Anda had taken a frugal breakfast of fruit and bread; Keisha wondered how he could accomplish so much on so little food. Her heartiest meal was breakfast. "Are there any new patients there at the moment?"

"There are always new patients there," Keisha sighed, but with envy rather than weariness. "Except in the dead of winter, the Sanctuary gets a new group roughly every fortnight. If what you want to see is Northerners fresh from the wilds and tired to the bone, that's exactly what you're going to get." She took an experimental bite of her own breakfast of stuffed mushrooms; they were cool enough to eat, and she didn't want them to grow cold. She gave Darian a glance; he took the hint, and picked up where she left off.

He's almost done with his breakfast, anyway. If I don't get something to eat soon, I'm going to start tearing out throats.

"The Ghost Cat people sent up a couple of messengers to the tribes they were related to," Darian explained, fully aware of how irritable morning hunger made Keisha. His meal was all made up of things that wouldn't be spoiled by getting cold, and he had no problem talking around bites of food. "Those tribes have been spreading the word that there's a place of Healing down here, but they are being careful the word doesn't get to tribes like Blood Bear—those were the barbarians that overran Errold's Grove. Either we were lucky or very careful. Those tribes seem to have gotten a lot of strange diseases out of the Change-Circles up north."

"We were careful," Anda said, after swallowing the last of his own breakfast. "After the scholars at Haven figured out the pattern for where the Circles would pop up, people were told. No one went near them until they'd been checked over. Sometimes they were sterilized by fire, if need be."

"But things still got away," Darian pointed out. "Animals, insects, some creatures we never could identify. We know that—and it happened here in Valdemar. My parents hunted all kinds of bizarre things that came out of those Circles. I'd have to say we were lucky, Anda; we could have ended up with the Summer Fever and Wasting Sickness as readily as Ghost Cat did. And—bless poor Justyn, but he would have been the first to admit to this—the Healer we had at the time wouldn't have had the power to cure it."

"But he *would* have the power to call those who did," Anda said firmly. "Furthermore, those he called would know the right steps to take, not only to cure the disease, but how to keep it from spreading further. Keisha, when can we go to the Sanctuary? Will this be an overnight trip?"

Keisha hastily swallowed the last of her mushrooms. "Overnight, yes, but longer than that, no, and we won't have to pack anything. But I think we ought to go first to Ghost Cat so they can explain how they deal with the pilgrims. *They* are the ones who are most involved, after all. You ought to see how this is benefitting all of us, not just the Northerners. If we leave now, we can go there, then to the Sanctuary, then be back by nightfall tomorrow."

"Then I'm ready." Anda stood up. "Shandi?"

"Ready enough." Shandi followed her Senior's example. "Karles says he and Eran will meet us at the Vale entrance. He'll have Tyrsell send a *dyheli* for Keisha."

Keisha could have allowed the two Heralds to go on their own; there was no reason why she had to come along. One of the *dyheli* at the Ghost Cat enclave could readily guide them to the Sanctuary without Keisha's help.

She didn't want to do that. She didn't want to take the chance that there was some serious illness, even a plague in the early stages, at the Sanctuary. Anda was perfectly confident in the abilities of the Sanctuary Healers to deal with such a thing, but the Sanctuary Healers would not be paying a great deal of attention to the healthy Heralds. All of their interest was bound up in their current patients, and it might not occur to them that the Heralds were exposing themselves to danger.

She, above all, knew just how focused Healers could be; when dealing with an incipient crisis, they concentrated on the problem in front of them to the exclusion of all else. Whatever ills were being treated at the Sanctuary, Keisha would be there to note the symptoms and the cure—and if Shandi or Anda, or both, showed any signs of illness, she would be able to treat them before either of them sickened too far. She would have the sense to get them isolated and keep them from the rest of the Vale; with the help of the *hertasi* (who could not catch human illnesses) she could get them through whatever they caught.

Besides, I want to see what's going on there! For that chance, she was willing to make the trip. She hadn't been to the Sanctuary in person for well over a year.

When they reached the Vale entrance, both Companions were waiting for them, already saddled with their lightest tack. With them was a single *dyheli* for Keisha. There was no need to pack anything, as they would be spending the night at the Sanctuary, which was more than prepared to host visitors. It wasn't as if they hadn't had healthy people there before.

They'll probably be glad to see someone who doesn't *need help. And Healers are even more implacable than Heralds. If Anda's in the way, they won't hesitate to push him aside.*

Shandi and Anda were in the saddle before Keisha had gotten her foot into the *dyheli's* stirrup. She was getting used to the way that Heralds and their Companions worked so incredibly smoothly together, but it took the *dyheli's* amused comment of *:Show-offs:* to make her realize that some of that was a deliberate—if somewhat automatic—attempt to impress.

Oh! she thought at her mount, not wanting to elaborate lest the rest of her thought leak over to the others.

The *dyheli* flicked her ears back delicately. *:Yes. They didn't have to link so tightly just to get into the saddle. And there's no real reason to try to impress us, is there? They're doing it to create an image, but is it an image they have to project all of the time?:* The irony in her tone colored every nuance.

Keisha always appreciated the *dyheli's* dry sense of humor, and never more so than now, but she was inclined to be charitable. *Maybe they're practicing,* she suggested. *You know, they haven't been together for all that long, and it's not easy to get a coordinated link that's natural and easy.*

The doe flicked her ears forward. *:Perhaps,:* was all she would say.

The journey to the Ghost Cat village took place without incident, and in a very short period of time. Sentries hailed them from posts among the trees without asking them to stop; the Heralds and their Companions were instantly recognizable, even at a distance. By the time they reached the village, Vordon and Celin were waiting for them. The Shaman was in his ordinary working clothes, not his talisman-bedecked ritual garb, and bits of bark caught in his beard and hair betrayed the fact that he'd been splitting wood when he was apprised of their imminent arrival.

"Hah! Kei-eh-sha!" Vordon hailed Keisha first, which rather pleased her. "And has our new brother recovered from his birthing? What brings you here, on this bright morning?"

"More or less, Chief," she laughed. "He is certainly up and

at all of his duties again, rather than sleeping like a man-shaped pile of rocks. My friends wish to know of the arrangements that Ghost Cat has with the pilgrims."

"That is correct, Chief," Anda said immediately, as the Chief and Shaman turned to the Heralds with faces full of lively interest. "If you will be so kind as to explain it to us, and show what you can."

The Chief, who himself had only dared to learn Tayledras with the help of Tyrsell, nodded to hear Anda salute him in his own tongue. "So you have braved the pain of teaching, eh? Well, this is good. I have begun to think such a thing is equal to the death of a bear in counting toward manhood!"

Anda rubbed his head ruefully. "I could not find it in me to argue with that," he agreed, and dismounted. "It's good to know you consider me a man."

Shandi and Keisha followed his example, but Shandi had to add to her Senior's statement. "Herald Anda must surely qualify for more than just manhood," she told Vordon, "for he has taken five tongues of Tyrsell at once."

"I am not sure if that was bravery or foolishness," Anda added hastily. It looked to Keisha as if Vordon agreed with that statement.

They chatted about gardens, roots, new babies, and leaf blight as they followed the Chief and the Shaman farther into the village, which had grown—indeed, doubled—in size, in the past year. There had been more additions than simple births or marriages. Some of the pilgrims had petitioned for adoption into Ghost Cat as their own tribes were so severely decimated by war or disease that they were effectively nonexistent, and Ghost Cat usually agreed to take them in. Darian was not the only outsider to have been formally adopted by a Ghost Cat family as an adult. He was just the only one thus far who was not a Northerner.

Many of those in Errold's Grove and k'Valdemar had been surprised to learn, once the tribesmen began to build, that they were capable of a great deal of sophistication in their dwellings. In fact, their village was as neatly laid out as any Valdemaran village. The Northerners built large, one-room circular houses, with an enormous common room in the center, and small cubicles built against the outer walls for privacy. Each extended family lived in one house—married children moved in with the bride's parents until the birth of their third child. It usually took that long for a young man to gather the resources to construct his own dwelling. Those who did not wed remained with their families, as additional hands, and suffered no decrease in status for doing so. The Chief had told Keisha that grandparents often bequeathed *their* homes to a favored young couple, then moved in with the oldest daughter's family. There was often much competition among married daughters to lure Grandmother and Grandfather to their home; there *was* an increase in status for those who sheltered such valuable repositories of wisdom as grandparents.

The Northerners used wood to build their homes, but no stone, with wooden roofs supported by four great pillars rather than slate or thatch. The buildings were made of squared-off logs with the chinks closed with moss and mud mixed, and the roof of rough planks laid over a radial pattern of rafters, which were then topped with rough wooden shakes.

The houses were odd to Valdemaran eyes, but it was the art decorating them that was so startling to those who were not out of the North.

The thick plank door of each house was carved and painted with the totem animal of the particular family in a kind of high-relief style. These were not realistic portrayals, but very stylistic and colorful, featuring patterns in red, white, and black. In good weather, beautiful blankets made of pieced fur were hung on the outer walls—both as a precaution, to chase out any vermin and odors, and to display the handiwork of the women of the house. Now that Ghost Cat had access to woolen fabric, they were making similar blankets of wool in bright, primary colors. Each blanket was a representation of the totem of the person it belonged to. There were always two poles outside each house, carved and painted with all of the totems of the family, and topped with the Ghost Cat.

Totem animals played a huge part in the lives of the Northerners; each tribe had a special totem (usually a very powerful predator). Each family also had a totem related to the totem of the tribe. And when each family member reached adulthood, he or she also got a totem—or as they put it, were embraced by one—in a special dream-ceremony presided over by the Shaman. Darian was an exception—Ghost Cat judged he already had his totem, in the form of Kuari.

Rafter ends that protruded beyond the edge of the roof were similarly carved and painted, but this time with the heads of spirits and ancestors. Inside each house the four great roof-pillars were identical to the poles outside the front door. The floor of a house was not *exactly* of earth, although the central hearth was a pit dug in the ground and lined with stones, with the smoke-hole through the center of the roof above and stones laid to some distance on the floor in case of sparks jumping from the fire. The floor of each of these dwellings was made of grass mats, many layers thick, laid over the pounded earth of the floor and added to on a daily basis. It was the duty of every member of the family old enough to do so to weave one grass mat in the morning and lay it over a place where the mats were looking shabby. As the mats below disintegrated, they were replaced from above; pine needles and herbs layered between the mats drove off insects.

Crude but adequate oil lamps placed on little shelves around the inside wall gave the place a fair amount of light, considering that there were no windows of any sort. But Keisha figured that was only to be expected, since these buildings were intended for much colder climes and a window was just one more place for cold wind to come through.

The little cubicles that family members retreated to for privacy were also used for storage. Basically, partitions were set against the wall with a distance of about six to eight paces between them, extending six to eight paces into the main room. A rope across the front made a place to hang a curtain for privacy; shelves built across the back and sides made a place for storage. People kept their personal possessions in the cubicles during the day; at night, they had the option of sleeping beside the fire, or in their cubicles with blankets over the rope to block out the main room.

Circular shelters, like the family houses but without walls, stood beside each house, providing a solution to the warmer weather that Ghost Cat had encountered in Valdemar. From spring until fall, this was where most of the work and living took place for each family; on the hottest nights, sometimes the entire family even slept in their shelters. Smoke from smoldering herbs in pots around the periphery kept insects somewhat at bay. And even those pots were decorated with painted decorations.

The longer that Ghost Cat remained here, the more of their village was decorated with painted carvings; Keisha expected that before long even the blank walls of the houses might start to sport their stylized artworks. No one had anticipated that, and a few traders had been eying the carvings and pieced-work with interest, wondering if there was any profit to be made from Northern art.

The houses were arranged in circles around a central building that was *not* the Chief's house, but rather was the storehouse for the entire tribe. As such, it was decorated only with Ghost Cat, repeated over and over, in an endless variety of poses. Each family had a cubicle within for the storage of raw materials of their own, and the center was reserved for common storage.

"So-ho, you come in a good time to see how we deal with the pilgrims come for healing, Valdemar-Herald," Chief Vordon was saying as they neared the central storehouse. "We have just sent on a family that came with riches, so you will see what we have had of them."

While Keisha had been admiring the newest carvings, the Chief had explained to Anda that Ghost Cat, in return for feeding and sheltering the pilgrims during their initial week of quarantine and continuing to shelter and feed those who were not injured or ill, received a toll of whatever the pilgrims brought with them. Being that some pilgrims came with little but desperation and hope, this was a very flexible toll. From the poorest, Ghost Cat often took nothing but a little labor— mat weaving, wood cutting, help in building, or carving if there were skilled artists among them. But there were plenty of pilgrims who had come laden with goods, and those made up for the ones that arrived with empty hands.

"See here—this was a tribe I do not know, but vouched for by those I do—and they are wealthy in fur and amber." The Chief gestured to the piles of goods laid out in front of the storehouse, and indeed, there was enough heaped there to make even Anda's eyes widen. "They have only lately been touched by the Summer Fever and Wasting Sickness, and are eager to pay for a cure that they do not lose any of their children." The Chief pointed to the piles of glossy furs. "There is bear, there beaver—there fox—that white is snow-fox—the small furs are what we call *goshon,* very soft and good, you have no name for it."

Indeed, even though Keisha knew the Ghost Cat language and got a mental image of the *goshon* (which was obviously in the weasel family), it was with the disorienting sensation that told her she had never seen one of these creatures with her own eyes.

Imagine what the senior Herald must be feeling! He has a skill I never thought of before—this Herald has the ability to act completely undisturbed by whatever he encounters even though it is so alien to him. He must have thousands of new concepts and images in his mind, from tunnel-spar designs of the hertasi *to thirty names for how a leaf tastes from the dy-heli to—who knows! And yet he still manages to travel and carry on a conversation without letting it overwhelm him. Incredible.*

"And here is amber, both the amber-of-the-sun and the amber-of-scent; these are *Seashan* tribe—" (another new word, and this one without any kind of mental picture of the live animal, but only the totemic rendering; so Ghost Cat knew the name and the carving that represented it) "—and they live upon the bitter-water where these things are found along the shore."

The amber-of-the-sun was the yellow, golden-brown, and red rough amber that Keisha knew was used in jewelry; these pieces ranged from the size of the end of the little finger to the size of a fist. But this amber-of-scent was an odd, gray-white substance with a faintly greasy look to it. There wasn't much of it, but from the way Vordon regarded the stuff, it was even more valuable than "real" amber. He held up a little piece and indicated that they should sniff it; Keisha did so, and was delighted with the fragrance, very sweet, heavy, and musky.

"A bit of this used in perfume, no bigger than a seed, and the scent will last for years," Vordon said with satisfaction. "Your traders will give us much gold for this, for there are those among the k'Leshya who know the use of it."

"I can see how you are raising the wealth of your tribe," Anda said with admiration.

"Not just of Ghost Cat, but of k'Valdemar and the Sanctuary as well. The *dyheli* of k'Valdemar have a share of this for their part, as does the Sanctuary." Vordon canted his head over, looking at them shrewdly. "We trade with the village for grain for the *dyheli* and the goods going to the Sanctuary are taken there with each new lot of pilgrims. It is good trade, all around, and trade is how we of Ghost Cat have always prospered."

"As opposed to war?" Shandi asked, and Vordon nodded.

"That is why, if we did not wish someone to see us, then like the Cat, we would not be seen."

He led them away from the piles of furs; Keisha cast a wistful glance back, and decided that she would try to bargain for some of those *goshon* furs, so glossy and soft, and a wonderful dark brown. They would be a joy against the face, and so warm lining the hood of her winter cloak. . . .

"And here is the camp of the tribe," Vordon was saying. "We hold them here until the Healers send the holy *dyheli* with the last group, making room for the new pilgrims. Those who are not ill remain while the rest go to the Sanctuary."

Here was an encampment very like the one that Ghost Cat had first made when they arrived at this place—the difference being that the people here looked healthy and hopeful, perfectly at their ease. There was a distinct difference in their artwork, which was displayed on their clothing and carved on their wagons. This was, so far as Keisha could tell, some sort of fish, with a large top fin. She wondered what on earth the real creature looked like.

They lived in the tents that Ghost Cat supplied, but unlike Ghost Cat, these folk had no herds. They were hunters, fishers, and gathered what foodstuffs they did not hunt or fish. Keisha wondered what they were making of the strange foods that Ghost Cat had learned to prepare from foodstuffs bartered from Errold's Grove.

"All of the sick ones that we sent to the Sanctuary were children; their mothers went with them to help tend them." Vordon finished. "So, now, are you ready to journey onward? There is really nothing more to see here, unless you wish to watch the division of the goods."

Anda smiled. "Not really; how you share your profits is your business, not mine. I would like to get to the Sanctuary before nightfall, if that is possible."

It was not only possible, it was easily accomplished; the

Shaman called one of the *dyheli* in the Ghost Cat herd to escort them, and off they went. Keisha had been this way before, but it was new to Shandi, and to Anda.

The *dyheli* took no one path; in fact, he made several detours through untracked forest from one game trail to another. This was all intended to confuse, and it succeeded admirably.

"I give up," Anda said to Keisha, after they had been traveling for half the afternoon. "Where are we?"

"Three-fourths of the way there," Keisha told him, unable to hold back a grin. "This is only one of the ways that pilgrims are brought to the Sanctuary; there must be at least a dozen, maybe more by now."

"All right," Anda replied, as Eran looked back over his shoulder at Keisha. "Why?"

It was Shandi who answered. "We want the Northerners to believe that the Sanctuary is a special and holy place, and that only the *dyheli* know the way there. We hope that will keep any renegades from getting the bright notion to come kidnap a Healer for themselves."

"I would say it works, since I've been *trying* to keep track of our route, and I'm hopelessly lost," Anda sighed, looking about at the forest surrounding them. There was no sign of any sort of landmark; no rocks, no particularly large trees, and no trace of a trail. There wasn't enough light filtering down through the trees to help, either.

"What happens when you climb a tree and look around?" Anda wanted to know.

"Nothing," Keisha answered with surety, as their mounts continued to follow the *dyheli*, who moved on his own secret "path." "All you'll see is trees. The Sanctuary is in a pocket valley, and they use some clever contrivances to disperse smoke from their fires, so you can't see that either."

Indeed, when they came upon the Sanctuary, they did so suddenly; one moment there was nothing but trees and brush, the next, the outer walls of the Sanctuary loomed up in front of them, walls of natural stone topped with slatted wood. They followed the wall around to the entrance; it wound around and through the forest in a most peculiar fashion, but it appeared as if it had been built without disturbing a single tree.

They passed inside the open gates, to find themselves in

one of the oddest complexes Anda had ever seen—because, once again, very few trees had been cut to make way for the buildings of the Sanctuary. Keeping the integrity of the forest canopy was important to keeping the Sanctuary secret, so instead of one big building, the Sanctuary was a complex of tiny ones, all of stone, linked by covered, raised wooden walkways, like tiny covered footbridges. All of the buildings were raised above the forest floor as well, in order to keep out vermin and insects; this was a precaution to keep illness from spreading further.

Anda took a wide-eyed look around, and suddenly grinned. "This is marvelous!" he exclaimed. "How ingenious!"

One of the Trainees, in the pale-green of one who was still a student of Healing, came hurrying toward them, his face anxious as he realized that the resident Heralds had arrived all unlooked-for.

"Heralds!" the boy exclaimed, shaking a shaggy brown forelock out of his eyes. "We weren't expecting you! Please, come this way, I'll take you to our Senior—"

Anda smiled down at the boy, then he and Shandi dismounted. Keisha did the same while Anda spoke to the boy in a casual and off-handed manner, conveying the idea that he hadn't wanted any special fuss or preparations. "It's quite all right; this is just meant to be a friendly visit, so I didn't send any notice ahead. Can you take us on a little tour, rather than interrupting your Senior? Let him finish whatever he's doing and join us at his leisure."

Keisha already knew her way around the Sanctuary, and let the Trainee lead the other two off while she led her own *dyheli* and the two Companions to the Sanctuary stabling. Since it was intended for intelligent *dyheli*, it would serve the Companions equally well. It was essentially nothing more than a large shed, open and airy, with thick straw on the floor and mangers and water buckets for food and drink. It was always left open so that the *dyheli* could come and go. Like the rest of the buildings, it was made of stone, with a thick roof of thatch.

When she had removed the tack, left it piled neatly in a corner, and given all three a brief brush-down, she headed for the heart of the Sanctuary, the infirmary buildings where new patients were kept.

Each tiny building held no more than four patients. This mimicked the pattern of the usual sort of structure, where the patients were kept in separate rooms. In this case, the Healers tried to keep as many family members together as possible. It was already traumatic enough, to find themselves depending on total strangers for a cure—to separate sick family members would have put too much stress on them.

Now that the weather was warm, there was no need to heat the buildings, but in the winter charcoal braziers or tiny fireplaces filled that requirement. Although the walkways connecting them were all of wood, the buildings themselves were not; they had been built partly of stone, the better to keep them clean. Their thick walls kept heat in during the winter, and out in the summer; windows covered with netting and flawed silk to prevent insects from entering were closed by glass windows *and* wooden shutters in the worst weather. At the moment, the windows were propped open and the shutters open wide to let in the fresh air.

Keisha found one of the Healers working in the third building she checked.

It was Kandace, someone Keisha knew quite well, a Healer with a great deal of experience and expertise with children. Her middle-aged, motherly face and figure tended to make children relax and trust her; she looked as if she had at least a dozen of her own—though, in fact, she was single and childless. With brown eyes and hair and a medium complexion, she could have passed as almost anyone's relative. This made her perfect to deal with frightened, wary Northerners.

Keisha stood just outside and caught Kandace's eye, then waited outside, rocking on her heels just beside the ladder leading down from the walkway. Kandace must have been nearly finished anyway, as it wasn't long before she came out, and jumped down to give Keisha a welcome hug. "It's been too long!" Kandace exclaimed. "I didn't get nearly as much time to talk to you at the celebration as I would have liked?"

"Neither did I," Keisha replied warmly. It was impossible not to like the exuberant, outgoing Healer; she treated every child like her own, every adult like a friend. Furthermore, everyone in her family was the same way; Keisha had met them all over the course of a year as they came to visit. All but one of Kandace's siblings were Healers, as was her father.

Her mother and one of her sisters were skilled cabinetmakers. "I came with the new Heralds," Keisha continued. "They wanted to see the Sanctuary."

"That *Anda* wanted to see the Sanctuary, you mean!" Kandace laughed. "I have never seen anyone so determined to find out *everything* in the shortest possible time!" She shook her head in disbelief. "If he wasn't so healthy, I'd be worried about him. That sort tends to drive themselves into heart trouble by working too hard."

She and Keisha shared a conspiratorial look. "I think you can depend on Nightwind to see he doesn't," was all Keisha said, but they both knew what she meant. "Since Anda wouldn't hear of not coming, I thought I'd better go along in case your current crop had anything different this time."

Kandace brushed her short hair back with one hand. "No, nothing different this time—just the Wasting Sickness that comes with Summer Fever, and thank the gods, the mild form."

Now they knew that the Wasting Sickness came in two forms—one that sickened and weakened, and sometimes left a victim with paralysis of a limb, and one that killed or left the victim totally paralyzed. With help, the victims of the weak form could recover much of what they had lost—but unless the disease was caught in its early stages, victims of the strong form could not return to their former healthy selves.

Keisha relaxed; Shandi was now immune to the Wasting Sickness, and even if Anda caught it—which was less likely, as it tended to attack children rather than adults—she and Nightwind could cure it in a few days.

"I've got one more set of patients to see. Want to help?" Kandace offered, knowing that Keisha would. Without waiting for her answer, Kandace skipped up the stairs and headed along the walkway, looking behind once to see if Keisha was following.

She didn't see a case of Wasting Sickness at all anymore, and she was right on Kandace's heels. They walked in single file with their footsteps sounding hollow as they headed toward the next building. Hung as decorations beneath the shelter of the roof were all manner of little talismans; there was no end to the variety of materials they had been made of—wood, bone, fabric, fur, stone—there were even some made of dried grasses or pine needles and twigs.

They all portrayed a single creature, the *dyheli,* and each one had been made as a thanks-token for a successful recovery. Some, made by the children, were crude indeed, but it was the thought that counted, not the skill. All of the walkways were hung with these tokens, which were never taken down or replaced, though wind and weather had rendered some of them pretty battered. The patients worked on their talismans as they recovered, and hung them themselves from the rafters of the bridges around the building they had stayed in.

"Ready?" Kandace asked, pausing on the threshold, and looking back at Keisha.

"Always!" Keisha said eagerly, as Kandace reached for the door to open it.

Now if only I could be so certain about the rest of my life. . . .

Ten

Darian was agreeably pleased when Keisha and the Heralds decided to head for Ghost Cat and the Sanctuary right after breakfast; he had a plan of his own, and if Wintersky turned out to be free for a day or two, all the better. He finished his own breakfast in a leisurely fashion, knowing that Wintersky was a late riser, and hoping to see his friend come into the eating hall before he left.

His patience was rewarded as he lingered over a mug of cooling tea; Wintersky did appear in the door, looking damp and cheerful from his morning swim. Darian waved at him; Wintersky acknowledged the wave with one of his own, then went over to the tables to fix himself a plate.

Wintersky was only Gifted with a trace of Mage-Talent; no more than half of all Hawkbrothers had enough of the Mage-Gift to perform more than the barest of magical tasks. As a consequence, Wintersky's black hair had only gone silver in streaks, and his eyes were still the intense blue of a Tayledras who hasn't meddled much with magic. Lean and wiry, with a generous grin and a long jaw, he was one of Darian's oldest friends.

He joined Darian shortly, his plate heaped with hot flatcakes and fruit. "What stirs you this morning, my friend?"

Wintersky asked genially, as he set down his mug and plate and took a seat across from Darian.

"Actually, I was waiting for you," Darian replied, as Wintersky applied himself to his food with a good appetite. "Did you have any plans for the next day or two?"

"Not really." Wintersky ate a few more bites before continuing. "I take it that you do, and you'd like my company?"

"Your company and your help. You're an expert at cold-tracking, and this track is ten years cold." He waited for Wintersky's reaction, which was just what he'd expected.

Wintersky gave him a long look, ate a bit more, and put down his knife and fork. He steepled his fingers over his plate, his eyes fixed on Darian's. "You want to see if you can figure out what happened to your parents."

Wintersky was good at deducing a great deal from a small amount of evidence—that was what made him such a good cold-tracker. "If I can. If there are any traces left at all." Darian shrugged. "I'm not deluding myself; I don't expect much, but if there is anything to be found, I'd like to know I looked for it. They wouldn't let me look while the trail was still hot. Now, though, anything that *was* left after a few years will still be there."

"Perhaps. I can understand that reasoning." Wintersky picked up his fork again and applied himself to his food. "Yes, I can understand that." He said nothing more as he finished his plate, returned to the tables for a second helping, and finished that as well. Darian didn't say anything about the subject either; he knew Wintersky, and knew that his friend was thinking the project over, weighing prospects for success against those of wasting his time for two days and finding nothing.

"If there's anything to be found," Darian added, "I can use magic to find it. After that, it'll be up to you to make what you can of it."

"All right," he said at last. "I'm your man. Between my tracking and your magic, if there's anything to be found, we'll find it in two days and figure out where it leads."

"And if we don't find anything, we'll know there's nothing to be found." Darian hated to say that, but he knew that it was only the truth. *I want answers, but sometimes there aren't any. Much as I hate that. . . .*

The more he had thought about his general feelings of unease, the more he was convinced that they all had something to do with that sense of *not knowing*. If he just had some notion what had happened, he might feel better.

"Let's find a couple of restless *dyheli* and our camping gear and see what's to be found." Wintersky pushed away from the table and paused again. "Is Kel likely to be useful on this trip?" he asked, narrowing his eyes at the sudden thought.

Darian shook his head. "Our birds will be good enough scouts to keep an eye out for trouble. Any tracking will be by small signs, on the ground. I doubt that anything will be visible from the air."

"Right enough. I'll meet you at the Vale entrance with my gear and food—you get your gear and the *dyheli*." When Wintersky made up his mind to do something, he got to it at once, and went at it with all his focus on the task—another thing that made him such an outstanding tracker. He was already out the door by the time Darian got to his feet.

He went first to the *dyheli* meadow, where he paused and sent out a general thought to the herd, which was divided pretty equally between those who were grazing and those who were taking their ease. Does had young at their heels, sometimes twins; young *dyheli* had all the wide-eyed innocence of any young thing, but were not much more intelligent at this stage than a human baby. Their bodies were capable of a great deal, but not their minds. When danger threatened, a doe would literally take over the mind and body of her baby to get it out of harm's way, controlling it so that it ran swiftly and surely at her side. And if the entire herd panicked, the king stag assumed control of *all* of them.

Darian did not leave the does out of his general message, although he knew that at this time of year, no female would leave the herd, not even a young or old one with no youngster of her own. Females were instinctively attracted to the babies, and willingly served as nannies and surrogate mothers, giving the blood-mothers time to graze in lush pastures on their own. There was no such thing as an orphaned *dyheli*; a youngster whose mother died was immediately adopted by one or more childless females, and any female with a baby of her own would allow the orphan to nurse. The youngsters stayed with their mothers for up to fifteen years, nursing for the first two, then continuing to learn as they grazed for the next ten to fourteen years.

Darian sent the equivalent of polite throat-clearing to get the herd's attention, then Mindspoke. :*Wintersky and I are going to do some cold-tracking for the next two days. We would like two friends to help us with this; is anyone interested?*:

Young adult *dyheli* were always restless and ready for an adventure, and at least nine heads popped up at that. He waited; there was some silent conferencing among the would-be volunteers and with Tyrsell, who had the last word, and then two young stags separated from the herd and trotted eagerly toward him. Their large eyes were bright with excitement, and they made no pretense of being anything but enthusiastic.

:*I am Jonti,*: said one. :*This is my twin, Larak. We have not been far outside the Vale before, and we hope that will not cause a difficulty.*:

"Then you should enjoy this," Darian said aloud. "We'll be off in a place where I don't think any of the herd has been before; you'll be first to scout it."

The stags switched their stubby tails with excitement, and followed behind Darian as he led them toward his *ekele*, heads bobbing with every step. On the way, he encountered a *hertasi* and requested it to bring riding gear for him; it nodded and continued on its way. Darian had long since decided that the *hertasi* were constantly in mental contact with each other— what other explanation could there be? This *hertasi* probably would not be the one to bring the tack, but *someone* would show up with saddles before he'd finished packing.

His camping gear was ready; it was always ready, since Meeren took it away as soon as he returned from a trip, cleaned, repaired, or replaced whatever needed tending to, and repacked it for him. He got the packs out of the storage chest where they stayed until he needed them, then rummaged through his closet for his oldest scouting clothes. He didn't think he'd need more than one change of clothing, but he packed three—because accidents happened, and wet clothing was an invitation to serious illness.

It didn't take him long to gather his things, but when he walked out of his front door, there was tack waiting beside the young *dyheli,* and no sign of the *hertasi* who had brought it.

Dyheli tack consisted of a saddle with belly, chest, and rump girths, stirrups, and a very thick saddle pad. It didn't take long to get the two stags harnessed up and his packs fastened to the saddle; he mounted up, and all three of them headed for the Vale entrance.

As promised, Wintersky was waiting, with his own packs and a waterproof pair of saddlebags containing their provisions. In no time at all, he too was ready and in the saddle, and they were on their way.

"So, where are we going?" Wintersky asked curiously.

"North of the village, almost directly north," Darian replied. "It's part Pelagiris Forest, part meadowlands, with the river running along one side, a couple of ponds and some streams. That's where my parents had their trap-lines. My thought is that we'll see if we can find anything left of the traps, first. If we can, we'll know that, whatever happened, nobody worked the lines and collected the traps."

This time both Wintersky and his *dyheli* turned their heads to look at him. "You think perhaps someone took them captive, then harvested their traps and everything in them?"

"That's one among many possibilities," Darian pointed out. "One of the more remote ones, I'll admit, but if that was what happened, I think it's important to know that."

:Blood Bear might not be the only pack of hunters who know where the village is.: That was Jonti, who sounded curiously unmoved by the observation.

"That's entirely true," said Darian, and left it at that.

They rode past the village without going into it. Darian didn't comment on that openly, but he felt that seeing the village and calling up all of its memories would unfocus his concentration on the task at hand. According to Darian's best recollection, his parents worked an area that was several days' distance from Errold's Grove. But they had traveled on foot, in the winter. He and Wintersky were going by *dyheli*-back, at a lope, in the spring. They should reach the area where his parents had last been well before nightfall.

They stopped at a stream around noon for a brief rest and

lunch, and in late afternoon, when they were close to the area where Darian expected to find things—if there was anything to be found—they stopped to set up for the night. It was time for Darian to try his luck.

Darian got down off Jonti, and stood quietly, closing his eyes, blocking out the world, bit by bit. Wintersky went straight to work, dismounting and taking care of the *dyheli* stags and setting up camp. It might seem as if he was the one doing all the work, but that was not the case and he knew it very well. Darian's search would take as much energy as he was using; perhaps more. That is how the Hawkbrothers were; as long as one did equal work, in one's own way, there were no complaints from others of the clan.

Darian did not open his eyes, since he would be exploring the forest for some distance around—perhaps a distance of a league or two—and the night was still young.

He himself had worked this area as a child; now he had to bring those childhood memories up from the back of his mind, superimpose them onto their current surroundings, and then—then he would invoke Mage-Sight, but he would be looking for two things. First, he would search for objects that did not belong in the forest naturally, such as refined and forged metals. Such things, even in a state of decay, might hold the traces of the humans that had made or owned them. Second, he hoped that his kinship with his parents would draw him to anything that they had once used.

It was not always easy to keep an objective pursuit as the hours of sifting went by. When he dredged through his memories for physical references to the landscape, he would come across one image after another of his mother's smile—or of his father trimming away a loose branch—or of him bending a trap-wire carefully while explaining to his young son how the spring worked. Darian would get such memories brought back to him, lit with intensely bright sun, in that way that only fond recollections seem to have.

It was fortunate for him, he knew, that the visions of Mage-Sight could not be blurred by tears.

Mage-Sight showed him the world as it was for those who could see the energies of life. On the surface, the living animals and plants, were each enveloped in a faint emerald glow, a mist of verdant power, thin but very real. This, rather than the deeper layer where the ley-lines were, was the stratum he wanted to examine.

His emotions were suppressed through practiced discipline just enough to be able to work safely. He existed in a detached and analytical state for this exercise in receptivity to power—at least, that was the ideal intent. The pace of his search was slowed by periodic pauses, while he collected his thoughts from the effects of one family memory or other. In the intervening times of emotional control, he searched for "holes" in the overlying mist, places where the nonliving intruded through the living at certain relative "depths."

He concentrated on each of those places, usually discovering that the "hole" represented a rock, or a place scorched bare by fire or lightning. Meanwhile, Wintersky worked quietly around him as he painstakingly sifted through each area he thought he remembered. With all of his concentration centered on his task, he was not aware of time passing. He was not aware of anything except the next pattern of radiant energy, from the next hand's breadth of ground. He felt the "glare" of someone approaching, seeming to his magical vision much like someone was walking closer bearing a torch while his eyes were adjusted to night and starlight.

Wintersky touched his elbow, getting his attention without disturbing his search. Like a sleepwalker, Darian allowed Wintersky to guide him to a place to sit, allotting just enough of his attention to keep from stumbling over his own feet. He continued his search without a moment's pause.

He sensed—albeit remotely—the sun setting; he felt it as an overwhelming, nurturing presence slowly sinking away.

In addition to searching out gaps in the fabric of life-energy, he used a more subtle "sense" in his examination—the Earth-Sense that made him a Healing-Mage. It was more like a sense than a skill, since it was not always consciously directed. As he examined each bit of ground, he let the earth tell him about itself. Had it been injured, had it been contaminated in the past? Was it under some sort of pressure, other than the normal pressures of life and change? Was there anything *different* about it? The more he listened to the earth, the farther that sense extended, and the easier it was to read the earth ways.

He expected to find at least one Change-Circle this way.

This area had not been checked for mage-storm damage or interference, except in a very cursory fashion, because the Changecreatures that had come out of it had long since been "dealt with," and whatever had happened here during the Storms had not been grave enough to disrupt the flow of magic to k'Valdemar. Eventually every finger-length of land *would* be gone over with the same painful care that he was using now, but such a detailed examination would take decades, even centuries. For now, only specific strategically important areas of the land closest to k'Valdemar had undergone such intense scrutiny.

He sensed a fire crackling nearby, sensed the cool of evening on his back and the warmth of the fire on his face and chest. Wintersky made the ideal partner in a situation like this one; quiet and unobtrusive, he kept his presence from impinging upon Darian's concentration, allowing the mage to do what he needed to do.

It was late, very late, and Darian was just about ready to give up for the night, when a distant hint of "other" distracted him from the area he was in the process of examining. His Earth-Sense, running out ahead of the conscious examination, had found something that didn't fit. Thirty-some degrees off from his current focus there was another sort of "glare," more akin to a reversed shadow. And it wasn't subtle either.

It was not an impulsive decision to abandon his examination and switch his focus; he was tired, yes, but this was something that needed to be looked at. The "nearer" he drew to the place, the more obvious it became that whatever was here, it didn't belong. There was nothing "wrong" as such—nothing that a Healing-Mage needed to put right—but this thing that had caught his attention was as obvious as a cabbage in a flowerbed. It was out of place—it had neither been born of this soil, nor had it been brought here long enough ago that some of the sense of it permeated the land around it. It was rawly new, stubbornly unintegrated.

He drew near enough to "see" its shape and form, clearly. *Ah, now, what is this?* It was a Change-Circle, all right, but the kind where territory was transported whole. What made it stand out was its sterility—and it was nothing but bare rock, so bare that not even moss grew on it. It had been planted in a scooped-out area of Pelagiris Forest. Tree roots did not penetrate it, though surface vegetation had spilled over onto it from erosion of the surrounding soil. Its surface was not level. In fact, it tilted slightly as a whole, like the side of a shallow hill scooped out by a massive ladle and dropped. The curvature of the stone carried true into the softer ground it had sunken into, and for the first time Darian had evidence that the Change-Circles were not *circles* at all, but spheres.

Huh! I wonder what those theory builders back in Haven will make of this!

He was about to leave the search altogether when something else caught his attention, very like the glint of sun on something small, but shiny and glittering amidst dark tangles of ground and greenery—

Only in this case, it was a faint calling of like-to-like. Or more accurately, of blood-to-blood. *His* blood, answering the faint call of blood that he shared—weak, old, but unmistakable—so faint that he had to clear his senses again and refocus. He fed it a wisp of power to reenergize it and make it more easily recognizable for what it was.

He had just found a possible first trace—the first sign—of his parents' fate!

He hardly slept at all that night; only good sense and the need to replenish the energy he'd spent kept him quiet after he'd burst out with his news to his traveling companions.

Knowing he would not sleep, he simply kept quiet and allowed his body to rest, although his mind refused to. He carefully catalogued all the possible things he could find, and made a simple plan for what he would do for each possibility. It was the equivalent of counting sheep—the only equivalent his emotions would tolerate at this point. At least he had the illusion of accomplishing something to comfort him. . . .

He dropped off to sleep from sheer exhaustion at some point, for the next thing he knew, Wintersky was shaking him awake and the stars were fading in the first light of predawn. They packed up the camp together and saddled Jonti and Larak, whose tails were twitching with suppressed energy and excitement. He and Wintersky planned to eat in the saddle, for Wintersky had brought journey-rolls for just that purpose. So they were on their way to the spot he had marked out, riding the *dyheli* and followed in the trees by their birds before the first hint of sun appeared in the sky.

He rode in a kind of fever, afire to be *there*, that very moment; wanting to hope, afraid to do anything of the sort. He couldn't even think, not really; his mind jumped from one thought to another without any real coherence. Kuari picked up his agitation, and flew back and forth, surging ahead of them, then swooping to the rear to check on their backtrail.

If it had been remotely possible to Gate there, Darian would have tried. During the entire interminable journey, his stomach churned, the muscles in his shoulders and neck were in knots, and his mouth was as dry as sand.

Their goal was as clear to outward eyes as it was to his inward senses. It loomed up, enfolded in the white haze of early morning low fog around its base as if it had shrugged off a mantle of clouds. A huge, perfectly spherical piece of gray-white rock, easily the size of his *ekele* or larger, reared up between the trunks of the trees ahead of them. The moment they spotted it, the *dyheli* went from their lope into a full-out gallop, leaving Darian and Wintersky to hang onto the handles built into the saddles and stay on as best they could.

The *dyheli* skidded to a halt as they reached the artifact, hips slewing a little sideways with the momentum of their run as they dug in their hooves, and Darian leaped from the saddle the moment they came to a halt.

The surface of the rock was perfectly smooth. Darian tentatively put out his hand to touch it, and the rock beneath his hand might as well have been perfectly polished by a jeweler.

"It's amazing. Look at this, Wintersky. Have you ever seen anything like it?"

But he had no thought for how that unusually smooth finish might have happened; what he wanted was on the opposite side of the boulder. He hurried around it to search in the grass at the junction of forest floor and rock. "It's near here," Darian murmured. "I felt the sign from near here, on the northwest side of the rock formation. In the soil."

Wintersky joined him, the two of them kneeling side by side and carefully parting the grass stems, pulling apart the leaf litter and dead vegetation of so many years, sifting through decayed grasses and earth for some tiny artifact—

Then, Darian's fingers tingled as he touched something small and hard under the surface.

He stopped dead for a moment—then slowly, carefully, probed at the object, fishing it up out of the moist, crumbling soil. His breath caught.

It was a bone; a tiny bone no larger than a thimble.

Now Wintersky took over, pushing Darian aside gently, and hunting carefully and methodically through the loam. Darian went to the *dyheli* who had followed them to this side of the rock. He pulled his ground-cloth out of his pack and spread it out beside Wintersky, numbly taking what Wintersky dug up, cleaning it meticulously with spit and a handkerchief, and laying it out on the ground-cloth. Of all the things that he had imagined last night, this was not one of them.

"Lay them out in the order I give them to you," Wintersky ordered after the third tiny bone emerged from the soil. He excavated the site meticulously, using the tip of his knife as well as his fingers, after cutting a square of turf going back to the rock and pulling it up. Darian obeyed him, and piece by piece, bone by bone, a pattern began to emerge.

Bones flared at each tiny joint, then nestled into the longer ones of the same general shape; bones gone gray-white from weathering, the surface cracked and pitted. Wintersky worked more slowly now, and there was a pattern to his excavation as he worked out the direction that the bones lay.

They were toes.

The heel—the ankle bones—then—

Right against the rock, flush with it, the joint end of the lower leg bones. But the rest of the bone had been sheared off cleanly, leaving only the rounded ends, with the cuts lying flat against the surface of the rock.

Slowly, Wintersky picked up the two bone fragments, cleaned them off, and handed them to Darian, cut-end first, so that Darian could see for himself that the ends had not been crushed, as they would have been had the boulder landed after a fall, upon the unfortunate owner of the foot.

Another few minutes and the remains of a hard boot heel and sole were excavated from rotted tatters of thick canvas.

—*Father*— He knew that must be whose foot they had found; he had somehow known it the moment he touched the first bone. He knew it from the lurch in his heart, the dryness of his mouth, the surge in his blood. His father always wore his boots to sleep in, in case there was trouble in the night. He wore canvas-bodied boots coated in the same neutral wax as his leggings, so he would not leave scent marks to warn the game. The waxing had to be restored every few weeks or it would let the canvas rot. This had to be his father's—

—but the ends of the bone were shiny, polished, as if they had been cut by a fine saw, then polished by a jeweler.

"Check with Mage-Sight. Is there any more sign?" Winter-sky asked diffidently, laying the two bones down with the rest when Darian did not take them.

Darian closed his eyes, extended his senses, and—shook his head. "Nothing," he said hoarsely, surprised at the sound of his own voice.

Together they looked at the bones, at the incontrovertible evidence that lay before them.

There was only one possible interpretation.

"They must have been caught in the Change-Circle," Darian whispered. He did not for a moment doubt that his mother had been with his father—otherwise she would have made her way back to him. "They were caught in the Circle, and sent—where?"

Wintersky could only shake his head. "I don't know, Dar'ian," he replied. "I just—don't know."

A few hours later, Darian had cause to bless the caution with which Wintersky had worked, for he had managed to preserve the very few representatives of non-native vegetation that had taken root around the boulder. How they had come there, Darian had no idea, but they were not part of the normal flora of the Pelagiris Forest. Perhaps seeds had drifted in with the air that had come with the rock—perhaps they had been caught in a crack at the top of the boulder, for he had discovered by climbing up on top of it that it wasn't *perfectly* sheared off. The top, flattened and cracked, looked like normally aged rock surface.

He carefully and reverently folded away the bones in one of his shirts in the saddlebag. He wasn't altogether certain how they could be of use—but Firesong would know.

Surely we can use them to tell me whether Father is dead or alive. That would be some sort of closure; he could weep for them, and know they hadn't come back to him because they couldn't. It was a disconcerting feeling, to almost hope they were dead just so he would *know* at last, one way or the other. It was sobering and distressing at the same time, so he pushed it away from his thoughts through force of will, as he had become accustomed to doing by his training.

The *dyheli* were as excited over their own finds as Darian was; with all four of them equally eager to return to k'Valdemar, the young stags alternated their easy, distance-eating lope with bursts of full-out gallop. Darian had only to hang on; they would get him home faster than any other means except by air—though now he was regretting that he had not brought Kel along. Kel couldn't have carried *him* home, but he could have taken those precious bones to Firesong.

He didn't dare send Kuari ahead with the bones. For one thing, Kuari wasn't that fast a flyer; for another, they needed his eyes when the sun set.

Which was going to be very shortly. . . .

The *dyheli* could see fairly well in the dark, but not at the breakneck pace they were setting now, and Darian was not willing to waste the power it would take to set mage-lights above and ahead of them; he preferred to use it to augment the *dyheli's* strength. They needed Kuari's night-sight, and the owl was happy to oblige.

Darkness gradually crept over the forest, and the *dyheli* linked their minds to Kuari's. The owl swooped down from among the branches and flew a little ahead of the racing riders, about an arm's-length higher than their heads. From this position, he could see anything that would trip the *dyheli* in any way—and so could they, through his eyes. Wintersky's bird had already come down and was riding his shoulder, gripping the padding and hunched down with his wings held close to his body.

Darian guessed that it was just about midnight when the first light of k'Valdemar glimmered through the trees in the distance. The weary *dyheli* found an untapped reservoir of strength, and broke into a last, tired gallop.

They stumbled through the Veil, and into the waiting hands of the *hertasi*. Wintersky had turned his own attention to notifying the *hertasi*—and thus the Vale—of what they had discovered as soon as they were within range. With Darian occupied in keeping up the stags' energy, he had no attention to spare for that particular job.

But thanks to Wintersky, not only were *hertasi* waiting, but so were Firesong, Silverfox, and Snowfire. The latter took charge of Wintersky, who was just as exhausted as Darian, and ushered him away for congratulations, food, and rest.

Firesong took one look at Darian's fever-filled eyes, and simply took charge of the bones and his pupil. "You won't rest until we know *something*," Firesong said wisely, and with unusual gentleness. "Come along; I think I can at least tell you whether your father is alive or dead."

He took Darian by the elbow, and guided him in the direction of his *ekele* and workroom. Darian didn't resist; he felt as if he was consumed by the need to know. It was a fire in his blood, a blinding light in his mind.

They went straight to the workroom, where Firesong already had shields cast and the room prepared for what they would do. When all three of them were inside, Firesong motioned for Darian to sit, and closed up the shields, sealing them inside.

He collapsed onto a stool, and stared hungrily at Firesong, who took the bones and carefully unwrapped them. Darian couldn't look away from the tiny white fragments; they drew his gaze and held it.

Firesong placed them down on the floor and sat cross-legged on a cushion beside them. Then he contemplated them for a moment, while Darian's heart pounded.

"First thing, I think—" the Adept broke off what he was saying, and closed his eyes, holding his hands palm down over the bones. "Link with me, Dar'ian," he ordered, but in a half-absent voice. Darian didn't question whether he had the strength available; he linked first with a ley-line, and then with his teacher, clutching the stool with both hands.

There was a moment of double-disorientation, as the raw power from the line rushed into him, then as he melded with Firesong. When he got himself straightened out again, Firesong was setting up a complicated relational field enclosing the bones. :*This was once part of a greater whole,*: the Adept said to him, quite dispassionately—but it was vitally important to be dispassionate when handling magic. :*You see what I am setting up here? I'm reestablishing a connection with the rest of the body this once belonged to—the plane of Power doesn't care about distance in our world, that's why we can Gate when things there are stable enough. By reconnecting in that plane what used to be connected there and here, I can learn something about the state of the rest of the body.:*

Darian watched with fascination that was not quite as dispassionate as Firesong's. The Adept was literally weaving a web of power between the artifacts here, and—and something somewhere else; a web that was possible only because they had once been connected.

When the last thread was in place, Firesong gathered up a little more power—surprisingly little—and gave it a command, in effect saying to it wordlessly, *Show me what you would be like if you were still one object.*

The power settled over the bones in a tenuous, visible mist, while all three of them watched with varying degrees of hope and fear. If Darian's father was dead, there would be no change—or the change would show conditions even less pleasant than a handful of dry bones.

The mist took on a pinkish tinge, swirled a little—

—then took on the ghostly outlines of a healthy, whole foot.

Darian hadn't realized that he'd made a sound until he heard it in his own ears—half a strangled sob, half a choked-off gasp. But he certainly felt the tears suddenly fill his eyes and blur the scene in front of him, then pour down his cheeks in an outpouring of the emotions he would not give in to while he was still linked in with the line. Silverfox rested a calming hand on his shoulder, a comfort and warmth that released some of the tension that had been building in him.

"Right; well, that's the main thing," Firesong muttered, and played a bit more with the relational field. He got no changes, however, and finally dismissed it with a sigh of frustration. Darian blinked burning eyes and told himself fiercely not to be disappointed; this was more, much, much more, than he had known yesterday at this time.

"I tried to get a sense of direction and distance, but I didn't get much," Firesong said, as Darian let go his own hold on the ley-line. This time Darian did not try to replenish anything; he needed the energy himself too much. "All I got was that it is north and to the west, and so far away that I couldn't get any reading on distance."

"But he *is* alive," Darian said, his own voice sounding forlorn even in his own ears.

"He is alive," Firesong replied, and smiled, patting Darian's knee, adding his comfort to his partner's. "Very much alive, and I think it far more likely than not that your mother is alive and well and with him. If he survived—with the loss of a foot—then she likely did, still intact."

The sudden outburst of tears surprised him, though it didn't appear to surprise either Firesong or Silverfox. It was over in just a few moments, but he felt as drained as if he'd just done his entire Mastery Trial all over again.

Silverfox helped him to his feet, as Firesong handed him a square of gauze cloth to wipe his eyes and nose with. "You've been through more than enough for one day," the *kestra'chern* said. "And since Keisha is off with the Heralds, why don't you stay with us overnight? I think you need company."

"I—think I do, too," Darian confessed, and followed both of them up the staircase to the *ekele*-above, his legs leaden weights, his head full of confused bits of thought that refused to come together into anything coherent.

They sat him down on a low sling-couch; Silverfox went out briefly and came back with food and something hot to drink. Numbly, Darian ate and drank without tasting anything, and listened while the two of them talked lightly of utter commonplaces. The longer he sat, the heavier his head seemed, until at length it felt as if it was easier to lie down than remain seated upright. Silverfox stepped over to him, uncapped a small brown bottle from a nearby shelf, and gently touched two fingertips to Darian's forehead just between his eyebrows. Darian focused on the unusual touch, and Silverfox waved the open bottle under Darian's nose while he was distracted.

Then, in spite of his certainty that he wouldn't be able to sleep the entire night—he closed his eyes for a moment, and knew nothing more until morning.

Eleven

Sleeping in the tiny, austere isolation hut, with the windows wide open to the night air, was very like sleeping in a hard-sided tent. Keisha enjoyed it as a change from Darian's *ekele*. Out here where the weather wasn't controlled, it still got quite cool at night, and she needed to use the blankets left folded up on her pallet. She woke up once or twice during the night at an unexpected sound, and smiled sleepily, as she listened to the life of the Sanctuary go on around her in the darkness, while she snuggled under the weighty warmth of her blankets. Helping out on the rounds had made her pleasantly tired, and she had gone to bed while Shandi and Anda were still deep in conversation with the Healers.

In the morning, they showed their lack of sleep with yawns and puffy eyes, but neither had lost an iota of enthusiasm. "When we get back to k'Valdemar, you can tell everyone that I've got enough to think about for a while," Anda told Keisha as they mounted into their saddles, with a cheerful wink that told her he knew very well that he had been driving some of the others to distraction with his incessant questions. "I shan't be pestering anyone for at least a week—and then it will probably be to find out who can help me arrange to build our headquarters."

"You won't have to pester anyone, since I can already tell

you—it's the *hertasi* chief, Ayshen. He schedules all the work in the Vale," Keisha told him as she polished off the last drops of her tea: "You *are* building in the Vale, aren't you? What are you going to call this establishment of yours? An embassy?"

"Yes, we're building in the Vale, and I think I'll let this Ayshen fellow pick a good spot," Anda told her. "As for what we're calling it—well, it's not a *way*station, and it isn't exactly an embassy—so I thought I'd just call it k'Valdemar Station."

"That'll work," Keisha acknowledged with hidden amusement. So, Anda didn't think it was an embassy, did he? *Wait until he's been here a year.*

The *dyheli* got them back to Ghost Cat in good time; Anda wanted to speak further with Chief Vordon and Shaman Celin, so Keisha decided to have a look at those fascinating goods that the Northern tribes had brought in.

Since she had spotted her old friend Hywel in the crowd gathering to greet them—now *warrior* Hywel, a fact he was burstingly proud of—she waved to him and got his attention as Anda and Shandi walked off with the Chief. He waved back, face full of delight, for the fact that he was great friends with Healer Keisha and Owl-warrior Darian gave quite a boost to his status.

She walked over to him as he waited for her; no man of the Northern tribes would come to a woman for a casual conversation, not even so high-status a woman as a Healer. It was nonsense, of course, and these attitudes were gradually changing even among the most recalcitrant of tribesmen—for this once, Keisha was willing to bow before custom.

"Greetings to you, Healer Keisha," Hywel said solemnly. He was trying very, very hard to look mature and warriorlike; he had shot up another hand's breadth in the last six months and was wearing a new leather shirt made from the skins of his own kills. The impression he was trying to make was utterly spoiled by the obvious youth of the face behind the new beard and mustache. He still looked to her exactly like the boy who'd been frantic to save the life of his brother, and willing to brave anything to do so.

"Greetings to you, Warrior Hywel," she replied, just as soberly, though it was all she could do to keep from chuckling. "Could you tell me who I would speak to if I were to wish to barter for some of the goods held in trust for Ghost Cat, k'Valdemar, and the Sanctuary?"

"Nothing easier," he said, brightening at the idea that he would be able to do so high-status an individual a good turn. "My mother, Laine, has the authority to barter for those goods for the tribe. I am sure she will be happy to bargain with you."

That was not in the least surprising; Laine was known to cut a shrewd bargain herself, quite as well as glass-maker Harrod's wife. The only reason that *she* was not in charge of Ghost Cat's dealings with the village was that she had not dared try the language exchange with a *dyheli*. In part, that was because she was strongly averse to any "meddling with magic and holy things" for herself, and in part it was because she didn't want to court the horrid headache that always followed such an exchange.

Not that Keisha blamed her.

Laine was learning Valdemaran the old-fashioned way, bit by bit, from her sons, who *had* gotten the tongues the "easy" way. This would not matter to Keisha, who spoke Laine's tongue with the fluency of her own.

"Come," Hywel said, gesturing grandly, "I will take you to her." Keisha repressed another chuckle at that; she didn't need Hywel to show her to his own house, she knew quite well where it was—but conducting her there raised his status another minute increment. The saying she had heard about the Northerners did seem to be true: "You are known by who you know!"

Not long after that, the two women were going over the goods in the storehouse, with all the pleasure of any two women anywhere in the lustrous furs, the warmth of the amber. His job done, Hywel had gone off to do "man things"— which basically meant sitting about with his young warrior friends, boasting about the animals they would hunt when fall came.

The familial resemblance between Laine and her sons was unmistakable; all three shared a distinctively high brow, deep-set eyes, and short nose. For the rest, they shared brown eyes, black hair, sturdy, muscular build, and heavily tanned skin with the rest of their tribe.

"Ah—these are what I wanted—" Keisha said, when she finally turned over a protective layer of cloth to reveal the skins she was looking for. "How many do you think it would take to line the hood of a winter cloak?"

"Six," Laine said instantly, the fringes of her leather dress swaying as she reached for one of the furs. She spread it over her arm, displaying it to Keisha, ruffling up the fur with her breath to show how thick and plush the hair was. "Yes, six. No less. You will not want the fur about the hindquarters, you see, and the belly-fur is thin. And were I you, I should have some wolverine as well, to put about the edge of the hood. The wolverine is so hot-blooded that the virtue goes even into the fur, and your breath will not freeze upon it."

Keisha very much doubted that "virtue" had anything to do with it, but she did know that the rest was true. She started to agree, when Laine spoke again.

"And here—I think that Clanbrother Darian might well like one of these," Laine continued, taking a cloth off another pile of what had appeared to be pieced and worked goods. She picked one up and shook it out—it was a vest, made of leather, but not tooled, dyed, or decorated in the usual fashions of the Ghost Cat tribe, but actually embroidered with designs. When Keisha examined it further, taking it from Laine's hands, she saw that it had been embroidered, not with thread or yarn, but very cleverly with tufts of dyed fur of some kind.

The designs themselves were nothing like those the Northern tribes used, although they seemed faintly familiar. But try as she might, Keisha just couldn't place them. They were more like some sort of foreign designs that the Northerners had tried to adapt to their own style.

"I think you're right, Laine," she said, as she held the vest in her hands, admiring the workmanship. "Darian will like this quite a lot. He's not the lover of decoration that Firesong is—"

"Ai, and who is?" Laine interjected, giggling, hiding her mouth behind her blunt-fingered hand as was the custom among Ghost Cat women.

"No one!" Keisha laughed. "But Darian does like to dress handsomely now and again, and this is just his sort of clothing."

She and Laine bargained spiritedly for some time, and eventually arrived at a price they both liked. Ghost Cat craved Keisha's dyes and the food-spices she raised—she would *never* bargain with medicinal herbs, but she had no compunction about using her spices as currency. The tribesmen had learned that spiced food was a fine thing; it was a taste they quickly acquired, for the spices gave their plain meals a savor they had never had before. In the cases of garlic and some peppers, it was quite good for their health, too.

In exchange for spices and dyes to be delivered by *dyheli*, Keisha carried off enough furs to line her hood and make mittens, and she also bought the handsome vest. She had stowed them away in her saddlebags by the time Shandi and Anda were ready to leave.

Darian is usually the one getting things for me, she reflected, very pleased with herself. *It'll be fun to see his face when I surprise him with a gift, for a change.*

It was at that moment that Anda's Companion picked up his pace, leaving Shandi and Keisha lagging a little behind. Shandi did not trouble to catch up, and the *dyheli* Keisha rode was in no great hurry either. Anda disappeared around a turn in the road, and only then did Shandi turn to her sister.

Shandi wore a stubborn expression; her golden-brown eyes narrowed as she regarded Keisha. "All right," the young Herald demanded. "What exactly is going on—or not going on— between you and Darian."

"Nothing!" Keisha responded before she thought.

"That's exactly the problem," Shandi retorted. "And I want to know why. You said you'd talk about it later—well, this is later, and we can't get any more privacy than we have now."

Except for two pairs of four-hooved, pointed ears, Keisha thought, looking resentfully at Karles' head. His ears were pointed back toward both of them, although the *dyheli's* weren't. She didn't relish the notion of having any witnesses at all to this.

"Come on, Keisha, you know I won't give up. I know you too well," Shandi persisted, turning in her saddle to face her fully. "You've got a situation here that's hurting both of you, whether you'll admit it or not." She sounded very sure of herself; too sure, Keisha thought.

"I don't see how you can claim that," Keisha said sullenly, looking straight ahead and not at her sister. She couldn't— didn't want to—meet Shandi's eyes. "I'm not in the least unhappy. I have a terrific life; it couldn't possibly be any better."

"Huh. You might be able to convince anyone else of that, but not your sister, and not an Empath," Shandi retorted energetically. "What's the problem? He's not discontent, and you aren't interested in anyone else. Are you afraid he's inevitably going to lose interest in you and go chase some other girl?"

Since that was precisely what had been troubling her, Keisha's head snapped around and she stared at her sister in shock. "How did—"

"It's pretty obvious, isn't it?" Shandi replied, staring into her startled eyes. "You never believed that anyone would ever think you were pretty enough to bother with when we were at home, and you don't believe it now. In your heart," she continued ruthlessly, "you're sure this is all some kind of accident on Darian's part, and one of these days he'll wake up and realize it." Shandi sounded calm, collected, and utterly unruffled; the very opposite of the way Keisha felt. "In fact, you're actually planning on it happening."

Put that way, so baldly and unadorned, it sounded ridiculous, and Keisha felt as if she'd been caught doing something very stupid. Embarrassed, resentful, full of chagrin—but it hadn't seemed foolish all those times when she'd been feeling alone and so unhappy!

"You haven't done anything stupid, sib," Shandi said gently, her eyes softening. "But you almost did. It's one short step from being sure that something good can't last to sabotaging it, and making your fears come true. You can't let things that you *know* don't make sense get in the way of a wonderful relationship!"

But Empath or not, Keisha was not about to admit anything to her little sister. Shandi was, after all, her *little* sister; younger, presumably less experienced. How dared she sit in judgment on her older sister? Besides, Shandi had no idea of the stresses on her. "Look, that's not all it is, it isn't even most of it. I have my duties, my responsibilities, and Darian has his—they aren't the same, and we're apart more than we're together. I *can't* trail around after him the way a wife is suppo—"

"Oh, *please,*" Shandi groaned, interrupting her, while Karles snorted in obvious scorn. "What god came down and told you exactly what a wife is *supposed* to do? Who set up rules like that?"

Keisha's temper flared as her resentment mounted. Just because Shandi was a Herald and didn't have to go along with
the kinds of conventions that *normal* people did, she had no
right to make any kind of judgments for her sister! *Keisha*
wasn't about to flout conventions! "Everyone knows what—"

"That's ridiculous," Shandi interrupted again. "When has
Darian ever told you—or even hinted—that he expects you to
sit home and bake and spin? *You* aren't everybody, you probably have more wits than any two of my old friends put together—and you don't have to put up with the small-
mindedness of village gossips if you don't want to. They won't
even know what you're doing if you live here, for one thing!
And for another—no one but you should be allowed to make
any decisions about how you live and who with."

Keisha opened her mouth—and closed it again. She had no
answer whatsoever for that, because Shandi was right—once
again.

"So when did Darian demand or even hint that if you two
got married, you had to become a so-called 'proper' wife?"
Shandi demanded.

"You can't answer me, because he hasn't, right?" Shandi
shook her head. "Listen to me, and think. What kind of cou-
ples has he had for comparison of what a good pairing is like?
I'm not talking about the villagers, either, because *he* doesn't
really think of himself as one of the villagers, he thinks of
himself as a Hawkbrother. He had his own parents—who
worked together as a team; his mother *certainly* didn't sit at
home and wash floors. He has the Hawkbrothers—who are
very careful about getting *into* a marriage, or whatever they
call it, but who don't make any demands that one partner be
subservient to the other! So *why* should he suddenly demand
that of you?"

Shandi was too logical, and fired off her arguments too
quickly for Keisha to respond. She felt a headache coming on,
a shaft of pain coming from her temple, even as she felt
flushed and very uncomfortable. Why wouldn't Shandi just
drop the whole subject and leave her alone?

Now Shandi changed her tone to one of coaxing; she lowered her voice and cocked her head to one side. "Keisha, just
because you get involved with someone, even marry him, that
doesn't mean one of you has to get swallowed up by the other.

Darian doesn't want that—if he did, trust me, you'd know it, and you have a good sense of self-preservation; you'd be running away as fast as a *dyheli* could carry you!" She laughed.

Shandi certainly did that, when Mother tried to swallow her up. . . .

But Shandi didn't make that comparison, which was probably just as well. "You say that you and Darian are apart more than together now that you're both taking on your full responsibilities—well, things change, and you have to change with them, you ought to know that by now! You'll probably have to work some things out, maybe make some alterations in how you work, but—"

Me? Why should I be the one to have to change? "I don't think it's fair for *me* to have to make all the compromises!" Keisha said—and cringed when she heard the whining tone in her own voice.

"So don't! When I said 'you,' I meant both of you!" Exasperation crept into Shandi's voice. "Listen to what I'm saying, and don't keep jumping to the worst possible conclusion! You make some compromises, he'll make some, you'll work out what's acceptable to both of you. But don't undermine your own happiness because you think you haven't got anything to offer him, and don't drive him away just because you're afraid of a commitment!"

I'm not afraid! Keisha wanted to snap—but she knew, instantly, that it would be a lie. So she didn't say anything at all.

Fortunately, that seemed to be the end of Shandi's lecture. Shandi left her alone then; she didn't ride ahead or lag behind, but she didn't say anything more. Finally Keisha thought of something to say.

She couldn't help it; she sounded sarcastic. "How did you become such an expert on—on—"

"On romance?" Shandi looked over at her, and winked, taking her question at face value and ignoring the sarcasm. "Forced into it. Between all the boys that chased after me in Errold's Grove, and all the Trainees who came to me with boy- and girl-problems, I got to be an expert fairly quickly." She sighed heavily. "*Everybody* goes to an Empath for a shoulder to cry on."

"Don't I know it!" Keisha said involuntarily, thinking of

the number of times that Shandi's disappointed suitors had done just that to *her*—and that broke the uncomfortable stalemate. They both laughed, Shandi heartily, Keisha weakly.

By unspoken consent they did not discuss anything remotely uncomfortable after that. Shandi changed the subject to something completely innocuous. They spent the rest of the ride talking about trivialities, nothing that used up an awful lot of brain power, which was just as well.

Shandi had given her a great deal to occupy her thoughts.

Darian woke in the late morning feeling just as much turmoil and confusion in his mind as he'd had when he went to bed. In fact, he hadn't really expected to sleep, but his exhausted body had decided otherwise. He turned himself out of the hammock he'd awakened in, in one of Silverfox's workrooms, and found (as he'd expected) a fresh set of his own clothing waiting for him beside the window. *And* cleaned boots.

The hertasi *were busy this morning.*

Getting dressed, he hurried up the staircase to Firesong's *ekele* above, certain that he would find his mentor there, probably engrossed in a magical text.

He was not wrong; Firesong looked up as soon as he poked his nose in the door. "Get over here," Firesong ordered, pointing to a low chair. In a moment, his teacher had Darian sitting down with food in front of him. Firesong turned his apparent attention back to the heavy book from which he was making notes.

"Don't say anything just yet," Firesong cautioned, without looking up. "Eat first." And he sat there with his arms folded across the pages, drawing delicate diagrams, while Darian did just that. Darian obeyed him, even though the food had no more taste than old leaves, and kept catching in his throat.

When he'd finished enough to satisfy the Adept, Firesong allowed him to set the tray aside and get down to a serious discussion.

"I've been doing some research, but I haven't found anything that was of much use. Charting the Change-Circle against our maps put it on a proper arc, in line with others we knew of already, but since no one has yet been able to find a provable correlation between source and destination Circles when they change places, I have no prediction of where what *was* initially in that Circle went. I also did a little more work this morning, when I was fresher, with Starfall's help," Firesong told him. "Unfortunately, we got pretty much the same result. Your father is somewhere north and west of us; how far, and in exactly what direction he is, we simply can't tell— except that it's a long way. Farther than a hawk would fly in a week." He sighed. "There still isn't enough clean, clear power about for us to be able to point to him with any more accuracy than that. Best scrying we can do at present gives us a general "feel" within a quarter compass, at this distance. It is like target shooting in a dense fog, when you haven't even seen where the target is placed first. We'd either have to have more power, or be a great deal closer to him to find him."

"And there's an awful lot of 'north and west' to be searching in," Darian sighed. "Firesong—"

"Don't make any decisions yet," Firesong cautioned. "We haven't begun to exhaust all of our resources. There may be someone among the tribesmen coming here for Healing who can give us clues, or even a real direction."

Darian grimaced. "And this is where you counsel me about patience. My head knows you're right, but—I don't *want* to sit around and wait, I want to be up and doing something!" He unclenched a fist he wasn't even aware he'd made. "I have been patient. I've undergone trials, travels, and ceremonies until my ears could bleed. I've been in fights that scared me to death and done responsible things for others enough to be Knighted, and even *that* was to better do the duties demanded of me."

Firesong nodded, and a lock of his snowy white hair fell over one eye. He said nothing in agreement, but also said nothing disapproving.

"I've given and given to this Vale. And to the village, and to Valdemar, and even the Northerners. I have had some wonderful times and great benefits, and I don't have too many regrets. I have not done these things so I could stack up favors to call in." Darian paused for a long deep breath then continued. "It is just that—the things I have done over the past few years have been almost all for others, but this is for me."

Firesong brushed the stray hair away from his face, still

seemingly impassive as he listened, then said levelly, "Go on."

Darian set his jaw and then concluded. "Firesong, I want this one. I want this one for me and for my family. I'm horribly afraid that if we wait too long, something will happen to them. . . ." His voice faded as he contemplated *that* terrible notion, that he would learn his parents were alive only to discover they'd perished just days before he could reach them.

Firesong shook his head slightly while he steepled his fingers. "I understand. But Darian, they've survived this long, surely they can survive the summer!"

"If I knew where they were, and what the situation was, I'd be more inclined to agree with you. But what if they're alive now only because they're being kept as a death-sacrifice by Blood Bear or some other tribe like them?" Darian protested.

"That is as may be, but it could as well have happened two years ago as not, or never," Firesong replied blithely. "What needs to be done is for you to balance and measure the likelihood of results with the risks to be taken, with what powers can be brought to bear with the time you have."

Darian looked unhappy with such an objective assessment, but he knew that Firesong was right. What they *did* know was that his father was in passable, maybe excellent health; the first spell had told him that much, and he had to presume that Starfall and Firesong working together had confirmed that. If a man lacking a foot and marooned in the far north was in *any* health after all these years, that argued for his continued survival.

But it was hard, so hard, to simply sit there and discuss logistical possibilities with Firesong, when what he wanted to do was to get a score of *dyheli* volunteers and go north as fast as they could carry him, carrying whatever food and equipment he could gather in a dash through his quarters, trusting that luck and his own magic would give him a direction.

But even at his most optimistic and foolhardy, he knew that such a plan would be ridiculous. Luck only favored those who didn't need it, an old saying went. . . .

Besides, Keisha deserves to hear about this.

That was another consideration altogether. He couldn't just go haring off without telling her.

"Of all the things in the world, I think being patient is the hardest," he moaned, and Firesong nodded.

"I know quite a few people who would agree wholeheartedly with that sentiment," his teacher replied, with true sympathy. "That includes the man I was for the first half of my life. As the Shin'a'in shaman say, though, 'Every scar is a lesson remembered.'" His face wrinkled in pits and creases as he smiled sideways. "I think that while we plan and prepare for what you will do about your parents, you ought to go find something useful that will occupy your mind." He closed the book firmly, caressing its spine before looking to Darian.

"I think you're right," Darian said after a pause, and got to his feet. "Have you any suggestions?"

But when Firesong also rose, a wicked gleam in his eye, Darian knew he had asked the wrong question.

"Of course, my dear student," Firesong said in tones of silk. "After all, just because you've become a Master, that doesn't mean you've stopped needing to learn, does it?"

The next several hours of magical work left him exhausted in mind *and* body; Firesong's idea of something that would "occupy his mind" was a set of exercises that took every iota of his thoughts and left him nothing to devote to his own problems.

He found himself juggling multiple ley-lines, plus Heartstone power, while fending off little stinging "annoyance" attacks from Firesong—and meanwhile he had to accomplish his stated task, which was to create a second outlet for his hot spring, since there was more than enough water flowing from it to supply two sets of hot pools. Ayshen had already voiced a wish for a supply of hot water for the kitchens so that they didn't have to use the smoke-belching wood-fired boiler that everyone considered a dubious compromise; adding blocks of native hickory sweetened the smell but still was not ideal. So, Darian just had to make a channel for the water from his spring. *"Just." Hah!*

What he'd actually had to do was find a series of cracks and weak spots through the bedrock leading to the kitchen, seal them from side pathways, then coax a tendril of the hot spring to take those cracks as he slowly forced open the weak spots, melted and sculpted the stone into a sealed channel, and finally bring the spring out near the boiler itself, so that Ayshen could use the existing boiler as a hot-water storage tank instead.

And meanwhile, hundreds of little wasplike attack "stingers" came at him from every possible direction—any he didn't deflect gave him a sharp reminder of his inadequacy. Twice Firesong even lobbed physical rocks at him, as he had during his Master Trial. He deflected both away—the second one, directly back at his mentor, earning a chuckle from him.

When he was through, Firesong laughed, congratulated him, and sent him back to his own *ekele* to bathe and change again. For a few hours, at least, he had been far too preoccupied to think of his father, but as soon as he set one foot on the path outside the workroom, it began again.

And Mother—how is she? I don't know anything *about her—but if Father survived having his foot taken off, she* had *to have been with him.* He could easily imagine her standing by and guarding him, hunting for both of them until he recovered, taking care of him. They worked together as seamlessly as a hand inside a glove; they'd both been hunters, but had switched to trapping so that they could include Darian in their treks. Trapping was no less work than hunting, but the danger was a bit less, and it had been something that they could all work at together, even when Darian was an infant. A crying baby wasn't much use on a stalk, but didn't make much difference in working a trap-line.

He opted for a quick shower, using a spigot high up on the wall, perforated with many tiny holes. It was his own idea, to have a way to get clean quickly in his own quarters rather than having to head for a hot pool or falls; Keisha liked it for washing her hair. He was just pulling his clean shirt on over his head when he heard hoofbeats coming toward the open front door.

He hurried outside, still barefoot, hoping to be able to catch not only Keisha, but her sister, and possibly Herald Anda as well. He wanted to tell all three of them what he had discovered himself. By now the news had certainly spread all over the Vale, and when any story spread, it tended to get changed, sometimes out of all recognition.

He was in luck; all three of them were together, and he managed to wave Anda and Shandi in before they rode off to the guest lodge. Keisha looked faintly puzzled, but she said nothing.

"Listen, I need to tell all three of you what's just happened," he said when the other two had dismounted. Then when the Companions shook their heads and snorted at him, he quickly revised, "I mean, all *five* of you."

The Companions looked mollified at his acknowledgment and he quickly outlined his search, the results, and the information that had come out of the magical investigation afterward. "And that's all I know," he concluded, looking mostly at Keisha for her reaction. "It's driving me frantic, because there really isn't enough to make a search on—"

"But you *have* to keep working on it!" Keisha exclaimed passionately, interrupting him. "Of course you have to! How can you come so close and just leave it at that? And when you do find out where they are, you've *got* to go looking for them!"

"I wouldn't advise undertaking a full-scale search on so little information," Herald Anda cautioned. This was what Darian had expected out of him, but suddenly Anda dropped his dignity and his caution and burst out with, "But—oh, hang it all! We'll all help you get a better idea of where to look, and the Tayledras and the Northerners, too, no doubt! Surely as many good minds as we have can come up with something!"

Darian stared for a moment, as Shandi nodded energetically. "I absolutely agree," Shandi seconded firmly. "No doubt at all; Karles feels the same. We'll *all* work on this together. It seems to me that with all the best minds of Valdemar *and* the Vales working on it, we'll surely come up with a way to figure out exactly where your parents are, and bring them home again!"

Darian did not know whether to laugh or weep with relief. He'd been sure that Keisha would support him, but he'd been half convinced that the two Heralds would oppose any attempt to find and bring back his parents, since it would mean his absence from Valdemar—and all his duties. "I—all I can say is 'thank you,' and that hardly seems adequate," he managed, after two tries to make words come out had failed.

"Thank us when we've got some results," Anda said simply. "Just know we're not going to oppose you, and we'll help you any way we can, starting by putting our own minds to work on this. Remember, I was trained in a couple of different 'schools' of magic; I might be able to think of something new to you."

He and his Companion exchanged a glance, then he and Shandi traded looks. "We all need some rest, and a chance to think, so we'll see you later," Shandi said by way of farewell, then she and Anda mounted again and rode off toward the guest lodge.

While they had been talking, Keisha had taken a bundle down off her *dyheli,* who then left them to find a *hertasi* to rid him of his tack. Keisha had held it clutched tensely to her chest all the time she'd been listening to Darian, and only now did she remember it. "Havens!" she said, looking down at the bundle in her hands in surprise. "I'd forgotten all about the present I got you! It doesn't seem like much after your news—"

But Darian was deeply touched. "I beg to differ!" he replied. "Thank you for remembering me—I'm hardly as exciting as the potential to see a brand new disease, after all!"

He saw by the gleam in her eye that she understood he was teasing her. "Oh, is that what you think, then? Well you might be right!" she teased back. "Maybe some day I'll leave you for a nice, exciting plague!"

He caught her up in his arms, and felt a new relaxation about her that delighted him. Whatever had caused this change, he hoped it would persist; she hadn't been this easy around him for months. "How about if I give you a fever instead?" he murmured into her ear as he nuzzled her neck.

She turned her head—and bit his ear. Not hard, but it startled him and he let her go. "You'll have to earn it by catching me first," she taunted, and ran into the *ekele.*

He ran after her, and for the next fever-warm candlemark or so, they were too busy with each other to think of anything else.

After a much more pleasant shower-bath, this time shared, and yet another change of clothing, Darian stumbled over Keisha's bundle in the middle of the floor of the outer room. He picked it up, saw to his relief that it was undamaged, and looked for a place to put it down.

"Oh, good, I was afraid we might have trampled that," she

said, emerging from the bedroom and tying her hair back as she walked. "Here, let me."

She held out her hands for it, and he obediently handed the bundle to her.

She sat down and began to unwrap it in her lap—first the outer square of cloth, which he realized had been her scarf. A scarf was something no modern Healer was ever without, since a scarf could be put to so many useful purposes. Inside the scarf was a bundle of soft, dark-brown furs. They looked rather like weasel or muskrat, but were much softer and the fur was more plush.

Keisha put the furs aside, and brought out something made of leather and lined with a coarser fur—she shook it out and held it up to him, beaming. "Yes, that fits—have a look, do you like it?"

He took it from her and turned it around—and almost dropped it, stepping back involuntarily.

He stared, struck dumb, as familiar patterns of embroidery branded themselves on his mind.

Keisha's smile faded and she looked at him with uncertainty. "You—you don't like it—I'll—"

"No, no, no, that's not it—" It couldn't be. It *couldn't* be—it was only a superficial resemblance, surely!

But he put the vest down, and went straight to the storage chest where he kept the few precious relics of his childhood that had pleasant memories attached. He opened it, reached in, and brought out a small, cloth-wrapped package of his own. This he took over to Keisha and opened, laying out the embroidered leather vest that lay inside next to the one she had brought him.

Though the colors of the second vest were faded and stained, the leather worn—though the motifs had been embroidered using wool and flax threads rather than tufts of dyed hair—and though the older vest was barely half the size of the new one—there was no doubt.

In all other ways, they were identical.

They stared at the vests, then into each other's eyes. And finally, Keisha managed to speak.

"Havens!" She exclaimed involuntarily. "They're the same! But how?"

"I don't know, Keisha," Darian breathed. "*Where* did you get this?"

Twelve

"Wait—" Keisha said, feeling that she had to slow all this down, at least a little. Things were happening too fast for her. "This could just be a flower, and flowers are a universal embroidery motif—"

"But it's not a flower," Darian interrupted. "It's a radial repeat of the Trappers' Guild symbol, see?" He blocked off all but one quarter of the spiky circle, and sure enough, Keisha had no trouble in recognizing the stylized trap. "It's Mother's own design, making it repeat like that; I've never seen anyone else use it."

So much for it being an accident or a coincidence, Keisha thought. "Well, I got it from Ghost Cat—*they* got it in trade-goods from one of the tribes that came here looking for Healing."

Darian started to move, and she put out her hand and pushed him back down into his chair. "It will keep for half a day," she told him. "If you wait until tomorrow morning, you'll be able to actually talk with someone; if you go now, you'll only have to wait until morning when everyone wakes up."

"But—" Darian was looking a bit wild-eyed, and she was in complete sympathy.

"I know, you need to do something, and the smartest thing

to do is take these vests to Firesong. Maybe he can make some sense out of them. Then—well, I think we should talk to the Vale Council and see what everyone else says." She was actually grasping at straws, but he nodded, agreeing with her, and she sighed with relief. The last thing she wanted was for him to go running off into the darkness to find a *dyheli* and ride off to the Ghost Cat village. Kuari or no Kuari, the mental state he was in was conducive to mistakes. Suddenly, she had a nightmare vision of Darian, his *dyheli,* or both falling on the night-shrouded trail and breaking a leg.

Or both legs. Or worse.

But at least she had managed to come up with an idea that made *him* feel that he was accomplishing something. She followed him out the door and down the trail as he set off at a lope for Firesong's *ekele,* knowing that it was going to be a very long night.

It turned out to be not quite as long for her; she kept dozing off, first while Darian and Firesong worked over the vests, then later, while Darian and most of the Vale Council of Elders discussed possibilities in endless detail. In fact, the last thing she remembered was half-waking as someone picked her up and laid her on a pile of pillows, covering her with a soft lap-rug.

She woke a second time when Darian shook her; when she raised her head, she saw from the thin light outside that it was dawn. Darian looked tired, but by no means discouraged; in fact, he appeared to be ready to set out for the north on a moment's notice. "Ready to go to Ghost Cat?" he asked, taking it for granted that she would want to be with him.

She caught herself just as she started to feel resentment; there was nothing to feel resentment about! She *didn't* have patients, except the ones at Errold's Grove, and they weren't due to see her for a few days. And he *knew* that; he kept as close an eye on her schedule as he did his own.

"As soon as I change," she agreed, rubbing her eyes and yawning. Then she looked critically at Darian's clothing. "You ought to also," she chided gently. "It won't take more than a moment."

He looked down at his rumpled, stained clothing, and blushed with embarrassment. *He might not be a peacock like*

*Firesong, but at least he isn't as slovenly as a great many men
I've known.*

"You're right, and I will. Firesong once said to me, 'Dress
your best. Heroes in paintings always look terrific, and you
never know when it might be your turn to become a legend.'
Perfect Tayledras reasoning, isn't it? Come on, then," he said,
and offered her his hand.

Before the sun actually crested the horizon, they were in
the saddle and on their way past the Vale entrance—but
Darian looked odd to her when Keisha glanced over at him.
He was preoccupied with something, his forehead creased, his
eyes narrowed as he concentrated. The tension suddenly
around him made her muscles clench.

"What's the matter?" she asked sharply, wondering what
had him so nervey all of a sudden. Both the *dyheli* flicked
their ears back at him; they sensed something strange as well.

"I'm trying to remember something," he murmured, rubbing his temple. "Something about dreams. . . ." His voice had
a distracted tone; whatever the "dream" was, his mood was
odd—as if the dream had overwhelming significance, and he
had to recall it at all costs.

It can't be that—it's just that he's not thinking clearly.

"What, have you been dreaming that the Northern Spirit
Cat has been trying to send you messages?" she asked, trying
to put a chuckle in her voice. She meant it teasingly, to try
and get him out of this mood, but he responded as if he had
just sat down on a tack.

Even his *dyheli* stopped dead, ears flattened, as he jerked
around to stare at her, eyes wide, pupils dilated.

What did I say?

"That's it!" he shouted. "That's it!"

But without bothering to tell her what "it" was, he bent
over the *dyheli's* neck. In response to an unvoiced command,
the young stag launched into a full gallop, and Keisha's followed, leaving her no choice but to stifle her curiosity and
hang on for dear life.

They reached the Ghost Cat village in half the time it
would normally have taken; the *dyheli* staggered into the village on their last bit of energy, and stopped, sides heaving.
Unlike horses, they were in no danger of foundering, or Keisha

would have been more worried about them than she was about Darian. Darian jumped down out of the saddle. As he sprinted for the Shaman's log house, with the bundle containing the new vest clutched in one hand, his *dyheli* began its own slow, careful cool-down. Keisha took her time dismounting, and followed, noting the curious looks that Darian attracted as he ran, a small part of her hoping that he hadn't lost his wits, the rest of her full of a faltering anxiety.

The second surprise of the day came. The Shaman *must* have been expecting Darian, for he flung his door open before Darian even reached it and beckoned him to come inside. And when he looked up and saw Keisha standing beside her *dyheli*, he waved to her as well.

The two men disappeared inside. She entered the door in time to hear Darian say, ". . . so *is* there a Raven clan?"

"I don't know out of my own knowledge, but the meaning of your dream and mine is now clear," Shaman Celin said somberly, and looked down at the vest spread out on the bench between them. "This, however—this comes from Snow Fox tribe. There are still folk from Snow Fox among us, cured, but not strong enough yet to travel, for the cure itself exhausted them. Let us speak with them, and perhaps they can give us the last piece of what we need to know."

Darian was on his feet immediately, so completely focused on the Shaman that Keisha might not even have been there.

And strangely, this didn't trouble her; she was too relieved to discover that, whatever all this was about, Shaman Celin obviously knew all about it as well.

As she trailed along in Darian's wake, she felt a real sense of relief and even anticipation, which completely replaced the anxiety she'd felt on the way here. This was real, something she could deal with, and a perfectly reasonable and understandable obsession; if it had been *her* parents rather than his, she would have been just as focused as he was.

Absolutely. They may drive me crazy, but they're my parents. *I know how he must feel.*

There was a log house in the farthest circle that had no tribal totems ornamenting it; instead, the house was decorated in stylized carvings of *dyheli*. Once again, the "holy *dyheli*" identified those who had come to seek a cure from Ghost Cat and the Sanctuary.

Here they encountered a slight difficulty, for the Snow Fox tribe spoke a different variant of the northern tongue. It took Darian and the Shaman several tries before the most senior of the men left in charge of the invalids understood what they were asking. Keisha couldn't follow him at all; he spoke so much faster than the Ghost Cat folk that he almost seemed to be speaking a different language altogether.

He wasn't all that old either; just out of adolescence, and probably newly come to full Warrior status. He was in charge of a band of young men his own age who had remained behind to guard and protect the three women and gaggle of youngsters who had not been strong enough to travel back to the tribal lands with the rest. The Shaman stood beside Darian as he and the young warrior sat facing each other on a bench just outside the door, with the morning sun full on them.

Keisha stood by and watched, rather than listened, as Darian grew more proficient in the Snow Fox dialect with each passing moment. She suspected from the faint tingling she felt along the surface of her skin that he was using magic to help speed his acquisition of the tongue. The young warrior, biting his lip earnestly, was a bit alarmed.

He must know it's magic—but it isn't dyheli *magic.* And Darian must look completely alien to the young man, with his Tayledras clothing and lighter hair and eyes than the Northerners had.

The Shaman saw this as well, and stopped the conversation to reassure him; after a few words, the youngster became quite charmingly cooperative.

Darian stooped and took a bit of charred stick from the ground to draw a crude map on the bench where they both sat, but the young man shook his head and put his hand over Darian's. Clearly he didn't understand maps; or at least, he wasn't able to translate what he knew to map form.

They do so much by rote— Keisha bit her lip, hoping Darian's memory was up to this.

Darian listened to him with fierce concentration as he described what must have been the journey here, committing every landmark to memory; frowning so, his eyebrows almost meeting in the center of his forehead, that Keisha knew he'd have a headache before this was over.

At last, Darian sat back, his frown fading and being replaced with a smile. He thanked the youngster—*that* much, at least, Keisha understood!—made some polite comments, then he and Celin took their leave.

Darian reached out and took her hand as he passed her, giving it a gentle squeeze. "I'm sorry if I seemed to be ignoring you, *ke'chara*," Darian said apologetically as soon as they were out in the open again. "I—"

"You were trying to get as much information as you could in the shortest possible time," Keisha interrupted, and smiled at his relief. "Havens, did you think I couldn't see that? But you had *better* give me a full explanation later on, and not leave anything out!" She squeezed his hand back, and his smile turned so warm she almost blushed.

"I will, on the way back, I promise." Darian turned then to the Shaman, squinting against the sunlight. "Celin, I can't begin to thank you—"

"Nay, do not thank me. It is the Ghost Cat's doing, and nothing of mine. If *he* wills you to this task, then I do no more than my duty to aid you," the Shaman said solemnly. "And you will be wanting a guide."

Darian was now the one looking surprised at Celin's words.

Celin laughed. "What, did I not tell you this was the Ghost Cat's will? You *shall* go northward into the white; this, he has told me. You will need one of us to guide you. I have thought upon it, and I believe your guide should be Hywel. In doing this, you will permit him to discharge his life-debt to you."

Darian and Keisha both knew better than to argue with the Shaman when he used *that* phrase. A life-debt was a serious thing among the northerners, and it was not something that any northerner wanted hanging over his head. By Keisha and Darian being instrumental in saving Hywel's brother, Hywel had incurred a life-debt to them both that would hold him back, socially and personally, in many ways until he repaid it. He could not marry, could not even court a young woman, and could not incur any other major responsibilities until this one was discharged.

Besides, Hywel would have been *her* first choice as a guide. He might be young, but he was sharp, intelligent, and observant.

"What you have done for us would oblige us even to your whims. This is more than a whim you have conjured as a game. It is a personal imperative. You go now to the Vale, and make your plans," Celin continued. "I will see to Hywel and Hywel's mother, making her easy with the journey her son must take with you."

Darian sighed, and accepted the Shaman's words without any argument, since it was obvious that Celin had made up his mind about all this.

Or the Ghost Cat made it up for him.

"We'll head back, then—we've borrowed two more *dyheli*. I don't want to impose on the two we rode on before; they practically broke their necks to get us here quickly." He must have already asked the *dyheli*, for two volunteers had joined up with the two cooling down, waiting for someone to come take the tack off the first two and put it on them.

"Go, go, go!" the Shaman said, making shooing motions at them. "Send one of the holy ones to come for Hywel when you are ready."

There didn't seem to be anything else for them at that point but to take the saddles from the backs of their weary original mounts and transfer them to their new volunteers.

They were out of sight of the Ghost Cat village before Darian took a deep breath, shook himself out of his reverie, and turned to find her staring at him expectantly. "I definitely owe you an explanation," he began sheepishly.

"Definitely," she replied, with just a touch of acid—enough to let him know that she was more than tired of waiting. "I have been *incredibly* patient, understanding, noble, forbearing—"

"Enough, I get the idea!" he cried, holding up his hands as if to fend her off. "I guess the place to start is— I've been having these dreams, except I couldn't remember them afterward."

"I know." When he looked at her oddly, she added, "It was like sleeping with a kicking *dyheli* fawn. Or rather, *trying* to sleep."

He blushed. "Anyway," he continued valiantly, "When you said something about the 'Spirit Cat' talking to me, I remembered suddenly what those dreams were about." He shook his head ruefully. "I don't know why I couldn't remember before."

"Maybe you were afraid," she said slowly, remembering the

aura of fear that had hung over him during those dreams. It had been the fear, and not the restlessness, that had awakened her.

He looked very thoughtful. "Maybe. Especially since I didn't have any notion that they were supposed to help me. They were *weird* through and through." He shrugged. "The point is, they all involved the Ghost Cat *and* a different totem, an enormous Raven. Not only that, but the day I was made a Clanbrother, the Ghost Cat appeared at the ceremony and left a raven feather at my place. Nobody seemed to have an explanation, and no one thought it was a bad omen, so I just dismissed it in favor of everything else that had to be done."

"Until I triggered your memory." Now she understood why he'd acted as if she had jabbed him.

"I just had this inspiration—no, that's too mild. I suddenly *knew* that the Ghost Cat was trying to tell me something— that I needed to find the Raven tribe, so that was why I wanted to see Celin—"

"Because you wanted to find out if there *is* a Raven tribe." She nodded slowly, as all of the pieces began to fit together for her. "And he didn't know for sure, but the vests came from Snow Fox, so he figured the Snow Fox people *would* know. I take it that there is?"

"Yes, and here's the best part. They make the vests as trade goods, usually to order, with someone's own totems on them. But sometimes they make the ones like *I* got—and what's more, they only started making them a few years ago." He looked at her in triumph, and she felt her eyes widen.

"So we're going?" she asked, feeling breathless all at once. *If he goes, I go. I have to. Is this one of those compromises? Maybe—if so, it's one I know I* have *to make.*

"We? You want to go?" He looked at her with doubt and hope mingled in his glance. "I thought—"

"I can turn Errold's Grove over to the oldest of the Sanctuary Trainees; they're about to make him a full Healer anyway," she said resolutely, a thrill of pleasure running through her at his reaction. *Yes. This is a compromise I have to make.* "You don't think I'd let you go traipsing off into the howling wilderness on your own, do you? You might get hurt, and then how would we both feel?"

* * *

Armed with this new information, Darian asked for an informal meeting of all of those who might be at all concerned with his proposed expedition. Shandi and Anda invited themselves to the meeting; he was pleased, but not surprised, given their earlier positive reactions.

He asked Tyrsell, because he would *have* to have *dyheli* if he expected to get from here to who-knew-how-far north in any reasonable length of time. The Elders of the Council were obviously concerned, given that *he* was supposed to become an Elder himself eventually. Shaman Celin and Hywel both arrived when he sent a polite invitation by *dyheli*. Hashi came because he wanted to, and Kel came because Kel wanted to know everything that was going on. Ayshen was there because he would have to see that the expedition was properly provisioned. Wintersky because his friend already knew what was planned, and had no intention of being left out.

There was an addition who was entirely unexpected: Steelmind. Why the plant expert would care where he went and what he did, he wasn't certain, but Steelmind and his buzzard were both in attendance.

He finished his summation of everything he had learned, and looked around the table. "I want to go north to find them," he said. "I know that's obvious; it should also be obvious that I can't do this alone. Shaman Celin and Hywel both think that Hywel should go as my guide, and I agree. Also, Keisha wants to go. *I* want to leave now; I want to get there and back before winter, and winter probably comes earlier there than here. So—" He spread his hands. "Are you going to let me go—and have you any ideas of your own?"

Firesong burst into laughter, as Snowfire grinned and Nightwind cast her eyes upward. "Do you *really* think we could stop you?" Nightwind demanded. "Whether we like it or not, this is something that's too important to you. You'd claw your way through a mountain if it stood between you and your parents, now that you know at least one may be alive."

"You might have some really pressing reason why I shouldn't go, and I *am* supposed to be the Valdemaran representative here," Darian pointed out mildly. "I wouldn't like it—"

"Be truthful, you'd be miserable and angry," Nightwind interrupted. "So the best thing we can do is not only agree, but give you everything you need to get you there and back safely. Which is—what?"

"Me," Kel interjected eagerly. "I am a forrrmidable foe. I am an outssstanding ssscout. You need me. I am *fierrrce*. I will frrrighten enemiesss jussst by being therrre!"

Kel seemed to take a great delight in being *fierce*. He was doing his best to look the part, too; head up, eyes bright with a predatory gleam, beak slightly agape, talons slightly flexed.

"Agreed," Starfall said immediately, to the delight of both Darian and Kel. "Since Keisha is going along, she can serve as Kel's *trondi'irn*. Keisha, Nightwind can show you how, enough anyway to handle most problems. You'll all be immensely safer with Kel along. What next?"

:I believe I should accompany him,: Hashi offered diffidently. *:You know that what Kel cannot see or scent on the ground, I can. I can work well with Kuari after dark. I am eager to have this saga at first hand. I am not vital to this Vale; there are others who can serve as the* kyree *representative as well as I. The fact that I have remained so is mostly habit on our part.:*

"Any objections?" Starfall looked around the table, and saw none. "So far we have Darian, Kel, Keisha, Hashi, and Hywel. Tyrsell, I take it that you can supply as many restless young stags as need be?"

:Hah. I would have difficulty holding them back. This will be a high-status expedition for our eager young stags. The young does will be greatly impressed.: Tyrsell's dry amusement at the expense of his younger counterparts had them all chuckling.

But Tyrsell hasn't had to exert himself to impress does in a very long time, Darian reminded himself, with rising sympathy for those "eager young stags." The only way a young stag became a father and potential harem leader was to do something impressive.

"Do you have to ask?" Wintersky said. "I'm going, of course. It's too dull around here. If I spend another summer shooing those Northern pilgrims onto the right trail, I'll go mad. I swear I will."

Starfall laughed at him. "All right, all right. I *think* you can be spared! That's Darian, Keisha, Kel, Hashi, Wintersky, and a herd. Who else should we ask to volunteer?"

"No *hertasi*," Ayshen said reluctantly. "It is very cold in the north, even in the summer."

"Not that cold!" the Shaman protested. "You speak as if there is snow upon the ground *everywhere* at midsummer!"

But Starfall shook his head. "No, I agree. This is not like our foray into Valdemar, where the *hertasi* were protected and we were in no great hurry to cover ground. This expedition will move too quickly, and have too many risks for any *hertasi* to go along safely. Ayshen, your people are fine fighters, but only in large numbers, and what's the point of asking for fifty *hertasi* to go and be chilled solid up North, when they're needed more in the warm Vale?"

"No argument here," Darian agreed, nodding. "Ayshen, I agree with you completely, even if it does mean I have to eat my own cooking."

That brought a laugh as he had hoped, and the talk turned to provisioning for a little while, until Shandi cleared her throat. That brought silence, and all eyes turned toward her.

She flushed a little but said into the quiet, "Karles and I want to go along. Actually, Karles and I think we *need* to go along."

Now *that* was a surprise! Of all of them, only Steelmind nodded, as if he had guessed as much.

"Anda and I talked this over very seriously before Darian went to the village, and spoke to the Snow Fox people," she continued. "Anda would like us to see what conditions are like up there. It is not intended as a slight to any of you, of any species, but depending upon what was encountered it could be very advantageous to have an official Valdemaran presence there. No offense meant, Shaman Celin, but we need to know if there are any more—" She paused to pick out the least offensive words. "Any more aggressive peoples, like the Blood Bear tribe."

"You need to know? You are not the only ones!" the Shaman replied. "We stand between you and any armies, recollect! And we have pledged to guard this place, have we not?"

"Well, there you have it." Shandi shrugged. "Karles and I put our necks into this, too, then."

Anda traded a look with her, then spoke to the rest. "This

is something that is very important to us. I would have hesitated to send her and Karles alone, but this is going to be a
group that is large enough—not to protect her, but that she
can work with."

This was not the first time that Darian had gotten the feeling there was a great deal going on between the two Heralds
that was not spoken aloud. There was an entire conversation
taking place—probably in personal Mindspeech—that no one
else was privy to.

"My Gift of Empathy can be pretty useful in figuring out if
someone is telling the truth without having to use a *vrondi*-
based Truth Spell, you know," Shandi pointed out. "And I
probably know as much about rough camping as any of you.
And I can do one thing that none of you can. Through Karles,
I can keep in touch with Anda and the Vale."

Darian raised an eyebrow at that, but said nothing; he could
read between the lines easily enough. Valdemar and the
Hawkbrothers were friends and allies, but . . . it was always
better to have a pair of your *own* eyes along.

He couldn't find it in his heart to feel resentful either; he'd
have felt the same if the shoe had been on the other foot.

*In fact, I don't think any of us here at the Vale would want
a set of Heraldic spies going up there without one of us along.
After all, we're the ones who'd be getting the arrows and
spears in our teeth first.*

But the greatest surprise of all was that Steelmind then said,
"And I would go, too, if you will have me."

From the startled look that Shandi threw at him, this was
a complete surprise to her as well as everybody else—except
possibly Silverfox. "Why?" was the question on the tip of
everyone's tongue, Darian suspected, but no one asked it, in
part because it was, frankly, no one's business but Steelmind's. "We can certainly use you," Darian said gratefully,
and left it at that.

*We-ell! There must be a great deal more going on there
than I had thought! And Steelmind's decision to come took
Shandi by surprise, too! I wonder why—unless it's that she's
closing off that Empathy of hers when it comes to Steelmind
. . . maybe because she didn't want to know what he was
feeling!*

Hywel and Celin had gotten their heads together and now

Celin said, "We two believe that it would be well if you went as traders. Traders have some protection among our people, more than any other outsiders; they tend to be left alone by all except wolf-heads and outlaws, for if the traders were molested, who would bring new goods in the coming year, or pretty things for our women?" He chuckled. "I tell you, our women would take our scalps for that, if the traders were frightened off!"

Darian didn't much like the idea of posing as traders. He didn't want to end up weighed down by a lot of clattering goods, and he *certainly* didn't want to be a target for outlaws because of those same clattering goods!

"Could we trade in dyes?" Keisha asked instantly. "I know your women really like the ones I have."

Oh, good thought, ke'chara! *Dyes are light, and a little goes a long way! We'd have a reason for not carrying much baggage!* He had not liked the idea of being loaded down with pure mass to maintain the ruse, or perhaps even being forced to bring a wagon for trade goods.

"Dyes would be good," the Shaman ruminated. "I tell you what you may ask for. Earth-amber, gold, and carved ivory. Dyes are valuable; we weigh them out, weight for weight, with such treasure. Those things will not weigh you down; you will look like proper traders, but wise ones, who are willing to move quickly and venture much for much gain."

Darian privately had decided that if anything threatened to weigh them down, he would discard it without a moment of hesitation. This was *not* a real trading expedition, and he had no intention of looking for a profit.

With that decided, the planning began in earnest.

When they finally returned to the *ekele,* very late that night, Keisha looked around with a sigh. "If I'd had any idea what this expedition was going to be like—" she began.

"You'd have volunteered to come along anyway," Darian replied confidently. He was already selecting clothing for the journey—and curiously, the first thing he picked was his Ghost Cat outfit.

Perhaps I'd better take mine, too.

"I don't know about that," Keisha muttered, but mostly to herself. It hadn't occurred to her that she was going to be camping rough when she volunteered. She'd scarcely been camping at all, and when she did go, it was with full amenities; tents, cook-stoves, plenty of food, and lots of *hertasi* to help out.

But there weren't going to be any comforts on this trip; no tents, no cook-stoves, and they'd eat mostly what they killed or found for themselves.

Thank goodness for Steelmind. He'll be able to tell what's good and what's not without our having to experiment with it. An all-meat diet would be very bad—though I doubt Kelvren would agree.

They'd be cooking over the fire, without pots for the most part. They'd be sleeping in hammocks, sometimes strung high in the trees for safety. If it rained, they'd each have a rain cape to drape over themselves and their hammock—or they *might* put up a lean-to, if they had time.

It could be worse. We could be sleeping on the ground, I suppose.

True, there wasn't much danger of anyone becoming sick, not with her along, and one thing was certain, she *wasn't* going to scrimp on her medicines. Darian could always use magic to keep them warm, if he had to, and maybe even sheltered from the weather.

Still.

"Heyla, you'll enjoy it," Darian said, putting his arms around her, as if he had been reading her thoughts. He probably didn't have to; her thoughts were written clearly enough on her face. "I know it's not what you're used to, but camping this way can be a lot of fun. You miss sleeping out under the stars when you're in a tent, and you miss waking up to the dawn."

"Insect repellent," she muttered absently, thinking about the black flies and nocturnal mosquitoes that Hywel had described. "I'd better come up with an insect repellent we can wear. There's a camphor balm I can mix up."

"Exactly. It's not as if we aren't clever enough to improvise, or as if we haven't done this before. You're the only one of us who's never camped this way." He turned her around and gave her a winning smile; a little reluctantly, she responded.

"I'll try not to be a burden on the rest of you," she told him, looking up into his eyes. "That's the part I'm really afraid of—

that after a week you'll wish I'd never come along, and after two, you'd wish you'd never met me."

There it was, out in the open. The confession had slipped out before she could stop herself. She pushed away from him, as he considered her words.

"You might say the same thing about me," he finally answered. "When it's cold and raining, and we haven't had any luck hunting, or when we're trying to sleep knowing that there's something prowling around at the foot of our tree, just waiting for a rope to snap or a limb to break. Or when I order you around—you might wish me on the other side of the world."

"I might," she agreed. She'd meant it to sound teasing; it came out as a bit waspish.

"So we're even." He didn't pay any attention to her sharp tone; he just grinned and shrugged. "We'll deal with it when it happens. In the meantime, we've other things to think about. *What* is going on with Steelmind?"

That's certainly changing the subject! "Why are you asking me? I don't have any more clues than you do." she replied, making no effort to conceal her own confusion. "I suppose it might have something to do with Shandi, but you know that he's far too steady to be doing this on a whim, or half-heartedly. Does it matter why he's coming?"

"Actually—no." He looked down into her eyes. "As long as I know why you are."

Once again, words came from her mouth that she hadn't intended to say. "For you," she whispered. "Just—for you."

It seemed to be the right thing to say.

Thirteen

Keisha fingered the talisman at her throat and stared at the mountains before her in disbelief, drawing comfort from the little clay owl figure on her necklace. Since Owl Knight Darian's induction into the clan, the Elder Women had been making the talismans along with their *dyheli* figurines. Each of them in the traveling group had one of the clan's talismans—given to them by Shaman Celin before they left, strung on sliding thongs in the Northern fashion. Hywel's featured cat claws, understandably enough; both Keisha and Darian had little handmade owl figurines and semiprecious stone beads on theirs. Hers featured the color green in its beads as a reminder of her status as a Healer. Shandi's had an odd sort of charm—a Tayledras-made chiming ball, enameled with a white horse. Steelmind's was a silver hawk on a crystal arrowhead shape. Wintersky's was a pair of hawk talons in stone, with a stone knot between them.

These talisman necklaces were meant to identify them to other northerners as friends to at least one of the tribes. Celin and Vordon had advised them not to wear their Ghost Cat costumes, at least not at first; the relationships among the tribes were complicated, and it was better to be thought of as traders and healers first, and allies of a particular clan second.

They were now altogether out of familiar territory; for the

past several days they had been taking a barely discernible track through hills that had been plenty tall enough for Keisha, but today they had come up over a particularly lofty range to see the *real* mountains.

Keisha could only sit slackly in her saddle and stare. Between the top of the hill where they were and the beginning of the mountain range was a wide river valley, a meandering river running through it that they would have to ford.

"Is there *snow* on the tops of those?" she asked Hywel incredulously, pointing to the white-dusted peaks looming against the blue sky.

"Probably," he replied, shrugging his indifference. "It doesn't matter; we won't be going up that high." The young tribesman was in his element now. So far as he was concerned, this trip was the height of pure pleasure. Not that he disliked living on the border of Valdemar, but here he was, ranging and hunting rather than staying in one place and herding, and doing it all by *dyheli* instead of his own two feet. This was a much superior form of travel, and Hywel very much enjoyed the experience.

Keisha had mixed feelings; she was finding more pleasure in this form of travel than she had expected, but that was leavened by the fact that she seemed so much clumsier at rough-camping than anyone else. Steelmind, Darian, and Wintersky were already part of a functioning "team." They had worked and traveled together for four years before Keisha had ever met them. That left Keisha, Shandi, and Hywel to fit themselves into the pattern somehow.

Hywel had insinuated himself into the working trio within a day; his role was clear cut, after all. He was the guide. Between everything that he had absorbed from his elders and the Snow Fox folk, and his own memories, he had a fair idea of where he was going. Between Hywel and the sole *dyheli* doe that had come as Tyrsell's representative—who served as their scout—they had clear courses marked out for them every day.

Shandi had learned the essentials of camping all through her two years at the Collegium, by going out with Anda on a regular basis with little more than a bow and arrows, a fire-starter, and a few essentials in a saddlebag. Within three days, Shandi also had fit herself into the regular rhythm of things.

It was Keisha who had remained out of step for the longest,

much to her chagrin. It took her a couple of days to get the hang of putting up her hammock so that it didn't fold her in half, nor slip down on one side or the other. She'd never cooked over an open fire before, so she watched, feeling useless, as Shandi and Steelmind made meals. About the only things she could do competently were to fetch wood and water.

At least I'm good at fetching wood and water—and Steelmind can cook.

The others were already starting down into the river valley below; Keisha's *dyheli* took it upon himself to follow. She stared at the mountains with the same fascination that she usually reserved for poisonous snakes. Beautiful, yes, but—

How far are we going to have to climb into those peaks? She'd heard all sorts of horrible stories about mountains— trails that ran out, leaving you on a tiny ledge too small to stand on properly, avalanches that swept down in white roaring walls of death, storms that came up out of nowhere, air too thin to breathe, and the dreaded "mountain sickness." The latter wasn't an illness as such; it was caused by the thin air; the symptoms ranged from simple shortness of breath to vomiting and delirium. . . .

And the only way to cure it is to get off the mountain, which could be a bit hard to do if you're vomiting and delirious.

Nevertheless, that was where they were going, and she had volunteered to go.

The river valley was pleasant enough at least, and they couldn't get farther than the very foot of the first mountain before nightfall. "Hywel, aren't there any northern tribes around here?" she called to the front of the group. "This place looks deserted."

"Oh, yes. This is part of Gray Wolf territory," he said cheerfully. "They are usually farther upriver this time of year; I do not know if we will see them. They do not herd at all; they hunt and plant some."

They had encountered two tribes thus far; Black Bear (not to be confused with Blood Bear) and Magpie. The latter, allied with Ghost Cat in the past, had welcomed them with great enthusiasm for the dyes that Keisha had brought with them. The northerners, like the southern Shin'a'in, had apparently never seen a color they didn't love, and combined colors in ways that made Keisha's eyes water.

Black Bear, however, had been wary and careful; the travelers saw only their warriors, and never had been invited to the camp. Keisha had asked about their Shaman and Healing Woman, and had been greeted with blank stares and no information. Still, Black Bear had not been actively hostile—or else they hadn't wanted to take on a formidable enigma like Kel—and had let them pass.

Kel was up above now. Hashi and the *dyheli* doe Neta were somewhere ahead, acting as advance scouts. Neta was years past the age of breeding, but was just as agile as a doe half her age. More to the point, she was wary, clever, and experienced. The young stags were half afraid of her, since she had acted as a disciplinarian to each of them at some point in his life. Keisha was very glad to have her with them.

As her mount Malcam began picking his way down the hillside, Keisha scanned the valley below. There were no thin streams of smoke from possible campfires, nothing moving through the small clearings among the trees, nor along the banks of the river.

The air was so clear that everything stood out in sharp detail, and the scents were more like those of early spring than of early summer.

"We'll camp early, on this side of the river," Hywel called back over his shoulder, then urged his mount on ahead to pick out a good campsite.

Good! Steelmind and I can look for edible plants while a couple of the others hunt. Now that she'd gotten the hang of things, she'd be able to help with setting up camp, too.

In next to no time, they were under the trees again, and the branches cut off all sight of those intimidating mountains looming over them. The *dyheli* continued to pick their way down the slope in single file, with Steelmind taking rearguard just behind Keisha. There was no discernible track, but the rocky slope didn't support much underbrush, so the way was clear between the trees.

It was a lot farther to the river than it had looked from the top of the hill; they were still making their way toward the river long past the time Keisha would have figured that they would have already been in camp.

They heard the water long before they saw it; a deep rumble that alarmed Keisha, though she saw no signs of worry in any of the others. When they finally came out into the sunlight, just on the riverbank, she saw why.

To her right, on the downstream side, a smooth and silky expanse of broad water passed into a much narrower and rockier channel. Instead of rolling placidly along, the river leaped over boulders the size of a house and roared along a series of descending cascades.

Yet to her left, there could have been nothing more peaceful. The channel was three times the size of the one to the right; the water was placid and relatively slow-moving. It should be no great problem to ford or even swim it.

Darian and his mount had already turned to the left; Shandi and Karles followed. There was no sign of Hywel, who must have gone ahead to a campsite upriver.

He had, and it took several more furlongs of moving westward before they caught up with him. Hashi, Kel, and Neta were with him, acting as perimeter guards while he made some of the initial preparations for the camp. The rapids were no more than a far-off rumble, not disturbing, but the noise might cloak the sounds of anyone or anything approaching.

Keisha dismounted, pulled off her *dyheli's* saddle, and set to work. Her job was to make a fire pit while Darian and Hywel went in one direction to hunt, Kel took to the air to find prey for himself, Steelmind to the woods to find edible plants, and Wintersky took fishing tackle to the river. That left Keisha to take care of fire and water duties, and Shandi to get out all their camping gear and decide how she was going to prepare camp for this night's terrain.

By the time the hunters, fisher, and gatherer had returned with their bounty (or lack of it), Shandi and Keisha had the camp set up and the fire ready.

By sundown, everyone had been fed except for the *dyheli*, who would graze on-and-off all night. Tonight they had eaten better than usual, since Wintersky had successfully hooked and netted a nice lot of fish. The ones that hadn't been eaten yet were smoking over the fire, along with strips of meat from the small rabbitlike animals that Hywel and Darian had killed. That would give them tomorrow's breakfast and lunch—that, and whatever else Steelmind gathered in the morning.

Tonight, with one side guarded for them by the river, Shandi had strung the hammocks at ground level and downwind of the fire where the smoke would drive away blackflies and other biting insects. Keisha brought in a last armload of wood before darkness closed in completely, and she and Darian set themselves up for the first watch of the night. Hywel and Wintersky took the second, and Shandi and Steelmind the third. The arrangement suited everyone well except Wintersky's bird, and that hardly mattered, since the handsome falcon was ideally suited for daylight scouting.

While everyone else went straight to their hammocks, Keisha carefully turned the strips of meat and fish fillets to make sure they cured evenly, and Darian made the first of his many rounds of the periphery with Kuari. When he returned, Keisha made a space for him on the pile of leaves she was sitting on—leaves that would eventually end up on the fire to make more smoke.

"Is there a ford, or are we going to have to swim tomorrow?" she asked, as he put his arm around her and held her close. It might not have been a very romantic question, but he didn't seem to mind that.

"There's a ford—Ghost Cat used it coming here," he told her. "Hywel doesn't think the water is much higher than it was then. It is bound to be *some* higher, since they came through in summer, not spring, and there's still snowmelt coming down off the mountains."

"I know about the snowmelt," she replied, with a wry smile. "I gave up on the idea of a bath the moment I dipped out the first bucket of water. It feels cold enough to have been solid ice a candlemark before I dipped it out!"

"That's why we're crossing in the morning—it'll give us the full sun to dry out in once we're across." Darian looked toward the water, and Keisha knew he had planned every moment of the crossing and just beyond. "Then we spend a full day hunting and fishing."

"*Oh?*" She craned her neck around to look him in the face. "Why?"

"Because when we reach the mountains, there won't be

much worth hunting," he said. "At least, that's what Hywel says. There's supposed to be a big pass going right through the range, but Hywel never went through there; Ghost Cat's traditional territory is in the mountains, but east of here on the other side of the river. We need to go west, though. Once we get across and into that pass we'll be following Snow Fox directions."

"Hmm." She put her head on his shoulder and tried to listen for noises beyond the distant thunder of water. "Well, we knew that was going to happen at some point."

He didn't seem at all tense or worried, so she made up her mind not to worry either. *How much farther do we have to go?* she wondered. All that she knew for certain was that the Raven tribe was said to be living near or on a large body of water, but also in the mountains. *I suppose it could be both,* she decided, and got up to put more green wood and leaves on the fire.

They spent the rest of their watch making rounds and tending to the smoked meat, then took to their hammocks when Wintersky and Hywel awoke to take over. And yet, in spite of that (or was it because of that?) she felt more relaxed and at ease with Darian than she ever had before.

Their hammocks were strung within easy touching distance, though not so closely that they would bump into each other, and they twined the fingers of one hand together every night before they dozed off. That little ritual had come about entirely by accident, but they'd fallen asleep that way every night since.

And she fell asleep tonight the same way, taking and giving comfort with that simple, wholly natural connection.

"Well, this is deeper today," Hywel said dubiously, eying the fording place. "We should have crossed yesterday; something must have happened up in the mountains. A storm, maybe, or massive snowmelt."

Hywel was right; the water was higher by a significant amount, and faster, too. It licked at the rocks just beneath his feet now; if he stepped down to the point where yesterday's waterline had been, he'd be knee-deep in the torrent. "Too late now; let's just swim and have done with it," Darian replied with a shrug. "It's not that wide; we're in good shape. We can get across."

"No, but the current is swifter than yesterday," Hywel pointed out. He peered upstream. "Look there. If we're going to swim anyway, let's pick where we want to come ashore, then go upstream from there and cross diagonally. That way we won't have to fight the current as much."

Darian nodded, and sent Kuari up into the air ahead of them. The owl often got a better vantage from above than they had. Looking through Kuari's eyes, he examined the riverbank on the other side. Kuari perched in a tree just above the ford, and looked down at the riverbank. Water swirled treacherously among rocks, creating turbulent eddies and vortices.

"I don't much like the look of the ford," he said. "Now that the water's high, there's a nasty current right there at the bank, and a lot of rocks for hooves to get caught between. But—" This time he asked Kuari to land right on the bank, as he spotted a much better candidate for a landing point. "Look where Kuari is—we've got a nice, shallow slope going up to the shore and no loose rocks—yesterday that was a stone shelf leading down to the water."

"There's quite a drop-off at the end of that shelf, but that won't matter since we're swimming anyway." Hywel considered what he could see of the bank from here. "All right; that's probably the best we're going to get. Let's go upstream and see what we can find for a starting point."

They checked spot after spot; they had Kuari drop chips of wood into the river at various points to gauge the current. It took the better part of a candlemark to find what they were looking for, which was another shelf to allow them to walk into the river, but by midmorning everyone was ready to make the crossing.

Half the *dyheli* would carry baggage only. The other half, and Karles, had handhold-straps fastened to either side of their saddles. Like it or not, the larger creatures were better equipped to make the crossing, and the humans would have to take advantage of that.

Those carrying the baggage went over first, and Darian ran downstream as they were carried by the current, anxious to see them safely on the other side. He was just as anxious to see how their initial guesses panned out.

Not well. He knew that as soon the *dyheli* were halfway across. They fought the current every bit of the way, necks stretched out, eyes fixed on the farther shore, legs pumping, nostrils flaring as they panted—and they were the strongest of the mounts. One by one, they clambered ashore, where they stood with heads hanging and sides heaving. They had barely made it to the assigned landing spot; if any of them had been any weaker, he could have gotten swept along to a point where there were no more places to climb out. And after that came the rapids, which were certainly much worse by now.

Darian came back to the group on the shore, and looked from Steelmind to Hywel and back. "What do you think?" he asked them; Shandi had already disavowed any experience in these matters, as had Wintersky.

"We can't rely on the *dyheli* to help us; they're going to have enough to do to get themselves across." Steelmind spoke first, and Hywel nodded.

"I think we can get across all right anyway. We're all strong swimmers." Hywel didn't sound as certain as Darian would have liked, though.

:I can help.:

It was a mind-voice, but it wasn't any of the *dyheli*, nor was it Hashi.

As one, they all turned incredulously toward Karles, who bowed his head and pawed the ground. *:I can stay downstream; if anyone begins losing ground to the river, I can come to help him.:*

Darian and Keisha, alone of all of them, knew how astonishing it was that Karles should begin talking to *everyone.* Darian decided not to make an issue of it; if Karles continued to speak to the rest of the group, all well and good. Maybe he had decided to take his cue from Neta and Hashi.

"I can tow frrrom the airrr," Kel pointed out. "I can have a rrrope rrready to drrrop to anyone who needsss help."

But that gave Darian an idea. "We can put up a catch-rope across the river at the crossing point; if the water carries any of us off, we can save ourselves with that. Karles and Kel can stand by in case that's not enough. That's three kinds of rescue, and that ought to be safeguards enough."

It would have to be enough; there was no one to help them here except the members of their own party. Three tries or a freezing, sure death in fast water that would batter them against the rocks, and still they were willing to see Darian through on his quest.

That seemed the best plan; with Kel's help, they strung a rope across the river from bank to bank. The unladen *dyheli* went over first, with Hashi paddling madly beside them. Then Karles, who had no difficulty getting across, unlike the *dyheli*. It occurred to Darian at that point that the Companion's strength must be enormous; he already knew that Karles' stamina was incredible, but his strength must have been incredibly greater than a horse for him to get across with such ease. Then, one by one, the humans crossed.

Steelmind—oldest, tallest, and strongest—went first, and instead of using the rock shelf, he dove directly into the water a little farther upstream beyond the shelf. If *he* had trouble, they were going to have to rethink their plan.

Like the *dyheli*, Steelmind labored every bit of the way, but did make landfall at the proper place. Without a pause, once he waved from the bank, Wintersky followed him from the same point that he had used. Meanwhile Steelmind gathered tinder, partly for a quick warming-fire on the other side, and partly so the activity would generate more body heat.

The two girls went next, one at a time; Keisha, who had been swimming every day in the Vale lake, just barely made the landing spot. Shandi overshot and had to catch herself on the rope lest she go farther downstream. Steelmind and Karles both waded in to help her over the last bit.

Hywel and Darian went in together; Hywel was not the swimmer that Darian was, and Darian wanted to pace him, just in case. Due to the life-debt, or perhaps friendship alone, Hywel did not want to be away from Darian.

The river was *unbelievably* cold.

Darian gasped as he hit the water, shocked by the temperature. He rose spluttering to the surface, and struck out for the shore, but the shock had driven most of the air from his lungs, and he had to fight to get another full breath. Darian realized that it was the life-sapping cold that they had not figured into their calculations. In no time he was numb and shivering uncontrollably; it was hard to get air as the muscles of his chest clenched from the cold.

He was too busy watching out for Hywel, swimming and

fighting for air to think; the swim was a nightmarish experience that required every fragment of his attention. His focus
was split between Hywel thrashing along beside him and his
own next breath, the next stroke of his arms, and kick of his
legs.

Then he was on the other side; Steelmind and Keisha
hauled him out onto the sloping shelf of stone. Beside him,
Shandi and Wintersky pulled out Hywel. They both staggered to the land, and dropped to the ground, shivering and
coughing.

But as soon as Darian could manage to *think*, despite gasping like a stunned fish, he seized the nearest ley-line and used
the magic—unshielded—to create heat. Without the shielding, the spell created more heat. The *dyheli* crowded close,
steam rising from their coats, and the humans relaxed and
stopped shivering. Hashi moved out of the way and shook
himself vigorously, then trotted back into the zone of warmth.
The heat made an enormous difference; as it soaked into
them, and they stopped shivering, it was easier to catch their
breaths, easier to regain lost strength. Steelmind returned
with an armful of driftwood and twigs, quirked a smile as he
realized what they were doing, then dropped the bundle in
place to join the group.

It was while they were still drying off that Kuari hooted a
warning from somewhere out of sight. Darian's head snapped
up, and the *dyheli* snorted in alarm.

:Men coming!: he told Darian. :With bows!:

They all scrambled to their feet; Darian dismissed the spell
and readied a trip-up, a variation on the first bit of magic he'd
ever used in combat, to make people's feet stick to the ground
just long enough to trip them. With their backs to the river,
they waited for the strangers to approach—weapons to hand,
but not at the ready. *Would* they approach, or would they slip
up to the newcomers to their land? And if they did, would it
be with intent to examine, or to ambush?

The warriors must have realized immediately that the
strangers had been alerted to their presence, for they did not
even try to approach unnoticed. They came openly, but very,
very silently—by Northern standards.

Not by Tayledras standards. Darian, Steelmind, and Wintersky heard them long before they appeared among the trees;

the crinkle of dead leaves, and the sharp snap of a twig betrayed them. The *dyheli* snapped their ears forward at each sound until the Northerners emerged from the forest, then they parted to show Kelvren lying at his ease in their midst.

The Northerners froze in mid-step, one by one, as soon as they saw the gryphon. They were clearly taken aback to see what to them must seem a monster lying like a pet dog beside the strangers.

Before anyone could move or speak, Hywel suddenly brightened and stepped forward. "Hiyo! Warriors of Gray Wolf, I greet you!" he said cheerfully. "I am Hywel, a warrior of Ghost Cat, and these are my friends, come to trade!"

That made all the difference. Some of the tension ebbed out of the group, and one of the warriors stepped forward.

"What, then, is—that?" asked the warrior, who boasted a headpiece made of a wolf's mask, with the rest of the fur serving as a cloak. He pointed to Kel, who stood up—slowly.

"I am Kelvrrren, a warrriorrr of the tribe of Sssilverrr Grrryphon; we arrre allied with Ghost Cat," Kel said genially, and cupped his wings. The warrior of Gray Wolf looked dubious, but wasn't inclined to dispute the word of anything as large and dangerous-looking as the gryphon.

Finally, though, the Gray Wolf fighters came forward. Although the Gray Wolf tribesmen still walked carefully around Kel, giving him wary glances, it appeared that they were ready to give conditional welcome to everyone.

"What have you to trade?" asked one, looking at their saddlebags curiously.

"Dye," said Hywel, and grinned. "Your women will bedeck you in colors of scarlet and blue, if you have amber or gold to trade for it."

That got their interest; Northern men were even more color-mad than the women, if that was possible. Hywel extracted samples of thread dyed with Keisha's colors and passed them around, causing the stalwart warriors to croon like happy girls over the brilliant shades. That loosened the mood considerably, and when Hywel remarked casually that they were trying to find the Great Pass to get to the north and Raven tribe, one of them commented that it would be no great matter to show them the way. In fact, once roughly a candlemark had passed, they were ready to do what no other tribe thus far had been willing to do—they offered to guide the group to their own encampment.

"From thence, we will take you through the mountains to the Great Pass," one of them said to Hywel. "If that will serve."

"Good; Snow Fox told us that the Great Pass will lead us to Raven," Hywel replied, as the others gathered up their baggage and the saddles that had been removed for drying and began tacking up the *dyheli* and Karles. Darian was very pleased with the way that Hywel was handling the contact, and had decided to leave him nominally "in charge" at least for now.

If Hywel hadn't been there, he might have hesitated in accepting the offer of Gray Wolf hospitality, but Hywel was perfectly confident with these folk. He even asked about specific individuals, and got answers—something that increased Darian's comfort level.

"And Shaman Rogare? Wisewoman Awhani?" Hywel continued with his interrogation as they took to their saddles and the whole cavalcade started out. "Have you had more trouble with the Summer Fever and Wasting Sickness, and have they learned of a cure?"

That certainly captured the Gray Wolf folks' attention; the fellow who appeared to be the leader (with a headdress made of an entire wolf-head, skull and all, and a cloak of several wolf-skins), and who hitherto had held himself somewhat aloof, suddenly addressed Hywel directly.

"Is it true, then, that Ghost Cat has found the cure for the Wasting Sickness?" he asked sharply—and anxiously.

Hywel started to answer, thought better of it, and looked to Darian. Darian motioned to Keisha to come up to the front of the group, and replaced Hywel himself.

"Warrior of Gray Wolf, I am Dar'ian k'Valdemar adopted of Ghost Cat, and it is among my people that Ghost Cat found their answer to the Wasting Sickness," he said. "What is it that you would know?"

The eyes of the Northerners widened to hear him claim kinship with Ghost Cat, and to see Hywel nod to confirm his claim.

"You have a cure?" the warrior asked sharply, showing no sign of surprise that Darian knew his tongue.

Darian nodded to Keisha, who answered the warrior with no sign of fear.

Star-Eyed, I'm proud of her! She acts as if she did this all the time!

"We have a cure *only* for the early stage of the sickness," she said gravely. "Once the fever has fled the body, little more can be done—but we have the means of that cure with us, and will share it gladly."

The warrior sighed; a mixture of relief and disappointment. "And are you, then, a Wisewoman?" he asked Keisha, with the aloof interest most Northerners gave to the female Healers—it was beneath their dignity to give females any notice outside of the home, but at the same time, the status of Wisewoman was nearly equivalent to that of Shaman.

"I am," she acknowledged. "And the holy *dyheli* have decreed that I am to impart what cures we have to *your* Shaman and Wisewoman, if they are able to master those cures."

The warrior nodded, then turned back to Darian, relieved that he no longer had to pay direct attention to Keisha. "I am Chulka, the chief hunter of Gray Wolf," he told Darian. "You will be *very* welcome among our people, with such gifts to impart."

The rest of the journey was made in silence, as the warriors of Gray Wolf spread out into the forest around them, leaving only one walking beside Hywel as his guide. The two young men—for the one that had been left was, if not Hywel's age, certainly very near to it—spoke with animation to each other. Darian didn't bother to try and listen, since it seemed to be mostly a mixture of boasts and hunting stories.

Darian knew that they were near the Gray Wolf camp when the warriors began appearing again, most carrying game, to close in around the strangers as a precaution against overreaction by their own folk. By the time they reached the encampment, there were curious children running alongside them, and women peering at them from the shelter of their bark-covered houses.

This was a temporary camp, not the kind of permanent village that Ghost Cat had established in Valdemar. Gray Wolf did very little in the way of husbandry, and as a consequence moved as they depleted the resources around their camp. In winter, they moved to a place where there were many caves that they used for storage and for living space during the cold months.

What they had here were movable shelters, made of flexible willow branches and covered with slabs of bark and pine boughs, intended to keep out rain, give a certain amount of privacy, and not much more than that. There were cook fires in front of each of these homes, with pots half-buried in the ashes, much like at Ghost Cat. The one striking difference between Gray Wolf and Ghost Cat was the presence of enormous dogs everywhere—huge, easy-tempered dogs who paid no attention whatsoever to the newcomers, even Hashi, who was about their size. Darian made a mental note to ask about the dogs later.

As was the case at Ghost Cat, the homes of the most important people in the encampment were nearest the center, so the Chief, the Shaman, and the Wisewoman had plenty of time to assemble to greet the visitors.

Their guide stepped back so that the chief hunter could make his introduction; Hywel introduced everyone, including the *dyheli* and *kyree*.

And Kel, of course.

Kel came to the fore of the group and bowed to the three leaders of the tribe. "Have no fearrr of me," he said, with a serious and sober inflection in his voice. "And do not fearrr forrr the game herrreaboutsss. I ssshall hunt upon the opposss-site sssside of the rrrriverrrr."

"That is good to hear," the Chief replied, just as seriously. "But it is best of all to hear that our allies of Ghost Cat have prospered in their new home. So, friends of our friends, before there is any talk of trade—will you share salt with us?"

A bowl of salt was duly brought forward, and everyone tasted it ceremoniously, even Hashi and the *dyheli*. That ceremony was all it took to break down the last barriers; the Wisewoman and the Shaman immediately took Keisha aside to interrogate her; Shandi went with them, and Darian, Hywel, Steelmind, and Wintersky found themselves seated at the Men's Fire, taking turns describing the journey they had taken and the condition of the land they had traveled through.

"Truly—the rumors we have heard are not rumors at all, then, but truth," the Chief said with unvarnished satisfaction. "Blood Bear is no more—having brought the Wasting Sickness upon us, they have finally sickened of it themselves. Had there been even a single war party, you would not have traveled past Magpie unmolested."

The warrior with the wolf-mask headpiece spat. "All the better, say I," he growled.

The others nodded.

"What rumors did you hear?" Darian asked, grimly curious to hear the details of the downfall of his oldest enemies, the people who had nearly destroyed Errold's Grove and who had succeeded in killing his first teacher.

"After their war band failed to return, they set to breeding sons on the orders of their new Shaman," said the Chief, his expression grim. "Girl-babies they exposed, that their women waste no time upon them. They sent out parties to capture more women to breed more sons. Then the Wasting Sickness at last struck *them*, and their new Shaman had not the cure for it."

"I heard that at the last, they had taken to sacrificing any who were stricken," offered the chief hunter. "The warriors took to eating the flesh of those warriors who had fallen, to take on their extra strength after their death. And that the women began to run back to their own people."

"And so—they are no more." There was no doubt as to the satisfaction in the Chief's voice, a satisfaction that Darian shared completely.

But he did not permit himself to indulge in it; an old Shin'a'in saying was that it was one thing to take pleasure in the defeat of an enemy, but gloating over it for very long made you no better than he.

"So," he said, allowing himself a single smile. "Let us talk of more pleasant things. Permit me, Chief, to show you the colors that we have brought. . . ."

And let me never have to think of Blood Bear again.

Fourteen

"Take slow, deep breaths," Keisha told her sister, who was struggling to get enough air. She wasn't feeling all that well herself, but it was Shandi and Wintersky who had been hit the worst by what their guide assured them was not a sickness, but due to "only the height of the mountain." This was mountain sickness, the illness of which Keisha had heard such unsettling tales. Safe to say, no one was making light of it.

Shandi leaned on Karles' shoulder, visibly taking calm from her Companion's presence. She was dizzy, felt as if she were choking, and nauseated; all symptoms, so their guide said blithely, of what he called "mountain fever." He insisted that coming down off the mountain would cure them, and since Keisha had not been able to find any signs of disease using her Healing Gifts, she was forced to take his word and the word of all the tales that she had heard for it.

Of all of them, Keisha seemed to have suffered the least. Steelmind, Hywel, and Darian were very short of breath and had killing headaches; Wintersky had both problems and was looking a bit green. Shandi had all of these and shook with cold; they'd bundled her up, but she still shivered, besides being sick and half blind with headache. The nonhumans all showed discomfort in some way, to a varying degree, except for Kelvren, who seemed invulnerable to it all.

Keisha only suffered from the headache, which was bad enough. *I suppose I should be happy with that,* she thought, and tried to will more air into her lungs.

"We must get over the pass," their guide insisted. "It will only get worse if we stay here."

"Worse?" Shandi moaned. "This can get *worse!* I can't see how—"

"It will," the Gray Wolf warrior said firmly. "Fever-dreams, or unconsciousness. We must get over. It will be better then."

"All right," Shandi managed to gasp, and climbed into her saddle. "Let's go, while I can still ride."

With her head feeling exactly like someone had tied a wire around it and was tightening it more with every passing breath, Keisha got into her *dyheli's* saddle and waited for the rest to mount. *How* was the guide managing to be so healthy?

I suppose he must be used to being this high, she decided. *It hardly seems fair, though.* They had been traveling through these mountains for three days now, but it was only today that they had started to feel so sick.

It was a pity they were all so miserable, because the scenery was spectacular; this last of the passes was actually above the clouds, though still below the snow line. It was about as cold in the shade as a late fall day in Errold's Grove, the full sun was intense and quite hot, and the little white puffs of cloud floating just below them looked like heaps of newly shorn fleeces.

Below and behind them lay one of many valleys, green and tree-filled; farther back, more mountains, growing blue with distance. Ahead of them lay the notch between two mountains marking the pass; mountains that in turn towered so far above the pass that it made Keisha dizzy to think about it.

This, so the guide assured them, was the final obstacle they needed to cross. Below this lay what the guide called "the Great Pass."

I can't imagine how Snow Fox got this far, laden with sick people! she thought. They must have been truly desperate to undertake the journey.

But then she remembered the children of Ghost Cat, so ill with Wasting Sickness they could hardly even feed themselves, and she knew that no parent could see that and not try everything to make it better. With the exception of the now-extinct Blood Bear, these people cherished their children no less than the parents of Valdemar.

She held on to the saddle-grip, enduring the jarring of her head with each step her *dyheli* took. She knew it was worse for everyone else—most of all for Shandi, who was as white as Karles' coat. Karles himself looked positively pale, even for a white "horse."

The trail they followed was a slender track threading its way between enormous rocks tumbled from the higher slopes and clumps of brush. At this height, colors had been leached from everything by the intense light of the sun; the bushes and grasses were gray-green, the trunks of the tiny trees gray-brown, the rocks around them pale gray. Here and there were spring flowers—pale blue, pale pink, and white. Only the sky held an intense color, a blue so deep and pure that Keisha longed to be able to dip fabric in it and capture it forever. The only other place she had ever seen a blue that beautiful was when she had looked into Karles' eyes, just before he had Chosen Shandi.

They plodded upward, and the top never seemed to get any nearer—then suddenly they were there, at the top of the pass, looking down . . .

. . . and down . . . and down . . .

Hywel whistled his astonishment; Darian shook his head in disbelief, and Keisha gasped. Even Shandi forgot her misery for a moment and stared.

Havens—it must be a league or more to the bottom! And it goes on forever!

"The Great Pass," their guide said simply. "And here I must leave you. The track down is plain, see? You no longer need my help."

He pointed to a much clearer track than the one they had used to climb up here, one that zigzagged down the steep slope (more of a cliff than a slope) from where they now stood.

The Great Pass; that was far from being any kind of a descriptive name for it. Keisha had pictured a mountain pass like any other—perhaps deeper, certainly longer, since it was supposed to go straight through all the way to Raven territory.

What she saw, however, beggared imagination.

It was as if someone had taken a giant knife and carved through the mountains to form a passage. The bottom was as level and flat as a good paved road, and it disappeared in either direction into the mists of distance. Right now the sun was high above them, so the bottom was in full light; she caught a glint of water down there, shining between the branches of trees made so small by distance that she could scarcely make them out.

"Gods of my fathers," Darian murmured. "Who could possibly have possessed the kind of magic needed to make such a thing?"

Only then did Keisha realize that it was magic, and not nature, that had created this place.

"Huh," Shandi said, rousing herself out of her misery. "I guess you don't know your history very well. The northern mage that Herald Vanyel fought, that's who—and I guess Vanyel must have had even more than he did, since Vanyel stopped him." She peered off into the south and east, following the gash with her eyes. "It'll come out just north of the Forest of Sorrows—or it would, if Vanyel hadn't blocked it. I had no notion this thing still existed."

Nor had anyone else, except the northern tribes, who clearly knew very well it existed, *and* provided easy access to the south. Only luck and Vanyel's Curse had kept them from taking it all the way into Valdemar in the past—and now, save for that final blockage, the north stood open to invasion.

Now it was more imperative than ever to find out what sort of state the rest of the northern tribes were in. They had joined together once to invade Valdemar, and only Vanyel had stopped them. What if they should band together again? They wouldn't need a great mage this time, only a strong leader and a good strategist—all the work of creating an easy path to the south had been done for them.

She was the first to break out of the trance of fascination that the Great Pass exerted on them, and ask her *dyheli* to start down the trail before them. Darian quickly shook off his own bemusement and followed her. One by one, the others did the same, as their guide remained on the top of the pass behind them, watching them solemnly as they began their journey downward.

It took them all day to make their way to the bottom, and once there, the great age of the place was self-evident. Far from being the barren cut it must have been for years after it had been made, a hundred thousand different plants and animals had taken advantage of the shelter it provided to move in and flourish. A stream ran right down the middle, fed by the runoff of the mountains above it, and where there is water, there will always be life. Leafed trees and evergreen trees had taken root here, and a variety of plants flourished along the banks of the stream. There was game in plenty, too, which was just as well, since the mountains cut off the sunlight and night would come very quickly here. There wasn't a lot of time left to set themselves up for the night.

So they didn't hesitate when they reached the bottom; they made camp immediately. They still had some provisions in the form of dried meat pounded together with dried berries, provided by their hosts of Gray Wolf. That would do for now; in the morning they could hunt.

"How are your heads, all of you?" Keisha asked the others as they quickly gathered deadfall for a fire.

She got variations on "Fine, now," from all of them, and Shandi in particular looked much more like her old self. Evidently their guide had been right; there was something about going up very high that made people sick—

Unless they're used to it! That must be it; Keisha didn't want to contemplate what it would be like to try and become accustomed to the heights. How long would the sickness last?

How long would I be willing to bear it before I gave up? That's the real question.

Perhaps it would be possible to become accustomed gradually, without the symptoms.

But I don't care to be the one to find out, she decided, and went back to gathering very dry twigs to serve as kindling.

Steelmind found a real windfall, in that he found a tangle of wood piled up against a rock, dry and ready to burn. But that very find raised the possibility of another danger. Flash floods were always a possibility in the mountains, and they were in a particularly hazardous and vulnerable place. A cloudburst could cause a flood leagues away—a flood that would sweep everything before it all the way down the Pass, and they would have no warning.

"Weather-Watching," Darian said to Steelmind, as they all came to that realization after a short discussion. "Have you ever done it?"

"Not often, but I can do it," the older man replied, unsheathing a hand ax, adjusting its weighting slide, then stooping to chop up the battered brush and limbs. Hywel and Wintersky helped him, as Keisha, Shandi, and Darian gathered up the armfuls of wood. Darian limbered up and hacked skillfully at some branches with his heavy brush-knife, while Kelvren helped in his own way by standing on long branches or small trees and snapping through them with his beak, even if they were as thick as a man's upper arm. It was getting dark fast, and even though the tops of the mountains above them still gleamed golden with sunlight, it was twilight on the floor of the Pass.

"Wintersky and I can watch, too," Darian said with satisfaction. "Good; there won't be a night watch when we won't have a Weather-Watcher too; during the day we can take turns. Kel will know more than any of us during the day; he'll be up *in* the weather we're watching."

:It is likely that we and Hashi will also be able to hear a flood before it reaches us—well in time for us all to climb to escape,: Neta said diffidently. *:So we will have twin defenses.:*

But Keisha wondered how well she was going to be able to sleep with the specter of a flood sweeping down out of nowhere hanging over her head every night. "Maybe we'd be better off trying to find caves above the waterline each night?" she suggested, dropping her armload of wood beside the fire and going back for another.

"We would—if we can find any," Darian replied. He didn't have to add anything; she'd seen the condition of the walls on the way down herself. There didn't seem to be much in the way of caves. "If I have to, I can use magic to enlarge a cave or fissure that is already there, depending upon the conditions at the time. I could maybe make us a shelter, before there were any rains, but that would put out an easily readable magical signature. It's best if we just make a camp as usual, though, because I'd rather not advertise to whatever may be out there."

They could camp on the trail itself, but that carried its own risks, and how many more trails would they find as they made their way up the Pass?

She resolved not to think any more about it. They would be vigilant, and improvise. There had been too many surprises on this journey already to try to anticipate all the possibilities and plan for them. Meanwhile, she could gather wood and water, and do what she could to make certain that none of them would suffer any long-term effects from their mountain sickness.

Steady marching brought them to the end of the Pass in three days, and they had pressed themselves to do so in that short a time. The terrain, at least, provided nothing to impede them; it must have been an easy trip for that long-ago army that Vanyel defeated.

The tall mountains around them never grew lower, but the valleys between grew broader—and wetter. More of their time was spent crossing valley floors, some of them thickly greened valleys that were filled with plants that were entirely new to Steelmind. Here they *did* find furtive signs of people, but never saw any. Kuari reported that the tribes he saw were all small, no more than twenty or thirty people altogether, and they kept away from the travelers and their strange beasts and stranger allies.

More streams joined with theirs, and they started to see fish more abundantly. With that, Wintersky began throwing his line in every time they camped, and they enjoyed the results of his labor.

The end of the third day brought them to the end of the Pass; it opened out into one of those broad valleys, heavily forested, green, and wreathed with mist. All that day Keisha had noticed the clouds becoming thicker overhead, and the air growing more humid, although there was no sign that it was about to rain.

"Hurrrr," Kel said, as he landed beside them. "Thisss isss like the Haighlei Forrressstssss, except that it isss not ssso hot." He looked about with interest. "The trrreessss arrre asss big, and it isss damp therrre, like thisss."

Moss and lichen grew thickly underfoot and on the trunks of the trees; and moss hung from the boughs high overhead. *All* of the trees were varieties of conifer or evergreen, and some were awe inspiring in their size, even to someone who was used to a Vale and the huge trees that grew there. These giants towered above their heads, so high that their tops were lost to sight among the branches of lesser trees.

Those trunks were like great, smooth columns, without any branches for such distances that Keisha couldn't see how they could possibly be climbed. This was how they differed from the Vale trees, which branched out no more than two or three stories above the ground; these trees went on forever without branching out. It was unlikely that anyone would be using *these* trees to house an *ekele* any time soon, unless they built from the ground up!

But the raptors and Kel all loved the new surroundings, and cheerfully went out on scouting forays while the rest moved away from the mouth of the Pass and found a secure site to set up camp.

They all returned at sunset, Kuari last of all, and as they ate fish caught by Wintersky and grilled over the fire, each Hawkbrother related what his bird was telling him.

And in the end, even Kel looked troubled by what they had *not* seen.

"Wherrre arrre the people?" Kel said finally. "We have flown herrre and therrre—and therrre isss no sssign of people."

"No sign that anyone has traveled the Pass recently either," Darian pointed out, frowning. "There were tiny tribes in the other valleys—shouldn't there be *some* sign of people here? Could another sickness have come through here and wiped everyone out?"

"If it had—why wouldn't Snow Fox have brought it with them?" Keisha asked. "They only had Wasting Sickness and a few other things we already knew how to clear up."

Hywel poked at the fire with a stick. "People do things differently, up here," he said at last. "It could be that they are off fishing."

"Fishing?" Wintersky said incredulously. "*Fishing!* What is that supposed to mean?"

Hywel looked uncomfortable. "I have heard—heard—that on the other side of that mountain there is a great expanse of water so far that you cannot see the other side, and it tastes of salt. This is where the peoples round about here get salt with which to trade. And I have heard that in the spring, there are torrents of fish coming up the streams. People gather at the rivers and catch these fish for as long as they come, and it is said that the fish are so thick in the rivers that one can walk from bank to bank upon their backs and keep dry feet. It is said that they can thus dry and smoke enough of these fish to serve them the rest of the year."

"That sounds like some sort of fable to me," Wintersky said skeptically.

Hywel shrugged. "It is only what I have heard. Also, I *have* tasted of this fish. Traders brought some back with them as provisions. It is good, very rich, and the meat of it is red, not white."

"Huh." Wintersky still looked skeptical.

"White Grrryphon liesss bessside sssuch a sssalty waterrr," Kel observed, tilting his head to the side. "We call it an 'ocean' or 'sssea.' Could thisss be the sssame sssea?"

"I don't know why not," Steelmind replied. "There is no reason why the coastline here could not be *much* farther to the east than it is where the Haighlei lands lie. It could be a larger lake than we can even imagine. But that doesn't address the question of where the people are."

"No, it doesn't, but we've only looked close to the mouth of the Pass," Darian said. "Now, if I were living up here, and I knew that this place existed and might be used by war parties or even armies, I certainly wouldn't want to live near it."

Nods all around the campfire showed that Darian had come up with a reasonable explanation—for now.

But Keisha had the shivery feeling that this was not the real explanation.

After half-a-day's travel, they had finally come upon signs of people—but the signs weren't good.

"I don't like this," Darian said, staring at the remains of the village. This place had been more like the permanent village that Ghost Cat had built in Valdemar, before it had been deserted.

Deserted? Maybe. Maybe not. However the village had become untenanted, it had been too long ago to tell if the people had left, died, or been taken away. All that was left were the moss-covered remains of the log houses, the carved poles, the other artifacts of life. The roofs had fallen in—but that could have happened in a single season; Darian had seen how the kind of roof the Ghost Cat folks built needed constant attention. As wet as it was here, moss would have started to grow inside immediately. Grass was knee-tall, but there were no possessions, nor the remains of any.

"Hywel?" Darian said, turning to their only expert.

Hywel looked just as troubled, and just as puzzled. "I do not know," he said, looking around at the tumbled houses, the fallen poles. "There are no bodies, and no belongings. Perhaps they—"

Then he shook his head. "No, I do not think they walked away, and it would be foolish to say so. I do not know what happened here."

Darian scratched his head. "Do you see any signs of attack?" he asked reluctantly. "What would we be looking for?"

"There would be no signs," Hywel told him. "If the tribe was under attack, the men would go out to meet the enemy, and the women and children would remain here. And if the men did not come back—" He paused. "Well, until Blood Bear began taking other tribes' women, the women and children of the defeated would have been left in peace to rebuild their tribe as best they could."

"But now—we don't know." He considered for a moment. "If they were attacked by Blood Bear, wouldn't the victors come here and carry everything off? They certainly tried to do that at Errold's Grove."

"What if illness killed most of the people here?" Keisha asked. "Would the survivors just pack up and walk away?"

"They might." Hywel brightened a bit at that. "It is tradition that girls go to other tribes to wed, and warriors take wives from other tribes, so there are alliances created all the time. It could happen that they would pack what they had and go, if there were too few hunters to feed the people, or too few people to make a tribe."

But this settlement had been huge, larger than the Ghost Cat village was now. Could sickness have wiped out that many people?

The ruins held no answers for them now, it had been too long since—whatever it was—had happened.

"We move on," he decided. "We're nearly to Snow Fox territory anyway. We *know* that they're all right. Maybe they can tell us what happened here."

He didn't have to add that they would *have* to be wary. They already knew what to do. With Neta taking point, the birds spread out to either side, and Kel watched their back-trail. Hashi ranged out in a fan shape in front, filling in wherever another scout wasn't. The one advantage they had was the forest itself; it was damp enough that scent lingered, giving Hashi plenty of information. The scant undergrowth and lack of low branches kept a relatively clear line-of-sight for them down on the ground, and a clear flight path for the birds.

But the forest was not continuous; there were huge meadows to cross, with acres and acres of waist-high grasses. They were beautiful, but dangerous; crossing them meant coming out of cover.

They had another one of those meadows ahead of them. This time, though, Darian was fairly certain that they would be safe, for a herd of deer grazed there, and Neta's probe of their minds showed that they felt perfectly comfortable here, which meant they hadn't been hunted recently. Darian was tempted to ask Kel to take one down for them, but decided against the idea. It was too early in the day to stop, and they would have to stop in order to take care of that much meat.

So they were the ones who spooked the herd into flight when they came out from under the shadows of the trees.

As the deer disappeared, the party moved warily out into the sunshine. Only now could they see the mountains towering on all sides of them; mountains with snow capping their peaks, rising through the thin clouds. It was Darian's turn on Weather-Watch, and he sensed that there were storms moving in from the west. There would be rain tonight.

Again.

He didn't know what the natives called this land, but he had a few choice selections. When they'd packed for this trip, he hadn't counted on facing rain practically every night. They'd been improvising with limited success; rain shelters made from boughs and rain sheets didn't keep the precipitation out all night long, and by dawn everyone was damp.

He used magic to dry them out, driving the water from clothing and hair. He had no choice, even though this simple act might signal their presence to an enemy; they could not afford to get sick, or pick up something that would rot feet or infect skin. Keisha had to preserve her own strength for things that could not be prevented.

Carefully, with all the birds in the air, they crossed the

meadow. Steelmind gathered plants as they walked, stooping over now and again to snatch something that *his* peculiar Gift told him was useful. Already he had a dozen different herbs that he wanted to try cultivating—someday. For now, he was content to add flavor and variety to their meals.

This time he walked practically bent over, pulling up bulbs that looked exactly like wild onions, brushing them off, and stashing them in the bag at his waist.

Darian knew that Hakan, Steelmind's buzzard, was keeping a sharp eye out for trouble; Hakan circled highest above the clearing and had the widest view. Hakan's type was not the same as the scavenger vultures; it was closer by far to the hawk families. Buzzards had fully feathered heads, mild tempers, and sleepy dispositions. They never exerted themselves if they didn't have to—but that mild and sleepy outward demeanor concealed a determined nature. Hakan would fly through fire to protect Steelmind.

Wintersky's little sharpshin hawk Kreeak by contrast was a bundle of nerves. Never able to stay still unless he was asleep, Kreeak was making a circuit of the meadow, while Kuari stayed in the trees at the point where they would reenter the forest. Kel was above with Hakan, in position to attack if he was needed.

Neta and Hashi kept their noses in the wind, staying beside the humans. The rest of the *dyheli* spread out all around them, for they were on foot, deciding that it would be better for the humans to present less of themselves above the grass as targets.

It was Kuari who sounded the warning, before they were a quarter of the way across the vast meadow—but through Kuari's eyes, Darian saw that the hunting party drawing cautiously towards the meadow wore the emblem of the Snow Fox.

"It's Snow Fox!" he shouted, and got into the saddle of the nearest *dyheli*, the rest no more than a fraction of a moment behind him.

Hywel, on Neta, took the lead; although he was riding on an unfamiliar animal, he wore the familiar clothing of another Northerner, and more, he carried with him a token from the Snow Fox women and children and the young warriors still with Ghost Cat. Darian let him race ahead of them; when he came close enough, he dismounted and finished his approach on foot. At that distance, he and the others were no more than dots against the shadow of the trees, but through Kuari's eyes Darian saw that the meeting was going very well indeed. With that as encouragement, he led the rest on at a brisk lope.

By the time they reached Hywel and the hunting party, Hywel and the strangers were acting like old acquaintances. This was a party of young men his own age, which certainly helped, and the faces that they turned to the approaching riders were friendly and smiling.

But they soon sobered after the introductions were made and the initial excitement of the meeting died down. "We must make a kill and return quickly," the leader of the hunting party said, with a nervous glance to the east. "We are too near to Wolverine territory. . . ."

They didn't elaborate, and Darian figured that questions could wait until later. "We will help," he offered. "We should not come to your home empty handed, after all."

The Snow Fox hunters were too young to hide their skepticism well, but politely said nothing. But of course the moment that Darian had offered his help, he, Wintersky, and Steelmind had sent off their birds to scout for those deer that they had frightened off earlier.

:Kel!: he called upward. :These are Snow Fox hunters; they need to make some kills and get out of here. When the birds find those deer, can you help out?:

:Hah! Easily!: cane the cheerful reply. :I will dive at them so that they run toward you—it will be your task to see that at least one or two do not get by you!:

Kreeak located the deer at just that moment, and Kel gave them time enough to get back across the meadow and in place before he began his flush. Darian felt his blood begin to heat and his heart speed up as they approached their ambush point.

"I beg your indulgence," he said carefully. "But there will be a herd of deer running here in a moment—will you make ready?"

Now the hunters exchanged thinly veiled looks of amusement. Of course they were amused. This was their land, and they knew the habits and movements of the animals here; how could strangers presume to predict that a herd of deer would come through a particular place?

Nevertheless, they were polite young men, and they did indulge this ridiculous foreigner. So when, after a short period of waiting, the herd of deer *did* come charging through the trees as if a terrible enemy was on their heels, they were understandably startled. Only two or three of them actually got shots off, and of those, only one hit.

Darian and the rest, of course, knew exactly when Kel spooked the deer—and knew that Kel had managed another of his infamous double-kills as well. Small wonder that the deer fled!

Darian and Wintersky targeted the same deer that the Snow Fox hunter had hit, and the three of them brought it down. Shandi held her fire, as did Steelmind; Hywel brought down a fourth deer by himself. That was more than enough to make them welcome at the Snow Fox village.

One for Kel, three for us; that's generous enough. Darian signaled to Wintersky and Steelmind to come with him; they found Kel with his two prizes, terribly proud of himself.

"Hah! Did I not tell you!" he shouted happily, holding his head high, his eyes shining. "I am asss good asss my worrrd!"

"Indeed you are," Darian laughed. "Would you like us to wrap it up, or will you eat yours here?"

"Sssome of both," Kel replied. "You will clean and drresss them herrre, yesss? Why wassste good food? I want sssome marrow, too."

So as Darian and the others gutted and dressed the deer, bundling the meat into the hides, Kel gobbled up the entrails and other parts they would normally have left behind. The *dyhelis* flared their nostrils in distaste at the scent of blood, but permitted their riders to load the bundles up behind their saddles. Their attitude toward deer hunting was remarkably pragmatic considering that they looked so much like *dyheli*. They didn't like it, but they didn't actually object to it. The general attitude seemed to be, "better them than us."

While they proceeded with the messy business of butchering, Darian Mindspoke to Neta, the *dyheli* doe. :*Neta, could you ask Hywel to carefully explain Kel to the Snow Fox hunters for me?*: he asked, once he had established contact with her.

:*Hmm, yes, I think he had better,*: was the thoughtful reply. :*I shall try to help him.*:

When Darian and the others rejoined the rest, Kel came along with them, walking sedately on the ground rather than making one of his spectacular flying entrances. Darian hoped that Hywel and Neta had managed to "explain" Kel adequately.

Then again, knowing the *dyheli* doe, she would have no compunction whatsoever about invading their hosts' minds and making *certain* that they wouldn't panic when they first sighted the gryphon.

He had some qualms about that. More than a few.

Should I have forbidden her to do any such thing? He could have done that, but that didn't mean she'd obey him. *Dyheli* had their own code of behavior, one that set the good of the herd above that of any individual, and that meant she would do whatever she thought was in the interest of her "herd," in this case, the entire group she was with. She would dispassionately disobey orders, and lie to him about it. Of all the known creatures with Mindspeech, only the *dyheli* could lie successfully when using it.

There was no way to compromise with his conscience. He could only accept what happened and try to make up for it afterward.

Whether Neta had a hand in it or not, when they came out of the forest and into the sunlight, although the Snow Fox hunters looked a bit nervous to see Kel, they didn't seem frightened. "This is our friend Kelvren," Darian said carefully. "He has made two kills of his own, and wishes to present one of them to Snow Fox as thanks for your hospitality."

Kel glanced longingly at the piles of offal laid to the side, but immediately turned his attention back to the hunters. "I am honorrrred to make thiss gift," he said, with a graceful bow, and a broad gesture of his taloned forefoot.

"It is we who are honored by your generosity," the chief hunter said bravely. "And—ah—are your tastes similar to those of the hunting birds? If so, would you care to take your choice of the—remains—before we leave this place?"

Darian was extremely pleased and a bit surprised by this display of tact and thoughtfulness. And it argued powerfully for the notion that Neta had only helped to explain Kel's appearance, and had not taken charge of the hunters' minds.

"Yesss!" Kel exclaimed. "And I thank you!"

The hunters tactfully looked the other way as Kel pounced upon the pile of discards with relish; watching a gryphon eat was something that took getting used to. It was all too easy to imagine what else that cruel beak and talons could do.

He made very short work of the meal—which was indeed a full meal even by a gryphon's standards—and they were shortly on their way.

With the meat that would ordinarily have burdened them loaded on the backs of *dyheli,* the hunters set off at a lope that made conversation impossible. Very clearly they wanted to be gone from this place, and quickly, too. Darian longed to ask them why, but knew that he would have to wait.

Whatever the answer was, though, he was fairly sure that it had to do with the Wolverine tribe—and that it would not be good news for them.

Fifteen

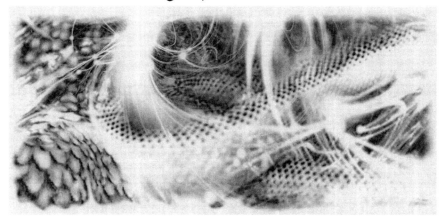

Keisha wasn't the only one who felt the relief in the hunters as they crossed some invisible line into "safe" territory. They slowed their pace to a trot from what had very nearly been a run; they began to talk among themselves and even make occasional comments to their guests. And at last they finally looked back at the laden *dyheli* with the satisfaction and anticipation such a fine take of venison warranted.

She decided to talk to one of the young men herself, and asked her mount to take her up to the front of the group. She "picked" the first one that looked over at her and smiled, thinking it would be easier to approach someone who showed some friendliness from the beginning rather than trying to coax a reaction out of someone determined to keep a stony visage.

"How much farther do we go to reach your home?" she asked him, thinking that would be an easy way to begin a conversation, and grateful that they had all learned the Snow Fox dialect via *dyheli* before they left k'Valdemar.

"Not far," the young man told her; he couldn't be much older than Hywel, and was possibly younger. "We are within the range of our sentries now," he added. And that was a curious addition, or so it seemed to Keisha. Why should that matter to her?

Unless he is reassuring me that no one can move upon his village without warning, she thought soberly. *Like a war party from this Wolverine tribe, perhaps?*

Their journey had brought them right up to the foot of the mountains, and soon it was evident that they were about to enter a kind of side valley, a cleft with steep cliffs on either side and a small, clear stream meandering along the base of the cliff on the left. If the village had not originally been situated with defense in mind, the setting certainly provided as much shelter as if protection had been a major consideration from the beginning.

Defensive cliffs, a water supply—the only thing they would lack if they came under siege would be food, and if they've stored enough, they might be all right.

"This is our valley," the young hunter said proudly. "It has been the home of our tribe from the time of my grandfather's grandfather's grandfather. The Snow Fox himself led us here, as the Snow Fox told our Shaman to send our sick to Ghost Cat, and then led our sick ones on the journey."

Ah! They didn't say anything about that back at the Sanctuary. But then again—they might assume we already knew something of the sort must have happened in order for them to find us at all. It seemed that the tribal spirits of these northerners took a very paternal (or was it maternal?) interest in their titular tribes.

:*And the other deities of you humans do not?*: came the impudent query from her *dyheli.*

:*Other deities have a great many more people to oversee, and rarely go so far as to personally lead their followers to help or safety,* she pointed out wryly. :*Perhaps it is easier when your worshipers number less than a hundred to intervene directly in their lives.*:

"I am called Bendan," the hunter continued diffidently, looking up at her, but not meeting her eyes directly. "May I know your name, Wisewoman?"

Hywel had found a way to get the tribesmen to grant both Keisha and Shandi better status than "merely female." Keisha was always introduced as the Wisewoman, and Shandi as something that translated as "woman whose soul is a man." Apparently there were a *few* female warriors in the history of the tribes, and they'd had to come up with a category to fit them into. "Man-souled women" who passed the boys' initiation trials could become hunters and warriors, but they sacrificed the traditional role of "wife and mother" in order to attain that status. They were considered neither male nor female—rather like the Shin'a'in Sword-Sworn, in a way.

At any rate, that was Shandi's role, and she went along with it, since taking on that persona at least allowed her to sit at the Men's Fire with the rest of the party, and not suffer a lonely exile to the company of the clan's women.

It said something for the status of Wisewoman that Bendan gave Keisha his name. A "mere woman" would have had to learn it obliquely, by overhearing it or learning it from one of her friends, for he would never have addressed her directly if she had not had that rank.

"I am called Keisha," she said. "Has Snow Fox a Wisewoman of their own, or does the Shaman conduct all healing?"

"We have only the Shaman, and he has no healing magic— that is why the Snow Fox sent to us to take our sick into the south," Bendan said eagerly. "Have you been sent by the Fox to teach our Shaman in the ways of southern healing?"

:Boy's a quick one, isn't he?: chuckled the *dyheli*.

"I have; your people reached us safely, as you know, and I came in answer to your need," she replied solemnly, taking the question as the gift it was. "That we bear trade goods is as a protection, so that others will not interfere with our passage."

"It is wise—though I do not think it would avail you with Wolverine," he replied, then shrugged and changed the subject, trotting along at her stirrup with no sign of effort. "We have some sick still with us; too ill to travel. I hope you will be able to help them."

"I hope so, too," she said sincerely.

When they reached the village, it was apparent that this was a permanent enclave, unlike some of the other hunting camps they had visited. Here were the familiar log houses, decorated and carved, roofed with slabs of bark; the characteristic poles stood prominently before each house with totemic animals and spirit representations carved into them. Even more than at Ghost Cat, there were piecework blankets on display, made of felted and dyed fur, and the costumes of the inhabitants were covered with embroideries made with tufts of dyed fur.

It was clear that this was a prosperous tribe; it was also clear that the invisible sentries had already alerted the Chief and Shaman that visitors were being escorted in. Women and children clustered at the entrances to the log houses—craning their necks and straining their eyes for a good look at the strangers, but also ready to bolt inside at a hint that there was something amiss. The Chief and Shaman marched forward to meet them, surrounded by armed warriors older and more experienced than the young hunters.

Hywel bounded from his saddle, and together with Bendan, came forward to speak with the leaders of Snow Fox. He displayed the token that the Snow Fox folk back in Valdemar had given them, and soon the faces of those around him were relaxed, even smiling. The warriors lowered their weapons, and with that sign that all was well, the women and children began to ease closer.

The Shaman headed straight for Keisha once the formalities were over; she dismounted rather than tower over him as he approached. Gray-haired and bearded, he was a handsome old fellow by anyone's standards, with strong features and lively eyes. Knotwork was layered down the front edges of his mantle, with points of antler serving as closures alternating from side to side. The colors picked for the tufting between the antler tips exactly matched his eyes.

"Wisewoman Keisha, I am Shaman Henkeir Told-True. I am warmed to see your presence. May your spirits bless you for coming to us!" he exclaimed, seizing her hand. "The Chief's woman and children are ill, as are several more, too ill to send to Ghost Cat with the others, and I have had no success with them. The Snow Fox told me I must wait for a healer out of the south—"

"Bendan told me," she replied, clasping the old man's hand. "Is it the Wasting Sickness? Summer Fever?" Those were both names for the same illness, the disease that struck the channels that carried the commands of the mind to the body, causing weakness and paralysis.

"Nay, it is something else, another new sickness out of the times of evil magic and heartsick skies; something that chokes the breath but does not weaken the muscles. So short of breath are they that we dared not send them over-mountain, for the mountain sickness would have killed them. When they move with any forcefulness at all, they become unable to breathe, but they cannot stay completely still," he told her, and she felt a little thrill of excitement, though she immediately was ashamed of being excited at someone else's misfortune. Still—the prospect of seeing something new—

"Let us go to them, and I will see what may be done," she said instantly. "All else can wait."

The old man's eyes lit up. "Hah! You are a true Wisewoman!" he exclaimed, leading her to think that perhaps he had encountered those who had not been as dedicated to their duty. "Come, and I will show you."

The sick folk had been isolated from the others in a separate log house. Although there were no windows, the roof had actually been propped up here and there to provide fresh air and ventilation. But the patients were bundled up near the fire, all of them weak, feverish, and thin. An effort had been made, using thick slabs of bark set upright in an overlapping-edged ring, to make sure that the smoke from the central fire was at a minimum; nevertheless, there was constant deep coughing coming from nearly everyone around the fire.

The Shaman told the stricken ones who this strange woman was, and in response there were murmurs of relief between rasps and coughing fits. Keisha examined the child nearest to her at the Shaman's urging, opening her shields and sinking her awareness deep into the body before her.

It didn't take her long to identify what was wrong—and it *was* a disease new to her, something that lived in the lungs, scarring them and turning them from a healthy honeycomb to a useless solid mass. But for all its toughness, for all that it was, if unchecked, absolutely deadly, it was no match for the forces she could wake in the body of its host with her power. It thrived because it walled itself off from those forces with scar tissue; she could break that wall down.

She gave the child a good first treatment before she emerged from her Healing trance, to see the Shaman staring at her with intense interest. "Have you the mastery of this magic?" she asked him. "The way of seeing inside the body, and going to war with sickness?"

"Nay, but my student has," he said instantly. "I could not

teach him, and he has been doing the best that he could with-out any learning, trusting to instinct. I shall go to fetch him, if you would deign to teach him."

That's a relief! "Please! That is why I am here. And if you would call upon the spirits as well, while we help the sick ones, it would be well," she told him. "It is not good to treat only the body and leave the spirit untouched."

He grinned broadly and got to his feet, leaving the log house only to return in a few moments with a very young man—perhaps fourteen or fifteen—and a bundle, which proved to be a set of drums, wrapped in a charm-bedecked cape. The boy bobbed his head awkwardly at her, and she smiled in a way she hoped would encourage him.

She could tell already that he had used his Healing powers in much the same way that she had at that age—crudely, be-cause he never had a real teacher. The Shaman at least recog-nized his power, but he was unable to teach him. Instinct and necessity had given him some direction, but to go any further, he needed proper instruction.

"You've done well by yourself," she told him, as the Sha-man donned his cape, and cast cedar on the fire. "You are like a carver who has been making good images with only an ax—I will give you fine knives as well, with which to do your work."

He brightened at the praise, and nodded enthusiastically at her explanation. "Yes!" the boy all but shouted. "That is ex-actly how I have been feeling! I know that there is a way to do things, but I cannot make them happen! Oh, Wisewoman, but show me the way, and I will speak your name to the spirits forever!"

"Exactly." She patted his hand, and placed it on top of hers, for the physical contact would help her make mind-to-mind contact. "Now, prepare yourself, and let me show you what I know. . . ."

Keisha worked with the young student until they were both exhausted; by that time, all of the people suffering from the illness that the Shaman had termed "Hammer Lung" had been given their first treatment. The disease was treacherous and tenacious, and would need many more treatments to be eradicated. The young student had gotten his bearings, and Keisha was certain he would make a fine Healer, in time.

Tomorrow I'll ask Shandi to give me a hand; maybe Darian, too. We'll get these people over the worst of their illness before we leave. Something in the back of her mind teased at her. There had to be a way to give this young man more of her own knowledge, but she couldn't make the thought come clear. Finally she let it go; if she didn't work so hard at it, it would probably surface by itself. That was how things seemed to work for her. When there was a problem that could be solved with quick thought, it would be at the forefront of her awareness, but if it would take a long time to solve a problem, then it would be mulled over behind her consciousness until finally popping up as a clear solution.

The patients were already feeling and looking better. She'd been able to advise some other things that let them breathe more easily, things that the Shaman could do in addition to his spiritual ministrations.

Although I have to wonder . . . I've never been able to work alone for quite so long before. Time seemed to move slowly for me, but it never dragged on. I am tired but not as completely exhausted as I would normally be. Maybe those spirits of his were helping out.

The student stumbled off to his bed, glowing with the satisfaction that only comes with accomplishment. The Shaman packed up his gear and offered to conduct her to the Men's Fire.

"Please," she said gratefully. It was very dark outside the log house, and she really wasn't up to stumbling around looking for the men. "I would appreciate that."

Henkeir beamed his pleasure, his beard practically bristling with cheer. This had been a good day for him, statuswise; the foreign Wisewoman sent by the tribal totem had deferred to him, requested that he specifically tend to the souls and spiritual needs of the sick ones, and now had asked him to escort her to the Men's Fire. If he had feared the possibility of losing status because of her appearance, those fears had been totally put to rest. Completely aside from her personality, for those reasons alone he would have liked her.

He led her out of the log house, as the patients settled into what must have been their first restful sleep for many weeks.

Soft calls of thanks and well-wishes faded away behind as the pair walked. Even though there hadn't been a lot of light inside the house, thanks in part to the smoke shielding around the fire pit, it was incredibly dark outside it. The cliffs on either side cut off most of the sky, and the moon was not yet up. Mist wreathed among the trees; the smoky air, cedar-scented and damp, penetrated Keisha's clothing and made her shiver. She was quite glad that she had accepted his guidance before they had gone more than a few paces, for the Men's Fire, as was the custom at Ghost Cat, had been sequestered in a remote pocket from the rest of the village. By contrast, the Women's Fire, which they passed as they walked between two more log houses, was right in the center of the village, with the women and young children clustered about it, laughing, talking, and eating. There was a wonderful smell of roast meat and some sort of bread, of wild herbs and onions. Her stomach growled.

The fire they sought was in a little pocket carved into the cliff when an enormous boulder came crashing down from above some time in the far past. The boulder itself, the size of one of the log houses, shielded the sight of the entrance to the pocket from the rest of the village, and even hid the reflected firelight.

The pocket canyon was as welcoming as a conventional hearth in a Valdemaran home. Firelight warmed the air and the stone walls, and if there was no roof, tonight at least there was no need of one either. The men "welcomed" her to the circle simply by making space for her beside Darian and passing a wooden platter loaded with roasted tubers, onions, and venison to her. She was famished, and with a nod and a word of thanks, set to her meal.

She ate as they did, with her fingers and a small, stubby eating-knife, keeping her head over her platter so that the juices from the meat dripped back down onto her food. The Shaman immediately took command of the conversation, telling the Chief the good news—both that his wife and children were on the way to being cured, and that the Shaman's young student would soon have the special healing magics of the southerners himself.

The Chief would not rush to thank Keisha here, in front of the rest of the men, but the look of gratitude he threw at her told her he would definitely be approaching her in private. She sensed that before their arrival, the conversation had taken a dark and foreboding tone, and that the Chief had welcomed the change their good news brought.

Meanwhile, the food warmed and filled her—and tasted wonderful, especially after the somewhat meager meals of the past few days. As her hunger eased, she started feeling how tired she really was; tired, not sleepy. She was content to sit beside the fire and listen to the men—and Shandi—talking. She had closed her shields in tight around her, knowing that she would be oversensitive after all her work, and as a consequence felt as if she were wrapped in a cocoon that kept the rest of the world at a comfortable distance. She had her footwear off, and her soles baked deliciously from their proximity to the slow fire, as she lay back and closed her eyes for a while.

The earnest conversation that her entrance had interrupted resumed after the Shaman described with great pride the work of his apprentice. *He's right to be proud; the boy outdid himself, and he's a fast learner. He's one I certainly won't forget.*

But already the conversation had gone back to bleaker subjects. "There is no doubt that Wolverine has taken up what Blood Bear left off," the Chief said, with a glance over his shoulder into the darkness, as if he feared that a spy from Wolverine tribe might be lurking there. "The difference, though, is that they raid, not destroy. Their raiding parties come farther south every moon; they take everything of value, male children less than five, widows and unmated females of breeding age. If a tribe dares to resist, they cripple the warriors after they have won."

"Ah, but first they come all smiles, and offer alliance—or rather, encourage their servitude to Wolverine—" the Shaman interjected. "It is only if the tribe fights that they raid."

Keisha was too tired to feel anything for herself, and too protected behind her walls to feel what the others felt, but the tension and concern beat against her protections and would flood her if she let it.

"Oh, but alliance means to surrender half of the provisions and goods, and all of the unmated females, and all boys down to the toddlers!" the Chief scoffed. "I do not call that generous!"

"They have not found us yet," the Shaman confided to

Keisha. "That is why we are unmolested. Our valley hides us well."

She nodded; she had not seen the mouth of the valley until they were practically inside it.

"Your sentries are to be given credit, too, I would think," Wintersky observed. Steelmind nodded, even as he frowned, and Shandi spoke up.

"It isn't just your location or your sentries, is it?" she asked, and looked directly at the Shaman. "You are—concealing. *You* are hiding the tribe, Honored One, using your powers. Aren't you?"

"Not I—the Snow Fox hides us, as he himself hides in winter," the Shaman protested, but he looked pleased. Darian raised his eyebrow at Shandi and smiled at the Shaman in a conspiratorial fashion. The Shaman gave Darian the same smile—Mage to Mage, exchanging the compliment of recognizing each other's handiwork.

"I do what little I can," the Shaman said modestly. "But too much done to hide our people would reveal, rather than conceal them. Wolverine has a Shaman, too, whose power is of the Eclipse, and he will see the use of power should I overstep myself."

"That's why the hunting parties are on their own." Darian made it a statement. He sighed. "I can't think of any way of concealing them that wouldn't betray them just as readily; you are perfectly right to be cautious."

"Our skill will conceal us," the chief hunter spoke up, with all the arrogant certainty of someone who has never met with failure—yet. "We can outwit any Wolverine scout."

This time it was the Chief who exchanged a raised eyebrow with Darian. For all Darian's apparent relative youth, it was clear that the Chief of Snow Fox realized he had a great deal of experience, and Keisha hid her own smile of pride.

"Why is it that you have no Wisewoman of your own?" Shandi asked, knowing now, after seeing so many other tribes, that when the Shaman was not a healer, his work was generally supplemented by a Wisewoman.

"She went to the ancestors before she could find a successor," the Shaman told her, sighing heavily. "That was many years ago. My pupil has the healing touch, and there is another boy who I will train in my own work when he comes to his manhood trial, but it is not fit that I seek out a girl-child to become a Wisewoman. In other times, the Wisewoman of one of our allies would have found and trained such a girl, but we have had little contact with our friends since Wolverine began raiding. We have not had the great Midsummer Gathering for two years."

Even as tired as she was, Keisha knew that was a very bad sign; even at height of the mage-storms, the Midsummer Gatherings had taken place. They were the only time that all the tribes came together under a truce banner; a time for trading, finding mates in other tribes, exchanging information, making alliances. If they had not been held for two years, none of these things were happening, and the peaceful tribes were becoming more and more isolated from each other.

He looked hopefully at Keisha, who grimaced. "We have another task," she said reluctantly. "It has been put upon us by both the Ghost Cat and the Raven spirits that we seek the Raven tribe." She did not say *why*, but no one would ask if she did not volunteer the information. It would be assumed that it was private business between her people and the spirits.

The Shaman's face fell; he had probably been hoping that she had been sent for the benefit of Snow Fox alone, and would remain until both his apprentice and a new Wisewoman had been chosen and trained. Keisha felt badly for him, and added, "I will do all I can to leave you with all that Snow Fox needs."

Not that I have any idea how to do that, she added to herself. *Healing isn't like a language that can be dumped entire into someone's head by a* dyheli—

Or—was it? *Could* Neta extract everything that Keisha knew about Healing and deposit it in the minds of the young apprentice and anyone else who needed to have it? And if she could—would it be more dangerous to do that than leave them on their own? Having so much information dumped into his mind at once might drive the poor apprentice mad . . . unless there was a way to *keep* it out of his conscious mind until he needed it.

I don't know. There has to be some terrible price hidden in it somewhere. Inventive or not, it seems too easy somehow.

In this world, we sometimes get lucky, but we never get things easy.

The best creature to ask would be Neta herself—and that would have to wait for morning. Now she *was* sleepy, and a warm fire and full stomach were contributing to that; for the moment, it didn't matter how much anxiety the rest of them felt, it couldn't penetrate to keep her awake. She wasn't the only one—there were plenty of hunters and warriors blinking their heavy eyes trying to stay awake. It wasn't long before the Shaman excused himself, and the Chief offered to send his guests to his own log house for rest. Darian accepted for all of them, and Keisha was glad; beyond the fire the mist was getting heavy, and there would probably be rain before morning. At least tonight they'd sleep dry. And she was too sleepy now to care about anything else.

Morning brought the unfamiliar sounds of children chattering like a tree full of birds near at hand, and Keisha woke all at once, with no intermediate drowsing between dream and wakefulness. She remembered at once where she was, partly because of the rush of unfamiliar smells, and stretched happily beneath her bright (and borrowed) blankets. There was rain pounding on the roof above her head, and from the sound of it, the storm was good for the rest of the day. If they'd been outside, they'd have started the day soaked again.

Would rain keep raiding parties stuck in one place? Now that she wasn't so tired, she remembered the conversation last night, and it wasn't just the chill and damp draft sneaking under her chin that made her shiver suddenly. Wolverine tribe—they sounded too much like the tribe that had almost destroyed Errold's Grove.

Not good news. And we'll have to get past them to get to Raven. That was worse news; would they have to skulk across the countryside from bit of cover to bit of cover? These raiding parties—how many were there?

I wonder if Darian wants to use magic to hide us? The existence of another enemy mage made that potentially as dangerous as going unhidden. How did these people rank mages, anyway—and how strong was he, how skilled? Journeyman? Master? Worst of all—Adept? Would they be unfortunate enough to encounter some sort of mage they had never even thought of, whose powers would be a total surprise?

She felt anxiety starting to get hold of her, and fought it off. There was no point in getting worried about something that was in the future—something she couldn't affect, for that matter. It was not that she disliked planning or even speculating, but there *was* such a thing as pointless worry in a case like this. This wasn't her problem—or at least, it wasn't her problem unless and until Darian asked her opinion. For now, *her* problem was to work with the Shaman—and she really ought to find out what his name was! No, wait. Hank. Henk. Henkeir. Henkeir Told-True.

That prompted the recollection of her thoughts the night before, about enlisting the help of the *dyheli* in transferring Healing knowledge directly to the young apprentice, and possibly, (if she could find one) a potential Wisewoman.

Language was at least as complicated as Healing; the problem with transferring it all at once was that Healing involved the use of power, a power very like mage-energy—and it involved using techniques that could leave the Healer's mind perilously open.

But what else did I think of last night—ah, I remember now. Would it be possible to transfer the knowledge in such a way that it only becomes available when the person needs it—

But no, that wouldn't work, because they might need it before they were ready to handle it.

Perhaps—it becomes available when the person masters something—keyed to that—

No one had ever tried anything like this before, not that she knew of. *But just because no one has ever done it before, that doesn't mean it can't be done. . . .*

Once again, though, she knew only that she didn't know enough. She would have to ask the *dyheli* Neta as she had thought last night, at the very least. Perhaps the Shaman might know something out of his own traditions that would help.

It would be so nice just to go back to sleep and forget this for a little longer, she thought wistfully. It had been *so* long since she'd had the luxury of sleeping until she felt completely rested—

But now that she was awake, her restless mind wouldn't let her go back to sleep again. *Too much to do.* She shoved the thought of drowsing away resolutely, and pushed the blankets aside. Like the loghouses of Ghost Cat, the loghouse of the Chief of Snow Fox had little cubicles around the walls used for storage and sleeping in a modicum of privacy. Presumably because Snow Fox was a *very* prosperous tribe, the barrier between the cubicle and the rest of the house was not a simple curtain, but was one of the beautiful piecework felt blankets.

It cut off the light from the central hearth fire much better than a cloth curtain would have; it was as dark as a cave in their cozy nest.

She sat up and swung her legs over the edge of the platform bed she shared with Darian, and he stirred. "Getting up?" he asked; he didn't sound sleepy, and she wondered if he had been awake and thinking as long as she had.

"I've got so much I need to do—" she began

"Anything I can help with?" He sat up, too. "I knew you were really concentrating on something, and I wondered what about. You seemed tense."

"I don't—" she began, then stopped as a thought interrupted her. Hadn't she been thinking that the power she used in Healing was like magic? And hadn't he added his power to hers in the past? Maybe he had an answer, or part of the answer she was looking for. Quickly, she explained what she had been thinking of doing. "Do *you* know of a way to keep that knowledge locked up until the person is ready for it?" she asked.

He pondered her question, giving it full attention; she couldn't see his face clearly, but she sensed he was concentrating, trying to remember something. "I think it can be done," he said finally. "You'd have to be awfully good, though. I—don't think I could do something like that. Maybe an Adept could."

She grimaced; disappointed, but not surprised. "I'll see if their Shaman knows of something that would work. You never know."

"I might as well get up, too," he said, levering himself up out of bed beside her, his long hair strung across his face in tangles. "There's a lot to get done. I think that we'd better stay here until the sick are healed, so we can have Snow Fox's full support when it's time to move on. It can only help." He sounded as wistful as she was, though. "Sometimes I wonder if the only time we'll ever get to be lazy is if we get sick ourselves."

"Don't even think that," she chided, and reached for her clothing, handing him his. "We can't afford to be sick."

They both got dressed and Keisha pushed aside the partition blanket, stepping out into the central room. The Shaman's wife hurried to greet them, handing them bowls of porridge made with crushed nuts and sweetened with honey. It was very good, and a nice change from the breakfasts of cold meat they'd been having.

They were the first ones awake from their group, although some stirring and muttering indicated that the rest weren't too far behind them in getting up. Keisha finished her breakfast quickly and got her rain cloak, heading out to find the Shaman and begin the morning's treatments.

The Shaman was waiting for her at the house holding all the sick, and before she and his apprentice began work, he made a point of offering her a second breakfast, this time of a kind of bread or cake made of the same crushed nut mixture. She was not at all averse to having more to eat, knowing that she would need all the energy she could get.

As they ate, the Shaman introduced his apprentice as Lother. Henkeir's wife made all the meals for the sick isolated here in this house, and had sent extra for Keisha, her husband, and his pupil.

"Your wife is extremely accommodating," Keisha said dryly, thinking how much work a woman of the tribes did just to keep her own family fed, clothed, and cared for—never mind adding on the care of a dozen sick people.

"My wife tells me just how accommodating she is on a regular basis," he replied, just as dryly. "But I agree with her, even when she is not nearby to hear it."

Keisha covered her mouth with one hand, stifling her giggles; young Lother laughed outright, and Henkeir grinned behind his beard.

"I think that this may be the case with all worthy spouses," Henkeir told them. "Perhaps they fear that if they are too silent, we will come to take them for granted." He put aside his cup of hot herb drink and stood up. "Are you ready for the morning's work?"

"More than ready," she told him, and the three of them approached the first patient of the day together.

After rest—and a noon meal that she ate so fast she didn't even taste it—Keisha went out in search of the *dyheli*. She was altogether gratified to learn from the Shaman that the *dyheli* and Karles had been housed in the communal storage house, rather than forced to spend the rainy night and day out in the weather.

The children, who shed the water like so many ducklings and evidently considered this to be balmy weather, were making a great game of going out and tearing up armloads of grass to feed to the four-legged guests. She spotted a group of them running into the storage house, shrieking with laughter, so laden with long, wet bundles of grass that they looked like so many little walking haystacks. She followed them, and soon discovered *why* the sport of feeding the *dyheli* was so popular.

The *dyheli* were earning their dinner by taking turns telling stories.

Of course, when a *dyheli* "told" a story, it appeared in the "listener's" head, complete with pictures, sounds, and smells. The children were absolutely enraptured. This was better entertainment than anything they'd ever encountered before.

It was not yet Neta's turn to tell a story, so Keisha was able to take her aside and quiz her on the possibility of transferring knowledge rather than language.

Neta considered the question, then diffidently asked Keisha for free access to her mind. Keisha sat down on a pile of furs and obliged—sitting, in case this turned out to cause the kind of reaction that a language transfer did, and she passed out cold.

She didn't drop over, although Neta's explorations left her with the oddest feeling, as if her mind was a box whose contents were being meticulously turned over and examined, one bit at a time. It felt strangely like the mountain sickness, crossed with being intoxicated on very bad wine, and then being flattened thoroughly with a rolling pin but not minding it at all.

:*I think the transfer can be done,*: Neta finally said, when she'd withdrawn her mind from Keisha's. :*The problem would be that Healing involves development and exercise of mental powers—rather like training muscles for strength. If a young one tried to use the knowledge before he had the strength, it could harm him. Worse than another Healer could fix.*:

Keisha ground her teeth in frustration. Not that she hadn't already been afraid that would be the case, but it was disappointing in the extreme.

:*Let me think of this, and consult with Karles,*: Neta added, responding to her frustration with a sympathy that surprised her. :*There may be something that we can do.*: The *dyheli* doe looked across the room at the Companion, who responded by joining them immediately.

Karles regarded Keisha with an unreadable deep-blue gaze, then turned his attention toward Neta. While the children in the corner giggled and exclaimed over the story one of the young bucks was "telling" them, Keisha watched the silent colloquy going on between the Companion and the doe, and wondered what they were talking about. Finally Neta turned back toward Keisha. :*If we think of knowledge as something to be* held, *then what you need is a container from which a little can be taken at a time, yes?*:

"More like a smart container that knows how much to dole out, but yes, something like that," she replied, intrigued by the analogy.

:*Karles suggests that we ask the Snow Fox to be that container.*:

Shaman Henkeir was at first surprised speechless, then briefly appalled—then intrigued by Keisha and Neta's suggestion. "It has . . . merit," he said cautiously. "If this could be done, it would mean that we need never fear the loss of a Wisewoman, for the Snow Fox would always hold this wisdom in its keeping. The old stories hold that the People give knowledge to the gods. That is why we do not become like stagnant water, for we can create and give that knowledge to benefit the totem. The Snow Fox might be pleased by this, yes."

Keisha did *not* ask why the Snow Fox didn't already have that knowledge to dispense. The tribal totems didn't seem to be so much "gods" as benevolent overseers and benefactors.

They certainly weren't all-seeing and all-knowing, or they would have been able to protect their own tribes from the depredations of others. It was said, even in Valdemar, that gods received power and support from their followers, and they in turn helped those followers prosper. She wondered if there was a kind of spiritual warfare going on among the totemic "animals," with the stronger paving the way for the conquest of the weaker as the totemic spirits defeated each other.

It was actually a rather frightening thought.

If that were the case, it was no wonder that the tribes spent so much time in strengthening their totems with prayer and worship!

"How would we find out if the Snow Fox was willing to be the vessel for this knowledge?" she asked aloud, and the Shaman's eyes widened as he looked over her shoulder.

She felt a cool breath on the back of her neck, and turned to find herself staring into a pair of amused, milky-blue catlike eyes. She flinched backward, which elicited a look of frank amusement from the manifestation.

The eyes were set in a head with a sharply pointed muzzle and a pair of blunt, pointed ears. The head was attached to a body the size of a small pony, but it was a resemblance in scale only. The furred body was a misty white, and translucent—just as the shadowy spirit of the Ghost Cat had been. Tiny sparkles of white light, like twinkling stars, fell away from the apparition in all directions, as slow as falling dust motes in sunlight.

Time seemed to slow for Keisha, and there was only one thing that she could think. *I—guess we have our answer!*

Sixteen

Another day, another deity.

On the whole, even after hearing from Keisha about the bizarre manifestation of the Snow Fox itself and its subsequent absorption of her Healing knowledge, Darian regretted leaving this latest tribe—but there was no choice. Something strong and true and part of him drove him on; if he gave up now, how could he remain himself?

They left Snow Fox better provisioned than they had arrived. Dried meat, nut-meal, and dried berries made their saddlebags bulge, and in the packs of trade goods, gold nuggets replaced packets of dye. Keisha now wore two token necklaces instead of one; in addition to the owl, she wore a string of tiny carved foxes of mother-of-pearl. The Snow Fox Shaman had given her that just before they left. Keisha tried to think little of what she had done, but inside, Darian figured Keisha knew she had just given an entire tribe of people an edge against the cruelties of the wild world. The customs of the tribes made effusive thanks from a male to a female unlikely; given everything she'd done to heal their sick, he figured she more than deserved that necklace, and it was one of the few ways that the Shaman could show his gratitude. In fact, by rights she should have been bedecked by a dozen such necklaces by now, one for every tribe she'd helped, and for every

Wisewoman and Shaman she'd tutored in the Valdemaran use of the Healing Gift.

I think that Keisha is blissfully unaware of what a huge impact she is having upon an entire culture, by what she gives so selflessly. The tribes may worship or thank the holy dyheli now, but it is Keisha and the others in green they talk about plenty among each other, I'll wager.

They had good instructions on how to reach Raven tribe—and the origin of the vests had been confirmed. One more stretch of mountains lay between them and their goal—one more stretch, that just happened to be claimed by Wolverine.

Every time he thought about Wolverine, an odd chill touched him for just a moment.

"This is as far as I can take you," their guide said at about noon on the second day after they had left Snow Fox. He looked out over the valley that stretched out before them with some regret. "You wish to aim for that pass, between those two peaks," he said, pointing. "On the other side is the Bitter Water, and the Raven tribe."

And between us and them is trouble. He didn't give any sign that he was worried, though; he just thanked the hunter with as much sincerity as he could show, and watched as the man trotted off into the shelter of the forest that Snow Fox called its territory, melting into the undergrowth almost like a Tayledras might.

He looked back over his own group; Keisha was worried, but he could hardly blame her for that. Hywel was as confident as any young and untried warrior. He happily bore the arrogance of ignorance. Steelmind was as calm as one of the mountain peaks, Wintersky impatient to be gone, and Shandi unreadable. The nonhumans displayed a similar mix of emotional stances.

"It's probably going to take us twice as long to cross this stretch as it's taken before," he said, mostly to Keisha and Shandi. "If you thought we were being careful before, you were wrong. We're truly going into enemy territory now, and we'll be moving accordingly."

Shandi nodded alertly. "Kel overhead, the birds out in front, the *dyheli*, Karles, and Hashi behind them, then us, following on foot. Right?"

"Absolutely right." He felt rather gratified that she had

caught on so quickly, but then, she *was* a Herald, and Heralds got some military training. The only difference between this group and a group of the Guard or local militia was that their scouts had wings, paws, and hooves. He dismounted, and the rest did the same, taking time to tighten every baggage-strap and harness-fastener so that the hooved ones wouldn't be hindered by loose baggage. Then every stirrup was tied up, so that they didn't dangle free either. If they had to run for it, having the stirrups out of the way would make mounting and riding harder, but not impossible, especially not since their mounts were *dyheli* and a Companion.

He gave the mental signal to Kuari that the owl had been waiting for, then called Kel.

:All right, Silver Gryphon—we're moving out! Take high point.:

:I am ready,: came the reply from somewhere aloft. *:The way is clear to the next stretch of trees. Dodge to your left to make use of the runoff ravine and follow it to the light-gray stack of boulders.:*

The *dyheli* and Karles spread out, trotting down through the waist-high meadow grass, heading for the trees. Hashi was with them, but invisible in the grass. He could have left a "wake" in the grass, but he didn't—and wouldn't. The *kyree* were masters of moving invisibly.

Now it was the humans' turn, and despite having been given the word that there were no enemies in the immediate vicinity, they moved cautiously across the open stretch, hunched down near the tops of the grasses. Those who had bows had arrows loosely nocked to the strings. Wintersky and Darian, as the two most experienced in this sort of movement, took point; Hywel took right flank, Shandi the left, and Steelmind the rear, putting Keisha in the relatively protected middle. Darian wondered briefly if that rankled with her, then centered all of his attention on scanning the territory ahead.

It was hard to remain on the alert when from all the signs there was no need to be. Tiny birds flitted through the stalks of the grass, or skimmed ahead of them, chasing the insects they scared up. Occasionally they kicked up a rabbit. Other than that, the meadow drowsed in the warm late-spring sun, with some puffy clouds around to the west beginning to develop darker bottoms that might promise (more) rain.

Darian figured that as long as he remained in a posture of readiness, the others would take their cue from him—especially Hywel, who might well need "reminding."

The greatest danger was that because the meadow was at least a league wide, enemies might appear before they had crossed it. The *dyheli,* and *kyree,* Kel and Karles ought to be able to spot them in time to take cover in the grass, but that would leave them horribly vulnerable.

But they made it into the shelter of the forest again without mishap, and Darian relaxed a little. But only a little. There was one advantage here; the giant trees were interspersed with "normal" trees, and that gave them an escape route and a hiding place—into the boughs of those trees.

They had gone about another league into that forest, relying on Kel and the birds to guide them towards the mountain pass that was their goal, when Hashi sounded a warning of his own.

:I scent a party of humans—many smelling of fear, the rest of fighting! They come from the northeast and are coming straight for you!:

Darian had been planning escape routes all along as they moved through the forest. "Steelmind—you and Shandi up that tree!" he shouted, pointing to a cedar. He turned and pointed to another. "Wintersky and Hywel, up there!"

He grabbed Keisha's hand and ran for a third tree, a black pine. All three had the advantage of very thick foliage as well as branches near enough to the ground to be hooked by the climbing stick, a hooked half-weapon and half-tool device, that all three Tayledras carried.

He pulled his own climbing stick from the sheath on his back as he ran, slung his bow over his shoulder and shoved the arrow he'd had ready back into the quiver. In a practiced move, he aimed the hook of his climbing stick at an overhead branch as he ran, and used his momentum to carry him up the trunk. He went hand-over-hand up the stick as he scrambled over the bark of the trunk, and once lodged securely on the branch he had hooked, pulled the climbing stick loose, and extended it to Keisha. She grabbed it, and he pulled her up beside him, then repeated the process with the next branch. Once they were high enough that the branches were closer together, Keisha could climb up by herself without his aid; at that point, he stowed his climbing stick and worked his way up the trunk until they were both well-hidden from below.

:*Kuari, I need you,*: he called.

:*I come!*: the owl replied immediately. As he waited for Kuari, he made contact with each of the outliers, making sure that the *dyheli* stayed well out of the way, the *kyree* hid himself, and Kel stayed high overhead.

Kuari came in to land just as he heard the most distant sounds of forest disturbance, the scolding of corvids. :*Go perch where you can see the enemy,*: Darian told the owl. :*Then let me use your eyes.*:

Kuari hooted softly, and ghosted down out of the tree, choosing a branch a little lower with nothing else between it and the ground. He perched there and set his feet well onto the branch, then relaxed—and Darian saw what he was seeing.

No doubt Wintersky and Steelmind were doing the same with their birds.

A bit higher on the trunk than he was, Keisha tied herself into place as a precaution against becoming unbalanced. Darian was so comfortable in trees now that he didn't need such helps; he could fall asleep in the fork of a tree without losing his balance—and had, in the past. He still preferred to live in an *ekele* firmly planted on the ground, but that was just a preference.

The scolding of crows came nearer, and through the owl's eyes, Darian got his first sight of the warriors of Wolverine.

There were more than twenty, perhaps as many as thirty of them; they were more heavily armed and armored than any Northerners that Darian had seen since his last encounter with the fighters of Blood Bear. Most had breastplates of boiled leather, and arm-guards and greaves of hammered bronze. All had bronze helmets and iron swords; they also carried javelins or short spears with iron points, and long daggers. A few were also armed with bows.

But they were not alone.

They had taken prisoners: many prisoners. The captives had been divided into three groups—young women, young boys, and girls. The prisoners within each group were strung out in single-file, and the women and girls (though not the boys) were tied together at the waist by a rope that led from one to the next. In addition, the older women were also tied at the wrists. The boys, all under the age of five, were allowed freedom of movement.

There must have been a hundred prisoners, and by the decorations on their costumes, they were of some fox tribe. Were they allied with Snow Fox—or even related to them?

Their captors were, without a doubt, of Wolverine. They bore the insignia of their tribe on everything—but they also bore the sign of the eclipse. The sight of that symbol, even though it was through Kuari's eyes, made his blood run cold, and a sour taste came up the back of his throat. The last time he had seen that symbol, it had been terrifyingly close, on a pendant around the neck of the Blood Bear Shaman—

But this time there was no sign of the weird half-human creatures that Blood Bear had counted among its warriors. These were "no more than" humans.

Very well-armed, very large and muscular humans, who seriously outnumbered Darian's group. And much as he longed to drop down out of the tree, slashing at them with his climbing stick, he knew better. He wouldn't stand a chance, and from the cowed and beaten look of the women, they wouldn't even be able to muster the spirit to use his attack as a distraction to make a break for freedom.

But it was hard to hide in safety and do nothing, when he watched one of the warriors trip one of the women with his spear butt and laugh to see her stumble—then when he saw the fear in the eyes of girl-captives barely into puberty. They knew what their fate would be as soon as they arrived at the Wolverine village.

Darian had to repeat to himself that there was nothing he or his friends could do, but his hands clenched so tightly on the tree trunk that the bark bit into his palm and his fingernails were white. He felt another's anger as well, and realized that Kel, circling high above, was also looking through Kuari's eyes, and was just as enraged as he was. Gryphons had *always* had an inherent hatred for slavery as a matter of principle, and this was making the gryphon's hackles rise, and quickly.

:*Kel!*: he called immediately. :*Don't attack! This is an order, Silver Gryphon! Stay aloft!*:

He felt Kel's wordless protest, and from the way that Keisha turned pale and clutched the trunk, so did she. It was the anger-surge of a great predator, immensely larger and more powerful than Kuari, a predator that *needed* to kill. Kel clamped it down after that first surge, but it left both Darian and Keisha shaking with reaction in the aftermath of the experience.

Poor Keisha; she's never "seen" him this way. I have; I know him for what he is. He is a killer with civilization. Kel was the sweetest and most genial creature alive, until his killing instincts were aroused. At that point, there was no creature Darian knew of that was more murderous and less stoppable.

They clung to the tree, silent, each alone with his thoughts, as Wolverine paraded their captives past them and on to their own village. Darian tried to concentrate on memorizing everything he could about the warriors—and that was when he noticed something odd. The Wolverine raiders were treating the women and girls with casual brutality, but the little boys, who were allowed to run free, were being indulged—even petted and spoiled. Any time that a boy made any kind of overture toward a Wolverine fighter, it was immediately reciprocated with a smile, a pat, a treat. And already a few of the boys were trotting at the heels of some of the men, looking up at them fearlessly.

Of course—they took these boys to make them into future Wolverine *fighters.* And the campaign to win their loyalty began the moment they left their own village.

Brutal they may be, but they are not stupid. Those boys would respond to the petting and spoiling just like any child of that age. In six months, they would be strutting around and imitating the warriors' contempt for the women, even their own mothers. In a year, they would belong to Wolverine.

He wondered what the others were thinking, if they had seen what he had, and knew what it meant. This was a harvest—of breeders and future warriors. The women were no more nor less than walking wombs, valued only for what they could produce.

Whether the Wolverine fighters treated the women of their own tribe any better remained to be seen, but Darian had an idea that they might. Putting their own women higher in the social scheme gave them an extra set of guardians for their captives. Making the captive women the slaves to their own women virtually ensured that every Wolverine woman would regard the slaves as property, rather than as a fellow.

The only reason we defeated Blood Bear was that they underestimated us. The only reason that Blood Bear is no more is that they made stupid mistakes.

All the evidence pointed to one thing—Wolverine was of the same ilk as Blood Bear had been, but they had paid attention to all the things that Blood Bear had done wrong.

And that made them all the more dangerous.

Kel was doing everything but frothing at the mouth with rage. He paced, he snapped his beak, he mantled his wings, he bristled his crest. "Jussst one!" he hissed, tearing up the sod with his fore-talons. "Let me have jussst one, Darrrrian!"

Kel had been like this since he landed. *He* wanted to launch an attack on the raiding party, right now—no planning, no waiting, no thinking about it. He could not bear what he had seen, and wanted to fix it. After all, he was Kelvren, the brave, fierce Silver Gryphon—he *should* be able to fix all of these things, by shredding those responsible for them!

Keisha had all of her shields up, and still felt the heat of his anger blazing against them. She just hoped that time and Darian's soothing would calm him down. Right now no one was arguing with him; they were just letting him vent his emotions, agreeing, when confronted, that it was a horrible situation and should not be allowed to continue.

Hywel was as angry as Kel, but was handling it better; he was white around the eyes and mouth, but hadn't said or done much. "Why aren't *you* frothing at the mouth?" Keisha asked him quietly.

"Because it would not do good," he replied, with a maturity she had not expected. She might have forgotten that he was a native of these parts, but he hadn't, and he was well aware of the harsh reality of life here in the north. "Darian is right; we are too few to do anything. But—"

He didn't complete the thought; he looked back along the trampled underbrush where the party of captives had passed, and anger flitted over his face. Perhaps he was well aware of the harsh realities of life up here, but that didn't mean he was inured to them. *Or this is beyond what even he is used to.*

Shandi had one hand on Karles' shoulder, and Keisha

guessed that she was sharing her thoughts with her Companion. Wintersky and Steelmind were impassive, and Keisha could not guess what was going on behind their masks. *These aren't our people,* she reminded herself. *I am sure that they care, but we can't help the captives.*

But she had an idea, and it might take Kel's mind off his anger—or at least give him an acceptable outlet for it. "Shouldn't we—" she began.

Kel stopped tearing the helpless grass, and all eyes turned toward her. She swallowed, looking up into Kel's golden glare.

"Shouldn't we go back that way?" She pointed in the direction from which Wolverine had come. After all, the trail was clear enough. "There may be people where they came from that need help. There may be survivors."

They stared at her in silence for a moment. Then Kel leaped into the air without another word, powering purposefully upward but remaining below the canopy of the mammoth trees so that he could follow the trail.

There seemed nothing else more appropriate to do, so without further discussion, the rest of the party mounted up and followed in his wake.

Keisha heaved a sigh of relief, which no one but her *dyheli* noticed. *:A bit difficult for you, are they, Healer?:* he asked dryly. *:Not the easiest lot to deal with.:*

She snorted; he knew as well as she the kinds of strain all those angry people were putting on her shields. Not that *she* wasn't angry, but perhaps because she *was* a Healer, she'd learned to be pragmatic. You couldn't save every patient—although you tried; you couldn't solve every problem—though you did your best. She knew from the moment that she saw all the armed fighters that there was nothing they could do for the prisoners, much as she and everyone else would like to.

Turning their attention to something they *could* do something about had been the one thing she could do about the situation. She was just glad that her attempt at redirection had worked for Kel; he needed an outlet, a constructive outlet, before he flew off and did something foolish.

Now she steeled herself for what they would find at the end of the trail of trampled vegetation. Whatever it was, she knew that it would surely put a different set of stresses on them all.

It was dusk when they reached the village that they would

later learn belonged to the Red Fox tribe, a group that long ago had split from Snow Fox. Kel had gotten there long before, had given them a grim summary of what they would find when they got there, then flew off on a mission of his own—and an important one, second only to the Healing Keisha would be doing when she arrived.

Kel went hunting, for there was *nothing* left to eat in the village, and at the moment, no one capable of hunting or gathering. Absolutely nothing edible of any kind had been left— the village had been scoured right down to the spices. Even leather, curing hides and scraped skins had been taken.

They did not need to follow the trail to find the village; the wailing of women led them there. But there was no heavy scent of smoke, for the raiders had not troubled themselves with burning any of the log houses. It was not their intention to leave the survivors without shelter, because it was not their intention that all of the survivors should die.

It had been candlemarks since the raiders hit this place; long enough for the women to gather their dead and lay them out for mourning on a single rough pyre, long enough for the wounded to receive the rough tending that was all a tribe without a Shaman could give them. The Shaman—much younger than the Shaman of Snow Fox—had been laid out with the rest of the dead by his wives, who were the source of the wailing. The rest of the women were too numb for anything but silent mourning—and at a single glance, Keisha knew they had their own internalized wounds to deal with. No one had touched the Shaman's three wives, possibly for fear of a curse, but by the condition of the other women, clothing torn, faces bruised, and the vacant look of someone who has endured too much, they had not shared this protection.

Forewarned by Kel, Keisha was armored against their pain, emotional and physical, as the group rode into the village. Hywel preceded them afoot, calling to the survivors that help was coming; by the time the rest rode in, it was too dark for the northerners to see what they were riding, which probably spared them the fear that would have come when they saw the unfamiliar mounts. They had already endured too much, and even a little more fear might well push them over the edge of sanity.

Keisha left the organization of the survivors to the others, and went straight to work on the most seriously wounded, concentrating *only* on pure Healing with her Gift. Shandi and Karles supported her, lending her new strength and energy when hers faltered—then, when they were exhausted, Darian took their place. It was very, very late when she finished with the last woman; the moon was high overhead, though obscured by thick clouds, and all she wanted to do was eat and sleep—not necessarily in that order. She blessed the darkness that hid the ravaged village; with no fires outside tonight, and all of the inhabitants drugged into a semblance of sleep in their own homes, there was finally a measure of peace in this shattered place.

Darian led her into a log house, which by the trappings had belonged to the Shaman. When they entered, and all three of the Shaman's wives descended on them, pressing food rations, venison and a hot herbal drink on her, she was too tired to be surprised, but she was very grateful.

The women left them at the hearth fire where the others had gathered—including the *dyheli*, Karles, and Kel, which *did* surprise Keisha, Kel most of all. "What are you doing here?" she asked, staring at him stupidly.

"The folk of Rrrred Fox arrre not inclined to trrreat a gift brrringerrr as an enemy," he replied simply, and left it at that.

Judging by the fact that all of the party were eating chunks of well-roasted venison, Kel's gifts had been generous indeed. "What can you tell me?" she asked, knowing by Darian's rigid expression that he had learned far more than he really wanted to know.

Darian's voice was tight with suppressed rage as he answered. "This wasn't just a raid," he said. "They hit this place at dawn. They took out all the sentries just before they were going to be replaced by the dawn crew, then hit the village itself. When they had taken the village, they started harvesting."

She was startled alert by the odd word. "Harvesting?" she asked, incredulously.

He nodded, his lips white with anger, a vein in his temple throbbing. "The warriors that survived they crippled—or didn't you notice all the missing index fingers on their bow-hands? They did the same to the older boys, so they couldn't possibly grow up to be warriors. Without an index finger, they can't pull a bow or use a sword."

"But—harvesting?" she repeated.

"You were Healing them—you know the secret wounds they had in common. The invaders did their best to make certain that *every* woman here would be left pregnant, regardless of her age. The ones that still had husbands were left behind, the ones that had infants were left behind with their babies, and girls too young to breed. The rest were taken, along with the older girls and younger boys, as you saw. They took every scrap of food, and anything that was valuable—but they left the bare essentials, and they left the houses intact." She actually heard his teeth gritting as he snarled silently. "They intend to come back, Keisha. They intend to come back as soon as these people have started to recover. They'll take girls old enough to breed, and young boys, and strip the place again. And they'll *keep* coming back, as long as there is anything left of Red Fox."

"These are not our people, Darian," Steelmind said, in that slow, deliberate way of his. "We have already done more than they would expect from an ally."

She reached for his hand and clasped it, as he controlled his temper. Kel hung his head wearily; the gryphon was just as angry, but they all knew that Steelmind was only telling the truth.

"We've done more than our share," Shandi added, her voice flat. "Remember why we're here. It's not to fight a war with people who don't even know we exist. It's to look for danger to Valdemar, and find your parents, Darian. If we take the time to get involved in this, we may never do those things."

He didn't answer; he didn't have to; Keisha felt his upset even though her shields were up and tight, as a sick feeling in her stomach and a dry lump in her throat.

No one else said anything; there didn't seem to be much that anyone could say. Eventually they all went to their sleeping rolls in silence—but Darian held her very tight for a long, long time, and she cradled him, projecting peace, until he relaxed and finally slept.

But the only reason she slept was because she was too tired not to.

*   *   *

She was the first to wake the next day, and after a sketchy meal that she ate only because she needed the energy, went straight to her patients. They were doing better than she had any reason to expect; the women had mustered the tattered remains of their courage and were tending to the wounded men. Each man had his own wife taking care of him, and usually at least one other woman as well. It occurred to Keisha that this might be in self-defense. Wolverine had not taken the wives of any man who lived through the raid, so obviously the best way to keep from getting taken was to become someone's second or third wife.

But whatever their motives, they were working as hard as the "real" wives, which was giving the wounded men some excellent care.

The Shaman's widows had fired the funeral pyre and were chanting and drumming the farewell to the dead—they might not be Wisewomen themselves, but they knew the ceremonies, and no one was going to dispute their right to see that the dead were properly taken care of. All three of them sat on the upwind side, two playing a large drum, the third playing a counterpoint on a smaller drum. Whatever they had built the pyre out of, it had gone up like an oil-soaked torch, and was burning hotly with very little smoke.

Keisha was very glad that the village was upwind of the pyre; as it was, the unmistakable too-sweet scent of burning flesh made her stomach lurch, and she had to fight her breakfast back down.

Slowly the tribe of Red Fox was reclaiming its village and its life. A few children had recovered enough spirit to play a counting game quietly together, and the prepubescent girls were restoring order to the open spaces between the log houses by the simple expedient of throwing anything that was of no use into a rubbish pile and dividing the rest among themselves.

There wasn't a great deal to divide. Although the raiders hadn't taken common clothing and domestic utensils, that was about all that they had left. Finished furs and trade goods in the storehouses were gone, as were "show" blankets, weapons, and every bit of dried meat and fish. The women had been too traumatized to go out gathering, and the stocks of perishable foods hidden away was low. Unless the remaining men could recover enough to hunt soon, they would be starving in a matter of weeks.

As Keisha made her rounds, she noticed Shandi and Karles watching the villagers thoughtfully, as if they were making some kind of assessment. Shandi glanced over at her once, but said nothing, so Keisha left her to her thoughts and continued taking care of the wounded.

She finished around noon, and returned to the Shaman's house. The pyre was nothing but embers now, for which she was very grateful, and the widows had thrown great heaps of green cedar, white sage, and juniper on the coals. The scented smoke had overcome the stench of the pyre.

A line of gutted deer carcasses hung upside down by their rear hooves in the trees just outside the Shaman's house; Kel and some of the others must have been very busy this morning. Ordinarily it wasn't like Kel or the Tayledras to take out an entire herd of deer, but under the circumstances, it was the right thing to do.

Maybe Red Fox won't starve, she thought with a little more hope. *This looks like enough to keep them going for a while.*

Shandi met her at the door as she approached, stopping her with a look. "How long do you think that will last?" she asked, nodding toward the line of carcasses.

Keisha counted the deer, made a quick mental estimate of the number of people left and how much they would need to eat, added a bit more for generosity, and said, "About a fortnight."

Shandi nodded, and sucked on her lower lip for a moment. "That was what I figured. How long before most of the injured can hunt for themselves? About a fortnight?"

"Pretty much," she said truthfully, wondering what Shandi was thinking. "I've got them about half Healed; if we left now, it would be about a fortnight before they could do anything strenuous." There was something going on in her sister's mind—but what?

Darian pushed the blanket over the door aside and joined them, looking sharply at Shandi. "What's on your mind?" he asked abruptly, the same question Keisha had.

"These people used to be in Snow Fox," Shandi told him. "They split off about three generations ago, but they're still a Snow Fox sept. Neta can put the directions to Snow Fox right into the heads of as many people as we need to. We can leave them with enough food to get them healed up, and they can make it to safety before anyone from Wolverine comes checking on them. There's your solution."

Keisha heaved a sigh of relief as the tension eased out of Darian. "There's our solution," he agreed, nodding, the worry lines in his forehead smoothing out. "They won't burden themselves down with possessions, because they don't *have* any to speak of. Snow Fox has to take them in; they're related. There's nothing keeping them here, so I doubt they'll make any objections, but let me check and see what Hywel thinks."

Keisha went back into the log house while Shandi, Karles, and Darian went over to the butchering area where Hywel was working to turn the deer into strips of jerked meat.

She ate without tasting what she was eating, stayed a moment to rest, then went back to her patients. Now she had helpers—helpers who were dealing with their own pain by giving themselves something to think about besides their own ordeals, and they were very good at obeying her directions. She gave the same instructions so many times she could recite them without thinking about it: "Wash your hands in water that's been boiled and cooled. Pull the dressing off carefully; don't touch the wound with your hands. Sprinkle the mold-powder on the wound, check for the signs of infection. Take a new dressing that's been washed and boiled, rebandage the wound." One man had the start of an infection; she used the occasion to call all the women together to give them a lesson in what infection looked like and how to deal with it. *If they aren't Wisewomen, they'll certainly have half the training by the time this is over. . . .*

By nightfall she was as exhausted as she had been the previous night, but when she returned to the group around the fire in the log house, the mood there was so much more cheerful that she nearly wept with gratitude. She didn't, but she quietly basked in the positive feelings while she ate, listening to the discussions of what to do to prepare Red Fox for the journey. The Shaman's widows joined in the discussion—not with animation, but with a determination that surprised and pleased her. They were ready to leave *now*, and anything they could do to hasten the date of departure would be dealt with.

"Neta already gave Gwynver, Rinan, and Dedren the directions to Snow Fox," Darian told her in an aside during a pause in the discussion. "They're going to tell the rest of the tribe tomorrow that their husband and the Red Fox spirit came to them in a dream tonight—the Red Fox turned white, and their husband showed them the way to their allies."

"Nobody will argue with that," Hywel agreed, looking more like his old self. "And who knows? Tonight it might well happen that way. If *I* were the Red Fox, I would certainly choose to do that for my people."

"Young man!" called one of the three women—who was certainly no older than Hywel—in an imperious tone. "Tell me again where in the stream to place the fish trap!"

Hywel rolled his eyes, but turned back to her with all the deference due that rare woman who ranked higher than a young warrior, and the conversation resumed. Keisha leaned against Darian and closed her eyes. There was no more tension in the air; even Kel was satisfied with the solution. No longer having to keep her shields reinforced, she relaxed further—then she heard the word *sleep* in a *dyheli* mind-voice and the next thing she knew, Darian was putting her into her sleeping roll.

She murmured her thanks, and unable to even get her eyes open, gave up and fell back into dreamless slumber.

Seventeen

If the people of Red Fox themselves had not been so determined to take Shandi's solution and follow through on it, Darian would have had a harder time with his conscience. As it was, it was difficult, very difficult, to persuade himself that the tribe would do as well without his help as with it.

But the survivors greeted the morning's "revelation" by the three co-conspirators with unquestioning belief and even enthusiasm. It didn't hurt that the eldest of the three widows confided to Darian with a look of wonder that she really *had* dreamed of the Red Fox spirit. Furthermore, she wonderingly said that in her dream the spirit had bestowed its approval of all that they had said and planned, and it had told her to tell the rest of the people to do as these special foreigners—the "Trusted Not-of-the-Tribe"—directed. Whether her own mind manufactured the dream, or it was a true vision didn't really matter at the moment; what did make a difference was the reverence. She almost palpably projected a glow when she told the rest of her tribe of the manufactured vision. Because the spirits had approved of it, it *became* true for her and for her two co-widows. Their belief was contagious; it didn't even require the mental nudging of the *dyheli,* which had been his private, emergency plan.

When one of the younger widows lamented her husband's

loss again, the older woman gained a sudden look of extreme serenity and replied, "The Fox says, 'Do not let yesterday use up too much of today,' child." Two heartbeats of utter stillness followed, and then the older woman bent to pick up some of her belongings to prepare for the journey. Whether that had been clever acting or an actual contact with the Fox Spirit he did not know, but the effect was startling. One by one, the rest followed suit.

Kel, Hywel, and Wintersky went hunting that day as well, making certain that the village would have meat enough to carry it through not only the next fortnight, but the necessarily slow journey to Snow Fox. Steelmind, Shandi, Karles, and the *dyheli* "hunted" growing edibles and collected firewood.

Perhaps "collecting" was an understatement. They hitched the *dyheli* and Karles to downed trees, which were then dragged to the village; before long there was an enormous line of them in the clearing, waiting to be chopped up. It was an exquisite irony that so many of Darian's youthful indiscretions had revolved around collecting firewood, and now here he was, in charge of firewood yet again.

Darian remained behind to help the survivors plan their journey, help Keisha, and chop the wood—with the help of the strongest of the girls, women, and any of the men fit to swing an ax or a mallet. Many of them were impressed by the high quality of the Tayledras axes, and marveled at Wintersky's folding ax. And from the fierce and controlled anger with which the women dealt with their woody "adversaries," Darian figured they were getting more than just stockpiled wood out of the exercise.

For him, the day passed quickly. He took a great deal of his own anger out on the wood; it felt good to imagine the faces of the Wolverine raiders and strike with his full strength behind the blows.

Everyone was so exhausted by the end of that day that they all went straight to bed relatively early. But there was none of the depression and gloom hanging over them that there had been; having a place to go and things to do to get ready for the migration had altered the entire mood of the tribe.

He had no illusions about the damaged psyches of the women, however. What they had endured would have to be dealt with eventually—but he trusted, having met and worked with him, that the Shaman of Snow Fox would be able to give them help.

Or if he can't, their own tribal spirits certainly will.

So he went to sleep feeling, if not cheered, certainly with his conscience doing little more than an occasional mutter.

They left only when they all felt that they had done as much for the tribe as was needed; there was firewood piled high, racks and racks of meat drying, all manner of stores to tide these people through the difficult weeks ahead. Keisha had done as much as she could, given the brief amount of time she'd had to work; time and their own bodies would do the rest. The women had a purpose again, the men a reason to heal and get on their feet. The despair was gone, and there was even a glimpse of hope, now and again. These people were ready to stand on their own feet. If they weren't to become dependent on their benefactors, it was time for Darian's group to leave.

So they rode out on the morning of their fifth day with Red Fox, though not precisely as they had ridden in. If there were no cheers sending them off, there *were* grateful farewells, hands pressed silently but fervently, eyes with life in them again. If Darian did not feel *good* about leaving them to carry on without any more help, he didn't feel *bad* about it either.

As they took their bearings and departed from that path of browned and dying underbrush, heading once again for the pass between two mountains to the west and north, Darian felt the weight of another responsibility descend on him. Now they *knew* that Wolverine was out there, raiding, looting, and killing. They would have to be twice as vigilant as before.

He also held a secret from Keisha and Shandi, which made him feel a bit guilty. It wasn't a major secret—but he wasn't sure how they'd react if they knew it.

Kel hadn't won the hearts of Red Fox with his gifts; the *dyheli* had insinuated the concept of friendly, helpful, protective gryphons into the minds of the tribesmen long before the group ever reached the village itself.

Now that was meddling, by any standard. The *dyheli* didn't think of it that way; they considered it as being helpful, easing the way, making certain that the humans of Red Fox got no more traumatic experiences. However, they had planted a concept in the minds of the unsuspecting without consent or permission.

Quite frankly, at this point, Darian was in accord with the *dyheli.* Things had been difficult enough without having to calm hysterics and panic. They *needed* Kel's help, and needed to be able to have him come and go openly.

According to Kel, their detour might have been a good thing in a tactical sense. There were no wide meadows between here and the pass, nothing but thick forest. At least the group on the ground would have cover the entire way.

Yes, but so will any Wolverine raiding parties.

Hardly a comforting thought.

:Excuse me,: Neta said politely into Darian's mind, *:but there is something rather badly wrong in these woods. I don't know what, precisely, but it's too quiet.:*

:I agree,: Hashi spoke up. *:There doesn't seem to be anything around here bigger than a tree-hare, and even the tree-hares are staying high up. I haven't scented anything of a decent size since we crossed that last big stream.:*

Darian didn't like the way the forest felt either. The trees were a little farther apart here, letting plenty of sunlight through, and it should have been correspondingly more cheerful. But it wasn't; the forest felt empty, hollow, like that deserted village they had encountered.

Could Wolverine have hunted this place out? he wondered. That might be the explanation, and yet it didn't feel right. For one thing, there wasn't any sign of humans hunting—the broken undergrowth, trail marker ties, remains of camps, that sort of thing. For another, he didn't think that even a tribe like Wolverine would hunt an area bare.

They had been climbing steadily all day; they had managed to journey over all the territory between Red Fox and this final pass without crossing paths with any more raiding parties. There shouldn't be any reason why they wouldn't be on the other side of the mountains by tonight. Then, provided the information they had was correct, they would be within touching distance of Raven.

And my parents?

The shadow of the mountain fell across their path; it wasn't just cool here, it was *cold.* Darian shivered, and out of the corner of his eye saw Shandi pulling her cloak closer. *I'll be glad when we get across, into the sunlight. Who would have thought it could be this cold at the beginning of summer?* Small wonder that the Ghost Cat villagers had not been prepared for the summer heat in Valdemar. He was just glad that for once it wasn't raining. In this cold, rain would feel like drops of ice.

There was another small clearing coming up ahead of them, one with a brush-filled ravine running along the left side. As they cautiously entered the clearing, Hashi and Neta were running flank guard, Kelvren was high above, Kuari was running tail guard, and the other two birds were in front. It was better to have the birds in front and behind; they could cover more ground than Neta and Hashi. *It's too bad they don't have a way to pick up scent, but—*

There was a flash of motion. Out of nowhere, something huge and white reared up from the ravine, stretching up and up, and Darian froze. He *couldn't* move; all he could do was stare upward, at the strange eyes that whirled and pulsed in the snakelike head two stories above the ground. . . .

. . . . how . . . incredible. . . .

Was there someone calling him? Well, it didn't matter. Nothing mattered but those eyes. He forgot everything, even his name; all he wanted to do was to stare into those eyes forever. They were beautiful. He'd have thought his Clan, his Knighthood, and his quest were all useless if he'd even been able to think of them. The eyes were all that mattered. All else narrowed to them, or rather—yes, the eyes engulfed him. There was nothing above or below or around him that was of consequence, or was even noticed as missing, for that matter. There was only those eyes.

Just as abruptly as the drake's appearance, his mount went from immobile to active in a heartbeat. The *dyheli* spun in place, wrenching his attention from those hypnotic eyes, lurched into a run, and fled back down the way they had come. Greenery and stone flashed past at incredible speed, making even the view through Kuari's eyes when they were linked seem plodding by comparison. Holding on for dear life, Darian's *dyheli* caromed off the side of another one laden with supplies, which went down into the underbrush. Darian's knee and shin hurt immediately from the crushing blow against the *dyheli's* ribs, but the fallen *dyheli* was nowhere to be seen now. He looked around desperately. The noise of cracking branches and clattering gear mixed with a climbing whine behind him—a shrill one he had never heard before, much like the death cry of a rabbit, but forced from larger lungs. The *dyheli* he had crunched against struggled to get back up and then vanished into a pillar of white—the cold-drake's open jaws crushed down upon the flailing *dyheli* and there were three swift thrashing bites. The *dyheli* was dead, somewhere back there, but the scenery blurred past and the line of sight was gone. He wasn't alone; all of the *dyhelis* were stampeding back down the path, with Karles and Shandi in the lead. He shook off his pain and hung on like a leech as his mount lurched down the slope just a breath away from a disastrous stumble.

That was a cold-drake. Oh, gods, that was a cold-drake! Now that he wasn't under the creature's spell, he knew the danger of what it was, and could put a name on it. He knew what must have saved them, too—Neta, out there free and not under the cold-drake's mesmerizing gaze. She had exercised her own Gift and had taken over the minds of every other *dyheli* and probably Karles, too. Then she had made them all stampede away from the danger zone; the cold-drake wasn't swift enough to keep up with them.

The *dyheli* traveled across the forest floor in huge bounds, snapping Darian's head back and forth until he got into the same rhythm as his mount. The *dyheli* didn't usually break into this "stampede gait" when mounted, and he could only thank his luck that there was a saddle between him and that knobby *dyheli* backbone. As it was, his neck muscles hurt, and so did his head.

As abruptly as they began their run, they ended it, bouncing in three or four steps to a halt a safe distance down the pass. The others came to a stop beside him, with the *dyhelis* shaking their heads so hard their ears flapped as Neta let their minds loose. Last to stop was Karles, and it seemed to Darian that as the Companion walked toward them, his expression was decidedly sheepish.

Now it hit him—how close they had all been to a distinctly unpleasant death—and he began to shake with reaction, the sour taste of fear in his mouth. *One more heartbeat, and we'd all have been dinner. Oh, gods.*

Keisha looked puzzled; Shandi still confused. "We lost—we lost Gacher. What happened?" Keisha blurted. "What was that? Why did the *dyheli* all run?"

:*Gacher has died. The herd ran because I made them,*: came Neta's mind-voice. :*As for what that was, I do not know; only that it was dangerous. It had you all spell-trapped with its eyes and mind.*:

"It's a cold-drake," Steelmind said flatly. "Thank you, Neta; that was precisely the right thing to have done. You saved us all—except for poor Gacher. I hope his death was a swift one."

:*It was,*: Neta confirmed.

"I don't understand. I've studied all the weirdlings we were likely to find up here. Cold-drakes are normally dormant in the summer," Steelmind continued as he wiped his hair back from his face. "I wonder what woke this one up?"

"What's a cold-drake?" Keisha wanted to know.

Kel interrupted the conversation, coming in beside them for a noisy landing, his beak agape with agitation. He swung his head around, counting them silently, and heaved an enormous sigh of relief to see the humans all present. "I sssaw the drrrake!" he said, "But you all rrrran beforrre I completed a ssstoop."

"It's just as well that you didn't connect with it, Kel," Darian told him, dismounting and clasping Kel's neck—even though his own legs were still shaky. "One gryphon is no match for a cold-drake."

"Will someone please tell me, what's a cold-drake?" Keisha repeated insistently. "And why couldn't I move or think?"

Darian and Steelmind exchanged a look, and Darian answered. "A cold-drake is a magical construct, like a gryphon; they were created during the Mage-Wars as offensive weapons, but the problem was that they couldn't be controlled, and turned on their own side as often as not. They're eating machines."

"But they use mind-magic," Steelmind continued. "They freeze their prey in place, then move in and strike, or dine at their leisure depending upon their mood. That thing caught all of us, every one that could see its eyes. If Neta hadn't done what she did, we'd be sliding down its throat right now."

Karles hung his head, as if he was ashamed that he had not somehow resisted the cold-drake's gaze. Steelmind noticed, and turned toward the Companion. "No one is immune from a cold-drake," he said, for Karles' benefit. "I don't care who or what you are. When you're in front of a cold-drake, you belong to the cold-drake."

Shandi patted Karles' neck sympathetically. The Companion didn't say anything that Darian could hear, but he understood the Companion's chagrin; he shared it.

You'd think I would be able to shake that damned thing off. . . . How had he managed to get so completely under the monster's power in so short a time?

I didn't even get a good look at it before it had me!

It took one look at Hywel to realize that he did not have the worst of it. Darian was, by comparison, a war-hardened general compared to the young Ghost Cat warrior. In his past he'd been routed, ambushed, beaten up, surprised, attacked, and scared out of his wits before. It was Hywel's first time for being totally, utterly helpless, face-to-face with death when there was nothing he could do about it. Hywel looked just as white as the Ghost Cat itself.

"How are we going to get past that thing?" Hywel stammered, aghast. "Does it ever sleep?"

"Yes, but they're like spiders; they sense the vibrations of the ground if anything bigger than a mouse walks on it, and wake up immediately," Steelmind told him. "I don't think we could drive it off or lure it away either—they are very, very territorial. If we want to get through that pass, we're going to have to kill it."

"Oh, great," Darian muttered, as Hywel's eyes went round. Being magical constructs, cold-drakes were, to some extent, designed to be immune to the effects of magic. "What I don't understand is why it isn't dormant—it's *summer.*"

"It's also cold." Steelmind looked over his shoulder at the mountain behind him. "With this shadow falling over the pass for most of the day, and being so high up, it doesn't ever really get warm. That's probably why there aren't any animals here—the drake has hunted the place bare, and the animals don't get a chance to recover their numbers in the summer."

"It could be awake because it didn't get enough to eat to

support dormancy," Wintersky said thoughtfully. "Unless it moves to a new territory, it's going to starve to death."

"Well, we can't stand around and wait for that to happen," Darian replied with irritation. "And it just got fed."

Kelvren dipped his head toward Neta and intoned solemnly, "I am sssorrry forrr yourrr losss."

Neta returned the gesture, and her gaze went from buck to buck. :*It is a risk Gacher knew he was taking by volunteering for this journey. He knew before coming that such things could happen to him. It is easy to be brave from a safe distance.*:

Darian could only nod, even though he knew Neta was speaking to the bucks and not to him. As much as he had questioned the human morality of Neta's powers, those same powers had just unquestionably saved their lives.

Darian's mind was soon preoccupied, thinking on the ways to get around the drake. Wintersky went from one *dyheli* to another, checking them for injuries and making a mental inventory of what gear was lost when they fled. *We're so close—*

"We could go back," Shandi pointed out.

Dead silence dropped over them all; Darian looked at each of his party in turn. Shandi wouldn't look him in the eyes. Hywel looked solemn and frightened; Wintersky thoughtful. Steelmind just shrugged. Only Keisha met his eyes completely, and looked just as determined as he was to continue.

"We can't stop now," Keisha said firmly, and cast a withering glance at her sister. "That would be giving up."

Shandi shrugged off the criticism. "It's no shame to give up under the right circumstances."

Keisha didn't even dignify the comment with an answer; instead, she turned to Steelmind. "Do you have any idea what we can use against this creature?"

"Not at the moment," the Tayledras replied, with a look of admonition at Shandi. "But we'd better think of something other than bows and arrows."

"Heat," Darian muttered, after half a candlemark of debate. "That's the key, I think. They thrive in cold, and even magically generate it. It might not be directly vulnerable to magic, but if we can weaken and confuse it with heat, we can kill it."

"You think," Shandi put in.

Darian was getting more than a little irritated with Keisha's sister. Every time someone suggested something, she had a quelling remark. "Look," he said finally. "You wanted to come along on this journey. I didn't ask you for your help, but you, and Anda, and your Companions decided you needed to be with us, so you came. We've established a safe route back through the tribes, so why don't *you* just go home? You've been helpful, but you aren't doing anything that we can't afford to lose."

Shandi sat straight up, offended; Keisha, on the other hand, moved slightly closer to Darian. Steelmind raised an eyebrow, and licked his lips. "Is there a problem, Shandi?" he asked carefully. "Why are you trying to discourage us from going on?"

"I—" She looked around uneasily. "We already have so much information about the Northerners—and we *know* that Wolverine poses a danger to us back home if they continue to expand. Don't you think we have a duty to get back with that information?"

"Don't you think we have a duty to help our friend find his parents?" Steelmind countered. "That was why we came here."

"Yes, but—" Shandi looked confused.

"You could go back by yourself, if you want to," Steelmind continued. "But it seems to me that you would be going back on the agreement you made with Darian if you did that, and I suspect that you feel the same way. Is that why you're being so negative, trying to get us all into agreement to give up and go home so that you won't have conflicting duties?"

Shandi flushed, and had a hard time meeting his eyes. She couldn't meet Darian's either. Something in what Steelmind had said had hit home.

"All right, then; you've tried and failed, so give it a rest," Steelmind said decisively. "Either be helpful toward our objective, or be silent."

Shandi flushed again and bit her lip; she obviously wanted to make a retort, and didn't want to do so in front of the others. Darian exchanged a knowing glance with Keisha, feeling conspiratorial. *The first lovers' quarrel? Could be. And I think he's going to hear about it from her when there isn't an audience.* He couldn't blame her for wanting to give up at this point—but he and Steelmind had faced other monsters in the past, and he wasn't going to let a mere monster stand between him and finding his family. They'd encountered spirit manifestations before, but this cold-drake was, for all of its fearsome power, still flesh and bone.

"What else can we do?" he asked. "Can Kel and the birds confuse and distract him without getting into range of his eyes or teeth?"

"We could drrrop thingsss on him," Kel said meditatively. 'Sssimple but effective grrryphon tactic. Rocksss. Trrreesss. Perhapsss, if my luck isss good, I could drrrop sssomething over hisss head?"

"Just before we're ready to go for the final kill—even if you don't get the thing over its head, you'll distract it. A shot at the eyes themselves is not likely except from directly in front of it, and we all know what the danger is there." Steelmind fingered the hilt of one of his watersteel knives, thinking. "The main thing is to keep it from freezing any of us again."

"Could we just sneak by it?" Keisha asked diffidently. "Wouldn't that be better? If you use any magic at all, Darian, you'll show the Wolverine Shaman where you are. He can't ignore the presence of a Master mage so near to them."

Darian grimaced. "I know—but we can't do this without magic, and no, I don't think we can just sneak by it. You heard what Steelmind said about how it's sensitive to footsteps." He stood up. "If we're going to get over the pass before nightfall, we have to do this now. It isn't going to get any easier as the air gets colder, and if we camp, it may come *after* us."

They took out bows and arrows from their baggage, even Shandi. Kel and the birds took to the air. In this instance, being mounted would not be any advantage, so the *dyheli* and Karles were to stay out of the creature's range, and only come in to rescue them if they fell under its spell again.

Darian alone was unarmed, as he would need to keep all of his attention on his magic. Carefully, watching the ravine with every step they took, they approached the clearing. Darian's heart was in his mouth with every step; his breath sounded very loud, and he had to control a start at every unexpected noise. When they were at the periphery, the birds went into action.

Diving and shrieking, they showed where the monster was

hiding and teased it up into the open. Their talons could not harm the creature, but they annoyed it, and it lunged upward the full length of its neck as it snapped at them in irritation.

Oh, gods . . . it's huge. How are we ever going to defeat this thing!

Now Kel joined them, sweeping in from the west, dropping clawfuls of stones and branches on the cold-drake. He was aiming for the head, but the drake was too agile for any of the weapons to hit the skull; most of them fell short, or bounced off the armored hide of the shoulders without touching anything. What Kel *did* accomplish, was to distract it from Darian down below, who tapped into the nearest ley-line and began the simplest of all magics—creating heat.

His heart pounded in his ears, but he couldn't allow himself to be distracted. With energy from the ley-line, he could pour heat into the ravine, warming the very stone around the drake. He concentrated on raising the temperature of the area surrounding the drake, though there was no perceptible effect for some time. They didn't have arrows to waste; the only time that any shots were taken were when they were sure ones—clear shots at the creature's eyes or nostrils, the only two vulnerable places on it.

None of those shots hit the mark; the cold-drake evaded the arrows even as it evaded the missiles dropped on its head—but it was angry, and getting angrier by the moment. If Darian had allowed himself to feel it, he knew he would have been terrified. The drake towered over them, its bone-white plates glinting with the sheen of ice. Its head was the size of a *dyheli*, the fanged mouth looked large enough to take in any of them whole, but they all fought against instinct to keep from looking it in the eyes. It hissed and snarled, snapping at the birds, threatening the humans around it with upraised talons. They had to keep it irritated and off-balance, but not get it angry enough to charge.

Darian shut his ears to the screams of the birds and of Kel, and to the battle sounds of the drake, which sounded like the tearing of canvas. *Heat.* That was all he dared think of.

The others came forward for a cautious shot or two, hoping for that lucky moment—being able to hit the eye and strike the brain. Kel must have given up on his idea of blinding the thing with a dropped tent-cloth, because he hadn't come back for one. The drake particularly wanted a piece of Kel; every time he came by, the creature clawed the sky in his direction and gave one of those harsh battle cries. Kelvren pressed that advantage, at great cost to his endurance, engaging the cold-drake in a duel of feint-and-trick while staying airborne. A dive from the left would turn into a slip to the right in an instant, drawing the cold-drake up onto his hindquarters. That would be followed in an eyeblink by a blinding twist in midair, and the attack would be mirrored as the drake dropped back down to all fours again. Showers of ice crystals sprayed from the beast's shoulders when Kel did get a solid contact in, but not even gryphon talons got a single blood mark on the drake. A well-aimed wounding strike was out of the question—Kelvren was using all of his skill just to stay alive and engaged.

Meanwhile, Darian kept concentrating, raising the temperature around the drake bit by bit. He could feel the difference in the air now, and by its behavior, so could the drake.

It was uncomfortable; it tried to move farther back in the ravine where the rock hadn't been heated, but Kel wouldn't let it, dropping quickly retrieved branches on it, stooping at it, hovering in the air just out of reach and screaming at it. For one fleeting moment, Darian wondered if he ought to call Kel off and let it retreat—but it was too late to change their plans now.

Darian kept pouring heat into the small space containing the cold-drake, and the beast began to react to the heat as a human would react to the cold; the swipes of its talons became less sure, it snapped its jaws on empty air, and its eyes took on an odd glaze. It was fighting off torpor, and they all moved nearer.

Then Steelmind let fly a shot that hit the mark—one in the nostril. The cold-drake screamed, but in a *far* different way than the battle snarls and cries from the combat with Kelvren.

The sound went right through Darian's head like a white-hot lance. He dropped to his knees, involuntarily clapping his hands to his ears.

Then Darian lost control of his magic; the birds shot away up into the sky, and Kel floundered out of harm's way, landing heavily onto his side, behind their lines. The *dyheli* fled, though Karles stood his ground; all the humans cupped their hands over their ears; the scream went on and on, a sound that ripped through the head and stabbed into the brain.

We hadn't—counted on—this! Darian thought with difficulty, his eyes watering with pain. The cold-drake clawed desperately at its nose, and finally dislodged the arrow; the screaming stopped, replaced by a whimper, as the monster dropped its head down on the ground and rubbed its wounded nostril against the earth. Steam curled up around the drake, and its body plates dripped with melted ice.

"That's *enough!*" Keisha shouted in anguish. She stood up and staggered, unsure of each step, but seemed to have a purpose. She half-screamed again, "That is enough!" and marched toward the drake, her hands curled into fists. Darian stumbled to his feet and ran after her, but she paid no attention to him. She concentrated on the cold-drake, and the cold-drake was so preoccupied with its wounded nose that it ignored this small and insignificant morsel of prey marching toward it. But suddenly its head jerked up, and it stared at Keisha with eyes blank and widened. Bright red blood smeared down its snout, and ran freely from the wound in the nostril. The drake raised one claw, then curled it under its chest, staring at Keisha, yet somehow unable to focus upon her.

Darian felt a growing illness in his belly, adding queasiness to fatigue and the pounding headache. Ahead of him, Keisha was within easy striking distance of the cold-drake, and from his point of view, her small body was entirely framed by the red-spattered white mass of the cold-drake. Her feet were ankle-deep in the water runoff, both from the drake's newly lost ice layer and the nearby landscape. Darian's limbs seemed to move far too slowly, as he tried to gain on her, and the terror rose up inside him—was he about to see his Keisha die? But Keisha wasn't affected by the eyes the way they all had been the last time. Could it be that *Keisha* was doing something to the drake?

"Yes!" Shandi shouted from behind him, and ran to join her sister, shoving Darian aside. The two women came to within striking range of the drake and stood there, staring at it. They were too close for Darian to dare shooting at the thing—especially with its . . . head down?

Then it not only blankly stared at the duo, it raised its head to the fullest extent, and its eyes were widened and completely dilated. If Darian had not seen the cold-drake's next move with his own eyes, he would never have believed it. It reared up and back—but not as if to strike. It bobbed its head and seemed to be cowering away from them, as if they were the most dangerous and threatening things it had ever seen. Its whimpers changed to a whine, and it slowly backed away from them, scrabbling backward across the rocks, claws slipping on the smooth, slick surface, without ever taking its eyes off them, moving up and out of the ravine,and then down past the openly stunned Steelmind, and more rapidly down to the edge of the clearing.

It reached the edge of the forest, still walking awkwardly backwards, its tail actually between its legs at one point. Its own bulk made the progress painfully slow. Then, just as a large branch it had pushed aside snapped back into place, obscuring for a moment its sight of the two young women, it turned and *ran*—ran off into the forest, crashing through brush and briar and making an incredible amount of noise.

What did they—!

"Now! Let's get past!" Shandi shouted, as Karles raced up beside her. She mounted; the *dyheli* each sought out a rider—no matter which one, they'd sort out the baggage later.

They raced up the pass at breakneck speed, following Shandi, who was in the lead. Kel kept watch behind, the birds in front. There was no one watching the flanks, but at the speed they were traveling now, they'd be past anyone on their flanks in short order.

Darian wouldn't have thought the *dyheli* could maintain this pace uphill, but evidently fear was spurring them on; as he leaned down over the outstretched neck of his mount, there was no slackening of their speed as they reentered the forest, charged headlong through it, and exited again, higher up the slope. Now there was nothing between them and the pass—

Then they were up to the pass itself, and over it, and if anything, their pace increased as they charged downhill again. They were out in the sunlight at last; the air was considerably warmer, and the hordes of birds and small creatures that startled and fled before their headlong rush testified that the cold-drake didn't hunt on this side of the mountain.

Darian got a brief glimpse of something shining off to the

west—it might have been water, but he didn't get a good enough look to tell for certain. Then they plunged into the forest shadows again.

The *dyheli* kept running for a good candlemark, and only when their flanks were soaked with sweat and their sides heaving did they finally slow and stop beside a trickle of a stream.

Darian was off his mount in a heartbeat, as were the rest. Snatching up handfuls of coarse grass, they began wiping their mounts down. They pulled off the tack and did what they could, then the *dyheli* themselves walked off to cool down and take occasional sips of water.

Only then did Darian turn to Keisha. "You got into its mind? What was it that you two used? Fear?" he asked.

She nodded. "Fear. But I guarantee you, it is not in a way you would have expected."

Steelmind commented, somewhat amusedly, "These two've certainly scared me before, so I can understand that. I thought it had to be something more. I didn't think my arrow was that effective."

Keisha grinned. "Effective enough. When you hurt it, that was the first time anything had ever touched it since it had left its mother and been on its own in the wilds. Literally it had never felt pain since the last time its mother disciplined it. And do you know how drakes discipline their babies?"

Darian shook his head dumbly.

"They bite the baby's nose!" She laughed breathlessly.

Steelmind knit his brow, and shook his head slightly. "I still do not understand. You two are just humans, not the cold-drake's mother."

Shandi stepped over, her sweat-scraper and curry-brush still in hand, after tending briefly to Karles. "I'll try to explain. The warmth Darian summoned was making it delirious and disoriented. It became more and more unfocused mentally, it felt more vulnerable as its armor's ice layer melted, and its eyesight clouded, too, much like a developing infant's. It thought about the last time it felt that way—when it was just a pup. So instinctively, even though we were just snacks for it, when that nose wound hurt so sharply, the drake *felt* as if we were bigger and more powerful than it for just a moment."

Keisha picked up the explanation from there. "It's like with a pony, if you pick it up off the ground as a foal, even when it's full grown, it will think you can still do that. Lessons learned early in life stay just as big in any creature's mind, and when someone is in pain they tend to act more childlike—that's something we Healers know and use. That wound-scream jarred me out of my own fear and my Healing knowledge sort of welled up, and I remembered where I'd sensed that sort of reaction—from other wounded animals, and some badly injured people. The cold-drake didn't know what was happening to it, and its instincts made it think of dear old mama. We just pushed more fear at it, using what we sensed its own memories of an angry mother were. I don't know if I could have driven it off by myself, but when Shandi and I joined, there was enough to push it over the edge."

Steelmind shook his head. "Empaths," was all he said, but it was in a mix of bemusement and admiration.

"Well, how many more doses of that scream could *you* take?" Shandi retorted, glancing around for Kel. "I thought blood was going to pour out of my ears in a moment. I was in such pain from the scream I was damned well going to *do* something about it!"

"I have no arguments with what you did!" Darian assured them, waving his hands in the air for emphasis. "It worked, and that's all I care about!"

Kelvren limped up, his left side somewhat scraped up but only slightly bloodied. "It isss good rrreasssoning," he added, sounding complimentary. "It isss the mind that trrruly winsss orrr losssesss each battle. Talonsss would not accomplish in ten daysss what one well-placsssed bad memorrry of Motherrr did."

Keisha frowned at the gryphon, and gestured with one finger pointing downward at her feet, then snapped her fingers. "Come here, hero. Let me look at that." Kelvren gave her a withering look, but approached obediently and gently mocked, "Jussst do not thrrreaten me with yourrr Fearrrssssome Powerrrsss, and I shall obey," as he lay down to be tended to.

Shandi's face abruptly clouded, and she looked back up the pass, anxiously. "Getting back, though—" she started.

"We'll worry about getting back when we have to." That was Wintersky, who had been dragging their belongings into a rough circle. "I've been checking what we have left. Anybody object to staying here for the night?"

Darian shook his head. "I feel like it was me carrying the *dyheli*, not the other way around."

:I am no frisking filly—my old bones ache after a gallop like that one,: Neta said ruefully. *:With any luck the ladies have affrighted that cold-drake into a new hunting ground—it will eat its fill and retire into torpor as it properly should, and we will not need to concern ourselves with it on the return journey.:*

Neta looked terrible—all the *dyheli* looked terrible, and Karles didn't look much better. Their coats were drenched and streaked with sweat and dust; they hung their heads, and their legs trembled with fatigue.

"You lot, go lie down as soon as you think you can without cramping up," he said in a quick decision. "We'll mount guard tonight without you."

:Thank you,: Neta replied simply for them all. One by one the *dyheli* folded their legs underneath them and dropped to the moss and grass; following Darian's example, each of the humans pulled a blanket out of their bedrolls and draped it over the prone bodies so that the wet *dyhelis* didn't take a chill.

Darian squatted down in front of Neta. "About the . . . loss of Gacher. I'm sorry. Is there any ceremony for his death that we should do?"

:It has already been done,: Neta mindspoke. *:What you all choose to do regarding Gacher's death is yours to determine."*

They made camp, although it was still light; the early stop gave them time to hunt and cook food for a change. Kel settled in beside Darian and Keisha after his own hunt; the gryphon still looked somewhat shaken, and settled down on his bandages as an easy way of keeping pressure on them.

"I did not know the thing would ssscrrream like that," Kel said finally.

"None of us did," Darian replied. "I don't know that anyone has ever gotten close enough to a cold-drake to find out."

"The only time I've ever heard of anyone killing a drake, it's been three or four Adepts at a distance," came Steelmind's dry comment. "No one has even been stupid enough to try to take on one on foot that I know of, and survive."

Darian smiled a bit. "We certainly qualify as stupid enough."

"Maybe, but according to Kerowyn, the Shin'a'in say that if it is stupid but works, it isn't stupid," Shandi added. It looked to Darian as if she'd forgotten whatever grievance she had with Steelmind.

Then again, she's probably storing it up to use some other time. When he least expects it.

"I can only say that I hope never to meet with such a thing again in my lifetime," Hywel told them all solemnly. "Killing such would make the Manhood trial for a legendary hero, and I am no such hero."

At that, Steelmind smiled slightly, got stiffly to his feet, walked over to the young tribesman, and dropped slowly to one knee. While Hywel watched, Steelmind handed the young warrior one of his own valuable watersteel fighting knives.

Hywel took it gingerly, appearing startled. "What is this?" he asked, perplexed.

"I have no place in my life for anyone who is sure he can do everything. You just realized—and admitted—that you're not invulnerable, or unbeatable, or perfect," Steelmind said solemnly. "By my reckoning, that makes you a *real* man. Now I completely trust you, and I'll have you at my back any time."

Hywel admired the knife—and what it symbolized—for a long moment, before Kelvren broke the silence with his own comment.

"If you want *rrreal* perrrfection, you mussst find a *grrry-phon.*"

Eighteen

$\mathfrak{F}$og surrounded the campsite; there had been no rain last night, but it was a damp, cool morning. Kel had gone out to scout out the way as soon as there was any light in the sky at all. Darian looked up at the sound of large wings, his breakfast uneaten in his hands. He couldn't see anything in the mist, but a moment later, Kel's wings blew the fog away enough for him to land beside the morning fire. Darian put down the broiled fish, uneaten. He'd been too keyed up for hunger anyway.

"If you rrride harrrd all day, you will rrreach a village at the edge of the waterrr, and it isss definitely Rrraven," Kel said, breathing heavily. "I sssaw the totemsss forrr mysssself."

Darian started to breathe a little heavily himself. *Don't get too excited,* he reminded himself. *Raven is only the tribe that creates the vests. Mother and Father might not be there.*

Oh, he could tell himself that, but it was impossible not to hope, impossible not to feel his heartbeat quicken, his nerves tingle. "Then let's get going—" he began, starting to rise, when a hand on his belt jerked him back down again.

"First, eat," Keisha ordered, frowning. He knew that look. He ate, though the fish was cold and tasted like wheat paste. He crammed it down as fast as he could, washing it down with water.

He wished he could use magic to seek out the village and *know* if his parents were there, but he didn't dare. Last night he'd felt the sweep of a search over them, someone looking for the scent of magic and mages, and had been very glad that he had *not* used any magic at all in guarding the camp. A mage, and a powerful one, had picked up the magic he'd used against the cold-drake, and was hunting for the one who had used it. He was under no illusion that the one hunting for them was friendly; there was only *one* powerful mage hereabouts, and that was the Wolverine Shaman. *An Eclipse Shaman. There is no way that he can be a friend to us.*

He'd hoped that the creation of heat was a minor enough usage of magic that it would have gone unnoticed, but in his heart he had known all along it was a vain hope. Maybe if the seeker found nothing, he'd assume the drake had eaten the mage that had tried to kill it. He would *certainly* find the drake alive and well—wherever it had gone to.

With the drake standing guard over the pass, it was no wonder that Wolverine hadn't gotten this far—nor that Raven was so isolated from the other tribes. Surely the pass could only be traveled during the hottest days of summer, and only then at midday, when the sun reached every part of the pass and even a hungry cold-drake would seek a cool cave to sleep.

Darian was in the saddle before the rest of the group had finished loading their belongings in their saddle panniers. He curbed his own impatience at them; he reminded himself yet again that at this point they only knew that Raven produced vests with motifs that *looked* like those his mother had used in her embroidery, and that was all they knew.

But the moment everyone else was ready to go, he was off at a lope, trusting to Kel and the birds for guidance through the mist, and to the abilities of the others to keep up. The way led literally downhill, down the slopes of the mountain to the water; that made it easy for his *dyheli*. Everything conspired to help him except the mist; there were clear game trails to follow, the trails themselves were easy and not strewn with rocks, even the mossy turf was springy and dulled the sound of the *dyheli's* hooves. His mount Jakir positively frisked his way through the trees, enjoying the run. He couldn't see much through the fog, though—the nearest tree trunks, the lowest branches. He could just as readily have been running over the same piece of ground, except that the paths always led downward.

The others caught up with him, but he kept the lead; they broke unexpectedly into a meadow just as the sun began to burn off some of the fog and startled a herd of deer into flight ahead of them. As the fog thinned, they saw more and more of their surroundings, and they were nothing short of amazing; as lovely as a Tayledras Vale in a very different and far wilder fashion. There was water everywhere; in tiny rivulets that trickled down the mountainside and made miniature waterfalls, in larger streams they crossed in a single bound, and crystal-clear brooks that laughed through stone-strewn beds, in still pools full of fish, in the cool but humid air itself. Moss covered everything; rocks, tree trunks, branches; it hung in pendulous beards from the branches overhead, and cushioned every step the *dyheli* took. And everywhere was green, a thousand shades of green, from the black-green of water weeds in the pools through the blue-green and emerald of the underbrush, to the bright green of leaves overhead with sunlight shining through them. Even the light was green; Darian glanced back at Keisha, and saw she was looking about her with enchantment in her eyes in spite of the hard pace they were setting. The cool, damp air was full of wonderful scents; green growing things, the sharp scent of crushed pine needles, the ghosts of flowers, the promise of rain. Unfamiliar birds called in bell-like tones that echoed down through the branches, and from all around came every sort of song that water could possibly make, from the musical laughter of the tiny waterfalls and the gurgle of the brooks, to the steady, soporific dripping of water on leaves. But rather than lulling, the surroundings conspired to make him exhilarated, ready to do anything and everything.

They were getting dripped on themselves, of course, but today in Darian's excitement it seemed more refreshing than annoying.

They stopped long enough for the *dyheli* and Karles to snatch a few mouthfuls and get a drink; the others dismounted to stretch stiff legs, but Darian begrudged even the time it took for that. He tried not to show his impatience too blatantly, closing his eyes to check with Kel and Kuari.

:*You're not far now,*: Kel replied, :*You're making better time than I'd thought you could.*:

:*It's all downhill,*: he replied, greatly cheered by this. :*How soon do we reach them at this pace?*:

:*Huh—maybe a couple of candlemarks, no more. But do slow down before you get too close—you'll raise an alarm, galloping in this way, and I'd hate to see you shot full of arrows.*:

Darian grimaced, but Kel had a point. Normal traders would *not* come riding in as if a cold-drake were on their heels. :*Give me an idea where to slow down, and I will.*:

:*Darian, I have to say that I have seen no sign of your people. All the folk here look like Northerners.*: Kel parted with that information reluctantly. :*Of course,*: he added, brightening, :*I know I haven't seen all, or even most of them. There are surely some out hunting, and women in the log houses.*:

Once again, Darian clamped down on both hope and disappointment, reminding himself that he was looking only for a direction, not for his mother and father in person. :*Stay alert for trouble.*: he warned Kel. :*I caught the edge of a magic-search last night.*:

He caught Kel's assent, and turned his attention to Kuari, who flew along just behind them, with Wintersky and Steelmind's birds, who were much swifter, taking lead. :*Anything to our rear, old friend?*:

:*Was tree-hare. Very tasty. No tree-hare, anymore.*: Kuari's mind-voice, overlaid with great satisfaction at an easy kill and the pause to eat it made him chuckle in spite of his anxiety.

He heard the others mounting up, and opened his eyes again. "Kel says we've made better time than he'd thought we would, and we're nearly there," he told them encouragingly. Shandi made a movement that caught his attention, and he looked over at her directly.

"I want to borrow you and Keisha when we get there, to give Karles a boost for his mind-voice," she said, in a tone that made it more of a demand than a request. Karles bobbed his head and stamped a hoof to emphasize the "request." "The information about Wolverine is too important; I *have* to get it back home, so that it gets there regardless of whether or not we make it back."

"That'll take magic," he said, with some reluctance, as his

mount shifted restlessly under him. "I'm not sure that's wise, given that—"

Shandi eyed him with disfavor, and Karles snorted, giving him a similar look. "You picked up a magic-sweep last night, didn't you? And you didn't tell us."

"So did I, and I didn't tell you either," Steelmind put in, mildly. "It doesn't matter; nobody was using magic, so who-ever it was—"

"—the Wolverine Shaman—" she interjected with annoy-ance.

"—won't have found us. He probably thinks the magic we used was a futile effort against the cold-drake, and it ate us." Darian finished the sentence for Steelmind. "But using magic again might tell him it didn't."

Shandi looked him square in the eyes, and Karles moved a pace closer. "This is *my* duty. I'm helping you with yours, it's only fair that you help me with mine."

Great good gods, they're getting more alike with every day. Are all Heralds and Companions like this, I wonder! Her logic was inescapable, however, and he knew that she was right, even though it seemed to him that she didn't have to be so forceful about it. He wasn't all *that* hard to convince. He shrugged. "I didn't say I wouldn't help, I was only advising you that we'll be putting up a big, thick smoke signal for any-one with the right kind of eyes to see it. If you believe it's worth that risk, then we'll do it, and try to do what we can to prevent anyone from noticing."

Shandi seemed completely satisfied with that; Karles tossed his head and gave a nod of agreement. "All right, then," she replied, and swung up into her own saddle, the last to do so. "Let's get moving."

Once again, Darian's heart was in his mouth, and his blood singing in his ears; the emotion filling him was a very close relative to the fear he'd felt against the cold-drake. As they walked their mounts toward the distant village, situated above an expanse of water so large he couldn't see an opposite shore, he tried, and failed, to keep from hoping to see a famil-iar face among the people coming slowly to meet him.

And as they neared, and he could make out the features of

the wary men approaching, he tried, and failed, to keep his heart from sinking with disappointment.

These were tribesmen just like any others; brown, lean, dressed in the felt and tanned deerskin garments of others they had met with. He saw vests on some, but they were all decorated with tribal totemic animals, chiefest among them being the beaky head of Raven. He stifled his own feelings, put on a smile, and walked forward with Hywel to introduce his group.

Of all the folk they had met so far, these were the friendliest, and the least suspicious—but that might have been because they wore tokens from Red Fox, Snow Fox, and Ghost Cat; tokens that were not given out lightly, from three relatively peaceful tribes. Learning they were ostensibly traders brought looser grips on weapons, and a few faint smiles.

"And what have you brought to trade?" the Chief of Raven asked, tilting his head to one side inquisitively. "I see no pack-animals. . . ."

"Dyes, oh, Chief," Darian replied, slipping into his role of trader as easily as slipping on a well-worn slipper. "Colors such as you have not seen the like of. We bring another thing, also, and that is the learning of our Wisewoman—" He gestured, and Keisha came forward, "—who has the means to defeat the Summer Fever and the Hammer Lung, if you should be cursed with either, and will teach these things to you, in gratitude to the spirits who permit us to bring these trade goods to you."

"Indeed!" The Chief looked impressed. "We have neither sickness among us, but we know of them. Can she teach such to our Wisewoman even if there are none so touched?"

Keisha bowed her head slightly. "I can, Chief, and gladly will. But since you have no sick in urgent need, would you look to our dyes?"

"We will; come, be welcome in the house of the Raven." He waved them on, but Darian raised his hand. "We have representatives of our totems, Chief, and an ally you might find monstrous. We wish you to see them before you welcome us, for you must welcome all of us or none at all."

The Chief nodded; as one, Darian, Steelmind, and Wintersky raised their arms, and their birds came in to the glove. Gasps of surprise, followed by admiration followed the ap-

pearance of the hawk and buzzard, but when Kuari came in,
everyone stepped back a pace. Kuari looked about—as fast as
his head could turn, for he knew how funny humans found
the way he could swivel his head in nearly a full circle—and
chuckles followed.

Then came Kel.

He did not drop in suddenly, he approached gradually, so
that the tribesmen could see him approaching in the distance,
with huge, graceful wingbeats, and become accustomed to
him. It was still a dramatic entrance, though, and Kel was still
an imposing figure that took even the Chief aback.

Kel folded his wings with immense dignity. "I grrrreet the
Chief of Rrrraven from the Chief of Ssssilverrr Grrryphon,"
he said, enunciating slowly and clearly. The Chief gathered
his wits and his courage to approach.

"You are called a gryphon, then?" the Chief asked, looking
up at Kel's golden eyes and immense beak.

"I am; my name issss Kelvrrren," Kel replied. "And in rrret-
urrrn forrr yourrr hossspitality, I beg you to accept my aid in
hunting deerrrr and otherrr larrrge crrreaturesss while we
arrre herrre."

"Gladly!" the Northerner said with alacrity; it didn't take a
genius to figure out that so large a predator as Kel could be an
enormous asset in hunting. "I thank you, and bid you welcome as well."

They followed him into the circle of log houses, escorted by
the warriors, who were relaxing more by the moment. Darian
saw at once that there were scores of drying racks covered
with a red-fleshed filleted fish, with smoldering fires beneath
them. That made sense—in this damp, fish would cure better
smoked than simply dried. But the sheer quantity made him
pause and wonder if those stories about fish being so thick in
the river that you could walk dry-shod on their backs might
have a solid kernel of truth to them.

Keisha and Shandi spread out the contents of the trade-
pack, together with the samples of dyed wool—drawn by the
colors and encouraged by the actions of the Raven Chief, the
women of Raven gathered closer to look. In moments they
were passing around the bits of wool, exclaiming over the colors, asking if they could be painted on leather or used to dye

quills or fur, while the men feigned indifference, coming up cautiously to Kel to discuss a future hunt.

As they clustered around Keisha and Kel, Darian looked in vain for one of the special vests, or any other sign of Valdemaran handiwork. He ached with impatience, he longed to take someone aside and ask about the vests, but he knew that now wasn't the time. They had to establish a relationship with these people before he could go about asking questions of them.

Keisha got free for a moment, turning the questions over to Shandi and Hywel, since Hywel's heart was truly into getting the best possible bargains he could, and Shandi loved bargaining. "Any sign of your family?" she asked Darian in Valdemaran, all the while smiling pleasantly, as if she was simply commenting on how eager these people were for their dye.

He kept his facade up as well. "No," he replied, a bit louder, so that the tribesmen wouldn't think they were making some sort of secret comments. "No, I haven't seen anything, not a vest, not even a bit of embroidery that looks familiar."

But just as he said that, something odd happened. A young girl at the edge of the gaggle of chattering women jerked her head up as if it was on a string and stared at him.

Then she was off like a shot arrow speeding to a target—the target being one of the log houses.

"What was that all about?" Keisha asked, having noticed it too. "That girl acted as if something frightened her."

"I have no idea," he replied, his attention more on his own concerns than those of a strange Raven girl. "Maybe she was just shy of being around *strange* strangers. Kel probably made her really nervous, then it scared her over the edge to hear a different tongue. It doesn't seem to have bothered anyone else."

Almost before he finished his sentence, the girl reappeared, pulling a seemingly reluctant woman along by one hand. The woman was protesting, and it was clear why. In her other hand she held a headless, gutted fish, and she had obviously been interrupted in the middle of preparing a meal. She was looking down at her daughter—for surely that was who the girl was— and laughing along with her protests. Then she looked up.

Darian felt his head start to spin. His jaw dropped; he grabbed Keisha's arm, and stared. Older—yes—gray in the brown hair, a face weathered and lined with the cares of ten years, but—

"*Mother!*" he shouted, and ran toward her.

As if the world had slowed, he watched her reactions. She stared, first without any recognition in her eyes, then with puzzlement, then the look he longed for dawned, and grew, and burst forth like the sun coming from behind a cloud.

"*Darian!*" she shrieked—the fish went one way, the little girl the other, and she ran for him with outstretched arms.

He caught her up in his embrace, a tiny part of him bewildered by how *small* she'd become, and held her as he'd hoped to for too many lonely years. She hugged him, laughing and crying at the same time; she put both her hands about his face, looked into his eyes, kissed him, looked again, kissed him again. His throat swelled, and tears of his own streamed from his eyes, though his mouth was stretched in a smile so large the corners of his mouth ached; the smell of fish suddenly became the most wonderful perfume in the whole world.

By this time, of course, they had gathered a substantial audience, and not only the little girl was dancing around them, but a second, slightly younger one, and a littler boy, all chanting his name and tugging on their mother's deerskin shirt.

As for Darian—he didn't care. His mother was in his arms, babbling endearments—he held her tightly, babbling nonsense of his own. No matter what happened in the next moment, or day, or week—he savored where he was, right now, and no one could ever take it from him.

Darian looked dazed as well as blissfully happy, and Keisha held one of his hands as he and his mother slowly caught up on the last ten years. They all sat on benches or flat grass-stuffed leather cushions on the ground in front of the log house. She had insisted that he go first, plying him with honey-sweetened berry juice whenever his voice grew hoarse.

"So strange," she marveled at last, shaking her head as a cool breeze toyed with strands of her hair that had escaped from her single braid. "Of all the things I had imagined you would become, a mage was not one. And a *Hawkbrother!* Your father will be speechless."

"Where is Father?" Darian asked eagerly.

His mother laughed. "Where would you think? Out on the

river, trapping fish this time, rather than four-leggers. You wouldn't expect the loss of a mere foot to slow *him* down, now would you? Kelsie's twin Kavin is with him." She ruffled the hair of the oldest girl, who watched her brother Darian with undisguised adoration. The younger two, solemn six-year-old Ranie, and two-year-old Tel, snuggled against their mother's legs. "I suspect that these littles came as a great surprise to you—"

"I'd be lying if I said they didn't, but they're a wonderful surprise," he replied, smiling down at the little girl Kelsie, then at her sister and brother. "I never thought of myself as a big brother before. But tell me what happened, from the beginning."

Darian's mother—*Daralie Firkin,* Keisha reminded herself, *Her name is Daralie, Dar for short*—sighed, caressed the hair of the smaller girl, and began. "We had just finished setting up camp, when—something happened. I don't remember what being caught in the magic felt like, and I suspect that's just as well. The next thing I knew, we were halfway up that mountain there—" she nodded at the mountain to the north of the village. Even at this distance, there was a spot of terrain that was visibly different—no doubt the sphere of Valdemaran land that had switched places with the piece of terrain originally there. "Kullen was screaming, and no wonder, since his foot had been cut off clean. The fire had come with us, and—I don't know where he got the presence of mind to do this—and he shoved the stump into the coals. That seared the severed veins off; if he hadn't, I think he would have bled to death."

Keisha didn't need to be an Empath to know that those simple words concealed fear and horror that Dar still felt, even now. Keisha could not imagine being in her shoes at that moment—utterly alone, thrown onto the side of an unknown mountain by an unknown power, her husband wounded, perhaps mortally—

She shuddered, then smiled wanly, and shook off the emotions her recollection called up.

"Thanks be to the gods, all our camping gear came with us as well—well, except for the corner of the tent that had gone along with his foot; I bound up the stump and dosed him with poppy. We had food enough for a while, so I nursed him while I studied where we were." Daralie smiled thinly. "The most I could say was that I didn't know. I put out trap-lines for small animals, and caught things that are like short-eared rabbits that live among the rocks, and built up our campsite into a small stone hut walled over with snow blocks—I had no idea how long we would be there, and I wanted to be ready for the worst blizzards. As it happens, we weren't there for very long, and the blizzards aren't bad as far down on the mountain as we were." More of that years-old fear drained from her, and she smiled. "You might not believe it, but down here in the valleys the winter isn't harsh at all; it seldom snows. And when snow does come, it doesn't linger."

"I have trouble believing that, indeed, given how chilly it is at the moment," Darian replied, "But if you say it is so, I will try to believe anything you tell me."

That brought a smile to his mother's face, and she continued. "I don't know what we would have done if we had been left on our own, but some of the hunters from Raven found us. They brought us here, and although we didn't know it, we were intended to become someone's slaves—but one of the Changed creatures attacked the camp first. By then, thanks to the Wisewoman, Kullen was up and about, and when the hunters couldn't get near enough to the creature to kill it, we showed them how to build a pit-trap to take it. Would you believe it? They didn't know anything but the simplest of snares!" She shook her head at the idea. "Well, that ended any talk of making us slaves, or so I'm told. We helped them trap any number of wretched Change-Creatures, clearing out the valley, and they adopted us into the tribe and made us their Chief Hunters. There isn't much more to tell," she concluded. "We taught them how to trap, and they taught us their ways. When we realized that we were right off the map, we gave up the notion of getting home. I knew that the people of Errold's Grove would see you were taken care of."

Keisha was glad that Darian had not mentioned the way he'd been treated by the Errold's Grove villagers now, and she suspected he felt the same. Why cause Daralie any more distress? What was in the past could not be changed, and if things had not happened the way they had, he might not be talking to her now.

"I never gave up hoping that one day we'd get some word back to you, though," she finished, looking up into his face with eyes that were the aged mirror-image of his. "That was why I kept sending the vests out. There was always that possibility that one day, someone in Valdemar would see one, would recognize the pattern, and ask about where it came from."

"And that was brilliant, Mother," he replied, kissing the hand that he held. "Of all the things in the world that are likely to travel, it is trade goods that travel the farthest."

She blushed with pleasure at his praise, and spread her hands wide. "Well, we learned to live here, we came to love it, we prospered, the children came along—that is the sum of it. Here we do not count the passing of time by the day, but by the season, for the days are very like one another."

Darian was saved from having to reply to that by the appearance of a fast-moving party of happily shouting tribesmen, with a limping man—Kullen, no doubt—and a boy in the middle. Darian shot to his feet, shouting "Father!" and reprised the running greeting he had given his mother, while Keisha stayed prudently behind.

Rather than joining her sons and husband, Daralie cast a speculative glance at Keisha. "Keisha Alder—your people are the Alders that lived south and east of the village?" she asked. "The ones with all the boys?"

Keisha nodded, and Daralie looked her over carefully. "A Healer and a Herald out of the same family—your mother must be very pleased and proud."

"My mother is appalled and shocked," Keisha retorted wryly. "Having her precious girl-babies turn out to be independent women with minds and vocations of their own was *not* what she had in mind. Husbands, spotless cottages, and grandbabies would have been more to her liking."

To her pleasure, Daralie laughed out loud. "Good for you, Keisha Alder!" she applauded warmly. "Be sure you keep that mind of your own! Any man worth spending time with will value intelligence over a spotless cottage and a milk-meek maiden, however pretty she is."

By the warm glance she aimed at her own husband, there was no doubt in Keisha's mind what Kullen's preferences were. Daralie was by no means a milk-meek maiden.

This is the woman that raised Darian— came an unbidden voice in the back of her mind. *So, what was all that nonsense you were worrying about? Something about Darian really wanting a honey-sweet maiden in his heart of hearts, and not being satisfied with you?*

But now the man and boy were approaching, with Darian between them, an arm around each shoulder. When Keisha got a good look at the boy, she was struck by how very like Darian he was.

Daralie followed her look, and smiled fondly. "He could be Darian at the same age," she said softly. "Kavin could not be more like his brother if they were twins separated in time."

But this little boy will never have his mother and father wrenched away from him, if fortune smiles, Keisha thought, watching how the child looked up at his father with undisguised adoration that spoke well for the man's parental skills.

Kullen Firkin limped heavily, and Keisha's eyes went to the place at the end of his leg where a wooden form poked out of the bottom of his trews where his foot should have been. It wasn't foot-shaped, but it wasn't the peg she'd expected; it seemed to be the narrow end of a fat cone, which was interesting. *I should try that shape with a patient some time. . . .*

Where Daralie Firkin was small and slim (despite bearing five children), with soft, dark eyes and dark hair going to silver, Kullen Firkin was fair going to gray, with hazel eyes and a tough, wiry frame. The children, except for Darian, took after their mother rather than their father—but neither parent looked at all like the Errold's Grove "norm," which was to be brown-eyed, brown-haired, and stocky—muscular in the males, plump in the females. Small wonder that Darian had stuck out as the odd one.

Kullen was in tears, making no effort to hide them, and Darian's eyes were wet again. Keisha almost decided to absent herself from the reunion, but the glance that Darian cast at her said so clearly, "please stay," that she changed her mind.

The entire family, including Keisha, retired to the log house, where Darian again told an edited version of his experiences of the past years. During the recitation, several women brought in all of the components of a good dinner—fish baked in clay, roasted onions and cattail roots, a piece of honeycomb and some of the flatbread they'd sampled at Snow Fox.

Daralie thanked them sincerely. "We saw your dinner go flying—and one of the dogs got it," said the oldest of the women with a wide grin. "It was no great matter to add food to our fire. You certainly have done it often enough for the rest of us!"

The fish was a new dish to Keisha, but it was something she thought she could get used to pretty easily. It had been rubbed with herbs inside and out, stuffed with onions, then folded into an envelope of wet clay, the whole buried in coals and ashes. Keisha had never tasted anything like it.

She felt very much the interloper in this family circle, but there was one thing that she could not help but notice. Daralie was no stay-at-home wife, no matter what she had been doing today when they arrived. It was clear from the conversation that Daralie and Kelsie would be minding the same fish traps tomorrow that Kullen and Kavin had tended today.

It was also evident that this was the ordinary state of things for them—and Kelsie and Kavin were given equal chores and responsibilities based on strength, size, and ability, not on sex. Tomorrow, in fact, Kavin would be helping his father cook, as well as doing some repairs to the log house.

During a break in the family conversation, when Kullen asked Darian some detailed questions about the fighting with Blood Bear, Keisha decided to be bold and ask Daralie a few questions of her own.

"How did the Raven people come to accept you?" she asked. "You aren't a Man-souled woman, you've got a husband and a family, but you act like one."

Daralie laughed softly. "Well, they didn't have a choice at first," she pointed out. "Kullen was in no shape to help them; *I* was the one with the trapping knowledge and the two strong legs to take me out into the wilderness. They had to accept me, but I can tell you they didn't like it! It was a bit of a struggle; they did what I told them, but I got no respect in the village. And when Kullen was able to walk about again, they stopped listening to me at all!"

"So what happened?" Keisha asked.

"I don't know." Daralie shrugged. "The men had one of their ceremonies, and something happened there that changed them entirely in their attitude toward me. But they won't tell the women what it was—and I don't care, so long as they don't treat me like a nonentity anymore."

I wonder if the Raven intervened? That was the only thing

Keisha could think of, and by the shrewd glance Daralie threw at her, she figured the older woman had come to the same conclusion. But of course, she didn't know Keisha, she didn't know how much exposure Keisha had to the totemic spirits and the beliefs of the Northerners. The average Valdemaran would not expect to find spirits intervening so directly in the lives of mortals, and might even greet such a revelation with thinly disguised disbelief.

"So—I take it that you and my son are—partners, after the Hawkbrother fashion?" Daralie then said, her glance sharpening. And before Keisha could answer, she added, "Do you intend to wed?"

Keisha felt the blood rush into her face, and she averted her eyes. "We had discussed it—but we didn't make any plans. And then, well, looking for you was more important."

"You would probably do all right living here with Raven," Daralie replied, nodding knowledgeably. "You are a Wisewoman after all. You won't have to fight for respect. They'll give it to you without asking, and they won't expect you to act like their own women; they already have a category you fit into."

That confused Keisha. "Why would I want to live here?" she asked, her brows knitting. "I'm a Valdemaran Healer—"

"Because Darian will be here, of course." Daralie looked over at her son with undisguised satisfaction. "Now that he's found his family again, he'll want to stay—and besides, Raven needs him. He's exactly what we need."

"What—what you need?" Keisha repeated, feeling uncommonly dense. "What do you mean by that?"

The glance Daralie gave her made her think that Darian's mother must feel the same. "We need his talents and training," she said, with a touch of impatience. "He's a mage. We need a mage. The Raven Shaman has only Healing magic, and our warriors are no match for Wolverine. Now that Darian is here with us, you can all help us destroy Wolverine for good."

Keisha had a queasy feeling, and her food had nothing to do with it. *Here with us! Our warriors! Help us! I don't know how Darian is going to take this, but—like it or not, his parents are Ravens now!*

Nineteen

The others had gotten wind of Daralie's assumptions long
before dinner was over, and it wasn't long after Dar and Kullen
excused themselves to put the children to bed that the entire
group descended on Darian and Keisha and pulled them off to
"discuss things." They had their own campfire, far enough
away from the Men's or Women's Fires that they were well
out of earshot. They settled down around it, and Keisha knew
what Shandi would say long before she said it. One look at
her face while Darian put Raven's case forward with all of his
persuasive power told Keisha that he would never be persuasive enough.

"No," Shandi said flatly, the moment he finished speaking.
"Absolutely no. We are *not* going to get involved here. These
are not our people, this is not our problem, and your parents
can claim protection as citizens of Valdemar all they
want—my answer to that is that they can pack up and come
back with us."

Shandi's eyes told the story; nothing was going to change
her mind. The girl who had seemed so sweet and gentle was
gone, and in her place stood a young woman who was gentle
only when she felt she could afford to be. She must feel this
occasion called for her to be hard and strong. Shandi was not
going to budge; she wasn't even going to compromise.

But Darian wasn't going to give up either. Not yet, anyway. "Shandi, they may not be our people, but this *is* our problem, or rather, it will be. How long do you think it will be before Wolverine eats up every little tribe north of the border and starts to contemplate taking us? I wouldn't give it five years— and maybe less. They've already taken everything Blood Bear had and more, and it's only because they've been going slowly and consolidating their conquests that they haven't come after us."

"So now you're ForeSighted as well as a mage?" Shandi retorted, with no hint that she meant it humorously. "It seems to me that Wolverine is far more likely to stay up here in the north when they've taken in all the tribes. Why should they come south, when every conquering army that's gone to Valdemar has come back in pieces, if at all?"

"Because in the south are riches," Hywel put in solemnly. "In the south are herds of cattle and sheep, horses, grain and fruit for the taking. There are women with golden hair and red, with skin like snow and slim bodies, to become slaves. There are spineless dirt-digging men to be made into slaves to grow crops so that the warriors need never soil their honor with the cultivation of plants. There is gold, silver, gemstones. There is woven cloth, such as the traders bring, for slaves to make into brilliant tunics, warmer and softer than leather. And there are Healers who can cure all ills. That is why they will come."

"They can trade all that for fur and amber, and not have to fight," Shandi retorted. "They *know* what will happen if they bring an army into Valdemar. If Blood Bear was thwarted by a single village, what chance would they have against the army of Valdemar? We need only fortify the border; we do *not* have to stop them ourselves."

Darian's whole body telegraphed his distress to Keisha, but she was torn herself. Shandi was right; now was not the time or place to confront Wolverine, regardless of what would happen to Raven if they didn't. After all, Raven could conceivably leave as a whole, and seek sanctuary with Ghost Cat if they didn't want to fight or ally with Wolverine. They could join with Snow Fox and Red Fox; the three tribes united might well have enough force to hold Wolverine off. Confrontation was not their only option.

But part of her agreed with Darian; wouldn't it be better to take care of the problem now, before Wolverine became an unstoppable force? Valdemar had faced a Northern tribes enemy before—wasn't that why the Forest of Sorrows had been called a "defensive border?"

So she stayed silent, dropping her eyes when both Shandi and Darian looked at her for support. *I can't support either of them,* she thought helplessly. *They're both right, and I don't know which of them is* more *right.*

From under her lashes she watched as Darian looked beseechingly at Wintersky and Kel instead, when he could not get backing from her.

Kel, at least, had no hesitation. "Darrrian isss rrright!" he hissed, his eyes narrowed as he glanced at Shandi. "You sssaw what they did to Rrred Fox!" His hackles came up and he snapped his beak for emphasis. "You sssaw with yourrrr own eyesss! How can you sssit therrre and sssay that we ssshould do nothing?"

"I think that what happened to Red Fox was a tragedy, but it's not *our* tragedy," Shandi insisted. "There are likely things like that happening in the Eastern Empire—or what's left of it—at this very moment, and it's very sad, but we can't do anything about it. Life isn't fair, Kel, and it's not our job to make it so."

"*Sssketi!*" Kel spat, clearly disgusted with Shandi and Karles together, since it was obvious from the way that they had drawn together that Shandi spoke for both of them. "You call yourrrssself a Herald, and sssay that? That isss cowarrrd'sss talk! If no one trrriesss to make the worrrld fairrr, then it neverrrr will be, will it? Ssso you will *alwaysss* have that to fall back upon! I do not think that the firrrssst Herrraldsss in Valdemarrr made sssuch excusssesss!"

Keisha noticed that Shandi flinched a little at that, but she did not back down. Now she looked at Wintersky and Steelmind, seeking supporters of her own. Steelmind licked his lips and sighed. "I can see both sides," he said reluctantly. "I can't see that one outweighs the other."

Relieved that he had put into words what she felt, Keisha looked up and nodded eagerly. "Exactly," she said. "Both of you are right."

"That's my feeling," Wintersky told them. "You know,

none of us have ForeSight, so how can we know for sure what's likely to happen? And—Darian, just what *are* we supposed to do; there's only the nine of us—sixteen, if you count the *dyheli*. How big a difference can nine creatures make?"

"That's a mage, a gryphon, a Companion, a Herald, three Tayledras and a seasoned Ghost Cat warrior," Darian retorted. "It's not as if we were nine plowboys!"

"It's not as if we were an army either," Shandi countered, glaring at him. "And what about our duty to get back home and warn Valdemar about all this? Karles and I can only send so much—Anda needs more than we can tell him—"

By the sudden light in Darian's eyes, Keisha knew that Shandi had given him an opening, and he saw a way to get her to compromise.

"All right. Then let's at least get him some real information!" he insisted. "We can do what no one in Raven can. We can get in close to Wolverine and see what their numbers are, and what their equipment is! Why, I'll bet we could even get in close enough to find out some of their plans, just by listening to the warriors' boasting!"

Which would make us close enough to work a little sabotage, no doubt? Keisha thought. She knew how Darian thought; once they had worked themselves in that close, there would be opportunities to disrupt the enemy tribe, and no matter what Steelmind and Wintersky thought now, they would not be able to resist taking advantage of those opportunities.

Shandi frowned fiercely, and Keisha had a good idea what was in her sister's mind as well. Shandi wanted, very badly, to object, but there was nothing she could really object to. She and Karles exchanged a long, wordless look, neither of them happy about the position they'd been placed in.

"I think that's an . . . acceptable compromise," Keisha said tentatively, and earned herself a frown from Shandi.

Of course, I'm not one of the ones who'll be going on these scouting forays—

"I think that's the best answer, personally." Wintersky sounded a lot more decisive than Keisha, but that was to be expected.

Kel, however, was clearly not enamored with halfhearted measures. "I ssstilll sssay we ssshould do morrre than that!"

he began, but a look from Darian silenced him, and Keisha sensed another mind-to-mind exchange like the one that Shandi had exchanged with Karles. Kel's beak snapped shut, and he looked a little happier; that was when Keisha knew that she had guessed right about Darian's intention of adding sabotage to the scouting forays.

Steelmind looked from Shandi to Darian, and held out his hands, palms up. "I think that will work," was all he said, with no elaboration on what he considered "that" to be. So he knew, or guessed, too.

Shandi gritted her teeth and glared, but it was obvious that she was outvoted. She gave in, but not with good grace.

Keisha, however, had extended a careful tendril of Empathy toward her sister, and there was more going on beneath that hard surface than Shandi was allowing to show.

I wonder—will she go off by herself—

To Keisha's satisfaction, that was just what Shandi did; she exchanged another look with Karles, and got up and left the fire. The men interpreted it as going off in a sulk; Wintersky raised his eyebrows at Darian who shrugged, and Hywel snorted derisively. Steelmind looked defensive, but said nothing.

Keisha waited a few moments, then when the men began to discuss possible "scouting forays," she excused herself and left. It was not at all difficult to tell where Shandi was; at least, not for her. Shandi might think she was away from all eyes, hidden in the shadows on the outskirts of the village, but Keisha followed a surer summons than vision.

Her senses led her correctly. Keisha approached her slowly; Karles was a white shape in the darkness and Shandi a dark, upright slash against him. "Shandi?" she said quietly. "Why didn't you just tell the truth?"

The dark slash practically vibrated with tension; upon closer approach, Keisha could see that Shandi was trembling, handling an arrow wrapped in red ribbon. "What truth?" Shandi asked, in a tone very like anger—except that it wasn't.

But Keisha knew what the emotion gripping her sister really was. "Why didn't you tell them that you're *afraid?*"

"Me? Afraid? What are you talking about?" That was bluster, and Keisha only needed to hear how Shandi's voice shook to know it.

"I'm an Empath, too, Shandi," Keisha said.

The reaction to that could only have been predicted by someone who knew Shandi as well as her older sister did. Instead of blustering further when her bluff was called, Shandi dropped the arrow, and flung herself away from Karles and into her sister's arms. Keisha held her as she had when she'd been much smaller, and had suffered an emotional, childish tragedy. Only now, she was a young woman, and this crisis was anything but childish.

Shandi shook in every limb, and sobbed wordlessly into Keisha's shoulder; there was no point in trying to coax her to talk until she was over the first bout of tears. As Karles stirred restlessly, Keisha led her sister to a fallen log and got her to sit down on it. It took a long time before Shandi cried herself out enough to speak, but Keisha was perfectly willing to wait as long as it took. *Poor Shandi! They taught her how to handle other people's emotions, but not her own.*

"A chick can't go back in the shell, and a young hawk can't unfledge. I'm your sister, Shandi. We've grown up together, but we aren't the same as we were when we were little. We've always trusted each other, so trust me now. You have to remember that when you wall things out, you can wall them in with you, too," Keisha said into Shandi's hair as she held Shandi's head against her shoulder. Her own eyes stung a bit as she held back tears of sympathy. "Shields can work both ways—bottle up fear and it will eat you alive, sweetling."

"But I'm a Herald—" Shandi wept. "I'm supposed to be strong and dependable—"

"Since when does that mean *never* showing fear?" Keisha countered. "You saw how we all acted, when the cold-drake caught us. Hawkbrothers, *dyheli*, and even a gryphon—we were all terrified and showed it. And since when is fear a bad thing? Fear keeps us from doing a lot of really stupid things. Hey, fear kept me from becoming a good little miller's wife, right?" She smiled, trying to cheer Shandi, and pulled her a little closer, feeling very much the Big Sister once again. "It's perfectly all right to be afraid about this. I know I am, and you can tell, right? I'm afraid—as far as that goes, really very afraid."

"How can you possibly understand?" Shandi retorted. "You've faced all kinds of terrible things without being afraid!

I can hardly stand the sight of blood! How can you know how I feel—"

"How? I've lived with you, sweetling, or have you forgotten?" Keisha almost laughed. "I don't even need to be an Empath to know, sister! You spent most of your life being a good maidenly daughter, then became the belle of the village—everything in your life was sweet, perfect, and predictable. Then suddenly you got Chosen—which is every child's secret daydream, but there aren't too many who would know what to do if it happened—whisked out into another world, with no family around, and put through strange schooling so fast it made your head spin. And as if that wasn't enough on your plate, no sooner did you get someplace where you thought you might be able to catch your breath than you were thrown onto a dangerous mission that goes right off the map without *anyone* who taught you to help or advise you! You've seen some horrible things that you'd never imagined in your worst nightmares. And now this idiot mage wants *you* to help him fight an army? You'd have to be crazy not to be in a panic, and I know you aren't crazy!"

Shandi had been silent through all of this—and now her body began to shake again as she clung to her sister. "How could you know—how did you guess—" she sobbed weakly.

"Because I'm your sister and your best friend, and I love you," was the simplest answer she could give—and must have been the best. Shandi completely dissolved in tears—and now, so did Keisha, tears that flowed down her cheeks silently, without the kind of painful knot she got in her throat when she was fighting to hold them back. But Keisha's were tears of happiness mixed with relief, for now, at last, she knew that Shandi was never going to wall her out again.

It was well past midnight when Shandi had talked herself out; by then, Keisha was cold and stiff, but she wouldn't have moved to save her soul.

"—and the worst was when Kel said that the first Heralds wouldn't have been so cowardly," Shandi said, in a voice made hoarse with talking and crying. "He was right, I knew he was right—I wanted to sink into the ground, but I knew if I showed anything, they'd all think that the only reason I was against Darian was because I was afraid! And it's not, it's not, I swear it!"

"If you hadn't spoken up, I'm not sure any of the rest of us would have said anything," Keisha told her truthfully. "I mean, after all, we may each have our own private agendas, but at the heart of it, this is Darian's personal quest we're helping with. With his parents asking for help—how could his best friends let him down?"

Only now did Karles take the few steps needed to move to Shandi's side and gently rub his warm, soft nose against her shoulder—and Keisha's hands. Shandi reached up and patted his neck. "Karles—tried to help me, but—"

:I am not an Empath,: Karles said simply, surprising Keisha once again by speaking to her as well as to Shandi. *:I cannot shield her from her own fear, when I am just as afraid—I cannot even shield her from mine! This is* not *Valdemar, and I am . . . out of my element.:*

"We all are, to some degree or other," Keisha told both of them. "Never doubt it."

:But Valdemar is home, *and I have never been away from it!:* The plaintive note in Karles' mind-voice came as a second shock; all her life she had been raised to think that Companions were near-invulnerable and infallible—

:We are different, with a few powers, yes, and more experience, but hardly infallible.: Karles sighed heavily, and nuzzled Shandi once more. *:Shandi and I are two halves of a whole; we complement and complete one another. That is the way of Herald and Companion. We are still as prone to weakness and mistakes as any other soul. If being Companion and Chosen made us infallible, think how many disasters in Valdemar's history could have been avoided!:*

"Good point," Keisha replied, but kept her thought of *and how nice of you to have finally admitted that!* carefully under shields. "Shandi, do take it from an *older and more experienced* Empath—and not just your big sister—that you are doing yourself no good by keeping those walls up, inside and out. You need to do a certain amount of shielding, but not to the point that you feel nothing from us, and let nothing of your own emotion show! We need to know how you feel about things as much as you need to know how we feel, otherwise we cannot work with each other. Out here in the wild unknown, that could cost a life, maybe even mine." Keisha smiled again and kissed her sister's forehead gently. "Neither of us would want that, yes? Now let's get some sleep, and see what matters look like in the morning."

Is Darian thinking clearly? Is he so caught up in trying to impress his parents, to give them anything they need, that he's not able to be objective? No doubt, Shandi was already thinking those things, without Keisha's experience with Darian to bolster her faith in him.

And Steelmind needs to know more of how you feel than all the rest of us put together, she thought, but also under shield, as Shandi got stiffly to her feet and gave her sister a hand up. It wasn't her place to give Shandi any advice about romance, and she wasn't sure that Shandi would take it, even if it was her place. Maybe Shandi and Karles hadn't seen it as clearly as Keisha had, as a result of how much they had tried to wall themselves off from their own emotions and others', but day by day there was much more in Steelmind's attitudes toward Shandi than a passing interest in a fellow traveler.

I've been lucky enough to find Darian. Maybe the best gift I can give to my sister is getting her to open up enough to see that Steelmind is right next to her. And, just maybe, when he sees she will open up to him now, Steelmind will open his arms to her. We are farther away from home than any of us ever imagined we'd be, and all we have is each other.

Darian woke up all at once, with the disorienting impression that Kuari was trying to dance a jig on the roof of the log house. Then what Kuari was trying to tell him penetrated his muddled mind, and a moment later he leaped from bed and was pulling on his clothes in grim haste, as Keisha stirred groggily beside him.

"What?" she managed, raising a face half-covered with sleep-tousled hair.

"We've got to alert the village," he told her, for there was no time to tell this gently. "Kuari's seen something. I think there's something bad—a tribal army coming straight for us."

:Kel!: he blasted into the gryphon's dreaming mind. :Kel, wake up!:

:?: The reply was foggy and inarticulate. :Food sleep preen mate fight what?:

:Up! Alarm! Enemies!: He kept his reply simple; it took a moment for Kel's mind to get working. A moment later, Kel's war cry ripped through the village, shocking everyone within hearing distance awake.

In another moment, Hashi's howl started all the dogs in the village up, which ensured that no one slept. Darian left Keisha struggling to organize herself while he headed for the door to get the village mobilized. He was already outside before his parents, reacting to the unholy cacophony, pushed their way out of their sleeping cubicle. Keisha could explain to them; he had to get the rest of the village alert so defenses were in place before the enemy arrived.

Steelmind and Shandi burst out of the door of the log house they were guesting in shortly after he stumbled into the ghostly mist that swirled around the log houses, a mist that clung damply to him in the half-light of predawn. Steelmind whistled shrilly for his bird, and Karles pounded through the mist to Shandi's side. She seized her saddle from the bench beside the door and swung it up onto his back as he skidded to a halt beside her. Hywel and Wintersky were next out the door, and the *dyheli* were all close on the heels of Karles, snorting and stamping with agitation.

Then the northerners began piling out of their houses, all sleepy, all confused, all babbling. Darian tried shouting his warnings, but his voice was lost in the general confusion and he despaired of making himself heard.

Then Kel put a stop to the noise by diving down out of the trees and braking with huge sweeps of his wings to land beside Darian, just as Hashi broke off his howl of alert and the dogs followed his lead. The wind of Kel's wings cleared the mist; his sudden appearance silenced everyone, with shock and alarm, for no one here was used to a gryphon's dramatic entrances. Darian took full advantage of the sudden silence.

"Our birds just alerted us, Wolverine is on the way, in force," he called out. "Whatever defensive plan you've got, you'd better put it in motion now. We've got until dawn before they get here, and dawn's not far off."

There was no more confusion; the men quickly sorted themselves into defensive groups and headed for the stored weapons; boys and some of the women went for hunting bows and arrows, while the rest began dragging tied bundles of thorny brush into a defensive barricade around the perimeter of the village.

Shandi pulled herself into the saddle and trotted Karles over to Darian. "What do you want us to do?" she asked; her voice trembled a little, and she was dead-white, but she seemed steady enough. In fact, Darian was just as glad to see her finally showing a little fear; it made him less worried that she would try to do something comprised of equal parts of bravery and foolishness.

"Stand by," he told her. "You're the only cavalry we've got; I just hope Wolverine doesn't have any riders. One person can do a lot if she's the only one on horseback."

Karles stamped a hoof loudly.

"Or on whatever," Darian added.

Hywel had grabbed a boar-spear and picked out a group of Raven warriors to stand with on his own; that was perfect. He knew how to fight alongside these people, in their style; Darian dismissed him from his mind. Steelmind and Wintersky retrieved their bows and every arrow they owned, then sent their birds out after Kuari. Kel lumbered back up into the air to perch on the rooftree of one of the log houses.

How long do we have? he wondered, and joined his mind to Kuari's. Through Kuari's eyes he looked down on the approaching throngs of warriors and recognized one of the slopes they had passed yesterday.

His stomach lurched. *Not long enough.*

Wolverine's fighters would be within hearing distance in a few moments; he didn't bother warning the rest, since they'd be catching the sounds of jingling harness and men trampling through brush in a moment. Wolverine was no longer making even a token attempt at slipping up unnoticed.

And just how did they know they don't have surprise on us?

The answer to that was clear enough as the second rank came into Kuari's view.

Striding alongside a guard of muscular fighters dressed identically in leather tunics ornamented with an eclipsed sun instead of a tribal or personal totem was an all-too-familiar-looking figure. Darian's nightmares were sometimes haunted by a similar, dark figure out of his past.

The Shaman of the Eclipse. Mage and Shaman in one, this fellow was in his late twenties or early thirties, bearded, shaggy-haired, and fully as muscle-bound as his personal guards. Unlike the guards, he had only token armor; a helmet, shoulder plates, arm braces. He also wore robes of cloth, not a leather tunic; black cloth, with the corona of the eclipse painted in scarlet on the breast. He wore the same style medallion that the last such Shaman had worn—the Shaman who had led Blood Bear to attack and conquer Errold's Grove.

A Shaman you killed yourself, with a lot fewer weapons and no training, he reminded himself, as the sight of the man sent atavistic chills down his back. He tried not to think about how huge a part luck had played on that long-ago night.

"Their mage is with them," he told the others—which now included Keisha and his parents, who had joined Wintersky, Steelmind, and Shandi. "He must have followed my trail from the pass." Too late now to chastise himself for using magic at all; he'd done what seemed right at the time.

"They're coming!" someone shouted from the barricade, and as the first scarlet hint of the sun silhouetted the mountains to the east, an unexpected breeze blew off the mist. The clearing in front of the village sprang up as if conjured from the fog—and there they were.

Darian swallowed, his mouth gone dry. Even if every man, woman, and child of Raven took up a weapon, they would still be outnumbered two-to-one. The only slim advantage they had was that they were the defenders. Their opponents, though not as well-armed as Blood Bear had been when they descended upon Errold's Grove, were still formidable; all of them were fit, tough, and looked to be seasoned warriors, armed with swords, knives, and throwing-spears, armored with hammered-metal helmets, shoulder- and breast-plates, with vambraces and greaves over their leather tunics and trews. Cold-eyed and wary, they didn't seem impressed with the defenders.

His heart went cold and sank into the bottom of his stomach. His chest went tight as the warriors of Wolverine lined themselves up before the defenses of Raven, making a loose formation of two ranks. The ones in the second rank had bows instead of javelins.

Oh, gods. It's not all Wolverine either. . . .

He should have expected this, but somehow it had never occurred to him that there would be fighters sporting the totem of Blood Bear allied with those of Wolverine. There they were—not the half-human, half-bestial things that their Shaman had created, but more than nasty-looking enough. And by the wicked snarls on their faces, they recognized the three Hawkbrothers, too—recognized them as coming from the same folk as the instrument of their defeat in the south, at any rate.

I've got a very bad feeling about this.

Shandi eased Karles over to Darian's side, and nodded at the Blood Bear contingent, who made up nearly half of the left flank. "Is that who I think it is?" she asked, in a voice that cracked a little.

"It is." He didn't take his eyes off the Shaman. If there was a single person commanding this force, it was this Shaman, and his control was absolute. After the fighters arrayed themselves in two ranks, they remained in place, and when one or two stirred restlessly, the Shaman quelled them with a single spearing glance.

Only when all of his troops had settled into immobility did the Shaman send his gaze questing over the Raven defenders. When his eyes locked with Darian's, it was clear enough who he had been looking for.

Darian returned his gaze somberly, determined not to show a hint of weakness or fear. *You want to start a staring contest? Be my guest. I'd rather we tried to stare each other down than started flinging arrows at each other.* He tried to judge the level of the mage's power without actually probing him, for a probe could be turned against him; the other man was probably doing the same.

The flows of power around the Shaman told Darian quite a bit—more bad news, since the Shaman had accessed a ley-line four furlongs behind, which crossed the trail the army must have taken. It wasn't the strongest line Darian had ever seen, nor the strongest in the area, but the fact that the mage was accessing it at all meant he was at least Darian's equal. *Higher than Apprentice and Journeyman. Master, at least. How experienced a Master?* There was no telling, but Darian felt altogether too new and raw in his ranking at the moment. *I am not ready for a contest of mage-against-mage*—he thought, as he accessed another power line.

But evidently the other was.

With a brusque motion to his guard to stand their ground,

the Shaman stepped forward from the rest. His voice, deep and mocking, with an underlying rasp, rang out across the clear ground between them. "Ho! Chief of Raven!"

With a tightening of his jaw muscles, the Raven Chief answered, though he did not step forward in turn. "I see you, Shaman of Wolverine," he called, raising his chin in a gesture of defiance. "What brings you to Raven at the season of fishing?"

"A friendly visit." the Shaman grinned, his teeth glinting whitely in the darkness of his beard. "You give us cold greeting."

Darian felt his skin crawling at the sight of that smile. The Shaman was very sure of himself.

"Do friends come as armies, visiting with weapons in hand?" Raven Chief countered bravely. The Chief held his head high, his voice clear and steady. If he was worried, it wasn't apparent.

The Shaman did not reply directly to that; instead, he allowed his gaze to drift back to Darian, then return to the Chief. "You have strange visitors," he said instead, with a heavy frown. "Visitors who bear a strange resemblance to folk who caused friends and allies of ours much grief, some few years ago."

"Ah?" The Chief tilted his head to one side. "That is odd; I had heard a different tale." He scratched his head and feigned thinking hard. "There was something about an attempt to conquer the southlands that was thwarted by the inhabitants there. Something about Blood Bear being routed by a few birds and a handful of dirt-diggers and children—"

There was a roar of anger from the left, and the Shaman had to divert his attention to regaining command of his own forces, while the fighters of Raven roared with laughter. Somewhat forced laughter, perhaps, but it served its purpose, which was to make the Blood Bear fighters angry and difficult to control.

Darian silently cheered for the Raven Chief; he was doing exactly the right thing, putting as much strain on the Shaman's control of the troops as possible.

When the Shaman had regained the upper hand and returned to his negotiations, he had not lost a bit of his outwardly pleasant and half-amused demeanor. "That was ill-said, Chief of Raven," he chided gently. "You have made our allies unhappy. I cannot answer for what they may do if you anger them a second time."

The Chief shrugged, as if it was a matter of complete indifference to him. "Whether you can keep any grip on your own warriors' collars is not my problem, Shaman."

Darian hoped he could keep talking for the rest of the day—while they were exchanging barbed witticisms (or at least what passed for witticisms among the Northerners) there wasn't any fighting going on. "Your allies are no friends to Raven," he pointed out. "Why not send them on their way? Then, perhaps, we will consider offering you a warmer welcome."

"Oh, Chief, I do not believe I can do that," the Shaman said silkily, shaking his head with mock-sadness. "Much as I would like to oblige you. I believe they have some business with these visitors of yours."

"I believe they do not. These visitors are related to Elders of my tribe and are traders; Blood Bear has no relatives here, and has never been interested in gaining goods by trade." The Chief's tone implied that the reason Blood Bear wasn't interested in trade was because they preferred to steal.

Raven-spirit, this Chief of yours is as clever as any of the feathered tribe, Darian thought. Darian saw what he was up to—he was trying to divide the forces. For some reason, the Shaman of Wolverine wasn't ready to attack yet, and might not support Blood Bear if they did. It would be much easier to handle the enemy if they came at the defenses a piece at a time.

"Really?" The Shaman's arch tone betokened mock-astonishment. "You have some strange blood in Raven, then."

"No stranger than a tribe whose warriors once looked as much beast as man," the Chief countered, grounding the butt of his spear for emphasis. He looked down his nose at the left flank, and the Blood Bear fighters stirred uncomfortably. "The blood in Raven is different, perhaps, but strong. The Raven is lord of the skies. Even the Eagle does not interfere with him."

"So you say; the Raven's calls sound like empty croaking to me." That was an open challenge, but the Chief wasn't lured into taking it. He knew as well as Darian that their advantage lay in keeping the enemy talking as long as possible.

"For those who have not the learning or the wisdom, all good advice sounds like empty croaking." There was the challenge turned back without having to answer it.

But the Shaman was losing patience. "You have one among your so-called visitors with *dangerous* learning," he warned, pointing directly at Darian, who responded by standing straighter and staring back stonily into the Shaman's gaze. "Or has he not told you? Chief of Raven, this man would make you think he is but a harmless thing, but he is a poison serpent among you. He has magic powers that he had not disclosed to you, that do not come from the spirits—"

"But he has," the Chief laughed. "He has told us all, and much more than you know. And we know him. You say he is a poison serpent disguised, but I say he is the guardian serpent across our threshold—"

The Shaman smiled, and both Darian and the Chief—and everyone else knew that the Chief had finally said the wrong thing, and given the Shaman the opening he'd been looking for. "In that case," the Shaman said quickly and gleefully, "Send forth your guardian, for a Shaman is a serpent-slayer, and let him contend with me. If you wish us to depart in peace, that is the least that we will accept. Send your guardian forth so that we will face each other, and see who has the greater strength; he whose power comes from the Spirits, or he whose power comes from nothing *we* recognize." His tone turned silky and coaxing. "You have nothing to lose by this, Chief of Raven; only send him out. If he wins, we will depart."

Keisha stifled a gasp of dismay, and Darian bit back a gasp of his own as his heart sank right down into his boots. Of all things, the very last that he wanted was a head-to-head mage-duel with someone whose power and abilities were a complete unknown to him.

And the Shaman had maneuvered them all into a position where that was precisely what he would have to do.

Twenty

Keisha stopped herself from grabbing Darian's sleeve to hold him back. Her lover closed his eyes a few moments, took a deep breath, and stepped forward. To her left, Daralie made a little whimper, but no other sound of protest, though she caught Kullen's hand in hers and Keisha felt fear coming from both of them in waves.

I'll bet they never foresaw Darian confronting this mage face-to-face. They thought he'd just wave his hands at a safe distance and the Eclipse Shaman would fall into dust. Her throat was so tight it hurt to swallow. *Too bad magic doesn't work that way. . . .*

Darian looked cool and untroubled as he stepped up to the barricade of brush and waited for the warriors of Raven to use fishing hook-poles to pull the thorns aside, so he could pass; only Keisha and Shandi could really know how apprehensive he was. The Shaman of Wolverine waved off his guard and stepped forward to meet Darian halfway between the two lines.

Keisha held her breath, as the two mages stared into each others' eyes while they established the stance they wished to begin with. There was some distance, to prevent the bystanders from being injured—maybe. Of all the clothing Darian could have grabbed in his haste to dress, Keisha thought it was interesting that he had grabbed the leather tunic and trews that he'd worn for his ceremony with Ghost Cat. In the war of minds that was almost as important as the war of magic, Darian had gotten a boost with that outfit—he was *supposed* to be an outland southerner, but he was wearing the clothing of the tribes. Some of the Shaman's power came from the belief his followers had in him—and Keisha sensed a stirring of unease among them.

Darian made a cool and calm backhanded insult to the mage he was facing, by turning his back to him for a moment—a wordless way of showing the mage was of so little concern he didn't even have to keep an eye on him. Darian spread his arms, with his open hands at waist height, and two horse-lengths away from each hand, a wall of force grew up from the ground. As he drew his hands together, the ground churned up as if being plowed and the wall rose, looking like flattened bolts of lightning along its leading edge. When Darian's palms met, there was a shimmering wall several times his height in a semicircle between himself and Raven, cupping him toward the Shaman's side. Raising one eyebrow slightly, Darian turned to face the Shaman.

The Shaman grunted, and reluctantly mirrored Darian's action—the intent being to keep the opponent's attacks from harming the mage's own forces. The churning earth sputtered up in large uneven chunks, less plowed-looking and more like they were hammered upward from below. There was a resounding thud when the force-wall kicked up a log. The semicircles were barely visible to those who could not see the energies and powers that lay beneath the skin of the world. They shimmered a little in the early-morning sunlight, as if each mage had a structure of the thinnest, most delicate glass built around them as they faced each other.

The two semicircles joined edge to edge with a visible flash, and Darian's began to glow a very pale silver, while the Shaman's restlessly flickered yellow. The effect faintly obscured the two mages inside, who backed away to get as much distance as possible between each other. No one would enter or leave now.

The Shaman struck first, abruptly; he leaped into action, arms flailing as if he threw a handful of stones, pelting Darian with what looked like white-hot shooting stars, so bright they hurt the eyes. Keisha moaned and flinched away, her heart racing.

Darian didn't do anything outwardly, but the shooting stars bent their paths to either side, and bounced off something just in front of him, two of them slowing in midair before accelerating straight back at the Shaman.

The Shaman reached out, caught them, and with a sly smile, drew his arms up in a slow arc. He displayed the catch to his men, and crushed the sputtering fireballs in his raised fists in a pyrotechnic show of dominance.

Darian shrugged, as if the tactic hadn't impressed him, and the Shaman's smile turned to a frown. *Is Darian going to attack next?* Keisha wondered, her hands balled into fists at her side as she watched. The Shaman was obviously expecting him to do something equally showy in response, and his frown deepened.

Darian didn't even shift his weight; he waited patiently, with no sign of agitation or anger. *Why?* she wondered. Steelmind had come up to her other side unnoticed; he put a comforting hand on her shoulder and she jumped.

"Darian is playing a waiting game," he murmured in her ear. "When two Masters contend, there is no question of one running out of magic energy, for they use the ley-lines. Instead, usually the one who loses is the one who becomes physically fatigued soonest. Darian is rightly letting the Shaman expend his own strength first; he loses nothing by this, but if the Shaman were to play the same game, he would lose face with his warriors, who expect him to be aggressive."

The Shaman tried another few volleys of those shooting stars, but however thick and fast they came, Darian deflected them without turning a hair. They *looked* impressive—as most of his magics likely were—but the blazing attacks were treated with such apparent indifference by his opponent, the Shaman must have realized this bit of flashiness was working against him.

The Blood Bear warriors, already keyed up and spoiling for a fight, had no patience with this one-sided battle. They had been moving restlessly and muttering among themselves since the Shaman stepped forward. Just as Keisha glanced over at them, alarmed at a sudden rise in their anger, they charged the Raven defenses.

Their screams of battle drowned out her own scream of fear, and she stumbled backwards and would have fallen if she hadn't caught herself. Steelmind had an arrow on his bowstring and another in the air before the enemy had gone more than a dozen steps.

With her mouth dry and her heart racing, Keisha backed up further, and set herself behind the shelter of a carved pole just as the first set of enemy arrows rained down on their lines. The war cries of the fighters and the screams of the wounded drowned everything else, and her stomach turned over with nausea as the metallic scent of blood reached her.

But something else pulled her out of her shelter; the need of those injured. She darted from cover, grabbed the nearest wounded man, and dragged him back to relative safety by his shirt. Then she went to work, blotting everything else out. Every man, woman, or child she could get back on his or her feet with a bow in their hands might give them a better chance. She couldn't help Darian, she couldn't wield a sword, but she could do this much.

And she would.

Darian watched the Eclipse Shaman through narrowed eyes, sensing the ebb and flow of power in the ley-line that the Shaman had linked to. He didn't think it had occurred to the Shaman to do the same, and that gave him an edge in knowing *when* an attack would come, if not *how.* Then again, Darian had the advantage of Tayledras training, and not merely the standard training, but also Firesong's version of that training. The Hawkbrothers were steeped in the precise and most efficient use of magic, passed on for many generations, and by comparison this Shaman was likely self-trained or tutored in rough skills at best.

The Shaman began to prowl his half of the circle, pacing back and forth, eying Darian with barely suppressed fury. Outside the circle, there was a battle going on; *someone* had broken the promise the Shaman had made. But neither Darian nor his opponent dared pay any heed to anything outside their wall of power; any distraction would give the other a chance to strike the fatal blow.

Darian began to move warily himself, watching the Shaman and nothing else, keeping the same distance between them at all times. Then the Shaman darted toward him, pushing his hands forward, palms out.

A massive wall of force hit Darian and knocked him backward; he'd have fallen if he hadn't been moving himself; as it was, he had to dance sideways and fend off a second invisible blow, turning the force aside and into the wall of the sphere. That put him almost within *physical* reach of the Shaman, who made a grab for him.

He dropped and rolled out of the way, jumping to his feet and putting the fullest possible distance between himself and the Shaman again.

Again he watched the line even as he watched the Shaman, and again, an ebb in the power-level warned him before the Shaman attacked.

Hands blazing with power, the Shaman lunged for him; there was no time to move out of the way, so Darian used the oldest of all of his defenses.

The Shaman's right foot caught on the earth for a critical moment; he stumbled and fell, catching himself with his outstretched hands. The power he had meant to use to blast Darian discharged into the ground, creating nothing worse than a blackened spot and the smell of scorched dirt.

As he fell, Darian ran out of the way again; the Shaman picked himself up with red rage burning in his eyes. Darian reacted to the immediate drop in power just in time by strengthening his shields; this time the weapon he used was anything but subtle. He lashed at Darian with levin-bolts, whips of power that looked and hit like lightning.

The levin-bolts arced into his shields with a *crack* that hurt his ears and an eye-burning light that made his eyes water. He held his shields against the bolts as the Shaman poured power into them and the air around him tasted of a thunderstorm at its peak.

Abruptly, the Shaman released the bolts; Darian could barely see. Blinking tears out of his eyes, he used Mage-Sight to watch the Shaman instead, seeing him as a form laced with little threads of red and yellow.

Those threads blazed up as the ley-line ebbed, but this time Darian reacted before the Shaman could; he made the Shaman's foot stick again as the man moved sideways before his attack. The Shaman hadn't expected an offensive move after so much defense; this time he fell hard, and while he was down, Darian lashed *him* with eye-burning levin-bolts.

He held the bolts on his still-prone enemy until his own eyes had time to recover, then leaped sideways just as he released them, and just in time, for the moment he did so, the Shaman hit him with the conjured weapon he'd been planning to use.

A massive sphere of energy rolled toward him, looking like fire with *teeth*, threatening to engulf him. He made a quick guess and assumed that the Shaman would expect him to run; he stood his ground instead, and held his shields. The sphere rolled right over him; it *was* dangerous in itself, for it immediately began to suck power from his shields, but it wasn't as dangerous as the jagged spikes of energy that blasted out a pit right where Darian would have been if he'd run.

That made another obstacle to avoid. He solved the problem of the sphere by puncturing its outer wall; it deflated like a punctured bladder, and vanished as if it were a flame out of fuel.

The Shaman was furious. He was about to have his temper cooled. Darian detachedly reasoned out his primary advantage against this Shaman. The Shaman's use of power was formidable, and his endurance considerable, but it was all oriented toward obvious, surface-visible effects—which was only logical considering he was a Shaman who also sought power among his people—when you want to discourage challenges and impress your followers, why not use the most awe- and fear-inspiring magics?

Darian, however, was able to work beneath the surface. There were springs everywhere underground here; they accounted for part of the verdancy, part of the humidity, and were doubtless under pressure thanks to the large body of water nearby. Darian found the nearest underground reservoir, and with a few deft hand motions to help in the mental process of sculpting the channel underneath, brought it powerfully to the surface, right beneath the Shaman.

Water blasted upward in a cold geyser, knocking the other to the ground, and soaking him in moments.

Two can play at making holes in the earth.

And while he was at it—in the next breath, he aerated the ground around the Shaman, creating an ear-numbing protracted thunderclap, then super-saturated the ground beneath the Shaman with water from that same geyser, turning it into a sinkhole. The Shaman predictably began to struggle, miring himself up to the waist—at which time Darian cut off the geyser's feeding-channel, leaving the pressure to build below the surface. Another twist of the magic and Darian chased *all* the water out of the mud pit, leaving the Shaman embedded in rock-hard ground.

Raven kept the Blood Bear warriors at the barricade; none got past the hedge of thorns backed by heavier pieces of tree trunk. Keisha pulled ten or twelve of Raven's wounded to safety, mostly struck by arrows. After the first three, she got into a rhythm; wait for a lull, dash out, seize the victim by the shirt, haul him to protection. Then break off the arrowhead, pull the shaft out, stop the bleeding. Once that was done, most of her patients went grimly right back into the fray without pausing for more than a drink of water. She could hardly believe it—they must have been in terrible pain! But they didn't seem to feel anything; as soon as she had them reasonably patched up with rough bandages and supportive bindings they grabbed another weapon and went for the barricade.

The noise and stench were awful; metal clanging against metal, arrows piercing leather and skin, men and women screaming and shouting, punctuated with Kel's war shrieks and the cries of the raptors—old and new sweat, blood, rancid grease, churned mud. It all overwhelmed the senses, impossible to block out. She couldn't ignore the chaos, so she endured it, and after the tenth (or twelfth) man ran back to the lines as she finished tying off the bandages on his upper arm, she looked around for another patient and discovered to her surprise that there weren't any.

There were no more arrows flying into their lines; the fighting on this side of the barricade was all hand-to-hand, but now the advantage was with the defenders. *They* could continue to rain arrows down on the back rank of the enemy without even taking combatants from the line—the women and young boys stood off at a distance, lobbing their arrows in a high arc over the Raven lines and into the back ranks of Blood Bear. Blood Bear hadn't managed to breach the barricade, as the thorns still held them at bay, and as bundles of thorns were broken and trampled by the sheer press of bodies, grimly determined children came dragging new ones to be shoved into place with boar-spears.

Boar-spears—strangely enough, *those* were proving to give Raven a real edge. They were long enough to reach over the barricade and stab at the enemy without exposing their wielder to the thorns. The blade, long and sharp to piece a boar's tough hide, was about the same size as the short-swords all of the fighters were using, and the iron cross-bar designed to keep the boar from coming up the shaft at the hunter made effective quillons. Anyone could use it to stab; really good fighters could use it to slash as well. Although the only fatal wounds to Blood Bear so far had been caused by arrows, the spearmen were holding the line.

But where was Wolverine?

Keisha stood on her toes behind the shelter of her carved pole, and craned her neck to look over the embattled defenders.

Wolverine had not moved a single pace forward. In fact, some of them looked *embarrassed!*

They broke the Shaman's promise, that's why, she thought, astonished. *Blood Bear has broken the promise the Shaman made not to attack while he and Darian were fighting.* This wasn't a case of Northerner against outland Southerner, where anything was fair and promises didn't matter—this was tribe against tribe, where strict rules held.

And Blood Bear had broken the rules. No matter who survived this fight, Blood Bear had blackened the name of their tribe. Even their own totemic spirit might choose to desert them, and no tribe or individual would ever trust the word of a member of Blood Bear again. That meant no alliances, no intermarriages, no trade agreements, no intercourse of any kind. Essentially, it meant the death of the tribe. The only way a member of Blood Bear could survive the shunning would be if he somehow convinced the Chief of another tribe that *he* had not participated in the oathbreaking; then he could be adopted into a new tribe.

Which means no adult warriors of Blood Bear, period. Only the women and children. Wolverine will throw them out as soon as the fighting's over. Skies above—I'm actually wit-

nessing the final death of the entire clan that attacked Er-rold's Grove.

Wolverine wouldn't raise a finger to help Raven, though. Their code of conduct didn't extend *that* far.

Another man fell, and Keisha dashed out to drag him into safety. This time her treatment took even less time; a simple slash wound, shallow, with no arrow to extract. In a few moments he was back in his place, boar-spear in both hands, punishing the man who'd managed to reach him with savage thrusts of the spear.

One of the fighters in the rear of the Blood Bear mob pulled himself back and out of the fight; it was this movement against the flow of battle that caught her attention.

The fighter, who by his elaborately decorated, heavy armor, was someone of high rank, whirled to face the combat between Darian and the Shaman. He grabbed a discarded bow from the ground, took an arrow from the quiver still attached to his belt, and took aim at Darian's back.

Keisha screamed, but her cry was lost in the general outcry. Her heart convulsed painfully, as she cried out a warning no one would ever hear—

But someone did.

A huge, white shape streaked from the far right of the lines, launched into the air, and sailed over the barricade with the grace of a swan in flight. It was Karles, and Shandi clung to his back, her mouth set in a taut line, her never-used sword in hand.

Just as the warrior loosed his arrow, Karles reached him; Shandi's sword licked out and, impossibly, deflected the arrow from its deadly flight.

Their momentum carried them on past; the warrior put a second arrow to his bow, cursing loudly in his own tongue. But now, Shandi was not the only one who knew what he was trying to do.

An ear-piercing shriek from above startled everyone into looking up. Kel had been voicing his war cries before this, but never anything like the one he produced when he realized who the bowman's target was.

Kel dove down out of the sky with terrifying speed, shallowing his arc the faster he went and the quicker he approached the ground, fore-talons outstretched. The fighter had only time enough to cringe down, trying (in utter futility) to hide. Kel hit him with more force than a levin-bolt, doubtlessly breaking the warrior's back in an instant, and pushed him level to the lay of the earth for over five horse-lengths.

Then Kelvren rose again into the sky, wings laboring, talons set firmly into the fighter's shoulder and torso. The man screamed shrilly, writhing in what must have been incredible pain, for Kel's talons had wrapped right around the protective shoulder plates and penetrated the joints between them and the rest of the armor, and the thumb-talon of the other foreclaw was surely right through the stomach. Blood oozed from the wounds, streamed down the armor, and splattered down on the heads of his fellows as Kel lumbered higher and higher into the sky.

Then he let go.

Still screaming, the man plummeted toward the ground, hitting it with a *crunch* that made even Keisha wince. The screaming stopped instantly and there was a moment of terrible silence.

Kel had dropped the man practically on top of the Wolverine lines. The Wolverine warriors drew back from the mangled body—then, incredibly, turned their backs on it. No one bothered to see if the fighter still breathed, or render him aid in any way.

The shunning had already begun.

None of this seemed to give the Blood Bear fighters pause for more than a few moments. A heartbeat after their fellow hit the ground, they were back at the barricade again. If anything, their fury had redoubled.

But now they had another target besides the Raven fighters behind the barricades.

A handful of them turned on Shandi and Karles; the Companion reared on his hindquarters, lashing out with forehooves, then dropped back to the ground to kick those trying to take him from behind. Shandi laid about her with her sword; together they accounted for three of their assailants, but more turned on them.

Shandi was screaming, but it was not in fear or pain. She was screaming, "For Valdemar's honor! For Valdemar's honor!" again and again, with each slash of the blade.

Steelmind vaulted the barricade, racing to Shandi's defense.

Hashi and Neta joined him, helping him fight his way through the packed fighters to Shandi's side. Steelmind wasn't trying to use any weapons; he seized fighters before they were aware that he wasn't one of them and physically flung them out of the way, while Neta used her horns and hooves to good effect in clearing the path, and Hashi attacked any pair of legs that wasn't protected.

Steelmind got to Shandi with only a minor gash on his head; once there, he pulled his climbing staff from the sheath on his back and began to use it with lethal efficiency. Neta and Hashi made a stand on her opposite side. Together, the three guarded Karles' rear flanks, allowing Shandi and Karles to keep their attention on the enemy in front of them.

Steelmind's staff—a deadly device with a spike on one end and a sharply-pointed hook on the other, with several grab knobs at regular intervals—seemed as light as a straw in the Hawkbrother's hands. His buzzard, no longer slow or sleepy, joined the battle with a series of heavy stoops, knocking helmets forward to obscure vision, knocking helmets off completely, then returning to lacerate the unprotected heads with his raking talons.

Kel remained above, kiting on the strong wind, keeping watch over Darian. Meanwhile Shandi, Karles, Hashi, Steelmind, and Neta began working their way back toward their own lines. Kelvren then folded wings in for a moment and dropped to attack again, someone unseen, identified only by a short scream an instant later and the gryphon taking off again with a human arm in his beak.

With a dry mouth and a pounding heart, Keisha watched the horrifying battle her friends were engaged in, oblivious to the fighting going on immediately around her, her hands clasped tightly under her chin. She was afraid to pray, for who should she pray for? Her sister, or her beloved? Her friends, or her family?

Please, please, she whispered silently. *Keep them* all *safe. . . .*

Darian wasn't aware he'd been in danger from outside until an arrow arced high over his head, piercing both walls of the magic circle. The Shaman's smile warned him that he'd become a target, but he didn't dare take his eyes off his opponent.

It hadn't taken the Shaman long to blast himself free of his earthy prison—but it *had* taken time and physical energy, and the Shaman's legs were badly bruised and lacerated from the effort. Darian had those few moments of rest, which the Shaman had spent in labor.

Now they circled warily; the Shaman staggered, somewhat the worse for wear, and Darian tried to split his attention, using peripheral vision, trying to spot the archer who'd taken that shot at him while keeping the Shaman under his eye as well.

Suddenly a shrill scream rent the air and stunned everyone on the field into momentary silence. Riding the scream down out of the sky came a bolt of golden-brown power, which hit someone in the melee and rose again, a shrieking bit of man-flesh dangling from his talons. It was Kel—and Darian hadn't known the gryphon could lift and carry a man off before this. He wanted to gape in astonishment, but didn't dare. He wouldn't underestimate this opponent for a moment; the Shaman still had plenty of raw power, and the will to use it.

But he had weaknesses. He didn't look for attacks that *weren't* purely magical power. He only used visible magic manifestations. And—

And he's focusing every attack just on what I do.

The Shaman's attention flickered away, as Kel dropped his screaming burden. The man hit the ground with a curiously wet crunch, and the screaming stopped. The Shaman turned his attention back to Darian, his mud-streaked face set in a snarl.

But not before Darian had managed to snatch up and conceal a rock in the palm of his hand.

They began to circle again, and Darian sensed the Shaman draining power for another strike. *Now I have to put you right where I want you—*

He circled, feinted back, moved forward again. The Shaman followed his maneuvers with narrowed eyes, suspecting something. Then he glanced to the side, saw the shallow crater where he had blasted himself free, and graced Darian with a grimace of contempt. With exaggerated care, he stepped past it, then Darian felt the quick drop in ley-line power that warned he was about to strike.

That was when Darian threw the rock at him.

Startled, expecting it to be a magical attack, the Shaman redirected his power and shattered the poor rock to powder with a single blast. In doing so, he faltered back into the crater he had so contemptuously avoided.

But Darian's meddling with the groundwater wasn't over. As the Shaman stumbled into the crater, he sucked the spring's water out of the area again; between his efforts and the Shaman's, that particular piece of ground was on the verge of becoming a sinkhole big enough to swallow a house, and when Darian removed the groundwater, the surface layer of sandstone gave way.

Instead of swallowing a house, it swallowed the Shaman, who disappeared into the earth with a hoarse cry. Darian fused the stone, using the same technique he had used to create the water channels for the bathing spring at the Vale, and the startled Shaman was buried up to his knees in sifting, crumbling earth while his ankles and feet smoldered.

Then Darian brought back all the water, and more, dancing back to avoid getting dropped into the sinkhole himself as the earth crumbled around the rapidly growing—and filling—crater.

Ten heartbeats later, the Shaman's half of the wall winked out of existence.

Darian took down his own half, and stood staring into what was now a roughly circular pond of very muddy water, but the only thing that arose from the depths was a few bubbles—then nothing at all.

He looked up, slowly, to face the Wolverine lines.

For a long moment, he stared defiantly at the warriors, who stared back at him wearing expressions of incomprehension and dismay. No one moved. He clasped his hands before him in the same gesture he had used at the beginning of the duel, and waited.

Then one of the men at the far right broke, babbling, and ran, stumbling away as fast as his legs could carry him. That was all that was needed; a heartbeat later, the retreat had become a rout, the brave fighters of Wolverine taking to their heels as fast as they could, even casting off armor and shedding weapons so that they could run faster.

In a sudden reversal of tactics, the Blood Bear fighters turned from the barricade and flung themselves at the easier target within their midst. Steelmind's staff moved in a lethal blur, but there were too many around him, fighting to take him down; he went down under a pile of bodies. Shandi wrenched Karles' head around and forced her Companion back, coming to *his* rescue; the Companion bit, lashed, and kicked like a demon-horse as Keisha watched in agony, certain she was going to see all three of them die before her eyes.

Then, just as suddenly, the warriors of Blood Bear broke and ran.

Keisha didn't bother to wonder why; as the Raven fighters pushed aside the barricade and poured after them, she followed, heading straight for the place where she had seen Steelmind go down.

She found him—and Shandi and Karles with him. Shandi was on her knees, clutching the front of his tunic and weeping over him. Keisha shoved her aside without a word, sending her tumbling, and took her place.

Oh, gods. This is bad, very bad. There were many, many internal injuries; someone had landed a terrible blow to his back, and another to his stomach. *He's bleeding in there and I—* She knew with dismay that neither she, nor she and Shandi together had enough power to save him.

But someone else did.

She looked up; grabbed Karles' dangling reins, and pulled his head down to the same level as hers. She looked defiantly into his eyes, and let him know without any words at all that she wasn't *asking* for his help—she was *ordering* him to give it.

He stared at her blankly for just a moment, then the power came flooding into her in a blue-white torrent.

If water were to be compared to power and energy, being caught in the midst of Karles' strength was akin to swimming that flooded river so many weeks ago. But she *had* swum that river, and she *would* direct this power now!

Fiercely, she flung herself into the battle to save Steelmind's life, just as fiercely as any Raven warrior had fought at the barricade. She transmuted the blue-white beam into the gentler green energies of Healing and the golden ones of strength, and poured both into the shattered shell that was the Hawkbrother. She pieced together bone, mended torn and bleeding veins and arteries, soothed bruised tissues, and reinforced Steelmind's own faltering strength. She did things she hadn't even known she *could* do, galvanized by the unending flow of energy. This was something like the time she had Healed Hywel's brother—except that this time she was in no danger of losing herself.

The moment that everything she needed to do was *done,* and there was nothing more to do except that which only time could accomplish—the power was gone.

She dropped abruptly out of her Healing trance with a mental *thud,* and opened her eyes to see Shandi bent over Steelmind, both of them taking turns babbling about how much they loved each other.

Karles looked at her, then at Shandi, and snorted. Keisha got slowly to her feet, wobbling a little, feeling more than a bit light-headed. Karles hadn't given her a single iota of power more than he'd had to, but somehow she didn't resent that.

After all, Companions are supposed to help us with problems, not solve them for us. Karles looked up again just as she thought that—and nodded his gore-spattered, beautiful head, winking.

Darian walked slowly toward what was left of the barricades, which were now being pulled apart by industrious women. The Raven warriors were on the heels of Wolverine and Blood Bear, making certain that they took themselves over the pass, the news of their defeat with them. More women, boys, and a few old men followed their own fighters, each carrying leather bags or small fishing nets—harvesting the discarded arms and armor. They were no fools; they could alter the style and fit of what was once Wolverine's, and make it Raven's.

He saw Karles first—then Shandi, Keisha, and Steelmind. For one horrible moment, he feared the worst.

Then Shandi helped Steelmind to his feet; she draped one of his arms over Karles' back, and the other over her own shoulder, then began walking him back toward the village. Darian heaved a sigh of relief.

Keisha looked up as a shadow went across them, to see Kelvren wing heavily overhead, returning from overseeing the Wolverine warriors' retreat. His landing was imperfect and he nearly buckled; it was not too hard to see why as his left side became visible. There was a deep gash from the top of his beak, through the cere, and a nick in his eyelid, clearly from the same blow. His nares freely bled distinctively dark red blood which flowed to mix with the lighter sticky red of his foes', most of which had dried with loose feathers, dirt, twigs and other debris glued into it. The broken ends of two arrows showed from the blood-matted feathers in the leading edge of his left wing, and in his left thigh. As he landed, clearly in terrible pain, he raised his head high and bellowed, "Arrre therrre any morrre left? Brrring them on!"

Keisha and Darian cried out, in unison, "Kelvren!" and quick-walked—since they had little energy left for running—to the wounded gryphon.

"Arrre therrre any morrre left to fight?" Kelvren demanded, eyes pinning, his gaze darting right and left. Darian grimaced, seeing what had happened to his good friend. "No more left, Kel. We won. They're all gone now."

Kelvren gazed off in the direction Wolverine had fled and then slumped down onto his hindquarters, leaning right, and finally collapsing onto his side without even folding his wings. "Hurrrrhhh—then I will rrressst. Darrrian, Ssshin'a'in arrre rrright—being conssspicuousss attrractsss arrrowsss."

Swaying a little, Keisha turned to Darian, with both hands outstretched. They fell into each other's embrace, and that was all he needed or thought about for a brief, but blissful moment, broken only by Keisha murmuring in his ear.

His heart lofted skyward with joy, and his heartbeat in his ears sounded like wingbeats.

They had made it through every ordeal, despite fatigue, pain, and fear. Together.

Keisha was in an awkward position, in quite a few ways. Physically, she had one foot under Kelvren's head, and her other leg across his neck, snugged around the nape and all but unseen underneath the mass of feathers. Kelvren himself was flat on his belly, with Darian straddling his back, keeping his wings safely folded by sitting on them. The gryphon had his beak clamped around a bedroll, and flinched every time she pierced his cere with the needle. Kuari, feeling drowsy, was perched atop a chair back nearby.

"I know you don't like this, Kel, but I have to get this gash stitched up," Keisha softly said, and she hoped she actually sounded as reassuring as she was trying to. "The powder is dulling the pain as much as it will, the rest you just have to cope with. Bite down on the bedroll instead of me, and we'll be through with this in just a little while, all right?"

It wasn't just her physical position that made her feel awkward and strained right now, though. They were also in the middle of a discussion with Darian's parents, who hovered off to the side and projected nervous tension like a thunderstorm sent out lightning.

"Father, you know that I love you, but I am a Knight of Valdemar now *and* an Elder of my Vale. I do like it here, I truly do—but I cannot stay here and be a part of Raven. There are things happening back home that I have to tend to."

Daralie nodded slowly, her expression very neutral. "And that does say it all, doesn't it—back home. There, in Valdemar, and at your Vale. We always taught you from an early age that home is a place in your heart, Darian. Sometimes the place in your heart can also be represented by a place in the world. If it is where you have to be, then you have to be there."

Kullen nodded, agreeing with his wife's words, though his expression was much more grave. "Darian, we are so proud of you that there are just no words in any language to tell you how much. When we lost you, we carried around a hole in our hearts for years. Even with what we were going through up here, we thought of you, or rather—we thought of you as we last knew you. When we were separated, our only influence on you was what we'd taught you already, and we hoped that you remembered. We wish we could have been with you, all that time you were under Justyn's care, but fate did not have it so. We loved you then, and as for who you have become—we do not love you any less."

Kelvren rumbled deep in his throat, not quite a growl, but close. He was reacting to the stitching, not what was being

said, but it made a strange counterpoint to the discussion. At
least the most delicate part—the eyelid cut—had been completed first. Wintersky limped by, conversing with Raven's
Chief, and glanced in at the tableau briefly. They both seemed
to surmise in the same instant what was going on between
Darian and his parents, and drifted off discreetly after no more
than a short wave.

Kullen shifted his weight off of his crippled leg. "Son—who
and what you have become, *we* could not have given you. You
are a wonder to us, and to all of Raven, too. You'll be spoken
of here for a long time—Darian, the Hunters' Son, the Owl
Knight, the Shaman of the Earth-mother who can call up foun-
tains and crack stone with a thought, to defend the people—
and more stories yet to come."

Darian looked from his mother to his father, and even
though he tried to soften the blow of his words, he couldn't.
They still carried a hint of bitterness. "I didn't come this far
to become a tribal hero. I came here for you."

"We know, son, we know," Daralie spoke, and then she
paused when Kelvren flinched strongly, biting hard enough
into his gag they could all hear the bedroll's stitches popping.
She resumed a few seconds later, filling the uncomfortable
silence of the moment. "All of you will be welcome back here,
I hope you know that. But—before we even came here to talk
to you, we knew what the outcome would be. We haven't survived this long without knowing how to listen to our hearts,
and—we can't go back to Valdemar with you. We also know
that you can't stay here with us."

Darian's jaw set and his muscles were visibly tense, but
that was nothing compared to what Keisha sensed from him.
He was angry, disappointed, frustrated—upset at a very deep
level over this news, yet—there was an undercurrent of relief,
as well. Keisha sensed that inside, this was one of the end
results that her lover secretly wanted. She sensed an undercurrent of—

Relief? Happiness at—freedom?

Kelvren growled, jarring her attention back to the task of
stitching the wound. Darian straightened his shirt, and replied.

"Mother. Father. When you were gone, I had only feelings

of fear and abandonment. I also had myself, and one more thing. I had my memories of you."

Darian's eyes clouded in introspection. "In a way, this entire journey was not coming back to you, it was a way of confirming that my memories were real—that even though I *remembered* that you loved me, I wanted to be *sure* of it. When you go from childhood to manhood, everything changes, until you're not even sure that the very things that *made* you were real. Now that we're reunited, we have found that it *was* real. Then. But then is not now. Now, we are new people, and we love each other all over again, in a new way."

Darian is good at this. Maybe he learned it from Firesong, or maybe Silverfox—how to pick the right thing to say, to soothe and support the listener so the meaning of what is said doesn't crush them. He has the heart of a Healer, that is for sure. That may be why I love him so much.

Kullen nodded, his arms crossed loosely, listening to Darian intently. Daralie rested against her husband's shoulder, squeezing his nearest hand slightly—something very natural between them, Keisha could tell, and long-practiced.

I wonder if, when we are that age—may we live so long—we will be that easy with each other, that comfortable. Kullen just lists to the side, already knowing that Daralie will be there. They do not have "powers" like Empathy and Healing, these Gifts, but just look at them. Being in love is enough.

"You have a new home now, and so do I. Mine is far away from here, but your hearts will always be my home. My heart will always be your home. I have to return to my work in Valdemar and the Vales, with the woman that I love."

Darian looked at Keisha with an expression that showed no doubt in that statement at all.

Another moment, and Darian looked back to his parents. "I love you both, so much."

"We love you, too, Darian," Daralie half-whispered. "We are so proud of you. And what you have done for this tribe is—"

Darian smiled a little and shook his head, holding up one hand. "—is done lovingly, for no charge, price or demand. It was done for the principle, for the honor, and for you."

Kullen grunted, and nodded once, in acknowledgment.

Kuari hooted softly, as if answering, then twisted his head to receive a slow scratching from Darian while his bondmate collected his thoughts.

Darian took a deep breath. "Personally, though I need you to do something for me."

Darian clasped his hands in front of him, and despite his own bandages he stood perfectly straight up and strong. "You have children now, my brothers and sisters who I'd never met before and, honestly—who I just don't know. I may never know them. We are siblings by blood, but not by culture, except for one vital link."

"The link is you, and your knowledge . . . the things that you can teach them. Teach them that their oldest brother is a Knight of Valdemar, and that he is a Hawkbrother, and teach them what those things mean. Teach them that his friends of many tribes, cultures and species came here to defend Raven, and them. Teach them that they can live, and love, and actually fulfill the kinds of duties and risks and grand adventures that you used to tell me about in hero stories when I was just your little boy, Mother. Teach them that it isn't beyond their reach, that they can be brave, and travel, and learn amazing things, and do what is compassionate at whatever cost, Father. Teach them for me, because I cannot be here to do it myself."

Daralie wept, and Kullen's eyes looked near to crying as well. Keisha held her breath, and as she knotted the last stitch of Kelvren's wound, a teardrop from her own eyes fell on the blotting pad.

Epilogue

"No," Keisha said adamantly, and Ayshen's face fell. "No flower arches, no procession from the village, and *especially* no ceremonial dance. I hate those rigid dances—too much structure. I feel like I'm spellcasting, not celebrating, when I'm stuck in one of those things."

Ayshen looked to Darian for support, and Darian shook his head. "We're all agreed on this, old friend," he said with sympathy. "You got your chance to drag me through all the ceremonies you wanted last spring. We want a *small* and private ceremony, a modest celebration, and that's that."

"No fireworks," Steelmind put in. "No invitations to every Vale within flying distance. No canopies carried by hovering gryphons."

"You *can* invite the *tervardi* to come sing, though," Darian added thoughtfully, and Ayshen's snout lifted a little.

"Couldn't we manage to combine it with the Harvest Faire?" he asked hopefully. "Think what a fabulous celebration *that* would make! And with all of the symbology of the coming fertility, and new births the next spring!"

Keisha and Darian exchanged a glance. "I don't suppose the Tayledras are familiar with the concept of *elopement*, are they?" she whispered, as Ayshen launched into another set of grandiose plans.

He laughed and held her closer, and she snuggled into his embrace without a shadow of doubt coming between them. "Maybe we ought to consider introducing it to them," he whispered back, and she stifled a laugh against his shoulder.

Ayshen glared at them. "This is your future I am planning! Aren't you paying attention?" he asked irritably.

All four of them exchanged a look, and burst out in helpless laughter.

"Ayshen, my friend," Steelmind chuckled, "Gods and spirits laugh their loudest when a mortal makes plans, and doubly so when they make plans for another."

Reluctantly, Ayshen backed down, sitting back on his tail. "It is true that weddings are not so much for the ones being wed, as for their loved ones. I suppose that after all that has happened, you just want peace."

Darian hugged Keisha's shoulder, and confided, "Just about now, some time alone together sounds very, very appealing."